The Bitch Captain (and The Lady)

Anne: Bermuda

J. Flynn and V. Yospe

The Bitch Captain (and The Lady)

Copyright © 2024 by J Flynn and V Yospe

All Rights Reserved.

No part of this publication may be reproduced, stored in a retrieval system or transmitted in any form or by any means without the prior written permission of the publisher.

Cover image: "Allegorical Painting of Two Ladies, English School" by Anonymous, used under public domain {{PD-US}}
(Link to the image page on Wikimedia Commons: https://commons.wikimedia.org/wiki/File:Anon_(English_School)_-_double_portrait_-_circa_1650.jpg)

Interior design by Booknook.biz

Table of Contents

Prologue — v

Tavern Rock — 1

Take Me Away — 39

Decisions — 55

Galley Breakdown — 83

Bermuda Landing — 93

Bermuda Hospitality — 141

A Sisterly Visit — 177

Prison Purgatory — 187

Prison Company — 189

Home Again Home Again — 217

Home Sweet Bermuda Home — 229

Not my Honeymoon — 295

St. George's — 335

Goodbyes — 351

Epilogue — 363

Prologue

"To tequila and marshmallows!" Izzy toasted the stars and took another drink.

"To rum and hamburgers!" I tossed one back and coughed on the flash burn of the alcohol. That was my one drink for the night. One. I was a lightweight and needed my wits about me to sail. I didn't need the alcohol. Izzy was having a great time, and I was delighted to warm myself off the edges of her joy.

"To bacon and wine!" She drank again.

"To whiskey and tacos!" I shouted back. We whooped with laughter as a wave came up and rocked the ship with an unexpected swell from the east, spilling our drinks. We poured another round and continued toasting the sea, the stars, the moon, and delicious plastic-wrapped snack cakes. I continued tossing my drinks overboard, she tossed hers back like a pro. The stars were brilliant tonight. We were far from any land and light pollution and you could see the arms of the Milky Way. I raised my glass to them.

The constellations had been my most constant and steadfast companions on my journeys. It was my habit and prerogative to always travel alone on my ship. In fact, it was among my top rules that no one stepped aboard this boat while I was sailing – this rule applied doubly to men. In my younger days I would occasionally take others out on the boat, like when I had taken my mother and Izzy sailing on little day trips around the bay when Izzy was home from school. But for a long time now it had been just me and the sky.

Now that Izzy was with me I wasn't planning to sail alone until it was time to bring her back home. I had this one summer with her, and after that it would be back to loneliness, back to me and the stars. One day, maybe Izzy would look up at those stars and remember tonight and remember me. My sister knocked back another drink…maybe I'd take a picture of tonight just to be safe. The way she was drinking she wasn't going to remember shit.

I smiled as she stumbled her way across the boards and piled her plate with the gourmet boat snacks she insisted I stock in the galley. I watched her sway and rock with the sea as she stuffed her face with some tomato-mozzarella mixture and thought to myself that, at most, there was a 60/40-percent chance she'd kill me. Maybe 70/30. Okay, fine. I had, at the very least, a 25-percent chance of surviving the moment when she figured out what I had done – which was kidnap her a little bit.

Izzy had stepped foot on this ship for one reason and one reason only: I'd begged her. Actually, I had done much more than beg. I had bribed, groveled, guilted, and connived her into getting on the boat. I had also lied my ass off. As far as she knew, we were on a fun, sisterly cruise, our destinations being every bar, beach, and cabana in the Caribbean. One slight wrinkle…we weren't doing any of that at all.

We were going a-time-traveling.

Izzy and I were the last descendants of an indescribably wealthy, old-money family. For generations upon generations my family tree had enjoyed wealth beyond measure until complacency and self-importance had driven the family patriarchs into making terrible financial decisions that bankrupted us. The extended family had pilfered and squirreled away what little we had remaining.

My father left us before Izzy and I could get into PG-13 movies. Good riddance to bad rubbish. Moving on, never looking back. My

The Bitch Captain (and The Lady)

mother, the esteemed blonde dynamo in heels and designer suits, Vivienne Nicole St. Germaine, spent our childhoods pulling the family fortunes up by their bootstraps. She leveraged every inch of land, every scrap of luxury, every brittle connection she could drum up to keep the St. Germaine name relevant in society. Don't be fooled, she did it for herself. I'd have been happy with peanut butter sandwiches and canvas shoes, but oh, no. "You are a St. Germaine, Anne, whether you want to be or not. Now go get yourself presentable. Mrs. High-Falutin-So-And-So's tea begins in twenty minutes, and you *will* be perfect."

She turned our house and land into Heron's Landing, a boutique resort with a picturesque natural landscape complete with glorious bay views perfect for your wedding, bat mitzvah, or next corporate event. I'd grown up in a sea of fancy dresses, wedding veils, dance floors, and strangers in my house. Our family was relegated to a smaller closed off wing, away from the muzak filled lounges, the tea room, and event space C. Therefore, every Saturday evening I enjoyed resort guests singing and shouting, congaing and electric sliding, and toasting their way across the lawn outside my bedroom window.

The only brilliant thing to happen to our family was Izzy. My parents adopted her, and she brightened my life like a shooting star in the dead of night. Though I'd never forgive my parents for my childhood, I'll always be thankful to them for her.

I left home soon after turning eighteen.

I did not pack my last name into my suitcase. Diane "Anne" Collette St. Germaine was packed into boxes piled high with old trophies and art projects in the attic of that house and there she would remain. Out here, I was Captain, and that was the only name I needed.

There was exactly one piece of inheritance left to Izzy and me that was worth a damn: a dusty series of journals, 400 years old, where written in the first entry was a description of something only a desperate soul would or should attempt: time travel. Enter me. Desperation is the cornerstone of my being.

As far as I know, I am the only member in our entire family tree who was bored and lonely enough to crack open the trunk with the collection of old pages and ledgers and attempt to read them for instructions. It was incredibly dull reading. Even the museums hadn't wanted to purchase them – and believe me, my mother had tried her best to sell them.

Yada yada yada. Some stuff happened. The rest is history.

"All I'm saying is we better hit land soon because I did not go full Brazilian for you and some mangy seagulls. Also, I'm going to need to restock on batteries soon unless you are looking to make a MAJOR lifestyle change," Izzy said as she sat down next to me with her plate of snacks. She had worn less and less as the days at sea stretched out, as if she was playing strip poker with the waves.

I'm not sure who was losing. Probably me. I was on sunscreen duty to keep her flawless skin even more flawless ("Even people with melanin need sunscreen, Anne"), and I kept having to dive in after her discarded clothes.

"We'll get there sometime tomorrow if the wind is with us." We better. I'd do almost anything for my sister, but I was not going to go down that road with her. I had a stash of batteries she could use if she didn't burn the motor out of her vibrator first.

The sky was clear tonight. What the sky and sea might look like four hundred years in the past remained to be seen. I handed her my special flask. She took a sip and spewed it out.

"Is that water??" She threw the container back at me like I was trying to poison her.

"Sorry, wrong flask," I said, and handed her the whiskey one. She drank it down and soon was snoozing, rocked to sleep by the whiskey and waves. Perfect.

Showtime.

I muscled her drunk ass downstairs and into her cabin, shutting the door tight for good measure. She'd had enough booze to tranquilize a

The Bitch Captain (and The Lady)

horse. She would sleep soundly through the portal and my first little stop, and then I'd wake her when we were on our way to Portugal. I rested my hand for a moment on her cabin door and sent up a silent prayer that, one, we'd make it through the portal's time current just fine and, two, that she wouldn't kill me. I had at least a twenty-percent chance of living through this. Don't look back, Anne, I told myself, never look back.

Up on top I stood in my familiar spot at the helm. The waves stretched out for leagues, and in that moment I felt that I was the only living, breathing soul in the history of the world. We were close to the portal, I could feel it. It was a combination of fresh salt air, impatience, and promise, all rolled into one massive invisible current. I took a bearing on the stars and tacked in close, riding the edge till I found an opening.

I looked back at the doors leading to Izzy's cabin and steeled myself for what might come.

"Second star to the right." I grinned. "And straight on till morning." The wind caught the sails and stretched them taut as I steered us into the portal. Away we went from everything my sister knew and loved and onwards towards immense possibility.

CHAPTER 1

Tavern Rock

There. I felt my exit coming up and eased the wheel toward the edge of the portal and out. Nice and smooth. The sun beat down late-afternoon light here, no longer the middle of the night as when we'd entered the portal. I took my first deep breath in what felt like months. The deed was done. Izzy and I were officially members of the historical society.

What are you going to tell her? A little wriggly voice had the nerve to speak to me.

Energy fizzed in my blood, and I scaled the main mast to get a view of the horizon. No ships or hints of sails as far as I could see. This wasn't unusual because we were far from any of the main shipping lanes. A new journey was always exciting, and this one had the promise of being my best trip yet: I was with my best friend and sister; I had a well-thought-out and manageable plan; there was only a fifteen-percent chance Izzy would kill me. I was feeling good.

My thoughts immediately transitioned into traveling mode, and I automatically set a course to the teeny little island only I and a handful of other sailors (read: pirates) knew about. There I had a contact (read: ass-face misogynistic thieving rat bastard thief who screwed me over in our last deal, so I spoiled the cargo in his hold in revenge, but there were few trading options on the sea in these times and we had to deal with one another) waiting with cargo for me. This cargo was the final payment on a castle in Portugal where Izzy and I would spend the summer. The castle was perfect, she was going to love it.

My sister was a Renaissance Faire nut, and I thought there was no better way to have a last hurrah with her than to take her to the actual Renaissance for a summer of big gowns, rich food, and sisterly bonding before I took her home and back to her life. Problem was, women here couldn't own property. My buddy Charlie had agreed to speak on my behalf for the castle in exchange for my buying and transporting this cargo to him. That rat bastard thief had Charlie's cargo and was expecting me. I'd be in and out of there before Izzy woke up hungover and wondering why the air smelled so fresh and the sea levels felt strangely lower.

The little island wasn't visible yet and probably wouldn't be for a few hours, longer if the clouds moved in. I breathed in the fresh air and felt the freedom of this era like a soft towel wrapped around me.

Our second stop was Bermuda. It would be quick. Just a side trip to replenish our stores and stretch our legs. Bermuda was a convenient rest stop in the middle of the Atlantic and a good place to let Izzy dress in costume and practice being among people before heading to the continent. Then it was on to Portugal, where our honest-to-god castle waited for us on the southern coast of the country. How could you kill someone who bought you a castle? I mean, come on. I had at least a ten-percent chance of survival.

I climbed down the mast and checked the compass bearing. Right on track.

That little annoying voice in my head nagged, *What are you going to tell Izzy?*

Later. I'd figure that out later.

Down in the cargo hold I opened a secret panel to reveal my traveling clothes and arsenal. Izzy was still quiet behind her cabin door, and I surreptitiously closed my own door before changing. She hadn't seen me undress since I'd been burnt at the stake, and I wasn't ready to answer questions about the immense scarring I sported. Life as a time traveler came with consequences. I was much more careful about my bearing and appearance since that episode. There was not a stitch of plastic or synthetic material in sight. At home I'd been able to launder everything and now looked at each piece with satisfaction: fine creamy woolen tunic and soft leather leggings, long jerkin, and sturdy boots. My only concession to modern clothing was a binder I wore over my chest, a tightly-fitting compression tank top that could easily be misconstrued as era-correct clothing and not inflame suspicions. Ever since the stake I was meticulous about not inviting suspicion. You get burned at the stake once, and the lesson really sticks. Bras were always trouble.

I took the time to massage the toughened scar tissue and stretch before replacing my jeans with the leggings. Burn scars aside, I bore the marks of several fatal and near-fatal incidents. I made a note that that would need to be among the details I shared with Izzy about my life: I could take fatal hits and keep on rolling. The second facet of our trip this summer included coming clean to my sister about *how* I time-traveled.

Over the tunic I put on the jerkin and a double shoulder holster that I'd specially designed back home. It would hold my prize retrofitted 16th-century pistols. They had cost a fortune, but I wouldn't have to stop and reload after every shot. I allotted four bullets to each gun for my meeting with that rat bastard thief. On arrival in the past, I practiced strict bullet rationing. I did not want to mess around with gunpowder horns and lead slugs if I was in a life-and-death situation.

What are you going to tell Izzy?

Shut up. She's still asleep.

I pulled on a sturdy pair of stomping boots with steel toes, and around my head went a long batik scarf to keep sweat out of my eyes. Then I stuck my wide-brimmed leather fedora over the whole affair. I fussed a little with the cuffs and smoothed the jerkin. Palpable relief flooded through me as I looked down at my attire. For the first time in months I felt like myself.

What are you going to tell Izzy?
I looked down at myself again. She didn't know me like this…
Later. There's still time.

I climbed the steps back to the top deck and scanned the horizon with the spyglass. There was a smudge a ways out that was the start of Tavern Rock Island.

What are you going to tell Izzy?
Hush.

Tavern Rock Island was exactly that: a loose collection of rocks just above sea level with a few docks and a tavern. It was run by whoever managed to keep it going or killed the previous managers. At this moment, it was that rat bastard thief. Before that rat bastard thief, it had been me. Food, drink, and beds could be bought by barter or by gold. Its most appealing feature was the fact that no European power had yet to plant a flag on it.

I sailed awhile in silence and watched a storm far off my port skirt us by several leagues. Next to the wheel was a weatherproof box where I kept my notebooks and latest sewing projects; it was my habit to keep my hands busy at sea. My needles I kept pinned in my hat with extra thread wrapped around the brim for easy access. I picked up a piece of embroidery and added some detail around a flowery bit I was stitching into this bodice. Recently I'd considered taking up knitting and crochet but hadn't yet committed to either hobby.

We were riding a charmed swell straight towards the island, and before long I could pick out features of the place through the spyglass. For instance, there were several ships docked there today. A good sign I could squeeze in a little extra trading.

What are you going to tell Izzy?
Well? What are you going to tell Izzy?
Shut up.

Nothing too big was tied off along those old docks. The largest ship only had two masts, and that was most likely that rat bastard thief's

The Bitch Captain (and The Lady)

ship. My ship, the *Try Your Luck,* would be the largest bark. I raised the glass again and tried to spot any insignia, but it was all still too far off and of little consequence. All the merchants worth a damn were killed off a few years ago in a big sweep by the British. The new crop of captains and sailors were cocky and trying too hard to fill shoes they had no idea how to lace.

What are you going to tell Izzy?
Well?
I had nothing.
Zilch.
Zero.
Goose egg.

At a loss for words, I opted to cook some breakfast, just a simple meal of pancakes, leftover bacon, and, of course, a pot of strong coffee. Izzy was the chef, not me, but maybe she'd eat it just to be polite. I took a plate up for myself and sat at the helm watching the island creep ever nearer as I ate. I looked again and again through the glass, trying to pick out any markings on the boats to see if I recognized anyone. Nothing. Again, that wasn't surprising. There were just so many new crews on the seas these days. Too many.

I trimmed the sails and adjusted our heading. We were about near enough to begin watching for signs of reefs. I picked up the glass again, wishing even one of the ships looked recognizable. It bothered me that I was anxious for a friendly face. This wasn't a social call, this was business. I put the glass down, and when it rolled away, I didn't go get it. There'd be nothing new to see.

It would still be another two hours before we docked. I stretched out and watched the waves then sat back and focused on the embroidery. How hard could knitting be? Next time I was home I'd pick up yarn and some books on the subject.

The familiar clothing and familiar scenery lulled me into familiar patterns. I was too used to being alone on my ship, and my thoughts were on the seabed, the meeting ahead of me, and what I might be able to knit if I got my skills up to snuff. A scarf to start, probably. Crochet was another option too, one hook instead of two needles.

The charmed swell kept us straight on course towards the island, and before long I could pick out features of the place without the glass.

What are you going to tell her?

Let her wake up first.

Well? What are you going to tell her?

She's going to sleep through this. There's time to think.

"Which bar is this?" Izzy's voice startled me so badly I dropped my plate of pancakes, syrup side down. Shit. I'd have to scrub that later.

My sister was at the stairs, my discarded spyglass at her eye. Damn her young and efficient liver! She was supposed to sleep all day. I wasn't ready. Izzy stood there in a string bikini and gauzy coverup, Jackie O glasses, thick curls blowing in the wind. This vision of modern promiscuity put the spyglass back up to her eye for a better look at Tavern Rock. In her other hand was the fake itinerary I'd made her.

Shit. "Right! So, funny story—" I began.

"What kind of place is it?" Izzy lowered the spyglass and blinked at me. "What the hell are you wearing?" It was hard to tell her reaction to my traveling regalia underneath the big sunglasses.

You've got to tell her something.

"It's called Tavern Rock. Because it's a tavern...on a rock." *You are a moron.* "It's an old haunt of mine but it's—" dirty, dangerous, not a place for novice time travelers, "—a little eclectic. I just have an errand to run there. I wasn't expecting you up so soon." I felt stupid using the word "errand" to sum up what was likely to be, at best, a successful transaction of criminal subterfuge wherein I'd obtain good cargo.

"Eclectic, huh?" She continued looking through the glass.

Tell her something now.

"There's an...aspect to this trip I was keeping as a surprise." I took a baby step towards confession.

Smooth.

Shut up.

"You know I invited you on this trip because our lives are going in such different directions. We're drifting apart, and I wanted a, kind of, last hurrah before your life takes off and you leave me behind. Don't deny it." She wasn't, but the words were for me, not her. "It is what it is. I can't hang around you forever."

The days of me tagging along with her as she flew from one event to another were coming to a close. She was getting older, and I wasn't giving up my traveling ways. This summer trip was meant to preempt a traumatic goodbye by giving her some great final memories.

"So I arranged things to recreate our best summer together. Remember the one? When we were at that pretend camp of yours? With the tents and the turkey legs and the jousting?" I asked.

"Yes." My sister chewed her bacon and I plowed on. If she swallowed this load of crap about a Renaissance reenactment, I could buy a few more days to work on how to tell her it wasn't reenactment but actual Renaissance.

"We had fun, right? That was one of my best summers with you." It was the only time in my life I hadn't costumed myself in modern clothing after returning from a journey. It was the only summer I'd resembled even a touch of the person I spent most of my life being. Izzy had rolled with my curious appearance that summer and given me hope that perhaps she could know me as I truly am one day and not as the person she grew up with in a room decorated with rainbows and unicorns.

"Really?" She was always surprised when it turned out I liked the same things she did.

I laughed at her expression; she was honestly surprised. But when had I ever turned her down when she invited me to do something with her? Never. She was good times.

"Yeah, so I thought we could recreate it this summer. I have this place in Portugal. Everyone dresses up." Literally everyone because it's what people dressed in in the 1600s. "I have stuff for you in a trunk. Good stuff. Not that glittery shit you got at craft stores." She looked like a horny elf most of the time she dressed up. This summer she was going to look like an empress.

"Portugal?"

"This is just one stop I needed to make on the way there. It's to fund Portugal." There. That ought to do it. No mention of time travel yet, we were just dressing up and having a lark. I relaxed a little.

"Yeah." She seemed to relax too.

The island grew larger, and I started to make a list of the preparations I still needed to complete before docking.

"What do you mean you have a place in Portugal?" she asked.

"I *will* have the place in Portugal after I deliver this cargo," I clarified. Charlie had spoken for me. The place was waiting for us, but I wouldn't get in or have clearance to occupy until I delivered the cargo. "I'll be an hour, three tops, and then we'll be on our way." We'd resupply in Bermuda, get fresh water and food, and then make our way to Europe.

"I see." Izzy kept eating her breakfast. I was glad she was enjoying it. "Wait, what? I can't come with you?"

My sister? Going into Tavern Rock? I quickly stamped out an involuntary laugh. Izzy's first experience in the 17th century was not going to be some pirate hidey-hole famous for black-market dealings and the occasional stabbing. No. I had a plan. I was going to stick to that plan. Get Charlie the cargo, go live in a castle, throw a massive party, take Izzy back home. End scene.

"This place isn't really your scene. It's rough. Just chill out here, stay below decks. We'll be on our way by sunset."

"Rough? Like a dive bar?"

"Picture the worst place you've gone and add a bunch of barnacles. There's still a bottle of your disgusting lavender gin in the fridge. Drink that, and I'll be back as soon as I've got what we need. It's just a quick

The Bitch Captain (and The Lady)

stop. Really. Go have a drink." A nice breakfast gin, a romantic comedy on her laptop, not going into a bar with violent sea criminals…I mean, what more do you need for a fun-filled morning? I looked at the sun, low in the sky. I guess it was evening now. We had exited the portal into late afternoon/early evening. I shrugged and went to get ready to dock.

That went better than expected.

We'll see.

"Hey!" Izzy yelled as I went to the steps. "My botanical infusions are not disgusting!"

"Yes, they are!" I called back and got ready for landfall. I held firm at my ten-percent chance of surviving the moment Izzy discovered how far from home I'd taken her.

Before docking I needed to finish packing up the gold and my sack of cake and cream "incentives." My wardrobe also needed a few final touches. There was a faded blue broadcloth-and-leather wrap that resembled a knee-length skirt full of pockets and loops and sheaths for holding blades. It was more like an apron made of sturdy fabric and leather. I wrapped this around my waist. I didn't love skirts, but they hid all manner of useful items from sight: pistols, pocketknives, smoke bombs, vaginas. Over everything went my leather trench coat lined with Kevlar. I cinched the ensemble with my sword belt: short sword and cutlass on my left, one-handed brass flanged mace and dagger on my right.

The sun was just beginning to set as I pulled into the dock. An hour or two of light remained before the stars came out. I wondered if Izzy would notice how short the "day" had been. I'd tell her everything once the ship was loaded with cargo and we were on our way. Dear God, I prayed, let this not go to hell.

God didn't answer.

My welcoming party was just leaving the tavern as I lowered the sails to slow us down. The tide cooperated, and I was able to bring the *Try Your Luck* in smooth and easy. Several grizzled men from the welcoming party came down the planks to help me tie off. I threw the lines to them, and they hauled me to a standstill. I didn't recognize a single one, but the sailing community is generally helpful when it comes to aiding a solo sailor coming into port. Plus I had a big box of gold for them, and they didn't want it sinking to the sea floor.

"My thanks, gentlemen," I called out to them as I put down the gangplank. They just stared back, hands on the blades at their sides, sneers on their shabby faces. When it was clear more conversation wasn't forthcoming, I shrugged and began lowering the sails and coiling the ropes. They didn't leave the dock.

"You going to go tell that bastard I'm here or just stand there watching with the gulls?"

"Woman shouldn't have a boat like this. Shouldn't be on the seas at all," one of them grumbled. "Bad omens."

"Yet here I am." I sighed. Breaking in my presence to unfamiliar sea rats was always a challenge. Their superstitious fears were rooted deep in their uneducated bones. The men didn't move an inch from their current positions. That rat bastard thief had more than likely instructed them to watch my every step from the second my ship docked. He was such an asshole.

Since they weren't leaving, I needed to make sure my passenger stayed out of sight. If one of them caught a glimpse of her…or if she caught sight of them…maybe I should have roofied her along with all the alcohol.

"No men on my ship," I warned them, including a glimpse of my pistols for extra emphasis, and went to find Izzy. I wasn't concerned they'd behave themselves. They hadn't gotten paid yet and wouldn't risk the rat's temper by ruining this deal with some good old-fashioned premature ejaculation.

Izzy was on her bed in her cabin, laptop on her lap. I would leave her one final reminder to stay inside before I grabbed the gold for that rat bastard thief.

"Wow." Izzy took in my full regalia. The blades were sure to take some explaining later (never mind the mace).

I decided to breeze past the issue.

"Hey, so just enjoy the solitude. Stay down here. Don't go up top. I'll be back in a sec." I ignored her blatant what-the-fuck-are-you-wearing stare. Tonight, when this island was far, far behind us, I'd sit her down and explain everything. I was happy to see that she had a chunk of pot brownie on a plate next to her; perhaps that would serve in place of the roofie I should have slipped her. "Want me to shut your door?" If only I could lock her in for safety. But she might have something to say about that. My hand was on the handle even so.

"Are you sure about this, Anne? It sounds...seedy." Her eyes bounced from her window to me and back again.

"It's fine," I lied. "I know this place. Just a little rough around the edges."

One of the men on the dock drifted into view of her window and I reached over and twitched the drapes closed before he could look in or Izzy could look out.

"I see," she said.

She was smiling. That was a good sign, right? I hoped I wasn't sweating through my trench.

"Are you going to watch *Hello Dolly* or *Twelfth Night* again?" I took a step out of her cabin and shifted the strongbox from one hand to another. In preparation for our trip I'd had her download her favorite movies because "the wifi will be really patchy in some areas." So I know she had several movies locked and loaded: *Miss Congeniality*, *Pride and Prejudice*, *The Notebook*, *Superman*, along with some others. She'd be fine.

"I haven't decided." Izzy was suddenly on her feet, her hand in mine.

The gesture startled me. I was not a physically demonstrative person by nature. Back home, Izzy might hug me occasionally, but she was the only one. While traveling – and particularly while on this ship, definitely not while dressed like this – I was never touched. My life was a solitary one, and the sudden physicality of another person's hand in mine was overwhelming.

"Listen, is there anything you need to tell me?" She wouldn't let go.

"I'm just running an errand." I finally disengaged her hand from mine. "Pretend I'm going out for some milk. I'll be right back."

Izzy reached for me again, and I shied away from her but put on a smile to temper the reaction.

"You don't need to worry so much about me," I insisted.

"Okay." She seemed unconvinced. "Everything is okay, you'll be right back, and there's nothing you need to tell me?"

Yes. So, so many things.

Not now. Later. There's a right way to do this.

Tell her!

"Not a thing." I smiled again. "I'll be one hour. Three tops. Love you." I made it to the stairs before turning back around. One more reminder that she was not to leave the safety of this ship. "Stay inside," I said in my most serious, captainly voice. I did not temper those words with any comforting grin.

The men were still standing diligently at their posts at the bottom of my gangplank, only now there was a new addition. I bit back an epithet as I saw the figure treading down the dock. I guess you ask the universe enough times for a familiar face and it'll deliver, whether you freaking want it to or not.

Failure gave me a soft kiss as he moved into view. Tall enough to look down on most but not a giant. Dark hair tied back by a length of fabric under a sturdy hat, brims folded up at the sides. All the men on the dock were leathered by the sun, however, I knew this man hailed from the Middle East and I wished he was there now. Marco.

"Annie," Marco greeted me, "been a while. Last I saw you, you were behind some very lovely and very solid bars." We'd been in that jail cell together, but I'd gotten out.

The Bitch Captain (and The Lady)

"Don't call me Annie." I went down the gangplank and muscled past the men. He knew I hated that name. He was being an ass on purpose. "Last I saw you, you were shortlisted for a hangman's noose. Sailing with rats again?"

"I'm sailing. That's enough," he grinned and followed me, "for now. Are you trading with rats now?"

"For now."

"Where you been, Annie?" he asked.

"On my boat under my own command. Don't call me Annie." Stay calm, I urged myself, batting at Failure's gossamer threads weaving in and around my ambition.

Marco had lost countless boats. He was just jealous I still had one when he had lost nearly every boat he'd ever stepped foot on. The sea floor was littered with his attempts at ocean crossings.

"Does that rat bastard thief have my cargo?" I asked.

"You'll be pleased."

"Who are your friends?" I gestured to the flunkies flanking him.

"That thieving rat bastard is good at making friends." He grinned his megawatt smile that earned him berths and beds and friends the world over. I did not return the expression.

"Press-ganged?" That was one way of making friends.

"Or shanghaied. That rat isn't picky."

"Clearly. After all, he let you on his ship." Now I did smile.

"To the quick, Annie." Marco mimed getting stabbed through the heart.

"If only." We'd reached the tavern entrance. "Are we doing this deal or standing around all day?"

"I'm in no rush." He stretched and yawned, but one of his flunkies knocked his hand down.

"Let's get it over with. I don't like this sea bitch. I want her and her cursed ship far away from us. Women are bad luck." The old sea dog was grizzled and unwashed. He'd likely been crewing ships since he was at his mother's teat, knotting ropes, eating hardtack, and letting the harsh salt air eat into his superstitions alongside the milk. The other men grumbled. I dropped my free hand to my short sword.

"I can't argue with a consensus. Let us adjourn to the dining room." Marco's smile was back, and he gestured for me to lead the way. The others weren't about to follow a woman and crushed through the flimsy door a few steps ahead of me.

Inside was the same moldy, stained tavern, stacked floor to ceiling with barrels and crates and sacks of goods. Looked like that rat bastard thief had been busy. There were several ships' worth of cargo stored here, and likely none of it was gotten honestly. Behind the bar were two Tainos, a man and a woman, who I could only guess that rat bastard thief had enslaved. When I ran the place, it had just been me behind the bar. The rest of the tavern was populated with the crews of the few smaller ships, who presumably were there to trade with that rat bastard thief. It was the busy season for merchants on the sea.

I dropped my sack and box by a table and took my seat, the position with my back to the wall. Marco went out and behind the bar where there was a small room that functioned as living quarters for the proprietor. Presumably he was announcing my arrival to that rat bastard thief. I scanned the various sailors and crew mates and didn't find anyone I recognized as a friend. I also didn't recognize anyone as a foe. I didn't recognize anyone at all. Unease crept through my joints, settling in my fingers and making them twitch. That rat bastard thief and Marco were the only known quantities now.

"Evening, gentlemen," I declared as I sat. "Any of you heading to England? I've got salt, pepper, and vanilla to trade or sell."

"Aye," a captain near the bar answered. "I've got some bolts of cotton out of Egypt. You could make yourself a nice get-up. Something with a skirt a man could get under." Low and sordid laughter oozed through the bar. As if I hadn't heard that line before. Cotton was a

The Bitch Captain (and The Lady)

great item to buy up; I'd deal with this ass if it meant he had something valuable.

"How much? I've got a butt load of salt for you if you have at least twenty bolts." I held back my own laughter at the "butt load." It wasn't as funny in the 17th century as it was in the 21st. Butt load. Hilarious. This comedy gold was wasted on them.

"Twenty bolts? You'll be including the vanilla then?"

"If you were in Egypt, you've got some glass and paper—"

"Enough, Reg!" The captain of another ship jumped on my negotiations. "Them goods were promised to me." The two then got into an argument about their verbal contract. This felt like old times. Even though the merchants were new, the business was not. And I was the best in the business.

I settled back and waited for them to reach that conclusion. I'd win. Salt wins every time. The other captains jumped into the argument as they'd all been trading and negotiating away the cargoes in their holds for a few days now. Now that "Reg" was considering this big deal with me, it threw their loose contractual agreements into chaos. I stoked the fires by working in a few other offers for goods that interested me. There wasn't a lot of value in their holds, but a few things caught my attention. The captain arguing with Reg had several casks of rum from a distillery I favored in the Caribbean. At some point in the ensuing argument, Marco returned and watched the uproar with amusement.

"Never one to let an opportunity slip past, are you?" He took a seat on the barrel next to me.

I just sat back and smiled. I could come out of this little errand better off than I thought. Charlie's cargo was always leaving with me… but if I could get more cargo from the other ships and trade it, sell it myself…I could add a tidy little profit to my name. Maybe after I explained everything, Izzy wouldn't mind if we made a tiny stop or two in Virginia and Canada, possibly Ireland too. I know she'd always wanted to go.

And just as thinking the name of the beast is akin to summoning it...the door opened.

Failure tittered in my ear.

The whole place went dead silent at her entrance. The setting sun framed my sister in golden light, that mystical light that gilded and softened even the sharpest edges of disaster.

Did you really think she'd stay on the ship?

Yes. Izzy doesn't lie – never lied to me before.

Don't just sit there. Move.

The one teeny tiny, itty-bitty piece of mercy was that Izzy wasn't still in her bikini. I'd seen my sister in a number of Renaissance outfits through the years; this time, however, she was dressed in the real deal, petticoats, corset and all. She was making an impression alright. Queen Elizabeth II going to a dive bar in the middle of Baltimore would have made less of an impression. The corsairs shielded their eyes from the sun in order to get a better view of my sister and her barely-contained chest.

Move.

"Well, well, well, Annie, what have you done? I never thought I'd see the day." Marco looked between us and tsked.

Shit shit shit. There was no hiding her now. Here Izzy stood, brocaded and bustled and female, for all the world to see. I couldn't send her back to the ship now, these men had seen her, she wouldn't be safe alone any longer.

MOVE!

I scrambled off my seat and raced to her side before the shock could wear off the tavern. I pushed aside the stunned men, some of whom were actually attempting to brush dirt off their pants, take their feet off the table, and sit up straight. Now that there was a proper lady in their midst, they wanted to make a good impression. Izzy's attention bounced between the shabby interior decoration, the crusty inhabitants, and me rushing to get to her. She took a few cautious steps towards me.

"Is everything okay?" She spoke in a whisper but might as well have used a megaphone. All ears were on us.

"Who's your friend, Annie?" Marco shouted out. Damn him.

"What are you doing? You said you'd stay on the ship!" My tone and manner were rougher than she deserved, but I was in my full regalia and prepped to go into negotiations with that rat bastard thief. Who I was with my sister was an entirely different person than the captain these men had all heard tales of, the captain who'd taken blood from both Marco and that rat bastard thief on more than one occasion over the years.

"You said she always travels alone," one of the men behind Marco growled.

"Annie is always full of surprises." He could go to hell on one of his sinking ships. As a rule, I was alone…always. Rule number five was no men on my ship. The women here wouldn't sail with me even if I did offer them a berth…which I didn't.

"You shouldn't be here. You were supposed to stay on the ship," I repeated. My stomach was a rock. Every muscle clenched to hustle her out the door, but it was useless. There was no hiding her now.

"I couldn't leave you alone here," she whispered.

Oh god, she came in here to protect me.

If only you'd thought of something to say.

Not the time!

"I like this surprise," another man smarmed. His hand disappeared under the table. "Think she's got any more girls on that ship?" This sea rat, along with all the others in the tavern, wouldn't hesitate to pay my sister's vagina a visit now that they knew she was on my ship, female, and unguarded.

"What's going on?" Her eyes darted around the dirty tavern, freaking out.

I couldn't sit in this indecision for long. Choices had to be made, and fast. Like a politician in a scandal, I had to get ahead of the story, here the story being a fresh, young, beautiful passenger in a pirate hidey-hole in the middle of nowhere 400 years before anyone who knew and loved her could file a missing-persons report.

"Shit. This is not good," I mumbled to myself.

"I hear men aren't allowed on that precious ship of hers," someone scoffed, and a few pirates whistled.

"They've seen you. You'll have to stay." I was heartbroken. My first stop out and I was unable to protect her. Despite the layers of cloth and petticoats fanning out around her she looked small. Dammit! This was not how our journey was supposed to begin.

"Is this what you've been up to? A patroness? Someone's finally turned you into a legitimate captain? My dear lady, you could have had me at half the expense." Marco's deep voice assumed the tavern's attention. The pirates then began to shout the prices they'd pay to escort my sister on their cut-rate rafts. "Patroness" – damn, that was good. Crap. I didn't need to be any more in debt to him than I was. I ground my teeth and kept my attention on my sister.

"Well? Are you going to introduce me to your friend, Anne?" Izzy indicated Marco.

She reminded me so much of Mom sometimes it was startling. Even in the middle of a gang of pirates in the Atlantic Ocean in the 1600s, I mustn't forget my manners and make the social gaffe of not completing formal introductions.

Izzy meet Marco. Marco, Izzy. Izzy enjoys volunteer work with unappreciative youths and spending her days around plants. Marco enjoys singing, pretending he knows how to sail, and negotiating with warlords. Do try the pinot noir paired with the taleggio; both are aged to perfection and ready to delight your palate.

I ignored her pointed dig at my lapse in etiquette. Plans were forming fast and furious in my head. She needed status, she needed a story, and she needed a name. The tavern waited for an answer to Marco's question.

"I suppose I'll have to," I concluded, feeling like I'd taken a step down a dark path we shouldn't be treading. Damn Marco to hell.

"Gentlemen," I announced to the tavern at large, "as luck would have it, my esteemed patroness wanted to meet you all. This is the Lady Isabelle. She is traveling with me and is more than happy to provide a few rounds of drinks for you fine fellows. The lady is under my protection. She'll be staying with me." I signaled to the barkeep to top everyone off and pour more drinks. There were a few coins in my pocket to cover the glasses of goodwill, and I tossed them on the counter. Only a few scattered mumbles of appreciation and acknowledgment met the gesture. Reg and the other captains returned to their talks of negotiation, but the tone was changed. Thoughts of sailing away with extra profits today evaporated.

I yanked Izzy's arm to make her follow me to my table. The fancy costume was working. The pirates gave her the space and respect due to nobility. However, despite the deference, there was a new edge to their behavior. A veneer had worn off their words and countenances revealing a glint of trouble hidden beneath the surface. It was as if Izzy's arrival had not only altered my plans beyond repair but theirs as well. She was an unwelcome quantity for everyone on this island, and we were all scrambling to adjust. The question was: what plans were they trying to rearrange? Why did they need to scramble? The dissonance set my teeth on edge.

She was quiet for all of two and a half shuffling, petticoated steps.

"What is going on here?" She yanked my hand off her. "This feels unsavory as fuck. We should leave, Anne."

"Of course we should leave," I hissed. "This place is a hole. But I haven't finished my business here, and now I have to figure out how to do that with you here. Here." I pointed her to my barrel and pulled a crate over for myself. "Sit."

"Maid's day off?" Izzy fussed about her seat. She was very into hygiene. I mean, she'd blow a bottle of hand sanitizer if it looked at her with bedroom eyes and promised to make her feel real good afterwards. "Do I have to sit? I'll ruin my clothes!" she whined.

"Have a seat, *Lady* Isabelle." I was unamused with her prissiness in the face of the fact that she could have been neatly situated in her cabin right now with that bottle of hand sanitizer instead of here ruining all my plans. Once she and her flounces were arranged over the straw-and-dirt floor, I leaned over to whisper in her ear. "These clothes, this air of wealth, this is your shield," I warned. "Do anything to break the image of wealth and nobility, and we are screwed. And I mean dead."

Marco watched our whispered exchange but didn't interrupt until I sat back. "My lady, please call me Marco." He held out his hand and Izzy took it.

I bristled at the casual touch. These were two people in my life who should never have existed in the same room, let alone have their fingers intertwined. Marco kissed Izzy's hand gently, holding on just a touch longer than necessary. I ground my teeth, wishing I could warn Izzy. Marco had had even more wives than boats.

"Marco, Lady Isabelle. Isabelle, Marco." I tried, but I couldn't pry my eyes away from their hands. Why did they have to look like they fit together? Why did she have to have such doe eyes and beautiful skin? Why was he smiling back at her?

"Nice to meet you, Marco," she responded. Izzy was ready to make her vacation fun-filled in more ways than one. Getting a partner into bed was never a challenge for her.

I ground my teeth together. She was here with me, she would leave with me, we were having our last summer together, and that was that. If I had to shoot Marco again to make it happen, I would.

"Pleasure is all mine." The fucker smiled up at her. Izzy and Marco's hands finally dropped to their respective sides. I didn't relax.

"Drinks, ladies?" he asked.

"Sure. Is there a menu?" Izzy's question caught both him and me by surprise, and we laughed. Izzy was used to establishments with tufted-velvet club chairs, tables with a high-gloss lacquered finish, and servers that had bathed in the past month. The tension in my jaw broke a little (a very little) with the laughter. Menus. God bless her, that was hilarious. The memory of her asking for a menu at Tavern Rock was almost worth all the danger we were currently steeped in. Almost.

Marco sauntered to the bar. The clock was ticking. I had to get this deal done. Where was that thieving rat bastard? I clocked Reg ambling off, back toward the living quarters. Surely he was going to inform that rat bastard thief about Lady Isabelle.

"What do you mean 'dead'?" Izzy asked.

"Just keep your head down." I kept my eyes on Reg. "Say nothing. If I could have done this before you got aboard, I would have, but there were complications." Complications as in I didn't want to blow up. Charlie's cargo was gunpowder and arms, and I didn't care to risk carrying that crap through the portal.

Marco leaned against the bar and ordered our drinks. The barkeep was still busy when Reg returned and met two stooges by the door.

"When we get out of here, we are going to have a very, very long talk." Izzy gripped my arm.

No shit. "Agreed."

The talk in the tavern died down to just a few muted conversations. It was as if Reg was the stage manager and he'd just called places. Aside from that rat bastard thief being a thieving rat bastard, I had not walked into this tavern anticipating any issues. The deal was to pay that bastard an absurd amount of money for Charlie's cargo, put it on my ship, and leave. Not to toot my own horn or anything, but I was not a person you wanted on your bad side. Even that rat bastard thief wouldn't want me as an enemy. I was far more valuable to the merchant sailing community alive than dead. My jaw felt wired shut with tension. Marco likely knew what was happening but gave nothing away, the fucker. That rat bastard thief continued to make us all wait.

Marco returned to the table with the drinks and a subtle amused look on his face. If I could get him on his own, I could get the information out of him. He put the glasses of dark rum in front of each of us, one to me and one to Izzy. The last he took himself and sipped slowly.

Izzy sniffed at her glass and took a small sip, coughing at the potency. I'd seen her toss back absinthe; she could handle a little rum. I wish she'd handle it a little quieter, though.

"Cheers," Izzy said suddenly in full voice and raised her glass. Damn it all if the rest of the pirates didn't raise their drinks along with her. I shook my head in begrudging amazement. How did she do this? Didn't matter if you put Izzy into an AP history class, Miami dance club, or 17th-century black-market shack, she made friends and stole hearts. She drained her cup and turned it upside down like she was at a frat party playing quarters.

I left my glass right where he'd placed it. Marco refilled Izzy then picked up my untouched drink. "I know, I know Annie. You don't drink on duty."

"Don't call me Annie," I warned.

Marco offered Izzy his hand again. I glared. What was he up to now?

"My Lady?" I wondered if Izzy could sense the capital L in "Lady" when Marco addressed her. "Perhaps a short walk down to the water while we wait? I would enjoy a woman's presence after months of nothing but these salty and fermented sailors."

A few of the more brazen men chuckled and heckled. I made out a few comments: "Bet she smells real good." "What's the matter, Marco? Can't have your fun in here with us?" The rats, all of them, laughed and sneered. The hackles on my neck rose.

What was the lesser evil here? Keep Izzy in the line of fire but where I could see and protect her? Or let Marco escort her out of the lion's den and secrete her away in a secluded spot? The image of her hand in his made my stomach tighten. There were lots of clandestine spots on this tiny island, and Izzy worked fast. So did Marco, come to think of it. If

The Bitch Captain (and The Lady)

this little errand of mine took much longer, more than just their fingers might become intertwined. I shuddered. The lewd comments continued while Izzy formulated her response. Marco was the most palatable of this group, but I didn't know if I should encourage her. There were many things Marco could whisper in her ear away from my intervention.

Perhaps if you'd told her earlier...

Shut it.

"I'm quite content in my current location, thank you." Izzy dismissed him like a good noble lady, but her finesse left much to be desired. She must be thinking of secret places in the rocks too. I suppose I should feel good that she chose me over Marco.

"Annie, convince her otherwise." Marco's hand was still out.

There were no good options now, and I wanted my sister close. "Call me Annie one more time and I'm cutting off a finger." I loosened my short sword in its sheath for easy access.

He shrugged and sipped at his glass. Mine remained untouched. I kept scanning the denizens of the tavern; my barometer reading of the situation was not good. We were in for a storm. This storm wasn't precipitated by my sister, but she was the storm crow heralding it. Slowly the conversation rose around us again as we waited for that rat bastard thief to make his entrance.

"How's Mr. Hard To Let Go?" Marco waited patiently to see if I'd answer his taunt. I narrowed my eyes and kept my silence. "Come on, Annie," he baited me, "it was a long time ago."

Enough of this. I wasn't going to wait on Marco and the rat's timeline any longer. It was time to trip a few land mines.

"I swear to god, Marco—" I shoved my chair back and started to draw my sword. The stress of the situation already had me humming like a piano wire, and there Marco sat, the cherry on top of a nuclear reactor tower about to melt down, smiling and drinking a glass of rum and calling me by that stupid name. I didn't care if I owed him anything, I would have his head.

Izzy made a noise of protest, but it was drowned in the sudden click, click, click, click, click coming from every direction in the tavern. Every pirate in the joint had pulled out a firearm and cocked it. The tavern was quiet enough for a moment that all anyone heard was the sea.

And a ding.

A very distinctive ding that anyone from the 21st century would be able to shrug off as commonplace. The ding of a cell phone notification. Dings like that didn't belong in 1649.

Oh, I was so going to die. Scrap any gambling odds. I was dead.

A particularly mangy pirate tried to clear out an ear, wondering what exactly he'd just heard. No one lowered their gun.

Failure clapped its little hands in excitement.

"Ah, Annie," Marco sighed. "That rat bastard thief was concerned you might let your temper run away with you."

Ding.

"All this for one little lady?" I asked in my most simpering southern belle impression. I wanted to keep the attention on me and not Izzy and her stupid stupid stupid! phone.

"No one wants another Kings Bay." He motioned for me to take my seat.

There was my answer. Kings Bay. Kings Bay had been a massive failure of this thieving rat bastard to put an operating ring together throughout the triangle. It wasn't clear who tipped the navy off to our presence, but here I was, a woman, and men were superstitious and mean.

If he wanted—

"Good morning to yoooouuu.

Good morning to yoooouuu."

Marilyn Monroe's sultry voice as envisioned by a cartoon unicorn sang out from that devil rectangle in Izzy's lap. My world froze. Wisps of smoke wafted up from under my feet. The roar of the surf morphed into the sound of religious zealots calling for my death.

"Good morning to yoooouuu."

The pirates looked around for the source of the alien song. I had no time. This group would seize any chance to burn me alive. Ignore? Distract? Run? Izzy and her damn petticoats could barely make it to the table, she'd never make it out the door.

Distract.

There was a woman at the bar. An enslaved woman. She'd have to be Marilyn today. My apologies, Marilyn. I'll make it up to you.

"Good morning—"

I smashed my sword into the table, whipped out my pistol, took aim, and fired. The shot exploded a bottle of whiskey just to the right of Marilyn's head. My actions were so stunningly violent, unexpected, and loud the entire tavern lay silent and paralyzed. Twenty-first-century guns are a hell of a lot louder than the pop-gun flintlock grandfathers in the hands of these mangy pirates. There was no attention spared for Izzy. The men looked between me and the woman at the bar, who stared at me in terror.

"I will not be made a fool of, and I will not be intimidated!" I hollered above the ringing in my ears. "Leave!" I commanded her. Probably safer for her not to be here anyway. The woman fled without a moment's hesitation. "Get that thieving rat bastard out here now or I'm walking." My words were directed at Marco, but the threat was to the tavern at large.

"He's almost finished." Marco glanced towards the back living quarters. I heard some grunting and moaning from a deep male voice and muffled female cries.

"Nut or get off her, Rat!" I shouted back there. "St. Kitts would love this gold." I shook the box. The grunting increased. I'd pay Charlie some other way. Nothing was worth this. "I'm out. Tell that thieving rat bastard to contact me if he ever gets his dick back in his pants." I stood and gestured for Izzy to get up. My sister's face was a mask of shock and horror.

Marco blocked my way. He motioned the others back into their seats and spoke to me in a low voice. "That bastard knows you're the best ship on the sea. He's ready to pay through the nose." Marco was buttering me up. "A little patience will go a long way today."

"Why does it matter? What's in it for you?"

"I'm playing a hunch."

"I thought you didn't gamble."

"Only on sure things. Right now, that's you." He was too handsome for his own good. I wanted to kick his ass.

There was even more going on here than I realized. Marco wanted me here too much; desperation shadowed his words. He didn't like that rat bastard thief any more than I did, but here he was, working for him. There must be a reason for it.

He sighed and threw up his hands. "Ten minutes?"

"Three."

"Five. You owe me."

"Fine. Go tell that thief to get out here right now." I sat Izzy back down.

Marco was famous for his ability to play a long con. He wanted me as a piece in his game now, and I did owe him for leaving him to hang in that jail cell. He made sure I wasn't going to run, then went to the back and knocked on the door.

I slowly sat back down, and the pirates placed their guns on the table. No one uttered a word. That rat bastard thief finally made his entrance, still buckling up his belt as he entered the bar area. He and Marco actually made an impressive pair, both tall, well built, not the most filthy individuals in the room, but one would leave you bleeding and one would steal your shoes as you bled out.

"Well, well, well, if it isn't the Bitch Captain of the Seven Seas herself. And a new friend," he said, addressing Izzy.

"'Bitch'?" Izzy exclaimed. "Did he just call you—?" I shot her a severe look. She settled, but the countdown was on to get the hell out

The Bitch Captain (and The Lady)

of here before Izzy lost it or I cut off that thieving rat bastard's prick.

That rat bastard thief laughed and smiled. I knew that smile hid a thousand lies and betrayals. He could con the czarina herself into bed with his words and touch, but she'd still end up with herpes in the morning.

"My apologies, fair lady. But your captain and I have long neglected our pleasantries." He smiled and Izzy stared back at him warily. Marco poured her another rum.

The bastard ignored her and returned his attention to me. "I told you I would not do a deal for coins alone. Do you have my special request?"

I patted the sack, and he began to drool.

"Prove it." He sat back and laced his fingers over his belly. He was a barrel-chested mountain of avarice held together with sail-canvas pants and a leather bandolier.

I reached in and pulled off a tiny piece of pastry from one of hundreds filling the sack. I placed the tiny bit of cake and cream between us. The rat bastard thief had a sweet tooth, and I didn't care whether he died because of a bullet or diabetes. It would all be a win for me. He gobbled up the bite of cake and drooled over my bag. It had been tedious work unwrapping these hundreds of cakes.

"How much do you want?" He kept his eyes on the bag of cakes.

"Charlie specified that you and he have already discussed items and amounts. I have gold to supplement if the cargo is sufficiently valuable. I am also open to buying up more than just what Charlie asked for. It appears you've got an abundance on your hands, and I'd be willing to buy some of it outright if the quality holds."

"Show me what's in the box." He tapped the top of my strongbox, almost as eager for the sight of gold as for the cake.

"I will not take live cargo," I specified before opening the small chest.

"LIVE cargo?" Izzy exclaimed.

"It pays better," the rat spoke to Izzy.

Izzy made a distinctive Black Girl Noise, and I thought that perhaps I'd give her the honor of castrating this rat bastard.

"No live cargo. Charlie has no need for that," he confirmed. "Besides, we all know the sea bitch travels alone." He eyed Izzy. "At least she did."

"Fair Lady, we would all love to know what goes on aboard that ship of hers." Marco sat down close to my sister and refilled her glass again. What was he playing at?

"Oh, yes. Do tell us a story," that rat bastard thief crooned. I noticed the other pirates were leaning in with anticipation too. Disgusting, head-in-the-gutter fools, all of them.

"Well..." Izzy was tipsy, and I worried she'd had too much to keep the pretense of her ladyship up. She hadn't exactly walked into the tavern sober as a priest on Sunday either.

"This box is bursting with gold and you want a bedtime story?" I cut Izzy off.

"I'd love to hear about your bed, Annie." Marco grinned like the devil himself.

"That's it!" I pulled out my dirk, pinned his hand on the table, and took aim.

"Annie!" Marco ripped his hand away and lunged for me. That rat bastard pulled Marco back, and the bar erupted with the clicks of guns cocking again.

"Enough! I will not have this turn into another Kings Bay!" the rat bastard hollered.

Everyone sheathed their weapons, including me, and had a seat. I felt Izzy's eyes on me but didn't dare take mine off Marco and the rat.

"Now, let's see that gold," he ordered.

I opened the box filled with glittering gold, silver, and gems, but the men looked at it with anticlimactic expressions. I think they would have actually sold Izzy the cargo for her stories of life on my ship.

The Bitch Captain (and The Lady)

"And the other?" The rat bastard thief indicated the sack, which I opened to reveal hundreds of preservative-filled snack cakes.

"We have a deal?" I cinched the sack back up tight.

"We have a deal." He poured me a shot of rum and one for himself, and we drank together. "Start loading her up!" he ordered his enslaved men.

I got up to oversee the loading, but that rat bastard thief grabbed my arm. "Not just yet, girly."

"I will cut your arm off," I threatened. He removed his hand but stayed close enough that I could smell his breath and sweat and cum.

"You owe me an apology for Kings Bay," he demanded right back.

"You made your own mistakes there. I owe you nothing."

"I lost my ship." His hands itched towards me again.

"You kept what mattered." He'd escaped with his life, a feat only Marco, myself, and a scant few others could boast of.

"All these fine gentlemen here lost ships as well. In fact, everyone lost their ships. Everyone except you. That's led us all to become mighty curious as to how those soldiers found us." He leaned back in his chair, awaiting explanation.

I had not called in the navy. One of the other desperate and dubious men there had ratted us out, if not this bastard himself.

"Life is full of mystery, isn't it?" I said, eyeing the door and planning my escape. Failure tickled up my spine. This was the real reason that thieving rat bastard had offered to do business with me. He thought I owed him a pound of flesh, and he meant to take it off me.

Izzy's quick and nervous breathing reminded me that I was hand-cuffed by her presence. *I* could probably make it out of this place, but she was a sitting duck. For so long I'd traveled alone, free from the responsibility of another life on my boat, carefree and reckless. Now Izzy was here. Now I wasn't a lone wolf anymore.

"Lady Isabelle, it's time to leave." I stood.

"No. No, I don't think so." That rat bastard thief stood toe to toe with me.

I dropped my hand to my sword. He didn't blink. He was the one with several crews' worth of backup. I was the one with a ball and chain in brocade at my back.

"I'm owed an apology," he repeated.

"The Bitch Captain of the Seven Seas doesn't apologize." I gripped the hilt, threatening violent responses if he kept this up. We could all still walk away. He just needed to prove to his men he was the big bad. I waited and watched his thoughts churn. Come on, give me the opening I need, you bastard. I'll let you play your charade, but it'll be on my terms.

That rat bastard thief laughed. "I'm not an unreasonable man. I can offer an alternative." He laughed again. "No need for any apologies. Words are cheap. I'll just take your ship."

"Like hell you will." I'd burn my ship before letting him close enough to sniff the teak.

He just laughed and stroked a finger down my cheek. I should really never have let him make out with me that one time. Sure, I made off with his cargo hold of tobacco afterwards, but was it worth it? Yeah, it was worth it; I made a killing off that haul in Calais.

"Perhaps a partnership? Now that you take passengers," he strayed a step inside my personal boundaries, "we could sail together." Guess he still had fond memories of our time in St. Kitts.

"No," Marco interrupted in a sharp, clear tone. "No men on her ship."

"You heard him." I walked that rat bastard thief out of my personal space with a finger to his chest. He backed off but kept the smile on his face.

"Have it your way. What'll it be? Your ship? An hour with you?" He sighted Izzy and a new avenue for his greed appeared. "I am not picky. I would take an hour with your fare." The bastard maneuvered

The Bitch Captain (and The Lady)

behind Izzy and wrapped his dirty hands around her hips. He sniffed at her hair.

"Get off of me!" Izzy screamed. She was on her feet now with a bright new shade of panic in her eyes. She gave him a sharp elbow to his solar plexus and broke free.

"Do not touch her, you thieving rat bastard," I moved in front of my sister.

Now, I knew this was just another bargaining ploy. Besides the fact that it took him the better part of an hour to get off before making his entrance, he had no interest in getting between my or anyone else's knees at this time. He just wanted to have his say, get high off seeing fear in my eyes and body, and perhaps get me to throw in another sack of cake.

All males in this era (all eras) loved to throw my virtue and my sex in my face as a way to denigrate my skills. Very few would actually make good on their threats as to do so would mean losing good business. I wasn't captain of a big ship, but I specialized in hard-to-find items and had contacts in ports all over. I'd earned that Bitch Captain of the Seven Seas title fair and square. Thus far, I was more useful to men in my ship than in their bed. Money talked louder than sex on the sea. Money bought you sails. Anyone could be bent over willingly enough in port or on the water if they got bored enough. Bending me over would only lose them money along with their favorite appendage.

Izzy did not know this. "This is a rough place," I'd told her. Izzy didn't truck with male nonsense. She was a savvy club-hopping, bar-closing, late-night-partying beautiful woman who had no illusions when it came to her own safety. She'd brought her phone. Why wouldn't she bring her own weapon? After all, I'd brought several of mine. Why wouldn't she have chosen some protection too?

The thieving rat bastard cried out in pain as the pepper spray met his eyes at point-blank range. The nearest pirates went down next, and soon we were all rubbing our stinging eyes.

The rat bastard thief was rolling on the floor screaming, "Witch! She burned me! Witch!" The rat was frenzied.

The other pirates were in a panic watching the rat bastard brought down by a woman who shot invisible fire from her hands. They took up the call, and I heard a faint crackling in my ear as the smell of smoke filled my nostrils. The stake reared its ugly head before my eyes, and my pulse quickened. It's not real, I told myself as my eyes stung with remembered smoke and chemical capsaicin. It's not real. It's just the pepper spray.

"Witch!" the rat bastard screamed again. The crowd had roared at me the same way, calling me witch, calling for my death.

The smoke intensified until I couldn't see through it, until I couldn't breathe. Izzy was shrieking. I met the rat with one hand gripping his beard and the other hand holding my short sword pressed to the delicate under skin of his neck.

"Back down," I cautioned and pulled the blade enough to draw blood.

"Thou shalt not abide—" The rat's shout cut off in a gurgle of his own blood as I slit his throat. My panic attack cleared as I took that rat bastard and all his threats out of this world.

Someone fired a pistol with a deafening bang, and my calf collapsed under me with a hot, heavy weight.

"Get your back to the wall, Izzy!" I ordered as the tavern erupted.

I pulled out my pistols, wanting a fast end to this fight. With four shots in each of my guns, seven pirates met their maker in a very fast and surprising way. The rat was still rolling on the ground around my feet, and I leaped over him to meet a cutlass mid-swing. Jab, cross, uppercut, throw through the window.

"Feel like jumping in here, Marco?" I shouted as I ducked a sword. I charged after the gunman and sliced through a series of arteries that brought him down in a wave of red.

"I need passage to London," he bargained.

The Bitch Captain (and The Lady)

"No men on my ship." I parried a sword, disarmed, and sank said sword deep into a belly.

"Cheers then, Annie," Marco toasted me.

"Don't call me Annie!" I used my last remaining shot on him and missed. I started to chase him but was hauled back by a pirate twice my size. One of them got behind me, and my right arm went dead as someone shot me in the shoulder. The mace dropped to ground. I scooped it up with my left and screamed in rage and cleaved his head open.

Curses and obscenities poured out of me as I went after more of the attackers, who were now afraid of me and regretting their life choices. No matter. They wouldn't have long to spend their remorse. After a decidedly distasteful incident in my early days of traveling, I had dedicated myself to learning several martial arts. My favorites were boxing and judo. On my boat there were a punching bag and a speed ball that I hung and practiced with on all those lonely days at sea. These lazy, drunken pirates were no match.

My shoulder and leg were screaming by this point when a slug found the back of my hand. I hissed and growled at the long, deep path the lead ball furrowed into me. Izzy was cornered and wielding a broken chair at some drooling mongrel, and I lost all sense and control. I can't remember much else of that fight except to register that Marco was at Izzy's back and for that I would owe him another goddamn favor.

In moments we went from screams and gunshots and rage to a dead quiet in the tavern. Failure lay sprawled on the floor amongst the bodies in a post-coital glow of ecstasy.

Just me, Marco, Izzy, and the now-freed Tainos were left.

I kept my blade trained on Marco. "Did your gamble pay off?"

He nodded. "My debts are settled now." He shoved the rat's body over. "He's finally where he belongs." Marco spat on him.

As much as I hated that rat bastard thief, I hated being used as a weapon. This was Marco's con all along. He wanted the rat dead, and there was no surer way of accomplishing that than setting me free on him. The rat had set the stage, but Marco had tipped us all over the edge. The fucker.

"Would you at least consider taking me to London?" he had the nerve to ask.

"I'm taking the cargo and Isabelle and leaving."

"I've never gotten in your way before." He looked around the tavern, strewn with dead pirates, and sighed, "Looks like you got me a boat after all. Thank you."

"Take your pick." He gave me a curt nod and went out to inspect his available prospects.

Izzy was wild-eyed and frozen to the wall where I'd ordered her. I was able to pull her outside but not much further. She'd be okay for now by the door.

I went back in and picked up the sack of cakes. The formerly enslaved people were surveying the carnage. As I approached them, they stood together and presented a united front, wondering what price the bloodstained fury in front of them might demand.

"The place is yours now if you care for it," I told them. I shoved the strongbox into the woman's arms. "I'd appreciate it if you would help load the rest of the cargo."

There was hardly an inch of space left on the boat once we were finished. I scavenged what I wanted from the dead pirates' ships, what I wanted from the tavern, and what was owed to Charlie. I'd make a killing in any port in the world right now. The *Try Your Luck* sat low in the water, and I made automatic adjustments in my head for the next leg of our trip.

The woman I'd handed the box of gold to led Izzy down to the dock. I nodded in thanks, and she departed back to the tavern. Izzy kept her eyes on the woman until she disappeared into the shot-up structure. Then my sister turned on me.

"Anne, what the fuck is happening?" Her voice was steady, but the rest of her shook.

I looked around for a blanket. She was in shock, and people in shock needed blankets and juice boxes. I didn't have any juice boxes. I should take off my coat and wrap her in it. My hands were shaking, and my coat was covered in blood. She needed a coat not covered in blood. Where could I find that? My boat, I could find that on my boat. Izzy still waited for an answer.

"It's okay. We're fine. We're safe." My head was still spinning with adrenaline, and I twitched at the least sound. I held out my hand, even though it shook, and offered to help her aboard.

She almost took it but then looked me over, head to toe, and backed away. I was covered in the stuff of nightmares. Izzy hadn't come out of this unscathed either, at least her dress hadn't. The garment was torn and sliced and stained in a dozen different locations with alcohol, blood, and dirt. I'd probably have to burn it. There was no salvaging that costume.

"Where are we?" Her eyes wheeled in the dim evening light.

What are you going to tell her?

"It's 'when,'" I answered.

"What?"

"'When are we' is the question. The answer is 1649, June 1649." I had to start somewhere. Might as well start here.

"Time travel?! Those were bedtime stories Da read us, not instruction manuals!" She'd always liked to hear every detail of the dresses and the fancy balls. She'd make him repeat the passages about silk brocades over and over again while I pulled the covers up and wondered...was it really possible?

"They were journals, not stories." Non-fiction versus fiction. A vacuum-cleaner warranty booklet versus Hans Christian Anderson. "They are true." I'm not going to say I was expecting her to cheer and rejoice as I had when I'd made that discovery. But perhaps a tiny bit of excitement?

Izzy rage-screamed at me and shoved me off the dock. It was a long drop and a cold splash down. I choked and sputtered in surprise once I bobbed to the surface. There was just enough light to see Izzy flip me off before stomping onto the now heavily-laden boat.

Dumbass.

.

.

.

I know.

"Mom's finally settled down," Izzy said as she flopped on the couch next to me. She handed me a sandwich, and I picked at it without eating. "You really have her worried, you know." I shrugged. I didn't want to go into it. "You worry me too by the way." She had me there. I didn't like to worry Izzy.

"I know. I don't mean to." I spoke to my plate since I couldn't look her in the eye.

"You can't keep running away like this." She turned my face to look at her.

"I don't mean to. I'm just not good at it yet." Izzy was like truth serum. I couldn't not talk to her.

"I hope you're never good at running away." She laid her head on my shoulder, and the gesture was so familiar and pure I almost broke down right there on that old corduroy couch.

"I'm not running. I'm...traveling," I tried to explain.

"Are you here?" she asked.

"No."

"Did you tell me where you were going?" Izzy wouldn't let me look away.

"No."

"Then what's the difference?"

"Nothing. I guess."

"Traveling. So what do you do when you...travel?" Izzy was trying to be patient with me, and I was trying to find a way to tell her everything I was desperate for her to know. I'd love to tell her what sunrise looked like on the untouched coastline of the Americas. How the world smelled before the discovery of fossil fuels. The absolute quiet of endless miles of unpaved land and empty skies.

"I just go see places. Went to Florida once." Once. That was a colossal mistake. "It's more like...more like... it's time traveling. Going back in time and just being free." There, I said it.

"Time traveling...okay," Izzy said. "Can you tell me any more about that?"

God, how I wished to tell her everything about it.

"How about I show you someday? Think you'd like to go sometime?" I asked.

"Maybe. Let's get through high school first, okay?" I don't think she understood what I was saying. She flipped on the TV to put on some stupid show. I loved TV. No thinking, just numbing.

"Sure." I ate my sandwich.

CHAPTER 2

Take Me Away

The cold Atlantic water quickly worked its way through my layers of clothing and pulled me under. I struggled to a dock post and began to haul myself up and out of the brine. One benefit of Izzy pushing me off the dock was that much of the blood from the tavern rinsed off me. I'd still be dyed a nice period-pantie brown for a while until I could clean the clothing thoroughly. Great.

The cold water also had a chilling effect on my fevered brain, still marinating in its adrenaline cocktail from the fight. I had killed before. It wasn't something I'd made a habit of or anything, but things happen on the sea when you travel alone. Taking the journeys I do required a level of risk and commitment. The eerie part was how easy it was to lose the ego in myself that vowed, "Oh, I'd never!" and become cozier and cozier with the aspect of my id that whispered, "See, we move on, we are whole, we are here." After the first few (by accident or design), their lives had left my thoughts and my heart as fast as their souls had left the earth.

Today was a different story. Today was a massacre. I felt the blood on my hands stronger than with others. Their souls passing quickly through my body left me nauseous and revolted. I had not planned this massacre, and it gained me nothing. I had not come there for blood. I did not want their blood, did not want to know the feel of their souls on mine. I felt cheated, robbed, raped, wrong. I scraped my hands extra hard on the barnacles encrusting the dock, feeling too much the Lady Macbeth inside me.

They are ghosts, I counseled myself. They are all simply ghosts. They were dead long before I was born, and no one will remember them. I took a few steadying breaths while I tread water. Ghosts didn't matter. Their blood, their souls were irrelevant, brief impressions on this planet, now blown away like sand.

I had learned a valuable lesson today: traveling with Izzy was going to be dangerous and costly. I thought I had prepared. I thought, I really had thought, that I was prepared. God laughed at me through the stars. I began to pull myself up the dock post, hand over hand, with my eyes on those laughing stars. Laugh, God, go ahead and laugh! But I had been born pulling myself up and damn it all if I was going to stop now. Finally on top, I stormed down the weathered planks, kicking at seagulls along the way. I swung onto my boat and sought out the cake sack and a bottle of rum.

Against a backdrop of moon and stars, I watched Marco put his newly-acquired ship out to sea. "Fuck you!" I hollered after him, mad for mad's sake and with a dash of my remaining blood lust. He was too far and too busy tacking to hear the epithet. I threw a snack cake at his departing ass.

Then I threw another tiny cake at the closest seagull. "Fuck you too, you stupid sea rat!"

I shoved one of the treats in my mouth. It actually complemented the taste of the brine that still lingered on my tongue. I ate another one. Threw another one at a seagull that had just landed on the prow, cream exploding everywhere, and I cursed again, knowing I'd just have to clean it up before it corroded the varnish.

I took a swig of rum. "Dammit!" I shouted and took another gulp. The sugar in the rum competed with the artificial sweetness of the cake, but I chugged it down anyway.

The Bitch Captain (and The Lady)

I had five hard and fast rules while traveling. Rule number two was to avoid alcohol. Fuck it. What the hell was another rule broken?

"Fuck it!" I hollered out loud to the gulls chowing down on the cakes now littering the dock and rocks.

The raging adrenaline from the massacre on my hands, mixed with the rum, mixed with the burning realization that all my plans were fucked sent me into a fit. I pulled off my wet and bloody clothes until I was in nothing but my birthday suit, threw the lines into the water, and mooned the island goodbye before I was too drunk to navigate away from the rocks. Just needed to get out to sea and then the winds could blow me where they may.

"You hear that!" I hollered to the winds. "Come on down, Zephyrus! I dare you to make a better plan, you breezy bastard!" I chugged more of the rum and relished the numbness seeping into my sickened heart. I cackled and coughed and screamed until the souls from the tavern quieted in fear of my madness.

I stumbled down to my cabin and found dry clothes. Who had left all this blood on the wall? On my door? On my drawers? Huh. I pulled my hand away from my shoulder glistening with red. Guess I was bleeding a little.

My leg collapsed under me and sent me sprawling. Shit. I reached into a drawer and pulled out a fresh wrap. There was an entrance and an exit wound in my right calf, leaking blood steadily down to my foot. The rivulets captivated me as my cabin spun and blurred. The shower turned on in Izzy's cabin and brought me out of my haze. I wrapped my calf as tight as my numb fingers allowed and put on loose pants, an oversized shirt, and slippers. The rum was waiting for me in the galley. I took another swig as I looked at Izzy's closed door.

Izzy.

Izzy was the important thing. I had vowed that if she came with me, she'd never know harm. First journey out and I'd almost gotten her killed. I had to be better. I had to do better. The damned souls melted away in the heat of that vow.

I returned to the wheel. Someone had left blood on the wheel too. And blood in my slippers. Rum is delicious. I drank more of it. The current grabbed the ship and the winds pulled at the sails. We were away.

Cold air rushed through my hair.

Warm rum inside my body.

The moon on my skin.

Take me away.

Take me away.

Take me away.

I calmed as the rum blurred my vision, and the open ocean swells rocked me in a familiar lullaby. I made soft corrections at the helm and sipped at the sweet anesthesia in my hand.

"What are we to do now?" I mumbled as a chill wind caught my breath.

"I was just about to ask the same thing." Izzy appeared on deck, dressed and showered.

"Great minds…and all that." I slurred a little and turned my face up to feel the moon. I really did just love rum. Snack cakes were also good too. Rum was good too. And cake. And rum.

"You're bleeding," she announced. "Where are you injured?"

"Yes." I was definitely bleeding in places. "Some places." She didn't need to know all the places. It would scare her. "It'll be fine. I'm always fine. Tiny cake?"

Izzy did not take the tiny, sweet, little handheld cake I offered. I raised my head back to the sky and offered the cake to the spinning moon. She'd love this snack. I chucked it as high as I could and watched it plunk back into the waves. That's fine. The waves were her children. Sweet little wet babies that kept my ship moving. It took me a few tries, but I got a few more sips of rum. I loved rum. This was good stuff too.

The Bitch Captain (and The Lady)

"You know, say what you want about that rat bastard thief, but he has good taste in rum." I took another swig. "Ha! Say whatever you want about him because he's dead!" I felt again the beat of his heart through my sword, saw his eyes looking straight into mine, calling my sister a witch, smelling of smoke and char.

"Hear that!" I shouted to his specter. "Dead! You bastard!" My right arm failed me as I tried to drink again. I switched the bottle to my left. The better to drown you with, my dear. "Fucking dead. All dead. Lucky bastards." Sitting atop the crates were all the ghosts of the men I'd taken out of this world. They smiled as I choked on their vapors.

"Sit down, Anne. You're drunk." She pulled me off the wheel and took over steering. Good. Probably less chance we'd die. I reached for another snack cake. *Slap.*

"Hey!" I reached for another. *Slap.* "Dammit, Izzy!"

Izzy tried to throw something over me, but I threw it off. I cackled and collapsed on the port bench. When I rolled over, the bench was covered in blood. Who shot my ship??! My poor ship was bleeding. I pulled a blanket over the ship's wound and patted it. There, there, I'll take care of you, Ship.

Izzy was a kind soul just like my ship. For some reason she liked me, cared for me. She dug out an old orange life preserver and clipped me into it, pinching my skin in the clasps. "Ouch."

The little pinches joined a multitude of other ouches, and I began to realize that I hurt. I hurt all over. I think I might have gotten shot a few times. I looked at my hand. Yup. That hurt. Rum would probably help that. I drank some rum. Then another rum. Probably I should get my special flask out. But one does not drink from that Fountain willy-nilly. I really did hurt, though. Yeah, it was time for Fountain.

"I need to go get a drink." I tried to take a step. I didn't succeed.

"For fuck's sake, would you just sit your ass down so I can bandage you up?" Izzy and her cake-slapping hand, poised for more cake-slapping, pulled me back to the bench, and I had no ability to fight her. I was out of fight. "I don't imagine there's any point in attempting to call anyone for medical assistance."

"Not unless you like leeches." I imagined trying to call for anyone out here on the ocean. It would just be me yelling off the deck into the vast nothingness. It was a funny image. Maybe a porpoise would jump up on deck and say *Dr. Porpoise here, looks like you've been shot. My prescription is fish!* Then it would jump back into the ocean and disappear.

My stomach hurt.

The heat of the fight still burned ember-like beneath my skin. I took another swig. Sobriety was for the birds. Tonight, rum was for me. Mmmmmm. Rummmmmm. Rum and after-school snack cakes.

Slap. "What the hell!" How did this keep happening? I focused on my sister – both of them – nope, three of them. That's how she kept getting my snacks: six arms. I'd show those arms. Come at me, arms. Want to fight, arms? *Slap!* I tumbled to the deck. After finding my own arms, I managed to haul myself back up. Rough ocean tonight, everything was swaying so much. I hurt in a lot of places. More rum would help that.

I lay back against a barrel and looked up at the stars. It was only partially cloudy tonight and I held up my hand to sight the distance between the Little Dipper and the horizon. Not too far off course. As my hand was up I contemplated the gash the lead ball had left between my fingers. The flesh was ragged from my wrist to between my thumb and pointer. The gun mustn't have had much charge. The furrow was not terribly deep but stung like a mother and was bleeding profusely.

"Anne!" Some basic bitch clapped her hands in front of my face. Oh! It was Izzy. Right. I remembered her. "Do we have a heading to follow?" Izzy asked from so high above me.

"Yes. That way." I pointed away from Tavern Rock...tried to point. My arm wasn't working well. "Not that way." I pointed backwards towards where all the blood and bodies still littered the crappy shack's floor. I felt again the pulse of that rat bastard's artery beating through my blade. He couldn't just leave well enough alone. I'd need to clean that sword really well, it was my favorite.

"Just how drunk are you?" I looked up at Izzy. Oh yeah, I forgot she was here.

"I don't drink on duty." I did my best Marco impression. He just had to be there today. He just *had* to be right exactly there to ruin everything today. "Fucking Marco. It's rule number...uh...three...no, two. Yeah. No alcohol. Rule number two." Marco. That fucker. "Damn him straight to hell. He did that on purpose. I need a drink." I swiped some cream off the deck and stuck my finger in my mouth. Not bad. I went in for a second swipe. Where'd that rum go?

"No! You're the captain, you have to captain." Awww, she was scared we'd drown. So cute.

"Captain!" I laughed. It was my very favorite name. I loved it when people called me captain. It's what I did. It's what I was. It's all I'd ever be...till the unlikely day I died. Looky there, another tiny cake!

"That's great. I need you to let me look you over." Izzy made a move towards me.

"Here I am." I struck a pose on the bench. All I needed was a big blue necklace to complete the look. My body couldn't stay stretched out, and I quickly curled in on myself. My leg seized up, and I hissed at the pain. I threw the bottle across the deck where it skittered into the ocean. I'd have enough trouble tomorrow without the rest of that rum in my system.

I needed to drink something else. I needed to drink the Fountain, and I really needed to shower. Izzy had already showered and changed. She was in shorts now. No longer Lady Isabelle, she was back to being my sister. She had looked so regal in Tavern Rock. Just as I'd envisioned her to look in that outfit.

"You looked good in that dress. I liked that dress. Shame about it now. Probably need to burn it." The blood had detracted somewhat from the regality.

"Yeah. I did." Izzy fingered the latches on the kit, itching to sink them deep into gauze and antiseptic goo. "Anne, please? I'm really tired, and I need to make sure you're not about to bleed to death."

"I'm not." She was worried for nothing. I wasn't going to die. "You can go to bed. Ocean's calm tonight."

Izzy finally sat and released her hold on the first aid box. As soon as she went to sleep, I could drink the Fountain and put this day behind me. She said she was tired, but more words kept pouring out of her like an unstoppable spigot of verbs and adjectives.

"You have a cut on your forehead." She sat down like she was going to war and chose her weapons: alcohol swabs and gauze. "I'm going to clean it and put a dressing over it. And I'm going to stay calm and not think about how Stockholm-y this feels. Because it really feels like I'm being a medic for my kidnapper. But that's crazy, right?"

"Not crazy. I did do that. Kidnapped you a little bit. Yes." She was not gentle with gauze. I shied away from her, but she was a wiry little bitch and I couldn't escape. "But I had a good reason. I swear," I protested.

"Right." I don't think she meant that. I don't think she believed I had a good reason at all. Well, I did. So there.

"So you've been time-traveling." She kept swiping me with cotton. "And now you've dragged me back to the Dark Ages with you. Why?"

"It's more like the late Renaissance." The clothing in the Dark Ages had less shape and shine. Also, there was that plague.

"That's not the fucking point and you know it. Why? How could you bring me here?" Once again with the yelling. The whales were going to start complaining soon.

Because I couldn't leave her again. Because I couldn't lose yet another person. Because I was a chicken shit loser. "One, it was written." I was such a coward.

So tell her.

"And two—"

Tell her why you stole her.
Rule number four: no goodbyes.
Tell her you need her.
She'll be scared.
Tell her anyway.

"And two, I didn't want to say goodbye. So I just took you with me a little bit." I should not have said that. She wasn't to know yet that this was my farewell tour with her. When I brought her back home, it would be the last time we ever saw each other. "But mostly the written one," I mumbled. "Yeah, let's go with that." The rum churned in my stomach, and I gritted my teeth against the pain.

"It was written? What the hell is any of that supposed to mean? I want answers, and I want them now!"

"Hold on. Hold on. Hold on. I'll be right back." I shoved her hands off my head and limped my way down to her cabin, banging into the stairwell and ship walls as I went.

Blood followed me wherever I landed. Blood always followed me. I hurt all over. In her cabin I pulled the false front off her dresser to find the books I stashed there, books that did nothing but gather dust and be more useless than our father's old suits. I hadn't used this cabin for a long time except to store overflow cargo. I tossed the false front aside and grabbed a stack of loose papers that were terrible photocopies of the matriarch's journal. I hoisted myself up and felt a new rivulet of blood run down my leg. That was going to be a problem.

I limped back up the steps to the deck and shoved the papers at Izzy. "Here."

"What the fuck is this? Just tell me why you dragged me here!" She kept screaming.

My head pounded in time with my heartbeat. I wouldn't be upright for long at this rate. I tried to get the papers into her hands but kept failing. My triple vision was down to just double, but I kept choosing the wrong Izzy hands.

"I believed our bastard father's stories. Yes, I did. And this is what he read to us at bedtime. The journal. The only piece of our inheritance worth a damn. Our family matriarch's journal."

Izzy was altogether too coordinated and fended off the papers. "If I read a story about a black hole sucking down a spaceship and found out it was real, I wouldn't fucking take you there!"

"What if you were really, really lonely? Maybe you would then." The words escaped me before I could wrangle them back into my throat.

It's the truth, but do you want her to know the truth?

Shut up, you stupid annoying voice, and go back to hell.

"What does that have to do with why you brought me here?" She was steadfastly refusing to look at the pages I'd brought her. The numbing rum was beginning to wear off, and I was starting to feel my wounds.

"Oh my god, so many words. All these words." God, my shoulder was going to fall off.

Sea spray launched over the port side, and I shrieked as the cold water hit my body and the salt stung my open wounds. The water woke me up, and I began to get upset. We were not supposed to exit the portal into a massacre. We were supposed to be learning about time travel together and enjoying a new aspect of our inheritance.

My sister was asking for answers and refusing to acknowledge the proof I was placing right in front of her eyes. All she had to do was extend herself a little and read.

"Look at the damn pages! Look! Look at them! Do you see? I couldn't believe it when I saw. Jesus, my leg hurts. Look at the pages, Izzy! Look!" The sea water brought pain to the foreground of my brain. My body was screaming now that the rum had loosened its gags on my nerve endings. "Look at the writing. Do you recognize it? It's your handwriting, Izzy. These pages, you wrote them. It's all you." I pointed again and again, trying to will her to see what I saw, but she wouldn't even look at the words. She knocked them all out of my hands, and the wind scattered the papers all over the boat and out to sea. I sighed as

The Bitch Captain (and The Lady)

I watched them fly away. Some landed on the deck. It didn't matter. I only needed one for evidence.

Izzy looked in bad shape. I had promised our mother that I'd take care of her, and here I was doing the shittiest job of caretaker in the universe. I was not a mother; I would never be a mother. I only had to look at Izzy to know how terrible a job I'd do attempting to raise and keep a separate life safe.

"Would you please just sit the fuck down and let me help you?!" She held up one of the first aid kits I'd packed for her as tears started flowing.

"Izzy! Don't cry!" I was the worst sister ever. Dragging her here, getting her in a bloody fight, and now making her cry. "What's wrong? Are you hurt? Where are you hurt?" I couldn't stand Izzy in pain. I patted her down, looking for any wincing or tell-tale signs of pain. "Don't cry. It'll be okay." My hand came away from her shirt bloody. She'd been hurt! "Oh my god! You're bleeding!" I touched another part of her shirt and saw blood there too. And blood on my hand. I touched a third area of her shirt to confirm my hypothesis. "Oh, that's me." Now I'd need to burn her shirt along with her dress. We were really working our way through her wardrobe.

"Sit the fuck down or I'm going to tell Mom every sordid detail about how you brought me to an oceanic nightmare," she threatened.

Ugh, I did not want Mom to know this. Mom enjoyed thinking of me as the screw-up daughter who had finally stopped embarrassing her in public. Getting confirmation from her favorite daughter that I was a screw-up beyond her wildest nightmares was not how I wanted to be remembered.

"Mean." I sat and pouted. It was cold out tonight. I pulled the blanket around myself and shivered.

"Thank you. Will you let me take a look and make sure you're not about to die? I really, really can't handle that right now." She looked tired and young. I remembered seeing her bloody and young in the hospital bed after the crash that stole her parents.

"I'm not going to die." I offered her the blanket; she needed it more than me. The air blew around me, and I shook as I held the blanket out. My shoulder was killing me, and I was afraid if I stood my leg would give out.

"Famous last words, Anne!" She did not accept the blanket.

"I'm fine." Blood clots, wounds heal. I just needed Izzy to lose steam and go to bed already. One swig, some god-awful consequences, and these wounds would leave me in peace. She continued to look young and small and tired. I was tired. I was so very tired and so very lonely.

"I stole you. I'd do it again. Our time was almost up and…I couldn't say goodbye. So I took you along with me." I had had nothing left before Izzy stepped on this boat. I'd have even less after she left. Izzy almost put a hand on my leg, but I pulled it aside. She would never see these scars, never touch them. It was bad enough I had to look at myself on a daily basis.

She would have noticed sooner rather than later that I was a time traveler. I had, at the outside, ten of her years left before she put the clues together. Part of this trip was planned so I could explain to her, gently, the direction my life had taken. I wanted to explain so that when she outgrew me, and she had already outgrown me in several ways, she wouldn't be left wondering why I wasn't with her anymore. She would know that I hadn't wanted to leave her, but that I couldn't stay. When I brought her back home, I would not return for her. I would let her go. That thought haunted my nightmares.

"Anne?" Izzy's voice pulled me out of my reverie.

I was shocked to see her sitting close to me. Carefully, she put an arm around me, and I froze. The touch and proximity were more than I'd experienced in years. I was captivated at the sight and feel of her arm wrapped around me in a loving and non-hostile manner.

"I know that right now, you're not feeling so well. You're in pain, and you're tired, and probably a bunch of other things I don't even know about." My sister put her hand on my head, and I thought I might fall into that gesture and live there forever. I'd started this day with promise and hope and ended it covered in gore and sin. But Izzy was still here and still wanted to care for me. Tears burned down my cheeks as I watched my sister stay by my side.

"All I want to do is to make it a little better. Please, Anne, will you let me help you?" My wounds were screaming at me and I'd lost track of where the rum bottle had skittered off to on the deck and I'd dragged my sister back in time and traumatized her and everything sucked.

"My shoulder hurts," I mumbled. Giving a name to the beast brought the pain to the forefront and I could no longer think around it. My other wounds lined up behind it, vying for equal attention.

"Okay." Izzy hugged me and looked like I'd given her a lifeline. She always was a sucker for the weak and pathetic, and right now I was queen of the pathetics. "Thank you. I can stop the bleeding and I have pain medicine. Will you let me move your shirt so I can start with your shoulder?"

I shrugged off the life preserver and hesitated only a moment before removing my shirt.

"Thank you." She sighed and moved closer to examine me with her cut-rate medical certifications.

I probably should have cared more that my shirt was off and Izzy was looking over my bloodied and beaten non-corpse, but I was empty. I kept my eyes on the waves. I couldn't look at her. She had seen some of my scars before; we'd shared a room for most of our formative years. She knew I had a tattoo on my arm and a brand on my neck, but some of the marks would be new. I prayed the moon wasn't bright enough for her to register some of my more offensive disfigurements.

"Jesus, Anne. If I had known it was this bad, I would have wrestled you to the ground to bandage you up," she rebuked.

I shrugged and put my head in my hands. I'd been in worse fights.

The rum rushed through my system. I'd passed the point of floating on the surface of the alcohol, now I was drowning. Breathing was a chore. Judging by the amount of blood in my boot, on the bench, clotted in my clothing, smeared on the deck…I might be experiencing blood loss.

"Sorry. This is going to hurt," she warned, a millisecond before jabbing me with cold, pointy metal.

"Son of a motherfucking bitch! Get that out of me! Are you trying to kill me?!? Fucking hell!! My god! Stop!" I tried to jerk away from her, but Izzy was strong tonight and I was an oozing pile of rum and stale adrenaline.

"It's a good thing you're current on your tetanus shots." Izzy blithely chatted in a bedside manner that would put a patient into a diabetic coma. Finally she pulled away the awful tools but kept me in a vice grip. "I can't imagine what's in these disgusting little things. And you're definitely going to need a course of antibiotics. "Can I look at your hand?" She slathered lidocaine cream over some of the bruising, and I started to breathe easier with the slight reprieve from the pain.

"Here." I shoved my hand into hers and let her have her fun. Maybe it would distract her enough that she'd stop looking further.

"Ooof. This is going to sting. A lot." Izzy brandished those forceps again.

I swore to the very strands of her DNA that I would seek my vengeance upon her for this. She wrapped my hand tightly, and I guessed I'd lose feeling in the fingers by morning. I ought to be grateful; the rest of me would be feeling plenty tomorrow morning.

"Alright. Nothing looks too serious." She packed up her kit. "I guess you got lucky, if you can believe that. We'll need to keep an eye out for infection. I'll take a look in the morning when I change your bandages."

"I need a drink," I grumbled and stuck my wrapped hand under my other arm to both keep pressure against the bleed and hide it from my sister and her instruments of torture.

The Bitch Captain (and The Lady)

"What about your leg? You said it hurt."

"Everything hurts!" I shouted to the stars and looked around for my rum. I couldn't let her see my legs. Hide. Hide the scars. Hide your life. Hide the danger.

She would want to help you.

Leave me alone.

I wanted Izzy to help me so much it registered as physical pain greater than the musket balls, but Izzy's life was hard enough without me piling on. She'd spent her childhood recovering from the car crash that took both her parents away. I could still see, clear as day, her little, broken body in that hospital bed. My job was to take care of her, not the other way around.

Let her help.

I spent too much time alone on my boat. That voice was becoming too corporeal for its own good.

Didn't she do a good job? Don't you feel better?

Even my sister, brandishing her forceps with heavy-handed schadenfreude and alcohol swabs, was better than taking a dose of Fountain. Maybe if I explained the scarring just right it wouldn't scare her too much. She should know the consequences of taking technology off of the ship. She should know about the scars. She should know everything. I firmed my resolve to reveal my leg scarring and wounds and made up my mind to tell her everything.

"You should—" The deck of my ship flew into my face as my legs and brain gave out.

CHAPTER 3

Decisions

The pull of the anchor against the tide woke me. I hadn't put the anchor in. I opened my eyes and shut them again, immediately regretful. I was hungover in a nightmarish way. Everything that wasn't swollen and painful was punishing me for drinking. I tried opening my eyes again. I had to get up and moving. I had to get the ship moving. I wrenched myself to a standing position by sheer force of will, feeling like Sisyphus rolling that stone up that hill. My skin and muscles were so stiff I thought I might crack.

I needed my flask of Fountain and I needed it now. The Fountain was a messy business. If I were alone, I'd sit on the drop-down platform I used to fish and bathe off of instead of the tiny cabin bathroom. My sister was asleep next to me with a clear view of the water. Izzy "hand sanitizer" D St. G would not be pleased to see me Fountaining in the ocean. To say she'd be upset at the sight would be putting it mildly. She'd probably opt to swim back to that rat bastard thief and give him a smooch rather than witness the Fountain running its course.

I tossed my blanket over her and unclipped the life preserver she'd snapped me back into in my unconscious state. She seemed pretty out of it, but I didn't want to waste any of my time. The Fountain was foul, and the sooner it was over the better.

Making my way down below was a challenge. My leg was stiff and painful and wouldn't take my weight. I stumble-fell down the steps and gritted my teeth against a scream as I reached out with my injured hand to stop myself from falling, splitting open what had managed to clot, and then pulled it back in reaction to the pain only to have my leg collapse under me and my shoulder slam against the wall. I blacked out a little again with that one. Once I could pick myself off the floor, I staggered into my room.

My cabin barely outranked a telephone booth in terms of square footage, but it was comfortable and filled with little trinkets from my travels. Up high was a prominent shelf with two helmets on it: one large with bronze detailing, the other my size and solid silver. Both were crafted in an ancient Hellenic style made in an era immemorial. I'd received the silver helmet at the same time I'd received the flask stashed behind it.

"Suck it, Ponce," I toasted and chugged a large swallow from the flask.

The Fountain worked in three ways. The primary measure was an automatic feature, a continuous drip of restorative that kept my immune system in top shape. I did not get sick with either minor or major illnesses, low-grade fevers weren't bothersome, food poisoning and other toxins were dealt with in a speedy (if unpleasant) manner. This first measure made alcohol and other drugs particularly potent. I couldn't metabolize them well and suffered massive hangovers. Processed food and modern preservatives also presented issues. Health was the name of the game, and my body rejected my attempts to poison and blindfold it with delicious, delicious snack cakes, processed joy, and bottled comfort.

The secondary measures took effect in cases of extreme peril. I would, in effect, be turned off and turned back on again. It was unpleasant.

The tertiary measure was this: drinking the Fountain straight up: neat, no chasers. The price was almost as tough to pay as the secondary measures, and I never chose to drink it if I had even a microchance of healing on my own.

The Bitch Captain (and The Lady)

The effects began immediately after swallowing. I rushed to the bathroom as fast as my legs could carry me. It was akin to feeling every cell in your body vomit for dear life. My intestines gripped, I gagged and stripped out of my clothes before out of me, from all ends, flowed the horror and tragedy of yesterday's parade of misery. I was scrubbed with steel wool from the inside out. It took well over three hours of heaving and choking and shitting before the Fountain left my system, taking with it all the shrapnel fragments: infection, inflammation, and whatnot. I lay shaking on the tiny bathroom floor, feeling better but regretful. The price of the Fountain never seemed worth it.

It took about eight buckets of water and an hour of mopping and scrubbing to clean everything off. My wounds had mostly scabbed over, and I could easily heal from them under my own constitution if I took proper care of myself. As I scrubbed at the bathroom, I swore off the flask for the hundredth time, even knowing right then I'd be back at that bottle sooner or later. The Fountain brought my body to a point where my wounds (and hangovers) were no longer fatal, but I would still have to heal and bear the scars of my failures. It was like drinking infinite time, bitter and ugly and enduring, but ultimately healing.

Once the place was clean it was time for a shower. I gently washed around the still-open and tender wounds. The one on my shoulder was particularly irritated from all the cleaning and hugging of the toilet. If I were smart, I'd fashion a sling, but feeling the pain right now felt appropriate. I'd just experienced a massive failure, why did I deserve to feel any relief? This pain was earned and justified. I braided my hair and went to find another set of clean clothes. Before I dressed I squeezed some lotion from a half-used bottle onto my scars in an attempt to keep the hardened, angry tissue appeased enough to allow my joints movement. While my injuries were better, I was still in pain. I couldn't let Izzy know how much pain or she'd freak out...more than she already had.

I put some coffee on to brew and fixed myself a sandwich. While we were at anchor I'd eat and relax some. There was at least a week of hard sailing ahead of us, maybe more. The ship was weighed down, and that meant we'd make poor time.

As long as I was down here, I'd better check the hold. Papers were strewn all about the galley, copies from the matriarch's journal. Izzy's journal, from the 17th century. A journal she was supposed to write in a castle in Portugal, surrounded by food and servants and fun. I crumpled the foolish papers up and tossed them against the hull – the hull which was smeared with my bloodstains from yesterday. How had it all gone so very wrong so very quickly? I stared at those bloodstains and cursed that rat bastard thief all over again. Cleaning those walls would have to be a task for later. Right now, the cargo needed securing, and a new course needed to be charted.

Charlie's cargo was the most important. It was mostly stacked in the spare cabin –

"Anne!" Izzy was screaming up on the deck. She kept calling my name. I looked myself over to be sure I was presentable and climbed up the steps.

"Morning. Did you manage to sleep okay?" Izzy was a storm of emotions under a veneer of self-control. I needed to tread carefully.

"Oh my god! I thought – never mind. How are you feeling?" She jumped to her feet.

I know exactly what she thought. She thought I'd succumbed to my injuries and fallen off the ship. I had so much to tell her. She approached with her first aid kit of doom, and I winced remembering her ministrations from last night.

"I'm much better this morning. Are you hungry?" She had to be hungry. I pushed my sandwich towards her. She was going to need a full belly and stable blood sugar to listen to all my stories with an open mind. Where should I start? Probably with the portal.

"Did you take a shower?" Izzy interrupted my train of thought with this odd question.

"Yes." I looked her over. She looked like crap. Her shirt was bloody too. I wondered if she had some cuts under the dirty shirt. I couldn't see any bandages. "Your turn. The shower is free and very clean. Looks like that shirt of yours might need washing too." My shower was bigger than hers. That's not saying much when it comes to ship facilities, but I thought the idea of a more luxurious space might get her on my good side again.

"Did you rewrap all of your wounds?" She had so little faith in me.

"Mostly. Everything looks much better. Nothing was as bad as we thought. All good." I had thrown some new gauze over the wounds for show but had done a lousy job of it. I didn't think she'd waste her naptime opportunity taping me up. Besides, the Fountain had done a decent job healing the major wounds from deadly to simply offensive.

"Mostly? Like we are *mostly* in the Dark Ages right now?" she screeched. It was the late Renaissance/Early Age of Exploration. Izzy sucked at history. "Sit your ass down. Like I can trust you to take care of yourself. Let's go!" I guess she was going to waste her time. She clapped her hands like I was a school child. I prayed for patience.

Izzy needed sleep, a hot meal, and a stiff drink. This sober, exhausted, controlling lady was not the sister I wanted on this trip. If only she'd have stayed in the damn boat and let me do my thing at Tavern Rock, this could all have been avoided. I was starting to think traveling with her might be trickier than I'd imagined. Her eyebrow raised and her foot tapped, and I was not strong enough to swim to the nearest shore. I sighed, sat down, and took off my shirt so playtime doctor dolly could use her first aid accessory bag (bag sold separately) and poke and prod at me some more.

"I still want answers, Anne." Izzy pulled off my hastily-wrapped gauze and started slathering me with stinging crap from a bottle.

I hissed and shied away from her ministrations. "I'll answer. You don't have to torture me."

Apparently she did. She roughly pulled at my already-swelling shoulder and tightly wrapped it. I was going to black out if she kept that up. I gritted my teeth and prayed for the moment she snapped and finally took her ass to bed.

"Stop whining," she ordered and moved on to examine my hand.

Everything should look better and not as dire as last night. Either she was being rough on purpose or these wounds were worse than I thought. I would put money on the former.

"What the hell?" she whispered as she moved back and forth over my shoulder as if the giant hole in it was a mirage or one of those eye trick pictures and if she moved me just right, the deep hole would once again reveal itself again to her.

I knew what she was seeing. The injury would look older, clotted, not the fresh raggedness of mere hours ago. It wasn't healed by any means. It was still tender, massively bruised, and in need of attention. If I didn't take care, all my wounds would get worse again, just like it would for anyone who was careless about their health. Even though she should be napping right now, if my sister could stand to nurse me a little bit, I stood a chance of not having to drink the Fountain again. With injuries this severe I would usually need several doses of Fountain before calling myself "healed." Izzy kept scouring me with her home brew of iodine and reproach.

"Why don't you go take a nap?" I offered again after a particularly stinging swipe. "Come back up with a clearer head. We can do this later." I tried to shrug her off, but this only resulted in her using twice as much gauze to mummify me. I would just have to lie back and think of England until she'd had her way with me.

"Yes, because a few hours of sleep will surely make everything better!" She jerked my shoulder as she wrapped up my hand.

That really hurt. That bullet must have fractured my scapula. I gritted my teeth and shut my eyes until I was sure I could manage myself and my reactions. I could not tell her how much pain I was in, she was

The Bitch Captain (and The Lady)

already so upset. Izzy had enough to deal with and didn't need my issues piled on top of her own.

"You need a sling for this arm." She held out a sorry scrap of cotton in the vague shape of a triangle.

"I'll wear the sling. Now go sleep," I insisted again and put the "sling" over my head. "We have a few days until we see land again. Plenty of time to interrogate me along the way."

"The way? The way where?"

"Bermuda. There's business I need to handle there, and then we'll be on our way to Portugal shortly after that."

During my first trip to Bermuda, I'd gone to town and gotten the shock of my life: Izzy, my 21st-century sister, dressed to the ancient nines, was wandering the city center of St. George's. My plans to bring her back in time started in earnest that day. If I hadn't seen her, I would never have dared a trip like this. I would never have dared the scores of the other trips I took in preparation for this journey either.

However, I did see Izzy in Bermuda, and therefore it happened/happens/will always have happened. The past doesn't change. That wasn't a rule; it was a fact. Law. I had brought Izzy with me for a variety of reasons, but in this instance I was simply the cab driver keeping her safe on the way to her appointment with destiny on that tiny island.

All that aside, the amount of cargo loaded onto my ship last night was double or triple what I went to Tavern Rock to obtain. Charlie didn't need all of it. Bermuda was riddled with independently-governed militias as the civil war in England raged and devoured young men and ordnance as they fought for King and Country and Cromwell. My cargo would be welcomed with open arms: hundreds of pounds of gunpowder, lead, and muskets. I could compensate myself for some of my losses with extra gold and tradable cargo. The abundant cash the excess powder and arms would bring in would be put to good use on my lands and investments there.

"What?! I don't want to go to any ancient ports, Anne! You need a hospital, and this is not the summer trip I agreed to. Take us home, now!" she shouted.

Yes, we'd run into a little trouble, but there was a castle waiting, and I'd gone to a lot of trouble to set up a fun experience for her, and I didn't want to let her go yet.

"Do I need a hospital? You just saw my injuries. I'm not in any danger."

"I don't know what I saw. I do know that bullet wounds need more medical attention than gauze pads, however." She was tired. A little sleep would go a long way for her.

"We just got here—" I started.

"Yes, and I've already been involved in a massacre! We need to go – can we even go home, Anne?" She needed to sleep. Everything looked better after sleep.

"Yes, we will get back there. But, Izzy," I opted for the truth, as cold and hard and biting as it was, "I'm not taking you home yet. So go get some sleep. We'll talk later." Instead of meeting her eyes I adjusted the gauze on my hand so I'd look at least a little compliant to her efforts. Perhaps it might pacify her a teeny bit.

"What the fuck do you mean you're not taking me home yet? I'm kidnapped and I'm going to stay that way?" The thin veneer of self-control corroded away, and Izzy hurled her words at me.

I steeled myself. This was not going to go over well. "Yes."

There were any number of excuses and fabrications and equivocations I could have given her, but I was tired and in pain and my creativity failed me. Yes was the best answer I could give. It was the truth. I finally met her eyes because I had another bomb to drop. The cargo I'd taken off Tavern Rock – the cargo Charlie had commissioned me to bring him, the hundreds of pounds of gunpowder – did not mix with my sister's favorite hobbies: smoking and cooking. Her proclivity to light up her joints all over my ship and cook meals on appliances that might arc or short would put us in real danger of sinking to the ocean floor on a fiery wreck.

"And also, I'm going to need you not to cook or smoke until we get there." One spark and our little adventure ended here and now. Of course, we did make it to Bermuda as the journals said we did and as I'd seen with my own eyes, but there was no need to float there on twigs because she lit up too close to a cask of black powder or decided cold-cut sandwiches were too bourgeois.

Izzy slapped me. I took it. I deserved it.

"Fuck you, Anne!" she snapped and finally made her way down to her cabin. My cheek stung and my eyes watered.

I'd failed.

Right off the bat I'd failed her.

I lightly ran my hand along the stinging skin and reevaluated my choices.

The mainsail began luffing, and I pulled the sheet back to taut and meticulously coiled the line. Maybe this was hopeless. The smell of pot wafted from the direction of Izzy's cabin as she self-medicated into a coma. I had no idea what to do with her.

Our little summer cruise was supposed to go like this: party through the portal, wake up and reveal to her the big surprise that we'd time-traveled (time freaking traveled!) and that there was fantastic power in the world and we were part of it. Instead of dive bars and sleazy ports, we were traveling to Portugal to live like actual freaking queens with servants, fancy balls, and amazing food. She'd get to live out fantasy stories straight from her historical fiction shelf, books she'd read until the spines were broken and the pages crumbling. It was supposed to be a trip she'd never forget. I was going to tell her all about myself and time travel, and reassure her that I'd always be there if she needed me, but that this was my true self, and I wanted her to finally know about the life I lived.

Rolling out of the portal and into a bloody massacre had not been on the agenda.

I limped over to the captain's chair and elevated my leg. The calf was swelling up already, and I tried to rub some of the ache away. Izzy was going to end up in Bermuda writing that journal one way or another. That was going to happen. I had thought it was now. I would have put money down that that timing was now.

I'm kidnapped and I'm going to stay that way?
Izzy should never have felt like I'd kidnapped her.
She should never have had to witness that level of bloodshed.
My sister should have stayed on the ship.
We should have been on our way to a castle in Portugal.
So many "shoulds." What a stupid word. This *should* have been this way. This *should* have happened that way. We *should* do this. We *should* do that. Stupid, stupid, stupid word.

What *happened* was I kidnapped my sister and she was taking it badly. What would happen now is I would make it right. *How* was the word to focus on. Scrap the journey now? Dump the cargo and run straight back home? Keep the cargo and risk sailing the portal on a bomb? Force Izzy to go to Bermuda before she's ready and while she's furious with me all so I can make a quick buck? I grimaced. More like hundreds of thousands of bucks. This kind of payday was a once-in-a-lifetime haul…and I'd paid for it with all those lives I'd taken at Tavern Rock. There was no scenario where I'd voluntarily dump this cargo. But what was more important here?

All my plans cracked and crashed around me as I thought over yesterday's events. Izzy was going to end up in Bermuda but did it have to be this Izzy, right now? She was furious and rightly so. Whatever else hap-

The Bitch Captain (and The Lady)

pened on this trip I wanted to leave her with good memories, memories that would warm her at night and give her hope for the future.

I looked around at my ship and rubbed my hands through my hair and absently braided it back. This was one nightmare I had the power to wake up from. Sleep well, Izzy, I'm taking you home. You'll wake up to the familiar skyline and I'll let you be for as long as I can manage.

Someday Izzy would be walking around Bermuda in 1649 but it didn't have to be this Izzy, right now. I lived and worked in a literal time machine. "Right now" was a fluid concept in my line of work.

The wind shifted on me as I changed course to the portal. I would not force Izzy into doing this. I don't know how that journal got written but I would not force my sister into living this same absurd existence that I lived. This was as rough a start to a journey as I'd ever encountered and taking her home was the right thing to do. There was more than one way to get her to Bermuda in 1649. I could take her home, calm her down, and try again later.

The jib twisted and I regretfully got up on my bum leg to go yank it back into position. The damn canvas was caught in the foresail and I had to hoist myself up on the boom to push it into the wind. My shoulder screamed at me and I felt it open up and the bandage stick in the new bloodflow. Shit.

I jumped down without thinking and my leg collapsed. Shit! I limped back to the chair and breathed through the agonizing screams I locked up in my throat. Izzy needed to sleep and her ass would be right back up here if she heard me crying out because I'd busted all of her hard work open again. She might be onto something about getting to a hospital.

Sailing this overstuffed behemoth through the portal would be an ordeal. Explaining to my mother what was on the ship while her favorite daughter screeched her head off over what I'd done was going to be an ordeal. Having the patience to wait and see how and when Izzy gets swept back in time without my assistance only to land in Bermuda with a journal and quill in her hand was going to be an ordeal. There was no winning. There was just choosing your hard.

I would choose to attempt to salvage what was left of our relationship and get her feet back on dry land.

At this rate of speed it would be a two day trip to the portal. I could walk there faster. I shifted in my chair. My wounds were swelling and I couldn't get comfortable.

Izzy had left the antibiotic pills by the helm and I picked up the small bottle and put a few in my hand. I had stocked these specifically for my sister. Now that this journey was scrapped and we were heading to a time of pharmacies and urgent care doctors, she wouldn't need them. I popped one and twisted the top back in place.

Solo sailing in this era was almost unheard of. No satnav, no autopilot, no weather reports or instrumentation to beep at you and wake you if there were danger. It was all celestial navigation and dead reckoning. Only a lunatic sailed alone. The fact that I attempted solo sailing and was successful at it, added to the fear I inspired in the merchant community. I was a woman, I sailed alone, and I was good at it. My name and my sails were infamous on the water. The men at Tavern Rock were justified in their fear of me.

Sailing alone meant no breaks, no cooking, and little sleep. I had a system of setting my watch alarm to vibrate after twenty minute catnaps, then staying awake for three hours, then another twenty minutes and so on until I reached my destination however far it may be. Even in the best of health it was a hard and arduous process. I raised the genoa to capture more wind and hopefully speed us along. My shoulder did not thank me and spots of blood started showing through the bandage on my hand.

By the time the sun set, I was feeling light headed and cold. I pulled on a jacket over my sweatshirt and set my alarm for twenty minutes. Twenty minutes was not enough. The wind picked up. I was grateful for the extra speed but it cut through my layers and I shivered through the night.

When morning came, the sun beat down on my beaten up ass. My head was splitting and I was stiff when I tried to move out of the chair. I lasted only a minute to get up, recoil some rope, and collapse back in my chair. I kept liquids down but everything else came up. I was pleased at our speed (such as it was), we'd be at the portal by dinner.

Izzy didn't surface. I thought I heard an occasional thump or clink from her cabin but I decided against disturbing her.

I'm kidnapped and I'm going to stay that way?

No, Izzy. You are going home. Once she could see planes in the sky and container ships in the shipping lanes, I'd go get her. Till then I'd let her rest and enjoy what vacation was left to her.

I continued to catnap through the day. Lack of sleep and my disregard of care had turned my injuries in a bad direction. I couldn't get uncomfortable. My calf was swollen and I hissed and cursed any time something brushed against it. It was inflamed. The primary measures of the Fountain zapped away at me but it was moving too slow. I wasn't taking good enough care of myself. There was nothing for it though, I could only pour more coffee and pray that the trade winds stayed strong.

At the advent of the portal I began the process of slowing us down and prayed. The ship was full of explosives, my sister included, and the portal was not always a gentle place. I wouldn't know for sure until we were inside it what the conditions were and that made me nervous. I was dizzy by the time I brought the ship to a standstill and didn't realize what I was feeling until my head cleared.

I felt thunder.

The skies here outside the portal were clear, not a cloud horizon to horizon. Yet a rumble of thunder vibrated through me. I shivered and opened the cabinet door that housed the engine controls. Right up next to the entrance as we were, the tide pulled at my hull in a way I didn't like. It produced a drawn and bitter feeling in my stomach. Though it was bright daylight, I could feel the impression of thunder through my bones.

The portal was a particular type of ocean current like the Gulf Stream or equatorial currents, only it coursed across time and space, not just the sea. Power created it and that power desired more power. It fed itself by entrapping lost souls in cataclysmic storms and ferrying them to places they did not want to go. I rubbed absently at the brand on my neck, the Nekydalleon. I'd been caught in just such a storm.

The silent thunder rolled through me again.

My ship was in no condition to battle the type of storm I knew to be raging through the portal right now. I heaved to, feeling new bleeds with every movement, then limped below. I had promised myself I'd leave her alone but I needed help with this decision. Her door was shut tight. I tapped lightly.

"Izzy?" I called, hoping I sounded non-kidnappery. "Izzy can I come in?"

No response.

I cracked the door slightly, she was asleep. Her room had a haze of leftover marijuana smoke, several bottles lay empty on her dresser. Her laptop was playing some simpering romantic comedy in front of her closed eyelids. She'd found some old reference books of mine and they were strewn over Maui's lava lava wrap like a second comforter. Maui, my nickname for her former boyfriend, Fetu, would have been the best comforter of all. He wasn't here though and from the looks of it my sister was barely here either. I would have to make this decision on my own. I slowly closed the door and grabbed a bottle of water before lurching back up the stairs.

Up on deck I could almost see the invisible storm raging just behind its invisible barrier. It pulled at me, tempting me to try my hand against it. My choices were different now. Risk a storm in the portal, or risk my sister in Bermuda. I rubbed at the brand on my neck. I would not put Izzy through that. I was not willing to risk Izzy's life like that.

In this rare case, better the evil I didn't know. Izzy was going to Bermuda.

The thunder boomed enough that I could hear it and feel the vibrations through my hull. I hit the engine start and brought us around. The battery gave out after an hour and I shut it down. I set my alarm for twenty minutes and passed out. We were officially en route to that tiny island in the middle of the Atlantic, now two days behind schedule.

Before I settled in for another night at the wheel I rewrapped my wounds and put on jeans and a t-shirt and my broad-brimmed hat. Izzy hadn't found the significant gash in my leg, and I did what I could to keep it clean and stable. The change of clothes refreshed my perspective and revived me for another night of catnaps to get us across the leagues of barren ocean. I tucked the pill bottle away, cursing myself for having taken any of them. Now, if Izzy got hurt or sick, her supply was lower.

Bermuda. It was hard to believe this was finally happening. Bermuda and I had a difficult relationship. The place was crawling with Puritans.

The *Try Your Luck* was heavy and moving slowly, but we couldn't be far, ten days, maybe seven if I caught a good wind. It was 1649. I still had time, not much, but some.

Late spring 1650 was when I was captured and burned at the stake right there in St. George's Bay. The old burn scars on my legs itched, reminding me of the ordeal. The Fountain had kept me alive (barely) until the fire ate through the ropes binding me. Then I had run, sprinting on burned and blistered legs, flames streaking behind me, until I reached the bay and dove in. I swam back to my ship from there. As soon as I'd climbed aboard my ship I'd gone straight to the engine and revved it. My ship, captained by a charred briquette, left port with furled sails, no wind, snores of the devil (the engine) following it, and belching acrid hellfire (gasoline). It was 1649 now; I had a year until then. I still had time. I rubbed my scars and prayed that I still had time.

I would avoid the place entirely except for a few reasons: One, we were close to it; two, the excess cargo I got off that thieving rat bastard would be easily sold there; three, I had people on that island I wanted to see one last time. And four, the wheel of time dictated that Izzy would be in Bermuda in the summer of 1649 and therefore that's where we'd be. By my estimation, we would be on the island for a week tops. Then I'd put that place in my rear-view mirror for good.

The next day I shivered in the beating-down heat. Even with my hat I was getting too much sun. I was hungry. I kicked absently at the empty box of cereal at my feet and picked at a stale cake. My shoulder and calf were stiff and swollen and getting worse. I gave up on trying to rewrap the wounds. I couldn't touch them without getting faint. I couldn't shower or bathe but managed to beat and scrub clean some of my clothes and hang them to dry on a line. I captained in a towel all day until something was dry enough to wear. Then I froze my ass off all night in the damp clothing. Nothing was ever really dry on a boat. I wrapped a blanket around myself and made some tea.

Izzy stayed in her cabin.

I have not been able to keep track of the time. The compass reads true. I think we are still headed the right way. Everything hurts. This sucks.

By the time she emerged from her room I was in rough shape. My wounds ached and distracted me constantly. The little snack cakes had run out, and I was sunburnt to a crisp. Despite the equatorial sun, I was

The Bitch Captain (and The Lady)

cold. My recent shore leave back in the 21st century had been longer than normal, and I'd lost much of my protective tan.

I didn't feel well. I was living off a dwindling cask of water and some emergency protein bars.

I missed sleep. Catnaps while sailing couldn't replace a real night of sleep.

I missed real food. Izzy and her chef-ing skills had spoiled me during her short time on board.

The safety rope dragged behind my harness as I checked the sheets and sails. The past few days I was beginning to hallucinate, seeing ports where there were none, smelling food no one had cooked, calling out to ships that blurred into the horizon. Yesterday I had almost walked off the boat and into the waves because there was a deli having a special on roast beef sandwiches just off my starboard rail. The safety line had saved me from going overboard.

The delicious smells were wafting towards me again, and I tightened the knot. A bowl of soup, my most glorious hallucination yet, appeared in front of me. I looked wistfully at it, not daring to blink and risk it vanishing. Bermuda was only another day or two out. I'd find some food and rest then. The bowl stayed faithfully at my side as I steered, and I thanked it for its company.

"Anne!" Izzy snapped her fingers in front of my face. "Hello? Answer me and eat the damn stew already!" She wrapped my fingers around a spoon for me. When had Izzy gotten here? Why were her fingers ice-cold? Was she sick? Wait, did she come through the portal with me?

"Did you make soup?" I managed to garble out of my dry mouth.

"Stew. And who the hell else would have made it?" she snapped at me.

I carefully dipped the spoon into the bowl and felt tears stream down my face as I tasted real, fresh, hot food for the first time in who knows how long. Eating this vision of a stew felt religious, sacred, sexual, intimate.

"Are you okay?" Izzy asked.

"What?" My god, I'd get this soup pregnant if I could.

"You are not okay." She ladled more stew into my bowl, and I had to sit down and cover my face. I was sobbing so hard at the beauty of it all.

Izzy took the wheel and scanned the horizon while checking the compass. "Where are we going again?"

"Bermuda."

"Why Bermuda?"

"To sell the guns. And the gunpowder." My vision whirled as the calories entered my bloodstream and my muscles relaxed, knowing I wasn't going to continue to starve.

"What?!?"

"We are going to sell it all in Bermuda." Then we'd make a U-turn and head for the portal to return Izzy home. "I can't have us navigating the portal on a ship full of explosives." I wiped my eyes and took a steadying breath and shivered. I ached everywhere and was still a little dizzy but felt I could stand up. "Good soup. Thanks."

"It's stew."

"That's what I said."

Izzy sighed the sigh of a patienceless woman begging the universe for an inch more endurance in her war against stupidity. "Why don't you take a break? You look like you need sleep. And...more." Her eyes scanned over me, and apparently I did not pass muster.

I was still in my jeans and t-shirt, but my shirt clung to my back where the blood was plastered to the bandage. The wrappings on my hand were stained and dirty from blood, sea water, and now stew. My leg was in awful shape, but the thick denim hid the damage from her critiquing eye. I'm sure she noticed more than I could see. I got pretty banged up in that fight. I brushed and beat at my pants to attempt to present a better image. It didn't really help.

"No. It's okay. I'll be fine. The soup helped a lot. You don't need to do this." I was exhausted but wasn't about to ask her for anything after what I'd just put her through. I put the spoon back in my bowl and wondered briefly why on earth she had cooked this for her kidnapper. Mutual survival was the only reasonable explanation.

"When was the last time you slept? Like, really slept? Have you been living on junk food this entire time?" She kicked at some of the wrappers around the base of my captain's chair.

I tried to answer her, but she rapid-fired the questions and my brain was mired in pain and stew. My boat had always been so quiet. Did Izzy always talk this much?

"You look like you're on death's doorstep," she continued her critique.

I had to laugh at that remark. I could knock knock knock on death's doorstep all the livelong day, and that bitchy harlot with her scythe and cloak would never let me in.

"Why the hell didn't you just heave to for a while so you could do what you needed?" Izzy finally took a breath for me to answer.

"I'm getting us where we need to go. I'll sleep when I'm dead." I laughed at my own joke.

"God, just move." She used her impressively sharp elbow to knock me off the helm.

I crashed into the padded port bench. My head spun and my feverish body flashed at the sudden movement. I have to admit to being a little tired. I passed out.

The morning we were scheduled to depart, I stood in the shower turning the knobs from cold to hot and back again, over and over, luxuriating in the convenience of indoor plumbing and a large hot water heater tank.

"Anne, could you please not use all the hot water? I've got company coming over later. I'll need a shower too." Mom flitted down the hallway without waiting for a response. It was time to get out anyway. I pulled one oversized towel off the rack and wrapped it around my body and used a second for my hair. Such luxury.

I turned the sink faucet on and giggled at how easy it was to get water of any temperature any time of day, any time of year. I always missed that. Toothbrushes, toothpaste, floss…the things you never realize are near and dear to your heart.

Back in my room I toweled off and reveled in the air conditioning. I put my face right against the vent and breathed in the chilly, controlled air.

I smelled the laundry detergent and fabric softener on my fresh clothing. Then mourned a little bit for the brittle chips my soft clothing would turn into after a few months at sea.

While it was still wet, I braided my long hair back into two thick, tight French braids and welcomed back the reflection I was used to. While on shore leave I kept my hair down, clean, and dry since I had access to brushes and conditioner on a regular basis. While at sea, my hair was braided back and out of the way, covered with a wrap and brimmed hat. Deodorant, oh, my precious deodorant, but how I wish you'd been invented centuries earlier.

Down in the kitchen I filled up on anything with preservatives as my mother skittered and twittered at me about my nutrition choices and tried to clear away my Sugar Flakes and replace them with something that grew on a tree. I batted her away. Eventually, she alighted on the chair across from me with a mug of tea and a calculating look at my hair. She knew what my braids meant.

"How long will you be gone this time, do you think?" she asked.

"Izzy and I are planning the whole summer."

"Izzy is really going with you?" She was honestly surprised.

"She made the decision." Honestly, I was still surprised too.

"I'm just going to miss her is all." Guess who she wasn't going to miss. "You will take good care of her, won't you?"

"Of course I will."

"You'll see she gets home safe to me?"

"I will."

"Keep her out of trouble. She's a good girl."

"I will."

"You promise? You'll bring her back in one piece?"

"I promise."

The tide pulled at the hull in an unfocused way and the motion woke me up. I couldn't have been out too long. The wind blew lazily against lowered sails, and my sister sat at the wheel, unconcerned by the condition and direction of the ship. My heavy body tugged at me to stay still and begged me to keep my eyes closed. I wish I could go to sleep for several days. The primary measures of the Fountain buzzed and zapped against the fever like Lilliputians with tasers in my bloodstream; it promised a few more days before I gained ground against the infections.

The sun was low in the sky and a new batch of soup steamed in a bowl by my face. I ate it greedily and tried to express my thanks to Izzy around the hunks of carrot and beef in my mouth. My hand had been rewrapped. The bandage was clean, and the skin around it was clean too. My shoulder was rewrapped as well. I flexed it, trying to work the stiffness out of my muscles. How long had I been out? Not long enough. Breathing felt like a chore. I tried again to express my thanks, but the words were drowned by my current spoonful of soup.

"We need to talk." Izzy didn't acknowledge my garbled thanks.

I swallowed and tried to keep my eyes focused on her instead of the ladle that lay tantalizingly close in the pot.

"Okay?" Stay focused, Anne, you can do this. My eyes begged to close and bring me back to dreamland.

"Bermuda," she started.

"Bahamas," I put a little tune to it and continued listing tropical islands. Food really brought out the music in me. Also, that fever might have advanced more than I was admitting.

"Don't you dare start singing," Izzy said, but I knew there was a smile underneath her displeasure.

"I know a good one about a sloop too." I bet I could still remember the harmonies. How did it start?

"Anne! I need to know what to expect there." Lady Buzzkill never appreciated my musical stylings even before I kidnapped her.

"It'll be fine." I brushed her off. "You'll stay in the boat – for real this time – and chill until I finish the deals—" Shit. No, she needed to get off the ship. Okay, maybe she could put on one dress and go for one stroll for one hour. " – then, if you want, we can do a little sightseeing for an hour before getting back underway. We'll be out of there quick. Like a week." I reached for the ladle, but Izzy beat me to it and rapped me on the knuckles. I almost cried. I could not stand much more pain or I'd crumble into a pathetic pile of sobbing sea captain.

"No. I don't want to stay on this boat. I'll find a hotel," she countered.

Izzy then launched into a long list of boat grievances and unrealistic demands for accommodation in Bermuda. Honestly, did she really think spas existed in the middle of the 17th century in the middle of the Atlantic Ocean? No, Izzy, there aren't any hotels. There are rooms above taverns. Most are occupied by whores, of course. Cabo aside, I don't think she'd appreciate lumping herself in with that crowd. No, Izzy, this is a backwater colony that the entire seafaring European community used as a gas station grab-and-go turnpike toilet. No, Izzy, there are no good restaurants. This ship is the only really safe place. No, you won't be safe all by yourself off of the ship. Haven't we already learned that lesson?

The Bitch Captain (and The Lady)

The soup was cold by the time we reached a compromise we were both unhappy with: Izzy would stay at the least objectionable inn we could find, but I was hiring her a chaperone/guard who would watch her Every. Fucking. Step.

"And one more thing," she said.

"For fuck's sake," I said under my breath, rubbing my temples. "What now?"

"I want you to take me home."

"Bermuda—"

"After Bermuda. Promise you'll take me home." Izzy stood at the wheel with her hands at ten and two like the perfect A-plus student right out of Drivers' Ed. Her eyes were on the sea, but her body radiated intensity.

This is what she'd spent all those days below deck building up to telling me. If the storm hadn't been in the portal and we were halfway home…but we weren't. We were here and we needed to deal with Bermuda. We'd be home soon enough, and she could continue her life, working all her jobs and playing with all her friends and having cocktail hour with Mom where they'd make blithe jokes at my expense between sips of bubbles and bites of microgreens.

"Izzy, it's—"

"What, Anne?" Izzy snapped.

I held onto my temper by one fraying thread. She'd gotten off this ship without permission, and the result was several new holes in my body. She'd refused to look at the journal pages or listen to my explanation, then she'd slapped me and locked herself in her room. I prayed for a better hold on my frustration and begged myself to remember that she couldn't know what she didn't know.

"The portal is not like a door you can just walk back through. It's powerful. It has agendas of its own. Even I can't always get where I want to go," I attempted to explain.

The portal wasn't some austere tunnel that led to one place. It was a strong current which ran worldwide throughout every ocean, complete with storms and hazards, rip tides, and monsters. There were eras I had attempted to get to where I was simply shut out by gale-force winds. Other times I'd set my course on a particular year only to be yanked and blown in a different direction.

"It sounds like you're prepping one doozy of an excuse." Her sharp tone sliced right through my last thread of patience.

"It's not an excuse!" I was on my feet, blood pumping hard through my head. I was tensed as if ready for an attack and had to calm down, but everything hurt and I didn't feel good and I wanted to go home and Izzy was just staring at me waiting for me to fuck up more. My head was going to roll right off my shoulders. My leg and arm screamed at me with every movement. I felt like throwing up. I had to get some rest, or the secondary measures were going to take effect.

I groaned and sat back down, heavy head in my misguided hands. "This was never supposed to be forever. It was just a small summer trip." I was so very tired. I just wanted to lie down. "Your life is so busy, and I just wanted to get a chance to have one more trip together before you went and moved on without me. But fine. Screw it." I knew a hopeless cause when it slapped me in the face. "You're miserable. I'm shot up. Let's get this shit off the boat and then get you the hell out of here."

"Great. I couldn't agree more. Now promise me." She turned to face me head on. "I mean, this isn't like 'I'll try to get you home before curfew, but you know how traffic is on Fridays.'"

I groaned and leaned back in my seat. For years I had apologized for that over and over. Mom hadn't grounded her for even half the length of time she'd grounded me. To be fair, we were only fourteen and I didn't even know there could be that much traffic or that there was such a thing as an emergency brake release.

"What do you want? A pinky swear?" I grumbled as I tried to massage my headache away with my good arm. God, I could feel my pulse

The Bitch Captain (and The Lady)

in my eyeballs. Only a few more days till Bermuda and then I could rest.

"I want you to swear in such a way that you can't wriggle out or loophole your way away from this. Give me a definite promise. Give me a concrete promise. Swear on pain of your precious boat sinking to the bottom of the ocean that you, Anne, my sister, will get me home."

"Never." I patted my ship lovingly. I would never swear such a thing on such a perfect vessel. Don't you listen to your mean Auntie Zee, baby. I would never risk you over a foolish promise I had no way of knowing if I could fulfill. "But maybe there's something I can do." I wrenched myself to my feet and had to hang onto the rail until my head stopped spinning, then headed towards the steps. Good lord, my leg was killing me. I gritted my teeth with each step.

"I don't suppose you'd let me help you!" Izzy called after me.

"Just hold on!" If I stopped moving, I'd fall.

I went below deck and grabbed three items: my flask of Fountain, a milkglass mug, and a scalpel-sharp silver knife. I had to stop and regain my balance a few times as I collected these items. I felt like shit. I wanted to go home. I stifled the tears and forged ahead. Just had to get to Bermuda. I could rest in Bermuda.

I swayed at the top of the steps and tried to cover my misstep by holding up the items and smiling. I didn't see whether she bought the act. My leg was about to collapse under me, and I was focused on not falling on my face. I plunked the items on the small deck table, opened the flask, and poured a small amount of Fountain into the mug. We wouldn't need much.

This trip was supposed to be the trip where I told her about myself... this was as good a place to start as any. Izzy was intrigued by my little setup and wandered closer to inspect the items.

"I'm going to make you a vow." I hoped she paid attention to this. With my third item, the knife, I sliced a seven-inch cut from my pinky tip to wrist. Izzy gasped, but before she could move away, my hand flashed out, grabbed her hand, and held it tight as I performed the same incision down the edge of her left hand. Then I wrapped my pinky around hers, our blood mingling, and vowed, "You will get back home where you will live out your days fat, happy, and rich."

Izzy stared transfixed at the blood running down her arm, finally shocked out of her endless vocabulary. With my free hand I dipped my middle finger in the Fountain and swiped a drop along her incision where it immediately healed, leaving only a thin and barely visible scar.

I performed the same move on my own hand. Then I toasted, "Suck it, Ponce," and drank half down, then put the mug in her hand.

Izzy lifted the glass. "Upon your precious," she toasted and threw back the rest. It was only a tiny sip each. She wouldn't experience more than a little undue stress on her gastrointestinal system. The Fountain was the most holy and important item I carried on this boat. Izzy wasn't a party to its full protections, but she was bound by it now.

I left her to pilot the boat for a few hours. "Just keep it upright," I said as I hobbled down the steps. I set my watch alarm for two hours, an absolutely indulgent amount of time, and fell into bed.

In my dreams I was sitting on a beach with Maui. "Heeny," his stupid nickname for me was almost as cheesy as mine for him, "when we win, what kind of world do you think we'll go back to?"

I was supposed to respond, "One where you shower. You stink, Maui." That's what I'd said back when we'd had this conversation, ages ago.

"We don't win," my dream self told him. He ignored me.

"As long as your sister is still in the world, we'll have won." He lay back and I threw sand on him. It always came back around to Izzy with him. "First chance I get, I'm taking her out dancing. I'll find her a romantic restaurant. Something dark and candlelit where I can—"

"I will leave your ass on this island and never introduce you to my sister if you finish that sentence," I threatened him. He just laughed and enjoyed the rest of his imaginings inside his big, dumb head.

"When we win…" He trailed off, detailing more idyllic fantasies about the world we were hoping to create.

"We don't win. We never win," I whispered as he continued talking. I just watched him and soaked up this stolen moment where my best friend was full of life and hope.

The dream wandered on as he told stories and we joked on that old familiar beach. Finally he exhausted himself and looked me squarely in the eyes. "Have a little faith, Heeny."

My watch buzzed. I startled awake, my heart pounding and my skin clammy. My whole body was stiff and achy. I pulled my leg over the side of the bed and sat up. Izzy had been up there a while, but I decided to borrow just a little more of her time so I could wash up properly, change my clothes, brush my hair, and get a handle on my resolve. It didn't matter how shitty I felt, we were getting to Bermuda. I would rest in Bermuda. I disconnected the oven range on my way back to the helm. We were on a ship full of gunpowder. The soup was delicious, but I wanted to live.

Two more days till we arrived in Bermuda.

Then I would do my utmost to take her home.

CHAPTER 4

Galley Breakdown

Izzy wafted back into her cabin after lecturing me about taking her medicine. I nodded and agreed, knowing full well I wouldn't be stealing any more of the precious medicine I'd packed for her. I groaned as I settled into my chair. The solar batteries hadn't fully charged the engine yet or I'd cheat and use the motor for a while. No such luck.

The stars were fantastic tonight. I was happy to see we were steady on our projected course. In my early days of sailing I'd dedicated myself to learning celestial navigation. It often served me as well or better than a compass. I had learned some on my own before Maui took my skills to the next level. Still, it had taken years of dedication to the study before I felt comfortable traveling without instrumentation. Splash me down in any ocean in any part of the world, and I could tell you where we were and how to get where you wanted to go.

Problem was, there were these things called clouds that often got in the way.

Clouds arrived shortly before sunrise and hung heavy and low. I prepared for rain. We were well within the Bermuda Triangle after all; storms came with the territory.

I shivered and wrapped myself in a camping blanket. It had to be 80 degrees out here, but I was shivering in the morning air. All I wanted was to sleep, to curl up in my cabin, and to rest. I tugged at my safety line for reassurance that I was still secured to the ship.

As soon as the sky lightened, I kept a close eye on the waves for obstacles and disturbances below. Izzy came up to offer me breaks several times, but I refused her. Besides me not wanting to make her work on her vacation, we were a day out from Bermuda now and the rocky shores and treacherous reefs could sneak up on you. I accepted her coffee and meals but continued to beg her to please stop cooking and smoking. Her response was to cook and smoke more. I kept the life preservers close. I was going to be really put out if I lost this boat. Damn Charlie. I should never have taken him up on his offer.

Izzy also kept trying to get antibiotics and fever reducers into my system. Those I did not accept. I had stocked the first aid kits and medicines for her. I was not at my best or even close to my best, but I would recover. If she became sick, I wanted her to have first claim on that medicine. The little pills went back into their little bottle when she wasn't watching me. Whenever she came up to check on me, I attempted to look healthy and put together, but the truth was I felt like I'd been run over.

The smudge that was Bermuda became distinct on the horizon. Last night's clouds accumulated into a collage of storms in the distance, but nothing threatened us yet. If we were lucky (haha), we'd just get a simple rainstorm or small squall.

I began scanning the area for a special outcropping of rock. If my coordinates were correct, we should be in the vicinity. I spied it after an hour: three fingers of rock jutting up to my starboard. Cursing and limping, I reefed the sails, dropped anchor, and lowered the small rowboat into the water.

It was strange to row away from my boat knowing someone was still on board. I spent so much of my life as a solitary sailor on that beloved boat, it felt wrong knowing that another heartbeat was on board as I drifted away – even if that heart belonged to my sleeping sister. The sooner I was back on board, the better.

I pulled the oars harder, cursing every time the wound in my hand

The Bitch Captain (and The Lady)

and shoulder seized up. I'd be bleeding again once this errand was done.

Floating a little away from the rock outcropping was a homemade buoy I'd set up several journeys ago. I picked it up and into the rowboat and hauled up the synthetic rope underneath until a tough, watertight plastic canister landed in the rowboat. I worked the top off and pulled out several sheafs of paper and chose the most relevantly-dated parchment inside.

March 13th 1647

Dom is 9, gifted him seashells and telescope.
Ellie is 3, gifted handkerchief.
Mary pregnant with another. She hopes it's another girl.
Edmund press ganged. No word of his fate.
Sea Wind Tavern – safe
Hogs End – safe
Tide Trader – burnt by Puritans
Kings Bay
Marco captured by navy. Left him there.
Andrews expects an answer
Davies is down on his luck
Puritans gaining strength. Be warned.
Remember 1650 you get burned.

Two years since I'd been here. One year until I'd get burned alive. I shivered in the chilly wind blowing ahead of the storm. I shouldn't be here at all. My scars tightened, and the smell of smoke lurked under my skin. I pushed the foreboding feelings down beneath the surface. Be present, I reminded myself, do not be miles away. Thunder rolled in the distance and lightning flashed. I repacked and resealed the canister and threw it back in the water then rowed with my exhausted muscles back to the big boat. My shoulder was screaming.

I had just tied the rowboat back in place when the first raindrops came down. Big, fat raindrops. I set another anchor to keep the ship as steady as possible then hunkered down under a makeshift tent of waxed canvas and resigned myself to getting soaked.

The worst of the storm passed about half an hour later. The boat was safe, the storm was ebbing, and I needed to go towel off and change. I was shivering almost uncontrollably. The winds and rain blew against the hull as I went down to my cabin.

Izzy was awake and in the kitchen. The inside of the ship was blessedly warm and smelled of bread. If smells alone contained calories, I'd weigh a thousand pounds just walking through there. My sister was unamused at my dripping wet attire and sent me back up top to strip in the pouring rain and line the wet clothes before coming down again to dry off for real. I shook like crazy as I wrapped my robe around myself in the driving rain. When I got to my cabin I had to brace against the walls to steady myself.

One year from now – less really, maybe three seasons – I'd be burned at the stake. Before I put on pants I attempted to rub vaseline into the tight scar tissue and almost vomited at the sight of myself. The Puritans came for me right off the dock. The heat, the smoke, the pain…one year. I managed to keep my lunch down but was clammy and dizzy. Izzy banged around the kitchen outside my door, and I shook my head in exasperation. She was going to explode my boat.

"Izzy, you have got to stop cooking," I begged her as I left my cabin. A wave came up under the hull and tossed me into a seat.

Izzy put some steaming dishes in front of me and waved her joint around in defiance. Fine. Let's just explode then. Maybe I'd finally get some rest.

Tea was in the mug. I sipped at it, figuring it was the only thing that might stay down. Angry wind blew at the porthole behind me, and I

The Bitch Captain (and The Lady)

stiffened. My skin crawled as if it sensed a threat. One year. *Remember 1650 you get burned.*

"Where did you go?" Izzy interrupted my thoughts, indicating she'd seen me out the window.

"Oh, I stash messages for myself all over. My Bermuda canister is out there, and I wanted to check my notes before heading over tomorrow. I'd forgotten about Davies." The wind slammed against the porthole again, and I winced, anticipating pain to accompany the aggressive sound. I kept sipping the tea and trying to rub feeling into my face. I felt like shit.

"Mmmm," she mumbled, not caring even a lick about the words coming out of my mouth.

"A man on the island. Nice guy. Bad businessman. I'd love to set him and Mary up. Hopefully Mary's husband died while I've been gone. She deserves so much better."

"Mmmmm," Izzy gave by way of response.

I let silence go on for a while. Weeks of silence would go by on this boat, and I was completely comfortable. Now, with Izzy so close and so close-mouthed, the silence chafed.

"Mary. She's my main crew on Bermuda," I offered up. "Hates boats and the ocean but what can you do?"

Mary was my life-saver on this crazy island. I sailed in, and she would bring all her kids and live on my boat as I took care of business. There was no need to worry about the *Try Your Luck* while Mary was aboard.

"Her son Edmund used to help her, but now Dom does most of that work," I kept rambling. Dom felt like a nephew to me. I'd watched him grow up and always tried to bring him and his siblings exotic presents like whistles and ornaments and shells.

Izzy didn't even pretend to respond. The rain and wind kept on pounding.

There was no going on deck to escape my sister today. Izzy was

87

better at this whole conversation and words thing. I gave up and lapsed into silence and listened to the storm outside and thought more about Bermuda.

Loose threads had worked their way out from the bandage on my hand. I picked at them and unwound it a little to see the wound. It was healing but slowly. All the rowing had broken it open again. I grimaced and wrapped it back up tight.

Andrews expects an answer. Yes, I suppose I would need to deal with that one. He had made it very clear that I was not to return to him without an answer. I'd avoid him entirely if it weren't for the guns. I needed his help with that.

An answer. Dammit. I couldn't pay the price he was asking of me, and here I was about to turn around and ask him for a favor. Just a year left with Bermuda, the price was too steep. My scars tightened again at the thought. One year. The sound of the wind and rain became a dull roar that began to sound like a crazed mob off in the distance. I rubbed my temples and tried to breathe the oncoming panic away. It was a distant memory, let it rest, let it go.

"What do you have to say for yourself? Explain this shit," Izzy burst out suddenly, slamming her hands on the counter. I jumped, startled out of my reverie. My body tensed in panic. There was a threat. There was danger. Where was it? How bad would it hurt? Izzy stared at me in accusation.

"Say what?" I asked.

She continued to stare and accuse me of...something. What had I forgotten? My heart sped with the sudden shift in her demeanor, and I broke out in a cold sweat. I looked around for a clue. There was bread in my hand.

"Oh, thank you for the bread. It's delicious." I took a bite of the bread to reinforce my words. It tasted of ashes and dirt.

"No!" She wheeled around and brandished the rolling pin at my face.

The Bitch Captain (and The Lady)

My muscles locked in place even though I wanted to back away from the weapon before it could break my ribs again.

"You kidnapped me – straight into a gunfight, I might add – and all I've been trying to do since then is make sure you survive the injuries you sustained!" She was livid. Her anger felt like a searing heat licking into me where I was exposed. "And now I'm trying to study for this fucking mess you've dragged me into, and you come in here and start chatting about your fucking secret friends from your fucking secret life!" Her accusations, my inability to explain myself, my hands bound and my face in the dirt—

No – no, that's not right.

I was in my ship.

It was 1649.

"At the very least you owe me an apology, and I shouldn't have had to ask for one, either!" she screamed out.

My heart was in flight and I tried to swallow. I was safe with my sister. I shook my head a little. Calm down. Please, calm down. My heart sprinted, and my throat closed under the oppressive smell of smoke. Izzy's long dark hair and angry face was not the same long dark hair and angry face that shouted accusations I could not possibly defend against.

"It's not the same," I murmured to myself in reassurance, trying to disabuse my memories of the shouting and furious mob. The oven was hot, preheated for the bread Izzy was about to bake. It was hot. It was very hot and dry in here. I tried to clear my throat and get enough oxygen. But the air was too thick with smoke, and the crowd was shouting at me. I pulled at my collar, trying to get more air.

"It is the same!" Izzy shouted back. "You haven't said you're sorry. Or maybe in this strange little fucked-up world of yours an apology requires a magic potion and ceremony too—"

The wind whipped up and shoved against the hull. The rain – no, not rain, people, crowds of people who wanted to watch me die – the noise of the mob overwhelmed me. The angry man with long dark hair swung a cane at me. He wanted to break more of my ribs. He'd already smashed my shoulder and leg. I could feel the ache from those wounds. I yanked the cane from his grasp and raised it to smash into his ribs, his face! Let him feel the blows, let him live through the nightmares! The horrible man crouched in the corner as I shouted and threatened to beat his head in for accusing me of witchcraft.

"Anne!" the angry man said from the corner of my tiny ship galley. His voice was different, high and ladylike. What was he doing on my ship? No men on my ship! I'd kill him!

"I'll kill you! I'll kill you and all your descendants! You'll never be free of me!" I roared at him. This time I wasn't bound to a stake. This time I wasn't held back by hateful men. This time I would watch him beaten into the dust.

"Diane!! Stop!" Izzy shouted at me as I held the rolling pin like a cudgel above her tiny form. "What the fuck is wrong with you?!"

The voices of the mob retreated back to the dwindling wind and rain against the hull. I was standing, in my full glory as Bitch Captain of the Seven Seas, over my beloved, my most precious sister. I couldn't relax. My adrenaline spiked through the roof. What had she asked for? An apology? No. The Bitch Captain of the Seven Seas does not apologize.

"I know what I did. I did what I did. I would do it every time," I managed to say. Then threw the rolling pin aside. My flask was right inside my cabin door. I grabbed it and marched myself up into the storm. I could not be in the same room as her. My ship was a place of freedom for me, and Izzy had turned it into a prison. I didn't feel the rain or the wind or the cold. I didn't feel anything. I put my head in my hands and focused on breathing. That man, those voices, it was all memory. Ghosts. Put them to rest in their graves, Anne.

I tipped back a measure of Fountain. I stripped, tied a lifeline around myself, and went to suffer the side effects in the open ocean during a rainstorm. I came back on board soaked but clean and fever-free. My deep wounds were still troubling, but I was a step or two further down the path towards full health.

I stayed up top until the rain abated and my heart rate slowed then went to find Izzy. I needed to explain to her what happened. She'd left the galley and locked herself in her room. The horror stories would have to wait.

I knocked on her door softly. "I'll let you know when we dock."

She waited a beat and only responded with "When we get back home, I'm moving out."

I couldn't blame her.

CHAPTER 5

Bermuda Landing

I sailed around the perimeter of the island until I was within sight of Mary's farm. There, I set off a small firework to alert her I had arrived and continued on to the small breachway that led to the caves. This area was riddled with caves that wouldn't be discovered for a few hundred years and was the perfect place to stash cargo.

When my mother took Izzy and me to Bermuda for our high school graduation, we'd taken a tour of these caves. I'd made note of their usefulness for keeping valuable cargo out of the hands of pirates and governments. I had dragged them all over the island on that trip. We'd visited every historical fort and setting, spent hours at the history museum, and combed every cove and beach. I'd committed every detail and speck of history to memory while evaluating landmarks and inlets for their possible advantage. I'd milked the modern foresight for every drop. Mom gave up shortly into day two. Izzy ditched me after the museum.

I anchored a little ways off the small beach and lit a few lanterns. This morning I'd ditched my jeans and sweatshirt and returned to my 17th-century regalia. While I waited for Mary and Dom in the cove, I pulled out a sheaf of paper and a quill. I owed Andrews his answer, but the woman, Yvonne, who managed his business interests would be very interested in the profits this cargo would bring to the estate. She and I hated each other personally, but we were united in our mutual quest to become filthy rich. There was a good chance she wouldn't even tell

Andrews I was here at all, and I could leave this island without him ever knowing I was back in town.

> *Yvonne,*
> *I am in St. George's. I have cargo to move that would greatly contribute to the profits of the estate. If he asks, my answer has not changed. If interested, send a note back with a place to meet. I have cargo owed to the estate in my hold ready for delivery. Bring a wagon.*
> *~A*

Chances were beyond good that Yvonne would burn the letter and I'd never hear from her and I'd have to move the cargo myself. Worth a try. I sealed the letter and put it in my pocket to give Dom once we were finished.

Slowly and carefully I loaded and lowered the rowboat with rifles and gunpowder and brought it to shore. On my fourth trip back, Mary and Dom, each leading a donkey, arrived on the beach. My shoulder was already on fire, and I'd bled through the bandage on my hand. I hugged Mary and ruffled Dom's hair. He was almost taller than me. Almost. I told him to quit growing, and he almost grinned his face off.

"What have we got?" Mary asked. I lifted the lid on a crate to display the arms and powder. "Oh, my. You'll have plenty of buyers. But you better be careful." Her voice lilted with the remnants of a British accent. "Dom, go with the captain. I'll wait here." Mary had refused to get on another boat after crossing the Atlantic. Her ship had crashed on the reefs, and she'd crawled to shore amidst the wreckage, all the while swearing off any and all future boats.

By the grace of God, Izzy stayed quiet and out of sight. Dom chattered on and on about his family and the goings-on of the island from the vantage point of an eleven-year-old boy.

"And then little Mary came down with the pox. That was a sad time. But The Father says the Lord has her in his arms now and she's at peace. Bettie is after me all day. She thinks she can keep up with me and my friends, but she's only ten and we can't be waiting around for her. Mother gets awfully upset when she comes home with torn skirts. After the last skirt Mother had to mend, she forbade Bettie from running off with me and my friends. She's learning to keep a house properly now. There's already been talk of promising her off to our near neighbor's boy. He's fifteen and will probably have a farm of his own before the end of the year. Father is not happy that he's Dutch, but their father is not happy that Mother is half Italian. Mother says everyone will make do because it's a small island and options are limited and Bettie is pretty."

I loved hearing the steady stream of gossip after so long at sea with only my own voice for company. "Is that Bertram's boy you're talking about? Big blond boy?" I remembered that kid. A bit of a brute at first but responsible enough. Not that my approval counted for anything.

"That's him. Haans." Dom frowned. "He's beaten me before. But I was smaller then. I could get a few good licks in on him now." Dom stood tall to emphasize his new height. I nodded approvingly and handed him more cargo to place in the boat.

"The navy has all but gone. Just a few remain and they aren't very highly ranked." Dom continued his recap of everything I'd missed. "Militias keep the peace now, although," and he hesitated, remembering a bad moment, "I don't know if all of them are peaceful."

"The war will be over soon. For better or worse, the militias won't be around forever." Dom was used to me saying things like this. I was too comfortable around them.

"That's good. I don't like them," he said. "Anyway, John and Rebecca are so irritating. They can't even read yet and they bug me every night to read to them. A man like me can't be reading to children. They are only four and five. And Edie is still a baby, only two. Was she born when you were here?"

"Must have just missed her," I said.

"She's cute. I pray every night that she won't be taken with the pox same as little Mary. Mother says we can't know, only hope and pray. So I pray." He took a break from talking in order to row back to shore.

"What news of your father?" I hated the bastard and wanted to make sure I knew his status before asking too much from his family.

"Father spends most of his time away at the sugar plantation by Hogs Bay. I work the farm with Mother. She says his new wife is rum, but I don't understand. The Father says he is being tested. I don't get that either."

"There is nothing to get, Dom," I told him. "Your father makes his choices. You must make sure you make better ones in your life." I worried that with 1650 approaching, I wouldn't get to see him again before I was burned as a witch. Looks like this trip will be full of endings. Not goodbyes. Endings. Rule number four: No goodbyes.

Mary had been busy while Dom and I rowed back and forth to get the last of the crates and casks to shore. She'd stacked crates near the entrance to the cave where I'd long ago rigged a winch and platform. Once everything was off the ship, I lowered Dom and a lantern into the caves below and began to transfer the cargo down. This was a much faster process than getting it from ship to shore.

"Are you up for helping me at the port?" I asked Mary once Dom was safely back with us.

"You know full well we are. Especially if you are still paying the same type of wages." Mary smirked. Of course I paid. I overpaid, and she knew it. We had a comfortable friendship based on money and how we both loved it.

"Perfect. I'll need to wait until daylight to sail there. Can you make it to port by morning?"

"I should be able to. It may take a little longer with all the young ones."

"I can wait. And you should know something else." Mary paused her departure preparations to listen. "I have a passenger aboard." I told her. Both Mary and Dom were dumbstruck. "She's a wealthy lady financing my travels this season. I'll be arranging accommodations for her. But in case you saw her about the ship I wanted you to know she has my consent to be there." Neither had recovered from their shock yet. I had never allowed passengers on my boat before. I traveled alone and everyone knew it.

"Wait—" Dom started, but his mother interrupted him.

"That is good." Mary hauled Dom onto his donkey.

I gave him the note for Yvonne. He was beyond thrilled to have an important errand to do. We weren't far from Andrews' estate, he would be back in time to come to town with Mary and the other kids later in the morning.

Dom was still searching for signs of my mysterious passenger when his mother pulled him and his donkey away into the dark. I'd see them tomorrow with the other children at the dock. Mary was sure to spend the rest of the night counseling Dom not to ask questions or request that he be allowed to sail with me on my travels, a thing I knew the boy had dreamed of since I'd first met him.

I rowed my way back to the boat and found Izzy on the deck watching my approach. I stored the boat and checked the anchor was secure. The deck and hold were finally free of all the ordnance and my spirit felt lighter and safer. My wounds were killing me, but my spirit rejoiced. Izzy was staring off in the direction Mary and Dom left from.

"That's Mary and her son. They are some of the good ones." I gestured toward the path they'd left on.

If Izzy showed any response, I didn't see it. My arms were screaming from all the loading, rowing, and lowering into the caves. I rubbed my calf and winced. I'd be limping tomorrow if I wasn't careful. It was bedtime at last. I fell into my small cabin bed and didn't wake up till the morning sun was high.

The sail to St. George's took a few hours. It was bright and hot and I was sweating and thirsty by the time I finally arrived at my favorite far dock. It was a long walk for me to get to town but also a far walk for the port authority to arrive at my ship. I dragged Izzy's dress trunk on deck and began filling it with a few changes of clothes, some daily necessities, and other essentials she'd need while on land. In the cargo area there was a series of false boards I prised out to reveal stacks and stacks of coins, precious metals, gems, and other riches. I swept a large amount into a purse and filled several smaller leather pouches I kept on my person to pay various townsfolk along my way. I replaced the boards and went to bury the large purse beneath Izzy's folded petticoats. I got dressed in my full regalia – trench, wrap skirt, woolen shirt, holsters, and sword belt – and knocked on Izzy's door.

"We're docked. I'm going to go secure you a room. I already packed your trunk so get dressed as best you can, and I'll help you with the rest when I get back." I grabbed a few canisters of goods from the kitchen and went up top to toss them in the trunk as well. Two soldiers were making their way across the busy port towards my ship, and I grabbed the relevant papers and met them at the bottom of the gangplank.

"Please present the captain of this ship," the first soldier, a lieutenant, ordered me. His mask of bored regal nobility was broken when he looked up to see me, a woman, standing and holding out my documentation. He looked me up and down with suspicion.

"I am the captain of this ship."

"Ladies are not seafaring captains." The second soldier tried to clarify his superior's command as if I didn't have the intelligence to comprehend it.

"I am the captain of this ship," I repeated. The two officers weren't sure how to continue. They conferred a moment. The lieutenant awkwardly took the papers out of my hand that announced I was under contract with the East India Company. The regal-looking officer looked semi-familiar. Kings Bay, that's where I knew him from. He'd been a

The Bitch Captain (and The Lady)

part of the naval force that descended and fought on the beach that day. He still looked too young to fight.

"Are you a royalist?" the young lieutenant asked.

"I am the captain of this ship." It was my version of pleading the Fifth. I had no allegiance to the Crown, but I did know that Cromwell was kicking ass over on the mainland and I wasn't about to throw my lot in with any political party. I was particularly uninclined to share any of my views with these two, who looked like the vernix had barely been wiped from their bodies. "As a woman I know not to dabble in the affairs of men. I am merely acting as pilot for the esteemed lady I am hired to bring across the Atlantic." The midshipman looked over my shoulder to see if he could see anyone.

"Where is she?" If the young lieutenant recognized me from Kings Bay, he gave no hint.

"She is dressing. I'm going to make accommodations for her as soon as we are done here. I wonder if I might request a guard for her while I am briefly away?"

"His Majesty's Royal Navy is not in the habit of—" the young lieutenant began when Izzy made an entrance.

"Anne! What on—" My sister shouted down to me, not realizing there were other people around. What she also did not realize was that the sun was shining bright and clear right behind her and providing a detailed outline of her body through the only item of clothing she'd managed to put on: a very thin, very white shift. Her hair looked beautiful though. She'd done something twisty with it.

"One moment." I excused myself and went aboard to hustle my sister out of the sunlight. I hissed a few instructions at her that mainly consisted of "Stay out of sight" and "Get dressed"' before hurrying back down the gangplank.

"His Majesty's navy would be happy to provide a guard. Roger here has volunteered." The young lieutenant slapped the other soldier on the back, who nodded readily.

"I am grateful. Thank you." Men, always driven by their crotches. "Where is the finest establishment? My lady is sparing no expense."

"I'd be happy to escort you," the young lieutenant offered as they closed up their books.

"Thank you. Much appreciated." I cast a glance back at my ship and prayed Izzy was busy hooking and lacing herself into real clothes.

"Lieutenant Commander Ian Alexander Coventry." The young lieutenant performed a perfunctory bow.

"Captain Anne Collette Silverspring, East India." I used this alias when dealing with nobility. The more syllables you could shoehorn into a name, the more at ease the upper class was with you.

Roger took up the guard position at the gangplank, ready to fight off any ruffians, his eyes creeping constantly to the deck hoping for another glance of the sunbathed lady.

The lieutenant exchanged a salute with Roger and motioned me to follow him into town. I tried my best not to limp and to keep a pleasant expression on my face. "It is not often we get a remarkable lady of such...stature here on this island," he said. "I'd love to have you both for a proper meal."

"That is very kind. I have some business to attend to first, but perhaps once that is finished? Perhaps the end of the week?" Once I'd sold those guns I was sailing away as fast as the winds would take me. We would not be around for dinner. There was no need to tell him this, though.

"Wonderful. I'll have my cook begin planning a menu." He snuck a look back at the ship, like Roger, hoping for another vision of this mysterious traveling lady.

"The Lady Isabelle will be delighted to have proper company. I'm afraid our time at sea has been rather rough on her. I am also looking to find a chaperone for her. A woman. A big, scary woman." In my mind I was picturing an ogre that would sit outside her door forbidding anyone from going in or out. Maybe she'd be eating a goat who trip-trapped across her bridge.

The Bitch Captain (and The Lady)

The young lieutenant chuffed and smiled the secret, emotionless smile of the upper class. "I think I know just who you need." He nodded and kept that strange grin on his face. He was not unpleasant to walk with. He kept up a lively stream of conversation as we approached town. He was particularly interested in where we sailed from, why we traveled alone, what family this new and radiant lady hailed from. I kept most things vague except where money was concerned. I wanted to impress upon this young lieutenant how wealthy and important Izzy was, the power and prowess of her heritage, and just how important it was that she be safe for the duration of our time here.

"How long might that be? If you'll need a guard long-term..." he mused.

"I have my own crew I use while here," I assured him. "As for how long we'll be here, I can't answer that. I'm due back in Europe by autumn. However, I have several matters to attend to here. Which is why I need the lady in the best accommodations possible."

The best accommodations possible turned out to be an inn, the Sea Wind. A decent-sized building smack in the middle of town. The bottom floor was a tavern, complete with passed-out drunks, smokey indoor and outdoor kitchens, and stray animals that wandered in and out. It was nice...for a recently settled island in the middle of the Atlantic Ocean.

The young lieutenant sent someone to fetch the proprietors, who were only too happy to boot someone out of a room upstairs when they saw the giant stack of gold I was ready to hand over. I arranged for meal delivery, bath service, stocking the room with wine and rum, and credit to cover any unforeseen expenses Izzy might incur. There was little likelihood she could possibly spend more money than I was plunking down for a first installment, but Bermuda was usually full of surprises and I wanted to be ready.

We crossed the street to a seedier establishment where it was not stray animals but stray soldiers and sailors wandering in and out of the whores' rooms up above. The lieutenant introduced me to Gerta. Gerta was old. Gerta was fat. Gerta was mean. Gerta was drinking a local man under the table. Gerta was perfect. The lieutenant excused himself for a moment, and I sat down to explain to Gerta the situation.

"I am escorting an esteemed lady across the Atlantic and need a chaperone and guard for her." I brought out a small purse and opened it. Gerta's eyes lit up.

"Ja, I am a good guard and chaperone for the lady." She reached for the bag, but I kept hold of it.

"No harm is to come to this lady. She is not even to stumble on a stray rock in her path. Do you understand?"

"Ja, Captain. I understand."

"The lady is to be kept fed. She is to have all the drink she wants," I instructed.

"Ja, Captain. The lady will grow very fat before she leaves this island." I let her grab the pouch, and her greedy eyes bugged as she counted the coins. "So very fat," she assured me.

"Lady Isabelle is to have her solitude. Anything she needs you will see gets delivered to her. There is no match for nobility for this lady on this island. She does not need to speak to anyone nor pretend to enjoy their company. Keep people away from her," I instructed.

"Ja, Captain. The lady is above us all."

"The lady should not be touched," I continued my instruction. "Any harm that comes to her I will visit upon you. If she bleeds, you will bleed. If she bruises, I will strike you. If a man defiles her, I will personally shove a broom handle up your ass." Gerta paused now, unsure of her commitment in the face of my threats. I brought out another pouch and curled her fingers around it. "So you know I'm serious."

Gerta nodded, speechless at the wealth in her hands. Then I pulled my dagger from its sheath and struck her across the cheek with the pommel. "So you know I'm serious." Tears filled the tough old broad's eyes, but she just kept nodding. "Fat, idle, and safe," I repeated. "The Lady Isabelle is to be fat, idle, and safe. Yes?"

The Bitch Captain (and The Lady)

"Ja. So fat. So safe. No men." Gerta pocketed the money when the lieutenant returned. If he noticed the growing bruise on Gerta's face, he didn't mention it. The trio of us went out to the road, where I hired a one-horse shay to carry Izzy to the inn. I thanked the lieutenant and lied about looking forward to our dinner.

I rode in the shay, and Gerta walked behind, all the way to the dock. Mary's family, complete with cookware, bedding, and foodstuffs, had made themselves at home on the ship's deck. Mary set up a terrific operation. The boat looked like a seaside tenement. No one could mission-impossible themselves through Mary's clotheslines to rob me blind. I loved that woman.

I steeled myself to let Izzy off the boat. Izzy's trunk was open and filled to the brim with additions she was planning on taking off the boat. I looked in and shook my head. Was she insane?

"Bettie, toss me a sack!" I yelled to Mary's oldest girl, who tossed me an empty canvas sack.

I rummaged around in the trunk and pulled out all the modern underwear with tiny bows and fruit printed on them. I pulled out pencils and perfectly-cut computer paper, flip flops, a lighter, and tampons. There were a dozen other toiletry and hair and nail care items I sorted through, and I banished the worst-looking offenders. I almost missed her tablet, one that was disguised as a leather-bound book, but found it and chucked it in with the rest of the contraband. In a last-second decision I tossed my dagger on top and shut and locked the trunk. I wouldn't give any of these townspeople a chance to accuse my sister of witchcraft. I went below and stashed it all in one of my smuggling areas within the boat. Gerta carried the heavy trunk to the shay.

Belowdecks, Izzy was still in her cabin trying to grow seven arms to lace herself into her dress. Without asking, I took over fastening the overskirt.

"I don't want your help, Anne!" Izzy wrenched herself out of my reach. I grasped the ties firmly and knotted the skirt tight.

"There is a horse and carriage outside waiting for you. You'll be staying at the Sea Wind." I started on her bodice. "Just stay there and hang out. I'll come get you when I'm done." I started fussing over her sleeves and stockings and shoes. A hat. She should have a hat too. Where did I put those?

"Exactly how long am I going to be stuck here in the middle of the Atlantic, in millions of layers, with no air conditioning for hundreds of fucking years?"

"I don't know. I'm due in Europe in the fall at some point. So before then?" My sister was unamused at the vagueness. "Just a few days. We'll be gone by the end of the week." I found a hat and stuck it on her head and stepped back to evaluate her. Good, not great. But she just needed to make it from the ship to the inn.

"At least cannabis hasn't been outlawed yet," Izzy muttered under her breath. As if the legality of her green plants had ever stopped her before.

"I'm going to give the driver his instructions. Wait two minutes, then come out. And, Izzy, I can't stress this enough: we do not belong here. Whatever happens, try to keep in mind that this is not your home. These people are not real. They've been dead for hundreds of years. They are ghosts. They don't matter. We don't matter. We'll be gone in a week. So keep to yourself and just – I don't know – try to enjoy the scenery." I left and went to speak a few words to the driver about trying to give Izzy a smooth ride.

Lady Isabelle finally emerged from the ship and stepped foot on a good and proper piece of 1649 real estate. My heart was in my throat. I felt like I was in the middle of pulling some huge con. I offered Lady Isabelle my hand to help her into the shay. She smacked me away at first, only to realize that hopping in and out of carriages with a corset and thirty-five pounds of fabric was a difficult ask. After several failed attempts, she relented and squeezed the shit out of my hand since she couldn't scream at me in public.

The Bitch Captain (and The Lady)

"Son of a bitch." I rubbed my injured hand and inhaled through my teeth.

I beckoned for Gerta to come forward. "Lady Isabelle, allow me to introduce you to Gerta." The two women regarded each other wordlessly. "She will be at your beck and call and with you every step of the way for our short duration here on the island." Izzy didn't respond. I turned to Gerta. "Gerta, you have your instructions. Do not forget them. I will be by to check on the two of you as soon as I can."

Izzy gave a stiff "Good day" to the woman and remained looking forward.

"But she is not a lady." Gerta leaned over and whispered to me in accented English.

"Yes, she is." I glared at the old broad.

"But her skin—"

"You'll be getting two more of those purses when we depart." I gestured with the hilt of my dirk to the bulges in her cleavage where Gerta had stashed her new gold.

"She is a very pretty lady, with very pretty skin. Ja, I see now." Gerta imagined the next fat purse with a fat smile.

"Fat. Idle. Safe," I repeated.

"Ja. The lady will be fat, idle, and safe. I understand." Gerta took her position behind the shay and signaled the driver.

"I am ready to leave, Anne," Izzy sang out. I prayed she'd have a relaxing few days. In the meanwhile, I'd work out how to explain everything to her on the way back home.

I went over to Izzy's side of the shay and stepped up on the wheel to get a closer look at her face. She was glaring at the town in the bright sun. I pulled her hat forward and double-checked that she looked every inch the wealthy patroness I was claiming she was. The driver had balked just like Gerta had, but his issue was mostly surprise, surprise that I remedied with a few coins.

"Gerta will know how to find me if you need something," I told her.

Izzy didn't respond. She sat there like a block of ice. The incident in the kitchen had been haunting me, and I didn't want to let her leave my side without letting her know how ashamed I was about that little slip-up.

"Izzy, I feel terrible about what happened in the kitchen. It won't happen again. I promise." I might as well have been talking to the wind. I didn't deserve anything better, I knew it. I'd try again once we were back on the water. "Stay calm. Stay relaxed. Stay in your room. I'll be back for you as soon as I can. Then we'll go home."

She leaned in close and growled, "Fuck off." I deserved it, I know.

I jumped down and the carriage took off with Gerta trotting behind. I watched till they were out of sight then turned back to the ship. Mary was watching Izzy's departure from the bottom of the gangplank, and I went to join her.

"She must be very special," she commented.

"She is. She's having a difficult time right now."

"Aren't we all." Mary went to wrangle her children, and I wondered if my eyes were playing tricks on me or if there was a small bump under her dress. I had dutifully ignored the bruises on her face and arms. I would love nothing more than to slit her husband's throat and leave him to rot in Shark Cove (and I'd offered such service to her), but Mary said if it wasn't him, it would be someone else. So she chose to stay with the evil she knew.

I was exhausted, but the day was only just beginning. Izzy was squared away with her chaperone/guard and would surely be able to manage a few days in the 17th century and then she'd go home.

I helped Mary finish setting up her "tenement chic" set-dressing on my upper deck, complete with tents and a stove and washing lines strung like spider webs across my rigging. The result was an unappeal-

The Bitch Captain (and The Lady)

ing ship to try and steal, especially since it would take hours of work to detangle the washing lines before being able to raise a sail. Dom came skipping down the dock not long after Mary and I had begun wringing out her first batch of laundry.

"Got it!" he announced as he leapt aboard.

"Any trouble?" I flipped the boy a coin and took the letter from him.

"None." He pocketed the coin and went in search of snacks. I was relieved until I opened the letter and saw the two-word response. Shit. Trust an eleven-year-old boy not to notice trouble. I was going to have to make the trek out there and deal with this. The ship was already decked out for Mary and her family, so I'd have to go overland. I could already smell the horse stink and feel the horrible roads under the rented carriage wheels.

"Is all well, Captain?" Mary saw the plans forming across my expression.

"Just an inconvenience. I'll have to go out to Andrews' after all." I called Dom back and told him to go fetch the shay and the driver back here again.

"Is that wise?" Mary knew my long and tangled history with that estate.

"Not even a little bit. But there's nothing else for it."

"Well then, you go. Perhaps clean up a little bit. Bring some presents, make a good impression. Having their help would go a long way towards selling all that cargo. Give me those clothes and I'll wash them while you're gone – or burn them." She sniffed me and grimaced.

"Wise as always." I laughed. "There are crates marked for the estate." I drew the marking on a scrap of paper for her. "Anything with this mark should be brought up and loaded on the shay." Mary called her oldest girls back over and sent them below to find and carry up the boxes and crates and sacks with the mark that matched the paper. It was easier to label some items with characters and logos.

In my cabin I lifted up my mattress and pulled out a box that was wedged between the back of the drawers and the hull. I carefully laid it on the bed and opened the top. It was my pièce de résistance, a gown I had made during all my long journeys. It was mostly constructed from pale silks bought on trips east. I had embroidered over almost every inch of the nine yards until it resembled a brocade: tiny flowers, sweeping idyllic countryside scenes, birds, and petals. I took inspiration from the glorious kimonos of Japan that I envied.

I'd built the collar of the bodice up into a mock standing Elizabethan collar and continued the stiff edges down to my waist. Gilt buttons adorned the top of the skirt where I'd gathered the waist into cartridge pleats. I had gone a little rogue with the sleeves. As beautiful as I wanted to look, I couldn't be dragging sleeves behind me in billowy waves. The sleeves were fitted to three-quarter length and laced through embroidered holes cinching them to the shape of my arms. I wore clean, stiff petticoats to fill out the gathered skirt.

I cheated again with the shoes. I had bought the shoes at a high end store back home. They were knee-length, gorgeous soft taupe suede with sturdy stitching and tough soles. Underneath all of it were as many daggers and pistols as I could hide on my body. I uncoiled my hair from its braids and brushed it out. I swept it into a low ponytail with jeweled hair combs and worked the long tresses into a few curls I artfully displayed across my chest.

Wealth and beauty were the biggest offensive weapons I could bring into play when it came to Andrews. Not that he didn't appreciate me in my regular clothes, but this was sure to make more of an impression, and I was going to need every edge I could get. In 1647 we parted company under bad blood. Today I needed to ameliorate that.

Putting the whole outfit on proved a great challenge. My right boot was too tight around my swollen calf and squeezed the injured muscle uncomfortably. I was having trouble getting enough range of movement from my shoulder to fasten the busk on my corset and correctly place the bodice over top. I gave up halfway through and found some aspirin and a whisky chaser before attempting it again. Lots and lots of screaming and cursing later I was all strapped in and gussied up.

One problem left: my hand. Izzy had broken the wound open yet again when she had squeezed it; this thing was never going to heal. I carefully unwrapped the linen and tried to wash and dress it. It stung badly and was growing warm. Later. I'd deal with it later. I rewrapped it and stuck on a pair of cream kidskin gloves.

My driver was back when I finally emerged from dressing. Mary and her family took in my outfit with appreciation and awe. Generally speaking, I rarely dressed in appropriate garb for a woman of the time, and when I did, it was never this fancy. Mary elbowed Dom to stop his gawking, and I winked at him to remind the boy that I was still the Captain he remembered. The smaller children toddled over to feel the silk and the threads.

Dom and Bettie had been busy bringing up the designated boxes, crates, and sacks, and the young shay driver had secured most of it onto the conveyance already. It was the same rented shay that had conveyed Izzy to the Sea Wind, but the driver didn't recognize me at all. I grabbed my valise, which had some candy, a sample of gunpowder, a flintlock mechanism I'd dismantled from one of the guns, and some money. Then I climbed aboard.

I bade Mary good luck and told her I hoped to be back tonight. It was a four-hour ride out to Andrews' estate if the roads and ferries were clear and we met with no trouble.

I hated traveling by land. The horse was smelly and pooped all over the road. Even though the driver was a skinny stripling of a lad, the shay was small and his leg kept touching mine. He tried and failed to hide an embarrassing erection that betrayed him at every bump in the road. He swallowed and apologized as we rolled over a pothole and I was almost dumped out. I lay back and closed my eyes and tried not to think about the horse (or donkey or whatever it was) or his furtive glances at my chest.

The main core of my plan had to do with spreading the word around to the various militias on the island charged with keeping the "peace" in the absence of England's military might, currently amassed in England fighting the Roundheads (or whatever was going on over there. It was England, they were always at war). This cargo of mine would provide a cutting edge for any group who managed to cough up enough dough to obtain it. The most likely outcome was that I would have to settle for selling it piecemeal to multiple militias as these backwater colonies were cash-poor.

Normally I'd settle for quality bartering of goods, but I wanted gold this time. I wanted that coin and no attachments. Andrews was the only man wealthy enough to buy it all in one lot, but he had no need for such arms. His little kingdom was so remote from St. George's he was rarely troubled by militias or rustlers or anyone stupid enough to try and catch him unawares.

I could smell Andrews' estate – fiefdom really – before I could see it. He kept his tanneries and tobacco houses far from the main house and neighborhoods where the labor was housed. His lands were huge; it was an entire working kingdom, complete with a port and smaller towns, here on the north shore of Bermuda. People were working everywhere.

When I'd first met Andrews, he was a skinny, wretched farmer straight off the boat. I'd brought him his first profits and helped him secure his first expansion. We'd worked together over the years, and with his share of the profits, he'd created the homeland he'd always wanted, a place he couldn't be kicked out of.

More land meant more people were needed to work that land, more people meant families, and families brought life to this forgotten corner of the island. Andrews employed anyone and everyone who came across

The Bitch Captain (and The Lady)

his path: indentured servants, renters, prison contract labor, free men, and enslaved peoples.

Bermuda at this time was just beginning to hint at the coming boom in human trafficking via the slave trade. As people arrived on the island in one condition or another, they needed a place to live and work and thrive. One person found a haven here on Andrews' land, then brought a friend who knew a guy who wanted his wife, and she sailed over with a cousin…and Andrews was male and white and rich and could sign papers and make the deals. As he bought up the failed farms and properties of his neighbors, they often included people who'd been trafficked to the island against their will. It was a busy place with processing houses, small farms, blacksmiths, mills, salt fields, coopers, fishing and cargo boats, distilleries, stables – everything a small kingdom needed to run and prosper was here. Brought to the island by force, kept here by leagues of unforgiving Atlantic waters, few chose to leave this odd kingdom. Any port in a storm. And the Hundred Acres was a safe and prosperous port. So many people, all laboring in their various positions, and Andrews at the top.

The place was an enigma of its time. It functioned like no other estate in the world at this point in history. The goods produced here went first to the people, the excess was sold, and the return reinvested in the property. Around and around and around it went until not a man on the island could claim more wealth than Andrews. Wealth, not cash. There was little actual coin available here, which was why I hoped they'd assist me in divesting the guns and powder. It would bring them a cache of gold I knew they'd find useful.

I held the letter tightly in my hand as we turned off the main "road" and onto his property. Rising beyond the hills I glimpsed the huge multi-story structure he'd built as a "screw you" to all the nobility he'd left scornful and laughing at his dreams in Europe. I had meant to never return here. I had last seen Andrews two years ago and had made it fairly clear that our association was over. Yet here I was. I worried the wound on my hand under the glove, and the sharp sting brought me focus. This felt like a huge mistake.

The children saw me first. All the children of Andrews' kingdom roamed free no matter who their parents were or what they did or what level of personal autonomy they had once held over their lives. The kids raced alongside the shay laughing and calling for me, knowing I always had treats for them. Which I did.

I started tossing them all candies, and they shrieked with glee as they chased the brightly-colored toffees through the air. The children raced off ahead of the shay to alert the household that I was on my way.

My shoulder ached after throwing all the candy and waving and calling out to the children I recognized. I inhaled sharply and tried to rub the pain away. I had the driver stop when I saw a pair of cobblers I recognized. I knew they had gotten married, and now she was beginning to show, I wanted to know if it was a first or second child. I hopped out to offer congratulations and ask how they were doing. This led to a bunch of other workers coming to greet me and ask questions about the business and the estate and offering me words of welcome. They wanted news of the outside world, the war, the gossip in St. George's, the colonies, any stories about my times at sea. There was so little physical want on this land that the hunger for stories and gossip was magnified.

Eventually I returned to the shay and continued on – only to stop and repeat this process at the distillery and the school, and even Father O'Shaughnessy and Rabbi Schmul were happy to see me and talk over the news of the estate and the island. If I wasn't careful, I could spend the next year here chattering away. I clutched at the letter in my pocket and reminded myself that I was strictly here for business. I resituated myself in the shay and directed the driver to carry on to the looming mansion and my questionable reception there.

Waiting for me at the front door were the three reasons for Andrews' meteoric rise to wealth and success: Angelica, mistress of the house and welfare manager of the people; Yvonne, business czar in charge of

The Bitch Captain (and The Lady)

expansion and acquisition; Helene, queen and proprietress of the entire estate, seeing to the profits and products of everything produced on site. I called them the sister wives.

They had each had a brief but productive affair with Andrews resulting in one child each for Angelica and Yvonne, and three for Helene. All three, brought to this island and eventually onto this estate as enslaved women. All three, now in charge of this immense kingdom. All three, wearing identical expressions of disgust and frustration.

I took a deep, calming breath before stepping out of the shay. Before I walked away, I left a wrapped sweet on the seat of the shay for the driver, who grinned and grabbed for it like the child he still was. I instructed him to bring the crates inside after me.

They watched my every step up towards the house. "Angelica. Yvonne. Helene," I greeted them. "Nice to see you again."

"You think you can just send a note and waltz back in here—" Yvonne began, but Helene cut her off.

"Two years. What do you have to say for yourself?" the formidable woman asked. Ugh, she was worse than my mother.

"I'm not here to make trouble." I put my hands up and tried to look nonthreatening.

"You are trouble," Angelica accused.

"You have much to answer for. Come. Lunch is served inside." Helene was the gatekeeper here, and she was inviting me in. One hurdle done at least.

"Where is he?" I asked before taking a step in their direction.

"He'll be in soon. He was all the way out at the salt flats," Helene answered without looking backwards. I motioned for the driver to follow me in with the crates. The other women had already disappeared inside as I gathered my courage to step through the door.

"Auntie Anne!!" I was rushed and tackled by five giant teenagers as soon as I crossed the threshold. They swarmed me and pelted me with questions as I hugged and kissed these children that I adored and missed so terribly. "You came back!" "I missed you!" "Where's your ship?" "Did you bring us anything?" That last one was courtesy of Magnus, Andrews' youngest, a thirteen-year-old boy who had grown taller than me in my years away.

"What on earth makes you think I brought you anything?" I teased him.

"Because you always do!" Yvonne's daughter, Sofia, fifteen now, wrapped her arms around me. I kissed the top of her head and laughed.

"You all think that in my incredibly busy and important life, I took the time out to search the world over to bring you back the perfect gifts?" They all responded with resounding yeses and affirmatives. "You're right! I got some really great stuff this time too." They all cheered, and we headed towards the crates.

"Wait." Angelica's voice stopped the party in its tracks. "Gifts after lunch," she announced to our crestfallen and sulky faces. The other two mothers were on Angelica's side, but such was the put-upon grief of their children that she just sighed. "Fine, be quick about it." We all dashed into the foyer.

I opened the first crate and pulled out sheafs of paper and a violin. "Beri, this is a new violin for you. I thought your other one might be getting a little worn." I handed Angelica's fifteen-year-old daughter the gleaming wooden instrument. "Now, the sheet music was written by a boy named Mozart. He wrote and composed music from the time he was four years old. I got to hear him play once. I thought to myself the whole time that Beri could do just as well." Mozart wouldn't play a note for over a hundred years, but I did indeed sit in that concert room thinking of my young Beri and how she was just as amazing a musician as this kid. Beri took the instrument and pages reverently and went to examine them in better light.

"Sofia, that whole crate there is yours." I directed the girl to the heavy crate, and she opened it to squeals of delight. It was filled with books. I had cheated a little with this gift. Many of the books were modern copies of classics bound in leather. My last trip home I had scoured used bookstores for books that looked appropriate on the outside and didn't have too much damning evidence of the future on the inside. I'd even gone so far as to pick up and leaf through some of Izzy's Regency romance novels to see if they mentioned technology or historical events that would stand out in this era. Just like my sister would have, Sofia picked up a book and was already lost in a copy of *The Once and Future King*.

"Me next!" Magnus muscled through his sisters to my side. I felt like a dwarf next to this baby giant.

"No presents for you until you stop growing," I teased him. He hugged me and kissed the top of my head. "Well, alright then. Just this once." Magnus had a special place in my heart. Of all Andrews' children, he and I were the closest.

I pulled out a beautifully-carved chess set I'd found in Italy. The board was inlaid with shell, and each piece was hand-carved, polished stone. Magnus and I shared a long tradition where he beat the crap out of me every time we played a game together. I stunk at board games, lost every time. He loved it and I loved it too…no matter how frustrating and humbling it was to lose Go Fish to a three-year-old for the billionth time.

"Amelia, where'd you go? There you are!" Amelia and Josephine were Helene's girls, fifteen-year-old twins.

I'd really broken the rules for Amelia's gifts. I pulled out a wooden case and opened it to reveal a kitchen knife set of ultra-sharp, ultra-expensive Japanese knives. Amelia spent much of her time cooking with her Aunt Angelica in the kitchens. Izzy had informed me that knives, sharp ones, were important for chefs. These were completely modern Damascus stainless steel with rosewood handles. I had dropped a small fortune on them. The girl took one out and marveled at the heft and balance.

"I was told that the most important tool for a chef was a good sharp knife. I got these in Japan. Do you know where that is?" The girl's eyes were riveted on the fancy metal, and she shook her head no. "That's because it's on almost the exact opposite side of the world from here. It's where I also got Josephine's present."

Josephine had been waiting patiently, and her eyes lit up when I called her name. "In Japan they have mighty warriors called samurai. I got this." I pulled out an ornately-carved sword and sheath from the crate, "from one of those warriors." Okay, I had gotten it from a shop in Tokyo, but it wasn't cheap or anything.

I pulled the blade out, and all the kids came to listen to the story. Magnus clutched his new chess set with glowing eyes. I knew the attention was almost as important to Josephine as the gift. The girl wasn't one to make waves or ask for what she wanted. She did as she was told and did it well, but when we spent time together alone, she wanted stories of my adventures at sea, tips on how to throw a punch, and what kind of armor would fit best over boobs. Helene did not like to see the two of us together; it made her nervous for her daughter.

"A warrior told me an amazing story of how this sword had been passed down through generations to him. A long time ago in a land far, far away, a hero fought valiantly against a masked evil villain." I climbed two steps to be slightly above my audience, and the children all listened as I waved the sword to catch the sunlight. "This villain had come to the hero's village when the hero was a boy and killed his family." I chopped the sword down fast, and they gasped and ducked, the perfect audience. "The hero grew up and vowed to kill the masked man. One day they met on a bridge over a deep, flowing river. 'You killed my father,' the hero accused the masked man. 'No. I am your father,' the masked man revealed before chopping off the hero's hand and shoving him into the roiling waters below!" I laughed evilly and held the sword over my head in victory. Then I broke character and handed the sword to Josephine, who promptly tied it around her waist. "Now, let's go eat before your mothers have a stroke."

The Bitch Captain (and The Lady)

Out of the corner of my eye I saw the sister wives waiting impatiently at the table for this impromptu Christmas to conclude. Angelica admonished the children for their comportment as they barreled into the dining room to show their mothers the gifts.

"You spoil them too much." Andrews spoke from the top of the stairs. My heart stopped when I heard his voice. It had been so many years since I'd heard him speak.

Slowly, so I wouldn't miss a moment, I turned to look at him. Graham Andrews was a tall, well-built man approaching his forties, with layers of muscle still present from decades of working his own land. He had a mane of blond hair that was just beginning to gray and a close-cropped beard that lent him a leonine appearance which won over many, oh so many, female hearts on this island. Like me, he'd changed out of his work clothes for this occasion. He was in a clean linen shirt, casual trousers, and polished boots. It wasn't terribly formal wear as far as this time period goes, but this kingdom was so far remote, the rules often didn't apply here. His cool blue eyes watched me cautiously, wary to see me again. I clutched the letter in my pocket to remind myself why I was here.

"My answer hasn't changed." I was going to hold onto my resolve and stay focused on the reason I was here.

Andrews began descending the stairs towards me. "So you said."

"I'm here because I have important business that concerns the estate."

"Clearly." He stepped up close to me, reached for my hand, and kissed my gloved fingers.

"I'm not staying long." Stay focused. Keep your resolve. Stay focused.

"So you said." He moved in close, and I could smell his freshly laundered clothes. He hadn't let my hand go yet. Andrews kissed my cheek, my forehead, my other cheek, and didn't move away. I closed my eyes. "That was too long away, Nanette," he murmured in my ear.

I turned to him and found his lips waiting. Stay focused – god, he had beautiful lips, and I knew just what they could do – stop it. Keep your resolve.

Andrews had used the name he'd called me from the first time we met, when he was just an immigrant on a scrap of land and I was a lonely captain in need of cargo. The fingertips of his other hand traced the lip of my bodice. Stay focused, I begged myself, stay focused – he pressed me gently against the wall and then we were kissing.

God, I had missed this man.

I missed his lips, his hands, his heart, his body. I'd been starving without knowing it until he was standing here in front of me. He pulled away just an inch to smile and look at me.

"I missed you, Graham." I caressed the side of his face, his smile broadened. I brought his lips back to mine and felt my whole body release. I wasn't supposed to come back here. When I'd left him in 1647, I'd left for good. Andrews pressed himself against me and I held him tight; there'd been too much space between us for too long. Thank god, I was here.

Our room was up the stairs and to the left, our bed was large and comfortable, and the windows let in the sea air and ocean views. Just a few paces away from where we stood on these steps and we could be out of these stupid clothes –

Angelica cleared her throat to get our attention. "Lunch is ready. Everyone is waiting." She tapped her foot and waited for us to disengage. Andrews kissed me one last time, then followed me into the dining room.

Magnus was standing over Beri, trying to cajole her out of her seat. "Please? Please?"

"No, you got to sit next to Auntie last time. Go sit next to Father. It's my turn." She pushed him away.

Magnus glared at his sister and turned to Josephine, who raised her new sword threateningly in response to his unuttered plea.

"Come on, I'm not such bad company, am I?" Andrews pulled my

The Bitch Captain (and The Lady)

chair out for me, the one which sat opposite him at the end of the long dining table, and led his son by the shoulder to his regular seat.

"Auntie..." the boy whined, begging me to intercede for him.

"Enough," Helene commanded from across the table. "Magnus, take your seat. Josie, no weapons at the table. Let's all thank Auntie Angelica and Amelia for this meal." Thanks went around the table, and everyone served themselves and began eating.

The three sister wives and I had long ago decided to make this family work by suppressing our animosity for each other. Each of us held a valuable position in this kingdom and were willing to put up with the others for the betterment of the family and the business. In front of the children we attempted (not always successfully) to speak with restrained kindness and respect. The children were allowed to determine their relationships with the various women on their own terms without pressure. When the children were absent, though, the gloves came off. I pulled my gloves off now and placed them to the side of my plate before picking up my fork.

"What happened to your hand, Auntie?" Josephine was looking at the bandage. There was a little blood still seeping through.

Shit. I had forgotten in all the excitement about that particular wound. The adults around the table froze. Besides our animosity for each other, we also attempted to hide how dangerous my work was from the children, a tall order as I typically arrived at the estate in dire need of recuperation from my journeys.

"Just a little rope burn. One of the sheets got away from me," I lied smoothly, fooling only the children.

Andrews pressed his lips together and took a steadying breath from across the table. I'd have to answer for this once the children were gone. I placed the offending hand in my lap and switched the fork to my left.

"I can't get over how big you all have gotten." I changed the subject.

"Things change when you are away two years. Sometimes for the better," Yvonne muttered.

"Sometimes not at all." I still hated her. That certainly hadn't changed.

"Because you left, we've had to contract with second-rate captains who let our goods rot in their holds."

"My ship was only one of several I set up—"

"You took—"

"Did you piss off all the other captains like this too?"

"No business talk at the table," the children all chided us. Yvonne and I glared at each other from across the table but backed down. No business talk at the table was a hard and fast rule here.

"This meal is delicious, Angelica. Is it duck?" Andrews drew the attention away from Yvonne and myself.

"Yes. It is duck," Angelica answered with strained cheerfulness.

Fuck, this was awkward.

Luckily Magnus swooped in to save the day. "I get to sit with Auntie tonight at the play," he pronounced. The other children erupted, shouting down his claim and pleading with me not to let him have his way.

"You always monopolize her. I want a turn!"

"You can't just shout things out and make people go along with that."

"Auntie is a girl and she gets to have girl time too."

"Father, tell him he can't do that!"

My heart was torn in five different ways as I listened to them fight over me. I couldn't stay for a show. I couldn't stay at all. I kicked myself for having come back. I needed to leave...I wanted nothing more than to stay.

"Now hold on. Don't I get a say?" Andrews chided his children.

"You'll get her all to yourself at the Wallingtons'," Sofia grumbled.

"Oh? Is there a party coming up?" I asked.

The Wallingtons were a major fixture of the stuffy nobility on the island. Every month or so, they dug up an occasion to celebrate some minor reminder of their home in England. It was a great networking

The Bitch Captain (and The Lady)

opportunity. Whenever my time here coincided with a party (and we couldn't find any excuses to get out of it), Andrews and I attended. Yvonne would provide us with a list of talking points and business opportunities we were to push during drinks and cigars – and we did that…when we weren't dancing and enjoying a night out alone.

"Yes. The party is in five days. We need Lavigne to commit—" Yvonne started, but all the children and Angelica cut her off.

"No business talk at the table." They spoke as one. Yvonne sighed and pushed her food around her plate, sulking.

"Tell me about this show. What have the players got planned tonight?" I asked.

"Oh! It's sure to be amazing," Beri answered. "One of the indentured men got to see a Shakespeare play before he left England. He was able to remember most of it, and the players are recreating it for us tonight."

"It's about this servant, Fallcane, who shipwrecks in a far country and has to dress like a woman to avoid suspicion by Henry the Fifth," Amelia expounded knowledgeably. "You see, Fallcane had made a deal with the devil to become rich, and Henry the Fifth was out to murder him for killing his uncle."

"But then," Magnus took up the story, "Fallcane is found out by Romeo and Juliet, who break the devil's spell on him by killing each other in a cave with poison on Saint Crispin's Day." Magnus pretended to choke and wheeze and act out a death scene until Helene stopped him and made him sit back in his seat like a gentleman.

"Then," Sofia brought it home, "Fallcane marries Ophelia and there is peace throughout the land."

The guns could freaking wait. I was going to see this show. "This sounds like the best play I've ever heard of."

"So you'll stay?" Magnus crowed.

"I don't think I can miss it."

"In which case she'll be sitting next to me." Andrews claimed my side. I warmed to the notion that I might spend the evening with him at one of these awful shows, like old times. He raised his glass to me, and I returned the gesture.

"There's much to be done before the show tonight. Auntie Anne and Auntie Von need to go through inventory—" Helene brought a list out of her pocket, ready to begin giving orders.

"My ship is in St. George's for now—"

"Why in god's name did you not sail it here?" Helene gestured to my dock outside. I gripped my fork and kept my temper in check. "We've been waiting—"

Yvonne interrupted her, "Your ship does us no good in St. George's. After the Wallingtons we'll need you to—"

"I had business in St. George's—"

"Two years, Anne." Helene slammed her hand on the table. "You had business here. I have a list longer than your dock out there of supplies and orders from the tenants. We have a backlog of—"

"No business talk at the table," they all reprimanded us. Helene, Yvonne, and I sat back, outnumbered. We ate in silence for a little while.

"Auntie, your hand is bleeding again," Josephine whispered to me. Shit. I'd forgotten to keep it in my lap.

"Nanette, what happened?" Andrews demanded from across the table. I had come to him too many times, broken and bleeding. My constant injuries were an old source of tension between us.

"It was close-range. The gun wasn't even loaded properly." I spoke only to him, attempting to downplay the wound and keep him calm. At least he hadn't seen my shoulder.

"Someone shot you, Auntie?" Magnus and the other children looked at me with wide eyes. I realized I had the attention of the entire table and flushed with embarrassment. "Why would they do that?"

"I can think of a few reasons." Yvonne chewed her duck with delight.

"I got into an argument with them—"

The Bitch Captain (and The Lady)

"Them? More than one?" Andrews rubbed the bridge of his nose.

"That rat bastard thief had his whole crew—"

"All children are excused!" Angelica stood up and commanded the children out.

They all protested this dismissal. They knew they were about to miss out on a good story. Once they were all out of the room the silence was deafening. Angelica dipped into the kitchen and back out again with clean bandages and salves. She sat down in Amelia's vacated spot and held her hand out with her stupid eyebrow raised and her stupid foot tapping away.

Reluctantly I gave her my right hand and let her unwrap the dirty gauze. She was long practiced in nursing me back to health. I wouldn't classify her bedside manner as gentle, however. I hissed and cursed as she rubbed the stinging ointment into the broken wound.

"Let's have the story, Nanette."

"It was an ambush. It was not my fault. I was just there for a straight-up cargo-for-coin transaction, and that lying rat bastard thief ambushed me and – and there were complications." I almost mentioned Izzy's name, but my plan was to have her off this island before anyone could even smell the smoke emanating from her room. "Long story short—" They all started yelling at me, knowing I was withholding details. "Long story short," I held my own against them, "he's dead, they're all dead, and I took all his cargo, which is why I'm here."

"What cargo?" Yvonne was finally invested in the conversation.

"Black powder, about 500 pounds. Twenty crates of muskets. Lead ingots and molds." Yvonne's eyes lit up with greed. I knew she'd appreciate this. "I have it all stashed safely away."

Andrews got up and stalked to my end of the table. "No. No. This is too dangerous."

"Ideal? No. But dangerous—"

Andrews grabbed my injured hand and pulled me to my feet. I winced at the pressure on the freshly-dressed wound. He quickly frisked down my arm to my shoulder. Stars burst in my eyes, and I sat down hard. He pulled the bodice sleeve and underdress away, exposing the deep wound there. The other women gasped, and Angelica stood to get to work on my shoulder. Andrews kept going and found a dozen other places that needed attention, and then he went to my leg. He knew better than to expose my scars to the other women and just sat back with his head in his hands.

"Tell me again how this isn't dangerous," he accused. "Let the cargo rot in those caves. For the love of god."

"I am with Andrews." Helene chose his side as she always did. "I don't want this type of danger following you onto these lands."

"Yes. It's too dangerous." Angelica threw her lot in with the other two.

"You're being short-sighted," I told them. "The profits from the sale could mean more housing, another school. You still haven't got a decent set of fishing—"

"I will not have you killed over a pair of fishing boats!" Andrews yelled. "Helene, Yvonne, I know the children are outside listening. Can you go assure them their aunt will not be in danger? Angelica, leave me the ointment and wraps. Nanette, a word in private. Now."

The ladies dispersed, but not before Yvonne came over to me and whispered that she was in and we'd talk later.

"Yvonne! Nanette!" he called out to separate us, but I knew I could count on her. We'd meet later.

Andrews and I went to our room where he helped me out of the fancy gown so he could get at my leg more easily. I sat on our old familiar bed and let him pull off my boots and stockings. He was gentle with the scar tissue and far more pleasant with the stinging antiseptic than Angelica had been.

"Two years, Nanette." His voice was soft as he tenderly cleaned the leg wound. It still stung, and I inhaled sharply with each pass of the ointment. He was being gentle, probably more than I deserved.

"I know. I should not have come back." He had every right to hate me.

"You shouldn't have left in the first place." Andrews wrapped my leg securely and looked up at me. "I regret the words I said."

"Me too." It had been an awful fight. We'd dug into old hurts and viciously hurled them into the other's face: how I continuously refused his proposals, how he'd had affairs with the women on his estate, how he knew nothing about my past or my homeland, how he needed to stop waiting for me and that I was leaving for good. Then, of course, I'd knocked him overboard and shouted horrible things to him as I sailed away.

I pulled him onto the bed next to me. He was only too willing to hold me closer. I traced the lines of his hand and worked on memorizing the veins beneath his skin. He brought me down to the pillows and wrapped his arms around me. The breeze wafted from the open windows across my skin. It was always peaceful here in our room. I relaxed into him and closed my eyes.

"When's the last time you slept?" he asked.

I made a noncommittal mmmmm noise and put my uninjured hand over his mouth to stop him from talking. He bit it playfully and kissed down the length of my arm.

"That wasn't an answer, Nan."

I tried to shush him again, but he captured my hands and held them fast in one of his while the other began exploring under my shift. Said hand traveled up my legs, my stomach, and settled over one breast. Andrews sighed in relief and kissed me.

"I should tie you to this bed. Never let you leave again," he said hungrily over my lips.

"Okay." I shifted myself closer and wrapped one of my legs around him. "But you have to stay here with me."

"Don't tempt me." He laid his weight against me and kissed me deeply. I laid back and enjoyed the feel of him. Andrews had just begun to undo his trousers when there was a knock at the door.

"Father? Auntie?" It was Josephine. Andrews rolled over and groaned.

"Be right there," I called out to her. I kissed Andrews lightly and went to grab a robe from my wardrobe. I tied the sash and opened the door to see Josephine's troubled expression. "What is it? What happened?" I invited the girl in and sat her on the couches by the windows. Andrews sat down next to me.

"Something happen, Josie?" he asked.

"No – well – no. I just wanted to give Auntie back this sword." Her eyes were puffy as she held the ornate samurai sword up for me.

"Sweetheart, that was a gift. I want you to have it." She had been so pleased to get the shiny weapon. Why did she want to give it back?

"It's just," her eyes flashed to my newly-wrapped hand, "if you are in danger and people are— people are shooting at you…" Tears started falling down her cheeks.

I shifted over to her and hugged her.

She took a breath and continued. "Then I want you to be safe and have all the protection you can. Maybe if you had used this sword, you wouldn't have gotten hurt…" Her voice choked off, and I hugged her tighter.

"I'm so sorry, Josie. I don't want you to worry about me. The only thing that matters to me is that you are safe and protected. This sword belongs with you. I promise I'll be more careful." I wrapped her hands back around the sheath and put it in her lap.

She wiped at her eyes and nodded and gave me a huge hug. My shoulder screamed at me, and I gritted my teeth together so I wouldn't reveal yet another wound to worry her further. Andrews came to my rescue and eased the girl off me.

"Why were you gone so long?" she accused as she wiped at her eyes.

"I thought I was making a good choice."

"Well, you weren't." She lightly touched the bandage on my hand.

I nodded. "You're right. But I'm here now."

I had a little under a year. I could smooth things out in that time. I could leave this estate in good hands with as little separation pain as possible. I dried the tears off her face and kissed her forehead just as I had done when she was a toddler and came to me with a scraped knee.

"Eyes up. Let's have a good day today, okay?" I smiled at her.

"Okay." She took a shuddering breath and I marveled, as I did every time, hearing my vernacular coming out of their mouths centuries too soon.

Andrews ushered his daughter out of the room, and I doubled over on the couch in pain as soon as he shut the door. My shoulder was throbbing, and I gasped and clutched at it until I could breathe again.

"They need you to say yes just as much as I do, Nanette." Andrews was standing over me. "Marry me."

"I cannot change my answer," I said to him, to myself, to the torrent of emotion and memories begging me to assent and live happily ever after in this kingdom I loved and built, with this man who I adored as my best friend and the love of my life.

No.

Izzy was here. I'd be burned at the stake within the year. I could not agree to a marriage proposal.

"So you've said." Andrews sighed and sat next to me. He pulled my legs onto his lap and ran his hands softly up and down them.

He was the first person I ever showed my scars to, the first and only. We stayed for a moment like that. I watched the sun playing on his hair and felt his familiar hands.

"Come to bed with me." His fingers inched up my legs further until they found their goal.

"Of course." I caressed the side of his face then gasped as he sunk his fingers into me. I brought him to me and kissed him, wanting him closer.

"I missed you, Nan." He kept exploring between my legs, warming me with his familiar and wanted touch.

"I missed you too." He watched me close my eyes and felt me respond to him.

Eventually Graham removed his fingers and carried me to our bed. It had been years since I'd had his skin next to mine, since I'd had him between my legs. He moved in a steady rhythm inside me, picking up in strength as we drove each other toward climax. I thought of the letter in my discarded dress and how I was supposed to be keeping my head and my focus. I held onto him tighter, kissed him deeper, ran my hands along his back as he thrust into me over and over again.

The letter had come back to me, my note to Yvonne crossed out and **"Come Home"** written in Graham's decisive script. Yes, I was home. I was home at last.

We collapsed on each other, and Graham smoothed the hair away from my face and kissed me. We'd been sharing our lives together long enough that we didn't need to speak our gratitude and contentment in words.

The sea breeze cooled our bodies as we lay next to each other in bed. I was relaxed here. The sounds were familiar, the smells were familiar. It was all too easy to lie in this bed next to Andrews. All too easy to slip into the ebb and flow of life here. All too easy to forget that, across the island, my real-life sister was waiting to chew my real-life head off in a room above a tavern.

I fell asleep listening to the sound of Graham's breath mixing with the breeze.

"Nan? Nanette?" Graham murmured in my ear as he pulled me closer. "We are going to miss the play if you keep sleeping." He kissed down my neck while one hand fondled my chest.

I rolled over to him, and he lightly pinched a nipple. I shrieked and swatted him. He just grinned his wildcat grin and continued feeling me up.

"Did you want to see the show? I hear they are adding a surprise ending." Graham was in new clothing, and the sun was lower in the sky.

"How long have I been asleep? Did you change?" I pulled him down to the pillows and kissed him.

"A few hours. I came to check on you, but there was work I needed to get done." He laughed, kissed me, then pulled me to my feet. "You are so peaceful when asleep. Looking at you snoring, one might never know how many people you've stabbed to death."

I threw my boot at him, then regretted it. Between all the sex and sleeping on my shoulder funny I was in a deal of pain still. I inhaled sharply and sat back on the bed. Graham sighed and retrieved the boot and helped me get dressed.

"I love this dress." He laced the sleeve. "I've always loved this dress. But you knew that, which is why you wore it." He curled my hand into his and kissed it.

"Perhaps," I teased him.

"You've added more to it since the last time I saw it." Graham indicated a beach scene with a flock of birds flowing over my shoulder.

"I pick it up as I sail along. Keeps the waves from stealing my mind." Graham finished lacing me up and kissed me again.

"I'm going to steal you away one of these days." He kissed me again.

"You already have me." Not in the way I know he wanted. But he had me regardless.

"Alas, poor Yorik. I knew him well.
  And in his mind did a secret dwell.
  I'll have these riches and that gold too.

And then I'll kill Henry the Fifth for you."

The actor playing someone who may or may not have been Macbeth scooped Ophelia into his arms and kissed her. The whole audience cheered. The play was going great. Already most of the English kings were dead. Everyone was cursed to kill their uncles, and all the women were ruling Illyria because they refused to have sex with their husbands. Food was passed around, the people in the audience (especially the young boys) joined in on the fight scenes. There were songs that we all sang together, and if an actor made a toast, we all drank. We were in the third hour of the merriment with no sign of it stopping.

Helene lit the bonfire when the sun went down, and meat was brought out to roast on sticks. Angelica was pulled up on stage for an improvised scene with Rabbi Schmul, where he attempted to marry her off to Romeo. Angelica was trashed and laid an enormous kiss on the young man, who returned it enthusiastically. The young man staggered backwards into the makeshift set, and Angelica took a bow to the standing ovation of the entire audience. Beri hid her face in embarrassment at her mother's actions.

The play went on for another hour devolving into old jokes and blue humor and finally people just getting up on stage to tell stories under the stars. Everyone was drinking and laughing, and the instruments would be brought out soon if this all went according to every other party in this strange kingdom.

The noise and merriment swirled around me and so did all the people I'd known and loved for so long. As if someone had opened a drain, into my bones a realization settled: this was my last time at a party like this. I'd detached my sister from her own time and space, and the price I'd pay for that sin was losing this kingdom of mine.

"Who's got another story for us!" Father O'Shaughnessy called out to the raucous audience.

"Auntie Anne!" Magnus shouted and tugged at my arm. The crowd took up the chant and shouts of "Captain!" "Auntie!" "Lady!" eventually

The Bitch Captain (and The Lady)

cajoled me into giving in and taking the stage to cheers, stomps, and yells. These were my people. I'd loved, cared, and provided for them – some their whole lives, I could give them a speech.

And there was Andrews, sitting and cheering with the rest. I remembered sitting not too far from where he was now, just the two of us, laughing and drinking over a tiny purse of profits and dreaming of the possibilities of this land.

My voice failed for just a second until I caught sight of Amelia, a book tucked under her arm. "My dear Andrews," the crowd cheered, "Mothers! Coopers! Blacksmiths!" They all whooped and cheered as I toasted and acknowledged them in the audience. "Farmers and salt miners! The distillery!" Everyone raised a glass to that one. "It's wonderful to see you all again! I've missed each and every loud and lousy one of you!"

They all laughed. I could remember, to a one, each of their entrances onto the property, their children, their needs, everything.

"Today is a great day for a homecoming." The rowdy crowd shouted back to me that they were happy to see me home too. "Alas, a scant few decades is far too short a time to live among such excellent and admirable folks such as yourselves." They didn't understand this reference but took my good-natured ribbing and threw it right back at me. I laughed and the feeling gripped me again: I wasn't going to be among them like this again. I shook it off and carried on.

"I'd like to – thank you, each one of you, for giving me a lifetime's worth of—" The crowd sobered at my sudden delve into seriousness. I couldn't leave them like this. I raised my glass. "To all the wind, waves, hardships, and hurricanes that have blown us to this corner of the world. You are the family I didn't know enough to ask for. I'm glad to be back home with you tonight." The crowd toasted and the music started playing.

A sudden gust of wind blew smoke into my face, and I rubbed the ashes from my eyes and I heard music.

The persistent finality of the moment manifested into a physical pressure behind my eyes. I massaged my temples and the flickering firelight flashed through my closed lids. It reminded me of the flashes of sunlight through trees as we traveled quickly down the road in a rented car.

"Anne." My mother turned down the volume of our car stereo. "We have reservations at six. Where are you taking us?" The Bermuda countryside flashed past us as I sped down roads I knew by heart.

"There's a place I know – read about. Very interesting. Historical. All the educational stuff seems more interesting here," I bullshitted her.

Izzy snorted in the backseat but kept her head in her book. The land fell away into the familiar swells and swaths that I knew.

The modern houses and buildings along the roads and hillsides were alien, but I could still feel the flow of the land under my feet as it passed. I pulled into a parking lot just south of the broken-down mansion. The mansion I'd watched get built over four hundred years earlier. I didn't wait for my mom or Izzy to catch up. I bought us all tickets at the gate and pushed my way through families of tourists. I walked straight through the front door, through the foyer, through the dining room and out the back door. My dock had been replaced long ago. Tourist boats were tied off on the shiny sheet-metal dock, but rotted posts still showed the location where my dock used to be.

I took a left before I hit the small beach and charged through the land to the only new/old addition to this estate that I could pick out: a graveyard by the tiny church. I stopped short before opening the creaking wrought-iron gate. There were hundreds of graves.

"Anne!" My mom was far back from where I stood. "This is supposed to be a vacation, Anne. You've graduated. No more school! Let's go to the beach," she complained. Izzy found a bench and sat down to wait for me to finish whatever this madness was that had gripped me today.

Then I spotted it.

The Bitch Captain (and The Lady)

Nanette? Nanette, come on back to me.

There was an old, eroded headstone with a name I knew.

Nan? Come on down.

There was another grave right next to it. My eyes were glued to the name written there. Not my name. Not my name because I was standing here over both graves, reading the names of my family.

I felt a hand in mine, but Mom had gone to sit next to Izzy. The hand was warm and strong and familiar and brought strains of music and laughter along with its touch. The graveyard erupted into the ghosts of my friends and family as they danced and partied around me.

"Anne? Can we please go now?" Izzy asked from behind her book. The ghosts whirled around me, dancing over their own graves.

"Nan? Come back to me." Andrews' voice filtered through the din of the car radio and party-goers. I blinked and saw the silk of my gown and felt the boards of the stage under my feet.

"Andrews? I – sorry. Just got a little lost." The sounds of the party returned to full blast, and I gasped a little at the onslaught.

"I know. Come on down, Nanette." I let Andrews guide me off the stage. He looked me in the eyes until he was satisfied I was back in the world with him, then kissed me. "Let's get you inside."

"No, I'm fine." I held his hand tight, not wanting to leave the party and these people yet. I wasn't ready to tuck them back into their graves.

"Anne." Helene marched over. "Explain that little speech."

"Sounded like a goodbye to me." Yvonne was smoking a cigar and holding a tumbler of whiskey. She grinned and winked at me. "Of course, I'm an optimist."

"Fuck off." I flipped her the bird for good measure. She cackled like the witch she was and returned the gesture with her cigar. Andrews groaned but knew better than to get between us.

"Nanette, let's get back in the house."

"No. I have to head back to St. George's tonight." I couldn't leave Izzy alone there. I wanted to check on her before morning, and as it was, I'd be traveling through the night. I caught Yvonne's gaze. "I'll be at the Sea Wind—"

"No!" Andrews, Helene, and Angelica all yelled.

Yvonne tipped her drink to me and sauntered off. I knew she'd do her part…and so did they, which is why they were now glaring at me.

"Do not visit a hurricane upon this family, Anne. Keep your danger to yourself." Helene walked off in disgust and Angelica followed, both shaking their heads and believing every awful thing they'd ever heard about me.

I had to get out of here. I dove into the crowd of dancers and found my driver from this morning. I yanked him off a girl and ordered him to get the horse ready. We were leaving. My valise was still in the foyer, and Andrews was hot on my heels.

"You are not leaving at this hour. Stay the night. We can talk about this in the morning."

"I have to go."

"Nanette. Stop." He grabbed my good shoulder and the valise. "I'll take you back to St. George's myself once the sun is up. Just stay." I wrestled my bag away from him.

"I can't stay tonight." Izzy was waiting. The gunpowder was waiting. I'd been here long enough…and I didn't just mean today.

"Fine. Dismiss your driver. I'll get the horses ready."

"Andrews, no. Stay here. They need you. If this goes badly—"

"They need you too. Two years ago you walked away—"

"You told me to leave. And not to come back unless I was your wife." I ripped the bag from his hands and marched out the front door.

"Why is this not enough?" He stalked after me.

I tossed my bag to the driver and attempted to get in the shay only to be hauled back to the ground, Andrews' arms tight around me.

"Why can't I be enough?" He brought me in for a rough kiss. I lost my resolve and held his face to mine. "Let it be enough, Nan," he begged.

The Bitch Captain (and The Lady)

"I cannot." I tried to push back against him and against everything in my body and soul that begged me to give in and live this life with him.

"Why, Nanette? Why? Why do you do this to yourself? You could be here. You could be safe! You could sit in that chair, at that table, eating real food every day! Instead, you come to me, season after season, a drowned, starving, wounded rat. You get well here. You get better here. I get better with you here. Then you leave and return in worse and worse condition! I can't keep watching you do this." He put his head in his hands. "Damn it all. Be with me! Be my wife!"

"You want to be my husband?" I shot back. "Is it so easy to give up your life? Break your contracts. Replant your trees. Sell your land. Give up your world for me. You want a wife? Leave all of this," I gestured to the house and beyond, "and come with me! The others can run the place while we sail out there together." I said this without thinking. My hand was outstretched to him of its own accord. I was just shouting words without my typical massive filter in place, and I inhaled sharply at the raw truth hurtling out of my mouth. More than anything, that's what I wanted from him. I wanted him on my ship and sailing away with me for as long as he lived. I wanted him to know everything about my life.

It terrified me.

Andrews firmed up his lips and looked away. He didn't take my hand. He was as unable to change as I was. And I would never make him leave his family.

"Yeah," I read the "no" in his eyes and dropped my hand, "I didn't think so."

"Be careful, Nanette. One day I just might."

"Say goodbye to the children for me." I pushed away from him and climbed onto the conveyance.

"No. You don't leave my children again without saying goodbye." He stood in front of the shay.

The driver looked between the two of us, wondering who to obey.

Andrews took a deep breath and tried to speak again with less venom. "Let the cargo rot. Let this boy go back to the party. Let this home that we built from nothing be officially ours together. Say yes to me, Nan, and come back inside." He held out his hand, his face a desperate mess of blond hair and yearning.

"I cannot change my answer." I spoke to my closed fists and felt the wound split on my hand again. There was a gravestone next to his, four hundred years in the future, and it didn't have my name on it.

"Go," I told the driver, who did whatever you do that makes horses go. Andrews backed out of the way of the large beasts but yelled after me.

"I'm not coming to get you this time. If you get into trouble, you can get yourself right back out again. I mean it, Nan!"

I didn't look back.

"It was a lively party." The driver attempted to strike up conversation. "Are there any stableboy positions? It's your land, right, ma'am? They all said it's yours—"

"It was." I had to begin thinking of that place in the past tense.

"If that were my land, I'd never bother with St. George's. I'm a hard worker, ma'am. I could—"

"Keep your eyes on the road." I had zero interest in this boy and his career. My interests lay in getting along this dark road without incident and without the horse falling over or bolting with us in tow.

The moon was bright enough to offer light, but we were relying on the horse to find the way. My valise was at my feet, and inside were my prize pistols. It was later than any highway robbers would care to stay out and sober enough for an attack, but heaven help them if they tried anything. The driver jumped at every snap of a twig and rustle in the

The Bitch Captain (and The Lady)

underbrush. I shook my head and tried not to judge him for his youth and naivete. He didn't know who he was traveling with, and I preferred he was alert and full of adrenaline.

The road spun out dark and unknowable ahead of us.

Right now, Yvonne would be sending out messengers to her contacts and associates across the island. I was trusting in her greed and desire to profit and prosper. She'd get the militias to me, I was sure of it.

Charlie's share was only a small fraction of what was stored in those caves. With the gold from this sale I could fund our – Andrews' – the estate for a year or two. The children would want for nothing. I would not be leaving the family without means.

He and I had been a team from the very beginning. He relied on me. He needed me. Next year, after the burning, I wouldn't be able to provide for them, and this sale would do for them in one fell swoop what a series of harvests could bring in over multiple seasons. Yvonne and I were not bosom buddies, but she was invested in the family and the estate and would want the profits from this sale the same as me.

I would not leave my – their family wanting for anything.

The dark road continued on and on.

Goddamn, this horse smelled.

We arrived back at St. George's in the early hours of the morning. My driver was shaking with fear and exhaustion from the long night out on the dark, treacherous country roads. I thanked him, paid him, and sent him home for his mother to tuck into bed. It was a relief to put distance between myself and that horse. I hated horses and they hated me. This dress was going to need airing out next time at sea, or it would smell of horse forever.

Mary sat up, sipping at a glass of wine and rocking one of the babies. She was surrounded by her sleeping brood on the deck of the ship. At her side was a selection of firearms and papers. She liked to read and write, and I made sure to have plenty of materials for her when I came to the island.

"I'm going to get some sleep. Have you rested at all?" I asked in a whisper so as not to wake the baby.

"When Dom wakes in the morning, I'll set him to watch."

The boy was in a hammock I'd strung up between the masts. I tucked the blanket further up on him and smoothed his hair.

"I'll meet you in dreamland," I whispered to Mary.

"Sleep well, Captain."

I was more than ready to ditch the fancy clothes and get my hair out of my face. I wanted my blades and guns in full view and a nice heavy coat that could turn away a sword. More than anything though, I wanted some sleep.

I pulled the letter out of my pocket and tacked it to the wall. Graham's **"Come home"** boldly ordering me from my cabin paneling. I would if I could. My heart and soul were sown into the foundation of that place.

Well, if I couldn't be there, I would leave them as secure as possible. I would get them their gold, danger and risk be damned. It was one of the last things I would ever be able to do for them, and I was going to do it.

The dress went carefully back into its box along with the petticoats. I took note of any areas that needed cleaning, repair, or improvement. There was hardly any space left on the garment at all. I could remember every stitch I put into this gown. The scenes depicted were my memories and experiences. If someone could read this embroidery like they could read Izzy's journal, they'd have a clearer picture of my life than any story I could write down.

I put the mattress back in place and fell into the soft foam. It had been a really, really long day. I set a timer on my watch. I was giving myself seven hours of sleep, pure luxury, and then I'd set out to meet with the lowlifes Yvonne was contacting and sending my way. It was a risk trusting her like this; the woman was one opportunity short of taking me out of this world. It wasn't just me she hated. Yvonne would set the whole world aflame and still seek out more destruction. Buried inside her was hurt and pain that only more pain and hurt could quench. I was merely a convenient target.

I fell asleep dreaming that Graham was in bed next to me.

The sun rose in the little window and the light fell onto our little bed in our little cabin. Graham's fingers pushed my hair from my face and the small touch woke me. His bare skin warmed mine. "Anne. Mine Anne," he murmured as he looked at me like I was something precious and whole. "Stay with me."

"Yes." I pulled him close and ran my hands down his young back, making him shiver and smile. It was a beautiful morning, and our future stretched out ahead of us, bright and lovely.

Seven hours later, my watch buzzed, waking me up. I felt like a new woman.

Before dressing, I opened a new container of lotion and massaged and stretched my scars from the toes up to my hips. This last journey back to Izzy and Mom had been great for my body. Simply having the opportunity to rest, eat well, and have access to over-the-counter medical supplies meant that I was feeling strong and my scars weren't bothering me as much as they would be in a few months when my supplies began to dwindle and it was time to ration. I slathered on the lotion then wrapped my legs from my ankles to my thighs in soft lanolin-infused wraps.

Over the wraps I pulled on a pair of leggings. I didn't bother with any type of skirt. My good one, the one with all the pockets, was still bloody and stained from Tavern Rock. I opted for a long shirt that I belted with holsters for my favorite sharp silver knives, a solid, well-performing dirk, and a longer cutlass.

I would not be bringing my retrofitted pistols. Izzy was here, and

I would follow the rules to the letter of the law. Better I be at a disadvantage in a fight than my sister gets dragged to the stake right next to me simply because she was associated with my ship and my company. I wore a sturdy waistcoat for additional coverage of my torso, heavy steel-toed stomping boots, my wide-brimmed hat (only slightly worse for wear from Tavern Rock), and my Kevlar-lined trench.

I'd beaten and scrubbed that trench coat for days until it was clean(er) and suitable for wearing again. That coat was a favorite. It was patched and repaired in so many places it was almost a new coat three times over. I fingered the hole through the shoulder where I'd gotten shot. That repair would need to wait until next time we were on the water.

I hauled a pin cask of tightly-packed gunpowder out of the hold and sat at the galley table putting together tiny twists of powder and paper. Those went into my valise with the other supplies. I put the cask, extra papers, and a powder horn into a crate and brought it all on deck. The sun was already low in the sky and the port was bustling, only outdone by Mary's children racing through the masts of my ship.

"I'll be gone a few more days," I repeated to her several times over the din before she finally heard me.

"I'll hold the fort down, Captain," she called back.

"Any trouble today?"

"Nothing out of the ordinary. Dom chased some rats away earlier. All has been calm since."

"I appreciate it."

"And I appreciate your gold, Captain." She patted the purse I'd given her earlier. If all went well, I'd get her more.

"Anything in particular you need? I left a purse in the galley for your use."

"I'm sure all will be well. You look after yourself. We'll look after your ship." Mary was one of my favorite people of all time. I wish she'd let me do more for her.

CHAPTER 6

Bermuda Hospitality

I took off down the road, crate in my good arm, valise in my other. The inn was not far, a mile at most. As I walked from the dock into town I looked around at the buildings and townspeople, now matching my ugly memories of this place almost perfectly.

It wasn't truly a year I had left, more like ten months. All these people would be there. The little street urchins running about would be running with scrap lumber and lit sticks. The merchants would hold their wives and babies in fear as the witch was hauled past their doors, trussed, bound, and bleeding. The laborers and sailors, the vendors and soldiers, everyone would be there, cheering for my painful eradication. My scars tightened and I walked faster. There's where they stripped off my clothes for evidence of the mark of the devil. There's where they erected the stake. There's where I ran flaming through the street to jump in the bay. A little street urchin got under my feet and nearly tripped me. She backed away in terror at my terrible expression.

"Get out of here," I ordered her, and she scampered. For all I knew, she was one of the ones who had called for my death with a sing-song smile on her face. The town square here had been packed with people, shoulder to shoulder. All of St. George's, all of Bermuda had turned out to see the Bitch Captain of the Seven Seas go up in smoke.

I took a minute to collect myself before my memories could overwhelm me. That was next year. Right now there was no smoke in the plaza, just people going their own way as I should be going mine.

The Sea Wind was right around the corner. Soft firelight flickered from Izzy's window, and I prayed a quick and silent prayer to the Almighty that, for once in her life, she was chilling the fuck out. If God loved me at all, Izzy was in her room high as a kite and snuggled up next to a strong bottle of wine.

The sun was just beginning to set, and my stomach rumbled. I knew from experience the Sea Wind had food and drink. It was the getting-them-to-serve-me part that was the problem. I decided to shortcut the issue by buying food off a street vendor just beginning to take his stall down for the day. It was a meal of meat and vegetables wrapped in pastry and smelled delicious. I bought a few extra in anticipation of them being my only source of food for the foreseeable future.

The Sea Wind tavern at night was teeming with locals and sailors and all the detritus that followed those denizens around. A group of navy midshipmen were treating their young and fresh livers to tankards of rum and mead. I saw the young lieutenant from earlier in the day among them, and he lifted his glass to me over the songs of his fellows. I nodded back to him and veered away from their tables and found a nice dark corner to set up shop.

The bartender scowled at me as I took a table. "Five bottles of your finest whiskey!" I called to him. He scowled and didn't respond. Well, I tried. I slid the crate under the table and arranged the seats so my back was to the wall. The room was noisy and crawling with soldiers and merchants. I stared at the section of ceiling that was Izzy's floor. Even though my militias could be here at any moment I had to check on her.

I quickly ran up the stairs to Izzy's room and shook Gerta awake. The woman startled and looked at me in horror. "The lady is fine. Not fat yet. I am working on it," she stammered out.

"Do that." I looked her up and down. Was she nervous with me so

The Bitch Captain (and The Lady)

close or was she hiding something? I couldn't decide. For the moment, there was little risk. All seemed quiet behind the door.

"Iz – Lady Isabelle?" I called to her and pounded on the door.

"What?!" my darling sister screeched through the door. That was as clear a message as any.

"Can I come in?"

"Fuck no!" Izzy hollered. She was a delight.

"Good night then," I said to the solid door. "Fat. Happy. Idle," I reminded Gerta, who nodded her head vigorously. I turned and dodged a small errand boy rushing up the stairs and passed servers in and out of the kitchens on my way back to my table.

Five bottles of whiskey sat on the crude wooden table, and I looked up at the bartender in shock. There was a woman next to him, and she nodded curtly to me as I sat. I was finally getting service here, just in time to never need it again. I ate my meager dinner and steeled myself for a long night.

From this vantage point, I had clear views of the room and an exit route through the kitchen. I pulled out a glass jar and candle from my valise and put it on the table. I surreptitiously lit a match and touched it to the candle wick. I was nervous to use anything so high tech as a match this close to my burning time but didn't want to bother finding a flame from another table.

My first clients arrived within the hour. I knew they were for me as the noise dipped in the room when they entered. I knew these bastards. They were a motley crew of farmers from outlying settlements on the island. They carried their weapons openly, and the crowds swirled and parted around them, eager not to get too close. I pulled the brim of my hat down and hunched over the table to disguise my silhouette. These assholes were not feminists.

I took one of the small twists of gunpowder and paper and tossed it into the candle flame. It was not enough for an explosion of any sort, but it burned and the acrid smell dispersed across the tavern. Several heads turned, but it was a common smell and was shrugged off as a fluke, especially since there was no accompanying bang.

My clients understood. That very smell was the reason they had come here. They turned as one rough and uneducated mass towards my table. The leader of the band pulled out a chair across from me, and his cronies took up positions on his flanks.

"I hear you have cargo to sell. Guns. Ammunition. Powder," he grunted through thick whiskers and greasy dark hair.

Show time.

"You heard right." I lifted my head and didn't bother to hide my high voice as it rang out its double X chromosomes.

The entire ensemble broke out in laughter loud enough to silence the bar area for a moment. That was okay. I'd been met with this reaction before. Let them laugh. I had what they wanted, and therefore they'd listen – or not and then I'd shoot them. Either way...

Once the laughing died, a man with white-blond hair and a hard expression barked at me to "Go home and fetch your husband to come talk with men."

"No. You'll deal with me, or I'll arm a different militia with these fine and superior weapons. Much better than what you're carrying." I pretended to sip my whiskey while his friends restrained him. He looked familiar. I did not like when people looked familiar, and I couldn't place them. It put me on edge. I decided then and there not to deal with them. "Deal's off the table," I said. "Have a nice evening, gentlemen."

"Now wait just a moment, woman," the leader said. "I didn't say we wouldn't deal. Marius was merely startled. Not often you see a woman pirate."

"Not a pirate."

"Oh? Then how'd you come across such interesting cargo?"

"A storm. A big one. Very dangerous. Killed this rat bastard thief and his entire crew. Can you imagine it? What luck for me." I pretended to sip again and speared a slice of pastry with the sharp silver dagger I

The Bitch Captain (and The Lady)

reserved for special occasions such as this, where men needed to see a good reason to keep their adrenaline in check and their genitals in their pants.

"No storm that big this season," Marius pushed.

"Have a nice evening, gentlemen," I said again.

"Listen to me, woman—" Marius slammed his hand on the table and raised the other one to strike me then paled as all the blood drained from his face. My lovely silver dagger now stabbed clear through his palm and an inch into the wood beneath. A matching dagger now appeared at his throat.

"I saw that storm with my own eyes, and guess what? It was heading this way," I threatened.

"I know who you are, you sea bitch, giving my wife all those books," Marius choked out. "I know your ship. We don't need to trade with you at all."

"Cargo is buried. You want it? You'll pay." I pressed the knife deeper against his throat and pulled a thin line of blood from his skin.

"I can still sink you," he continued.

"Enough of this," the leader said. "Release him."

"I'll release him last. The rest of you leave. He'll be home by dinner tomorrow."

"If he dies, we will come for you and your boat," the leader threatened.

"Stitch his mouth closed and there won't be a problem."

The militia got up and left, but Marius stayed under my knives. A rivulet of blood reached the end of the table and began a pleasant plit plit plit onto the floor. The woman who'd procured me the five whiskey bottles brought another chair over, and I shoved Marius down into it. I tipped her and poured him a glass.

"You are my guest until my business is finished here. One wrong move, one wrong word, you'll be reenacting the stigmata." He grunted and tried to move, but my dagger was sunk in deep. Unless he wanted to slice his hand in half, he was stuck. Personally, I didn't care.

Another militia group appeared, and I lit another twist of gunpowder to get their attention. They only wanted to speak with Marius, who hurled insults at them and spat at me. They wouldn't trade with a woman, I was bad luck, they said, and left.

By this time, the moon was rising, and an old whaler and his enslaved man replaced the midshipmen at the bar. I eyed them and lit the twist of powder, but if they were here for me, they weren't ready to make their move. Shame. If he was a successful whaler, he could be worth trading with.

Militia number three would trade with me, but they were poor with nothing to offer. They were a ragtag group of starving fishermen off the far end of the island. If I were to wager a guess, they were mostly escapees and refugees. The amount they offered must be the full sum their families could combine. It was mostly scrawny farm animals, a few crates of fish jerky, and a scattering of coins. Marius laughed at their pathetic offer. I flicked the tip of the dagger handle, and he gasped and failed to stop tears springing to his eyes. The blood dripped merrily, and I sat back enjoying his pain. I'd seen Mary's bruises. This was a small measure towards retribution. Izzy would be all about working with this group, but I pushed their offer back to them and advised them to try their hands at planting rice. I needed cash. I wasn't here to barter.

It was breakfast time and two militias later (who quailed at the sight of Marius's hand), and I was running on fumes when the door opened again to let in a large group of men from south of town. Marius was losing color. A man from the last militia had slipped on the puddle of blood on his way out. This group of men was numerous and dressed in dark and sober clothing. They brought a haze in with them. I wondered if the kitchen had set up a fire pit outside. I blinked to clear the smoke from my eyes. I needed to be alert, and this place did not serve coffee.

The Bitch Captain (and The Lady)

The man in the lead pecked at my memory the same way Marius had.

It was hot in here.

I pulled off my jacket and hat, tugged at the front of my shirt. The lead man was tall, well over six feet, with long, smooth hair cropped into a disciplined line at his shoulders. The dust and sand that covered most of this island didn't touch him. I swallowed against the stink of burning meat. What the hell was the kitchen cooking up?

Marius said something, but I couldn't hear him through the crackling flames. I couldn't answer anyway with my throat closed against the smoke. The barman pointed the group towards my table, and I saw that I did indeed know this man. His name: Closer To You My God Cowlishaw. He wouldn't know me for another year. But I knew him now. His face was different, a little younger, handsome, missing a distinct series of scars and burns drawn across his cheek. It was him for sure. Sometime between now and the fateful day when I docked in St. George's and got hauled off my ship by these fuckers, Closer To You My God would be sliced up by someone and burned. Bless that unnamed soul and his sharp blade. The smell of burning cloth and hair drifted into my nostrils, my legs twitched as the flames licked across my shins.

Puritans.

I hate Puritans.

The as-yet-unscarred Closer To You My God pulled out the chair across from me. He saw the knife stuck through Marius's hand and turned his attention to me.

"A harsh punishment. I hope it's deserved." He sat with the unwavering calm of a man who was assured his place in heaven.

"It is," I wheezed.

"My fellows and I hear you have a bounty of arms. I would hear your price."

"I will not deal with Puritans." I hoped my voice did not sound like the deflated tire I was.

"My good woman, you will." He was not being an ass. He felt every inch of his power, purity, and masculinity. He commanded and I was to follow; that was the way of it. "Now, let us hear your offer."

I took in the whole crowd of them and tried to breathe. I touched my chest to reassure myself that the ropes I felt constricting me were not in my present — my past and their future, yes — but for now I wasn't on trial at the stake.

"I will not deal with Puritans," I repeated. Marius scoffed and drew their attention for a second.

"You should have taken our offer, sea bitch." Marius was drunk from blood loss. His hand was growing red with infection already. "But these Puritans, ha! They have gold for miles. Bleed it out of everyone in exchange for heaven. Tell me, Closer, what need do you have of guns if your land is in the hereafter?"

"I would defend my people against their early occupation of a heavenly home," Closer To You My God responded. "But you, my brother, look indisposed. I will need to speak with the woman for the nonce. However, the kingdom of heaven is ready for you when you are free of your bonds here. Brother, I shall welcome you with open arms." His deep voice rattled as he began to address me. "Woman, the flawed man to your left is stricken by more than your knife. Demons cloud his eyes and drain his spirit even as we sit. It is not worthy of a man to sit thus. Let him free."

"You are neither my maker nor my mate. I will not deal with you." It was too hot in here. I tugged at my collar again. Sweat ran in rivulets matching Marius' blood splatters. There were too many of them for me to force my way through. I'd need to keep my place until they chose to leave and stopped stealing my oxygen with their fire and their lungs.

Closer To You My God was still and silent, perhaps in prayer, perhaps in anger. His women were supplicant and quiescent. I was not. Coming from this unmarred and handsome face, his silence was more dangerous, more patient. I could be patient too.

The Bitch Captain (and The Lady)

But Marius could not.

"She's hidden the goods. Won't tell a soul where," he slurred, and his non-stabbed hand reached out and knocked the mostly untouched whiskey bottles over. The alcohol mixed with his blood and my sweat and poured over my lap onto the floor.

I cursed and slammed the blade harder into his hand. He screamed and failed to stop his own tears from falling.

"Woman held a secret once and man fell from grace," Closer To You My God mused. "No," he continued, "No. You will tell me where the arms are hidden, and your confession will further the kingdom of God on earth." He crooked his finger, and his cronies moved as one in a well-practiced woman-abusing team to confine and kidnap me.

Under the table I pulled open my bag of gunpowder twists and threw them in a pile on the table. I overturned the candle and the papers ignited. I was just looking for a distraction. A few fireworks to cover my run to the kitchen. I neglected to factor in the potency of the Sea Wind's whiskey, now spilled over tables, chairs, my clothing, and the crate below the table. The liquor ignited and I realized the danger right away. I pulled my Kevlar-lined trench over my head and ducked just in time for my corner of the barroom to blow. My ears rang for real this time, and the sight and smell of real smoke cleared the phantom smoke away.

I grabbed my belongings and began climbing over the blasted and singed Puritans. Closer To You My God's face was closest to the explosion. He was burned down the left side, but he still had the wherewithal to reach out and grab my ankle. "Thou shalt not suffer—" I grabbed the knife out of Marius' palm and swiped at Closer's face. The red burst from his cheek in a clean line that looked oh so familiar. I stared at the knife in my hand and breathed in the smoke, this time in savage glee. Closer staggered back and tripped over an upturned table. I jumped on top of him and straddled him using my knees to pin his arms against the floor. I swiped again at his face, and bright red blood sprouted from another line. And what's more, I knew just where to put the rest. With delicious vengeance I carved out the rest of his scars until he matched the face I knew from my nightmares and spat on him.

"Suffer me you will." I took my time with the last cut, deliriously happy with the seeping wounds, an artist in her crowning glory. It was poetry: a silver knife and a pulsing artery mere inches away from joining. The chaos in the barroom was delightful muzak to my ears, and I sighed in contentment, thankful for this moment of pure beauty.

Alas, Time, being the little bitch she is, was too short. Loud and simultaneous gunshots quieted the bar. Marching feet dispersed the crowd, and rough hands hauled me off Closer To You My God and restrained me at gunpoint. Another soldier was restraining Closer To You My God and his dripping face along with several members of his posse. Marius melted away in the chaos. The old whaler's enslaved man came up close behind me and said, "If you live, we will trade," and he gave me the whaler's location. What a glorious day indeed.

I was frisked, and all my weapons handed over to soldiers too chicken to approach me themselves but brave enough to pocket my arms. The soldier restraining me kept up a steady barrage of insults and instructions along the lines of "Stay on your knees, sea bitch," and "Stop kicking, woman," and "You should count yourself lucky that I don't fight ladies," and "Ow, that was my thigh."

They divested me of all my blades and bound my hands tightly behind my back. As the madness siphoned off, I looked at the space where Izzy's room was above my head. Maybe she was still asleep and hadn't heard anything. The hole in the building was catty-corner to her quarters and wasn't likely to bring the building down. Probably. It's possible I should have been more concerned about my sister and her well-being, but Closer To You My God's face was a dripping masterpiece of satisfaction and all I could feel was a sense of deep calm and justice.

Once the soldiers had cleared the barroom of civilians and chained

The Bitch Captain (and The Lady)

all us miscreants, the young lieutenant entered the room. I sagged back in my irons. An idealist like him would make a meal out of a situation like this. He took in the hole in the wall and blanched.

"Order and discipline will be maintained on this island." He began what sounded like a well-rehearsed speech but petered off with another look up the stairs. "The Crown – " He lost steam again with another look at the ceiling. He probably thought this whole place was going to come down and bury him...the coward. "Take them away. Lock them up. I will deal with each individually at the fort. Rest assured each of you will be flogged in due course." With that he ran to inspect the hole I'd blown in the wall.

I was happy not to have to suffer a long primrose speech about character and honor from the young lieutenant, but honestly, I didn't get what he was so worried about. I had blown way bigger holes in way bigger walls. This was a tiny hole in some random bar. I mean, you'd have to duck to walk through it.

"Lieutenant!" I shouted to try to get his attention. I was going to request he check on my sister, tell her where I was going, and apologize that our dinner plans with him would now need to be postponed as I'd be unavailable.

The young lieutenant didn't stop his inspection, and the soldier behind me struck the back of my head with the butt of his musket. The world went black for a second until the soldier hauled me up and quick-marched me out of what was left of the Sea Wind (which was a lot. Again, I'd made bigger holes in much more impressive walls. Everyone could chill out a little bit). I had paid Gerta well. She could mind Izzy for a few days in my absence. I wasn't worried.

Fort St. Catherine sat along the rocky shoreline just outside of St. George's. It was a modest fort, but it got the job done. Right now it was nearly empty of officers and soldiers; the English civil war had called away most of the men and left just a few lower-ranked men and green recruits. These men paused in their activities as they watched the

Puritans and myself marched through the yard. I'd been here plenty of times and knew the way. My soldier was needlessly rough with me. I wasn't fighting him. Deep inside me, a knot had come undone. I'd gotten my revenge on Closer and was walking among the clouds. There'd be time to consider the consequences later. The familiar fort sat bathed in sunshine, and I turned my face up to drink in the last rays I might feel for a few days.

My cell was the same dark, dank hole I'd been imprisoned in several times before. It was just a large room with a tiny window showing the rocks, waves, and a square of sky. Iron bars bisected the main room, making two holding cells. I was separated from the Puritans because I was a woman, and I sat leering at them through the bars with my feet up and a clear view of my crotch (I was in pants, relax). They refused to look my way and began mumbling prayers until it was a dull buzz, a continuous white noise.

Last time I was here was right after Kings Bay. Both cells had been packed with people at that time. Marco and I sat back to back, keeping an eye out for each other. This time it was just me and the wall.

Last time I was here, Andrews came for me.

I'm not coming to get you this time. If you get into trouble, you can get yourself right back out again. I mean it, Nan!

I was on my own this time. But that's okay, I counseled myself. It was time to move on and relearn how to live without him. It had to be okay. I had to be okay. There was no other choice. So stop crying and toughen up.

I forced myself to think of other things and to sleep.

Dungeons and jails had a soporific effect on me; I was alone behind sturdy bars, I was not in danger of sinking into the open sea, and I had nowhere to go and nowhere to be. Today I had carved up the face of my enemy, I had made a sale, and I had stabbed Mary's husband. It was a good day. I was asleep within moments.

Closer To You My God was moaning and complaining when I

roused around sunset. His pathetic cries to his maker to ease his suffering and drag my soul to hell woke me from a sound slumber.

"Go to sleep. Your prayers aren't getting answered tonight," I yelled over their incessant murmurs.

"Our prayers will be answered in God's time, not our own," one of them responded. He'd only suffered minor burns on his hands and was tending to Closer's face.

"Just shut up. We'll be out of here soon." I tried to beat some of the dust and dirt from my hat and rebraid my hair.

"Yes. We will be free," one of the other dark and sober men responded. "You, however, will always be twice cursed: God made you a woman and the Devil made you a witch."

"You are unwanted." Closer finally joined the conversation. "You are unwanted in heaven, hell, and here on earth. If you manage to obtain release from this man-made prison, I warn you not to show your face in St. George's again, witch." They turned their backs to me as one and resumed their prayers.

I repositioned my hat and tried to breathe in a calm and natural pattern. The room was not filling with smoke despite the sting in my eyes. Although these voices belonged to the same men who lit me on fire, I was not burning now. I would not burn again. The event was still in their future but was long since past for me.

Still, it smelled like smoke.

I hunkered down and closed my eyes, but sleep didn't come again.

I'm not coming to get you this time. If you get into trouble, you can get yourself right back out again. I mean it, Nan!

The floor was just as hard as it was after Kings Bay. Andrews had come to get me then. I should stop looking at the door, wondering if every footstep I heard behind it belonged to him. He wasn't coming. I had to accept that.

The prayers of my fellow prisoners drilled into my head, every syllable a special note of irritation. I had to make it stop. I sang "It's a Small

World After All" over and over and over again until the guard came in and shouted at the lot of us to quiet down or, by god, he would talk to the master of this prison and see that we all got the maximum amount of lashings due to us plus ten. The Puritans didn't waver. I moved on to "This is the Song that Never Ends." We were all going to get beat to hell. I watched Closer To You My God cry in pain as he prayed and sang all the louder. Worth it.

The sun rose, and a surprise delivery of a half-eaten tray of breakfasty-type food was shoved through my bars. A man with a case passed by me and went straight to the Puritans' cell. He went right in and began examining Closer's face.

"Not that one," the guard slurred, a mostly empty bottle in his hand, "that one." He gestured vaguely in my direction.

"This one gets my attention first." The man, claiming to be a "doctor," brought out what looked to be salves, antiseptics, and clean bandages.

Of all the luck! I sat back hard against the wall and cursed under my breath. Did this island have the one, and I mean the one, competent doctor in all of the 17th century?

Closer moaned and hissed and prayed all the louder as the doctor debrided his wounds and wrapped him up tight. I knew the Puritan wasn't going to die from the cuts, but until this moment I'd held out hope. Hope always slaughtered me. Over and over, I'd hope that something in my timeline might change – something in any timeline – but nothing ever did.

I memorized this asshole doctor's face. When I got out of here, I was going to hunt him down and fill his bed with poison oak. When the doctor finished with Closer, he attempted to come examine me.

The Bitch Captain (and The Lady)

Such audacity. He left with tears on his face, a bloodied nose, and what would grow to be a beautiful set of black eyes.

I carefully rubbed at my newly-split knuckles and my (now-reopened) hand wound from Tavern Rock. I maybe should have at least accepted bandages from the man. There were not going to be any sterile wrappings for me here.

The half-eaten tray of food shoved in my cell just prior to the doctor's arrival lay where it had landed. Andrews wasn't coming for me. I knew he wasn't. He'd drawn his line, I'd drawn mine, neither of us would bend. But perhaps he'd tried to see if I was okay? I knew he was due in town soon for the Wallingtons' party and the story of the Bitch Captain of the Seven Seas blowing up a local inn was sure to reach his ears.

It was also sure to reach Izzy's ears. I cringed against the stone wall. Even through the cocktail of pot, alcohol, and pure distilled rage my sister was marinating in, she had to have registered the explosion. Would she put the pieces together that I had caused the damage? Did she wonder if I'd died in the blast? She would care if I died, right?

Right?

She couldn't be so mad at me that she'd be happy to learn I was possibly killed.

I don't know. Izzy was really mad. Maybe she wouldn't care.

I counted every syllable of the Puritans' moaning prayers, marking the time until I could harass a guard into delivering the message to Izzy that I was still alive.

The sun was out of range of my little square window when the outer door finally opened and the young lieutenant stepped inside, followed by a retinue of guards.

"Lieutenant!" I rushed to the bars. The young soldier would be sure to make finding Izzy a priority. He even knew she was staying at the Sea Wind since he'd assisted in arranging the room for her. "Lieutenant! A word, please?"

He ignored me as he directed the soldiers into the Puritans' cell, where they bound the shitheads, and ordered them taken out to the yard for punishment and release. The men of god and the men in uniform filed past me. I stepped back to allow room for my door to open and a soldier to come for me, but none made a move to enter.

"Lieutenant?" I asked as he was just about out the door. "Lieutenant, will I be released today? I need to get a message to my lady!" I called.

He stopped, one foot out the door, and finally paid me attention.

"Your lady was informed yesterday that she would need to find other accommodation across the seas." He closed and bolted the door and left me in silence.

Well, shit. Did that mean she was told I was dead or that I was safe and sound in this delightful hole? I judged the amount of noise outside in the offices just beyond the outer door and decided it was safe to run. This wasn't my first time locked up in Fort St. Catherine. It wasn't the second either…or the third. You get the idea.

After my first stay I'd gone back in time and made a few changes to the blueprints and stashed tools and escape mechanisms for future stays at this establishment. It was one of several prisons across the Atlantic where I'd gone back to the time of their construction and built myself escape routes. I couldn't change the dirty floor or the drab décor, but I had a way out and several sharp implements within reach if I was locked in here with others.

I couldn't let Izzy think I was dead or that she was stranded here. I was two steps towards freedom when the outer door opened back up and a guard stumbled in with what looked like the remainder of the tray of food he'd shoved in the cell earlier. There was a bottle of wine with this tray and another one, clutched and open, in his hand. What did Andrews think? That I'd relent my stance on marrying him if he got me drunk?

"Bitch Captain!" the guard shouted, and I froze in my tracks. "Sit down and don't make any trouble," he slurred. My spirit sank as the

The Bitch Captain (and The Lady)

guard dragged in a chair and collapsed into it, following his own directions.

The cracks of the whip and the screams of the Puritans echoed out to me from the courtyard. Why wasn't I out there too? It was a drain on the fort's already limited resources to keep a guard on one prisoner longer than necessary. It's not like I intended to stick around and put the town in danger. I had a ship and no intention of staying. The sooner I was out of here, the sooner I was off this island and out of their hair. Keeping me here unflogged, under guard, and longer than necessary was a strange departure in protocol.

I sat down. This man would pass out eventually, and then I'd leave.

He did not pass out.

Around midday he was replaced with another young soldier carrying another tray and another bottle that were both shoved through the bars to join this morning's tray. I didn't touch this one either. Accepting food from Andrews felt too close to accepting his proposals right now, and this was not the time or place to start a marriage.

The food taunted me.

I was getting hungrier...and there was a mouthwatering smell coming from a pastry. No. Best not cave yet. I put the food aside. They wouldn't keep me in here much longer, and I'd be able to return the whole lot to Andrews with a clean conscience.

A new guard arrived around sundown with a new tray. I wasn't feeling like making trouble at the moment. I watched the sun crawl across the stone floor and threw my shoe at the rats who dared to peek out of cracks and sniff the aroma from my trays of abandoned food. The guard jumped every time my shoe hit the wall. His discomfort eased my irritation, so I looked around for loose rocks that would make a louder noise.

Footsteps echoed down the hall and attracted both of our attention.

A woman's voice sounded from under the door, and I sat up straighter. The door opened, and another young guard escorted my dear friend inside.

"Mary!" I exclaimed and went to the bars to meet her.

"When you didn't show up for a few days, I concluded you must be here. Dom is watching the boat." Her eyes flitted to the guards, and I saw her words filter through carefully curated layers, layers that kept her safe from men like her husband and these guards.

"I owe you so much." I didn't know how she made it in here, but I'd be sure she was well compensated for her lies and efforts.

"Yes." She looked askance at the guard again before continuing. "Anyone I should contact for you? Andrews?"

"No." I'd sort Andrews out myself later. I was surprised he hadn't come by the ship already and talked with Mary. What I needed was to get the sale of the guns and powder started. Mary could handle that for sure. "If you could get word to my dear father, though. He's a whaler on the south shore, he must be worried sick about me. I'll be fine, but his heart is weak, you know."

"I know. Does he have any resources?" Mary played along without skipping a beat.

"Some. I'm sure it'll never be enough to get me out, but any little bit helps." The guard was clocking my every word. These damn fresh-off-the-boat recruits were so annoying. Give me a jaded pervert any day over a wide-eyed greenstick Boy Scout.

"I'll make sure he eats tonight." Mary was the picture of a caring and devoted friend.

"Oh, and do you have a paper with you? I'd like to write a note for the lady I'm traveling with." The thought just occurred to me that Mary could also get word to Izzy. My friend pulled a scrap of paper from a fold in her skirt as well as an old charcoal pencil I'd gifted her a few journeys back. I put the paper up to the wall and scrawled a short note.

The Bitch Captain (and The Lady)

Lady Isabelle,

I've been detained but you shouldn't fear that I'll be restored to you. We will be back on the seas shortly. Do not unpack too much of your trunk. Do not wander too far. I'll be along to get you soonest.

Your obedient servant,

Capt. Anne

Who knew what Izzy would make of the old-style language, but hopefully she'd get the gist. I was imprisoned but fine. I'd be out as soon as I could get one of these guards distracted long enough to escape. Stay put. I was coming to get her, and we'd be out of here.

Mary folded the paper into her skirt again and bade me to stay out of trouble so that I would be released, instead of hung, and would therefore be able to pay her. I beamed at my friend and assured her I would. Of course, if they did kill me, she could keep all the profits herself.

I would buy Mary a whole island if I could.

Either way, I'd make sure she came out of this journey better than she was when I arrived. Her young guard escorted her away, and I was left playing the staring game with my own guard.

This sucked.

The sun set.

The guard changed after another hour, and I realized that I wasn't going anywhere for the time being. I put my hat over my eyes and slept. An added benefit of the enforced inactivity was that my wounds finally started to heal now that I wasn't taxing them with rowing and running and Andrews.

Still…I'd rather not be here. I flexed my shoulder and did my best to stretch and make the floor more comfortable.

At least I could hear the ocean.

Damn guard still didn't sleep.

"Hey." I tried to strike up conversation with him. "You ever been to the colonies?" This guard looked a little older than the others.

The boy hesitated a moment. He was surely under orders not to speak with prisoners but we were both bored.

"I was headed to Maryland when my ship foundered," he answered.

"I know Maryland. Where were you going?"

"Kent Island. I have an older brother working at the gristmill there."

"I know Kent Island." Mom ordered special bottles from the distillery there, and when I was a kid, we'd had a few field trips to the old colonial sites that were still standing. I probably saw this poor brother's gravestone.

Ghosts. All ghosts. My fingers itched towards a bottle. For the first time since their delivery, I wished for a drink. I closed my eyes. It would be good to get as much sleep as possible while I was here. Once back on my ship I planned to push us hard and fast across the ocean, and that involved forsaking REM cycles for weeks on end.

I'm not sure I ever fell asleep. It was at most that alpha kind of sleep where I was keenly aware of the ocean and the moon and the pain from my still-healing wounds but where my mind drifted across the years, moonlight briefly illuminating waves of memory throughout the night.

"Paul and James came to me with the offer last week." Andrews, his face young, clean and unlined, looked at me across the fire. "Both farms are failing, and their friends at Virginia Company are getting replaced. The Somers Isles Company isn't interested in extending any credit. It's a good offer, and we have the money – you have the money," he amended, and I scoffed. He and I both knew my funds were his funds. We were in this together. "Still," he sobered, "I don't know if I can work that much land. Ansel's gone, you spend weeks at sea. There isn't much in the way of skilled labor out here. I'm nervous about expanding if the land is going to lie fallow."

"You've barely got five acres to your name here. You make good use of it—"

His turn to scoff. "It'd be nothing without you."

"Okay, we make good use of it. Imagine what we could do with more." The fire danced as we both contemplated the future. "Are both James and Paul going back to England? Would they stay on as extra hands?"

"Perhaps."

"How were they working the land before?" I stoked the fire and watched the ashes drift skyward.

"They bought a few slaves. James has two, Paul one."

"No. I won't be a party to that."

"You and I are doing fine on our own." He grinned that wildcat grin at me. He loved that it was the two of us against the world. I did too. "We can afford to hire out seasonally. I think I'll turn them down."

"Let's take a look at their farms together tomorrow. It can't hurt."

We were unprepared for their desperation.

The land abutted our western border, ten acres in one plot, sixteen the other. It would more than triple our holdings. Paul and James were both interested in staying on and proffered that they would like to start a distillery on the premises. If we could grow it, they could turn it into alcohol. I walked the grounds while the men discussed features of the soil. Andrews would give me the land report later. I wanted to take a look at the shore.

"He listens to you?" The voice was pleasant and deep and accented from Africa, likely one of the coastal countries along the Gulf of Guinea. The woman appeared from the same trail I'd just exited. This must be James' enslaved woman. Had she followed me? "Men do not listen to women." Her eyebrow went up on that last part. I wasn't attired as a woman here ought to be. I had decided this morning I wasn't going to traipse across fallow farmland in petticoats for a sale we were likely to turn down.

"Andrews is smart. He's a good partner."

"He is your husband?"

"Not yet." I sensed a proposal coming. He was established and gaining success. We spent every moment possible together. If he asked, I intended to accept.

"Will you be buying this land?"

"I don't think so. The parcel includes you and the other men. I won't hold anyone in bondage."

"Myself and the other men will be sold and sold cheaply if you and Mr. Andrews decline. I'd prefer not to experience that again."

"I don't buy people."

"Do you help them?"

"Not really." My sister was the one who helped people. Best I could do was not make anyone's life worse. "What's your name?"

"Helene. And yours?"

"Anne." The woman stared at me without blinking. There was power in her. She wanted control of her own destiny and who could blame her?

"Anne, I can do more than cook bad meals for bad men."

"I don't doubt it."

"I can be more than this." She gestured broadly to her position in the world. "But not if I'm sold to ignorant men who do not value me." She had me there. I knew that feeling all too well.

"I'll cut our offer by a third. Extend the length of their contract.

The Bitch Captain (and The Lady)

I can also take you where you want to go. I have a ship. I'm a good captain—"

"If I ever go on the sea again, it will be too soon." She balked at my offer.

"Then what do you want?"

"A partner." Helene was determined to make this deal and to make it with me. We both looked over to the men, currently pointing to aspects of the land and trees and rocks. They were mere facades this day; this deal would be made between Helene and me if it were going to be made at all.

"You want to partner with me?" I asked. Clarification was important here.

"Yes. Will you work with me?

"Yes."

We gave her the first house. Andrews and I moved into the almost-finished mansion. I liked her a lot.

It was not my name on the grave next to Andrews.

Up till now I'd done most of the driving on the island. I let Mom drive us home after the graveyard. Then I found my way straight to a bar. Mom and Izzy wanted every beach they could find. Myself, I wanted darkness and to drown myself in the bottom of every glass handed to me.

"Anne, get up." My mother rebuked me as she opened the curtains and the sun burned across my eyes. "You can't lie in this hotel room all day. Are you sick?"

Even if I was sick, she intended to get my ass up and moving and be part and parcel of this vacation she'd meticulously planned. My life was over. He'd chosen her, not me. What did I have to live for anyway? What did it matter if I smiled in pictures or ate dinner or felt sunshine ever again?

"Up!" My mother had lost patience. I shoved my feet into shoes and dragged my ass to whatever meal it was time for.

I would go back to him; we had business left to accomplish. But I could never marry him, I could never call him mine. He was hers. I was a thief and an interloper.

"Amelia and Josephine are Helene's girls. Beri is Angelica's. Sofia is Yvonne's," Andrews confessed across the pillow from me, his face glowing with pride over his daughters. "They are all mine. Nanette, I – I didn't understand. You were gone. You'd never gotten with child. I didn't realize…I was so surprised. Helene is expecting another."

"Congratulations." My heart ached, but I was happy he finally had his children.

"Do you ever think that you might be a mother someday? If we tried—"

"I will never be a mother. You know this."

"Come home. I need you there. I want you there."

"Do they?"

"Please. Come home."

The changing of the guard woke me. I must have slept a little as I didn't recognize either guard as the one who was supposed to be working a gristmill on Kent Island right now. It was early. The sunlight had only grayed the light coming in the window. I closed my eyes, but sleep was over. I hadn't gotten this much consecutive rest in what felt like years. My body was ready to move…if only there was anywhere I could go. I eyed the guard as he shoved yet another tray of food under the bars. The

The Bitch Captain (and The Lady)

rats had found friends, and they'd feasted during the night. I kicked at a few and got up to stretch.

My legs were killing me. The scars were tight and uncomfortable after days of stillness and no change of clothes. I needed to stretch. I got up and shrugged off my heavy coat, hat, and various wraps until I was in my leggings and loose tunic. Yoga was the best exercise to do in solitary confinement. I started a long and sequenced sun salutation. My guard was fascinated but sat silent on his stool. I lasted until parvatasana before thoughts of my sister intruded on my calm.

I should not think about Izzy. I would get back to her soon.

I moved on to the next steps in the sequence.

It was useless to expend energy worrying about her. She was safe in her room. She was provided for. Mary was sure to have given her my note. Gerta was sure to be protecting her. Izzy wasn't spending her days worrying about me; I needed to spend my days worrying about myself.

I would not think about Izzy. Period. End of sentence.

I moved through ashtanga namaskara into bhujangasana. The rats had really done a number on the old trays of food. I was going to need to start shoving some of that shit back out of my cell for removal before the rodents started snacking on me. I glared at the guard. I needed only a moment, one single moment, and I could escape.

I would not think about Izzy.

I would not think about Izzy.

I would not think about Izzy.

I spent the day thinking about Izzy and fretting that she was okay. Maybe I'd find a way to send her some supplies. Mary might come back at any moment, and I could send her with instructions to get Izzy food and money.

It wasn't just the constant guards that kept me in here. There was always the option of knocking one of them unconscious and bolting, but the young lieutenant who'd put me in here knew that I traveled with Izzy. He knew where she was and how to get to her. If I escaped and couldn't reach her before the lieutenant could, he could have her bound up and captive and at the mercy of whatever cruel will he possessed. My sister was turning out to be an enormous liability and anchor.

My square of sunlight traveled across the cell floor as the day waned. I caved and ate some of the next food delivery. Just enough to take the edge off. One bite of forbidden apple (or in this case cornbread) couldn't make this situation much worse. Voices in the corridor caught both my and my guard's attention. We both straightened as the door opened. At first glance I thought it was Izzy and jumped up to greet her. It wasn't Izzy.

"Yvonne," I growled. Why was she, of all people, here?

"Anne." The woman surveyed my accommodations with a slight grin distorting her perpetual resting bitch face. She eventually came and rested her arms along my bars.

I stood as tall as I could and crossed my arms, waiting for her to speak first. She sucked her teeth as she committed the sight of me behind bars to memory.

"Andrews has sent me to discover if you are in need of any assistance." I imagined Yvonne yearned to immortalize this moment in paint and hang it in a gilded frame if she could.

The woman was a shark. She hated the whole world, and I was an easy target. She and Andrews had had a one-night stand all those years ago, it was over, there was no jealousy between us about the liaison. We just had no love for each other. She was a shark, and I was a boat stirring up her waters.

Assistance. I yanked my thoughts back to her words. Andrews wanted to know if I needed his assistance. I chucked the cursed cornbread back onto the tray where a rat scuttled out to snatch it up and slink away again. Now Yvonne was even happier.

"If I say yes?" I asked.

"Then he will come with a priest, and you will marry him before you are released from these bars," Yvonne stated.

The Bitch Captain (and The Lady)

I crumpled inside. It was a genius plan. Andrews had learned his lesson well. I stayed frozen; not a trickle of emotion would cross my face, not in front of her. She smelled the blood regardless.

"You should know none of us want that," she said as if that wasn't clear as day. "You should know," she leaned into the bars right up close to my face, "we think you, Captain Anne, are a hurricane. Destruction. Chaos. No remorse." She would have reached into my chest to squeeze the heart out of me if she could. "Stay away, Hurricane Anne," she commanded.

"I'm trying."

"Try harder." She spat, the spittle landing just shy of my foot.

"Watch it," I kicked dirt over the gummy wetness, "or maybe I just will become his wife, and where will that leave you?" I shot back. It was an empty threat, they all knew it was an empty threat, but it was a threat they all dreaded nonetheless. If Yvonne wanted to pick this fight with me, she could just bring it on. I was backed into a corner and desperate and dangerous. I knew I was going to lose him. I knew I was going to lose my life with that strange drain trap of a property and people and family. I was about to lose everything and everyone. I knew that and had accepted it. Why did I continually have to repeat the information to myself over and over again?

"I'll still be a mother. What have you got to love you? A cold ship and a man who jumps into another woman's bed the moment your boat rows away."

"Go to hell," I said, low and cold.

"Just where exactly do you think you are?" She ran a finger along the outside edge of the bars.

"I was with him long before any of you." At the start it was just me and him, and he wasn't jumping into bed with anyone else.

"And we are left here long after you leave, cleaning up your mess." She sniffed at me and wrinkled her nose.

"Yeah, why don't you go on and clean something?" I retorted.

"Rot in jail, sea bitch," she snapped. Yvonne took her sweet time walking out of sight, opening and closing the outer door several times just because she could.

She wasn't gone thirty seconds before that fucking guard was back to deliver me yet more food. As soon as he set it down, I threw it at the back of his head and screamed. What the hell was going on here? How had this lovely fort prison gone from a relaxing vacation to social hour at the fat farm?

I sank down the wall and covered my eyes. Stupid Yvonne, it was a sailboat, not a rowboat. And it wasn't always cold. I took good care of that boat, I loved that boat.

A phantom weight grew in my arms, and my insides twisted. Yvonne was a mother. Yvonne had a child who loved her. A child who loved her with the man I loved. The phantom weight grew heavier as I denied it. To any child of mine, I would be the ghost, haunting their life throughout time. I would not do that to such a beloved soul as my child. No, Yvonne can have her child. I had my ship and that had to be enough.

Funny how the tears keep coming even after you tell yourself to stop.

Several days later, I was still in this stupid cell. Mary was successful with the whaler. My friend was not allowed back into the prison but sent a note explaining everything.

> Captain -
> Left your father with 12 loaves of bread, two sacks of rice, and some clean plates. He left me with the stinking bill. I won't be going back there. But he thanks you ten times over.
> Mary.

The Bitch Captain (and The Lady)

It was not as big of a payday as I'd hoped: twelve guns, two powder kegs, and a few lead ingots for approximately 100 pounds of ambergris. The ship would stink to high heaven, but it would keep thieves away. So that was a start. Now how to unload the rest? I was sure there'd be more buyers if I could just get out of here. I toyed with the idea of buying another boat, something I could transport lumber on, but that required staff and I was having enough trouble with just Izzy on board.

I didn't want to think about Izzy.

I liked to picture her chilling in her room, high as a kite, and enjoying the copious amounts of bacon available on the island. I'd get her back through the portal, and she could just repress this as a bad dream and move on with her life. It was not fair to take her so far from home and cast her in the role of family matriarch against her will.

I lay down in the corner of my cell and tried to do some deep breathing. Calm down, Anne. Calm down. After all, I had lost nothing but time.

I could live with everything I'd done. I just couldn't live with myself anymore. That's why she was here; I was greedy for her company. I wasn't ready to give her up, and I'd selfishly concocted this trip to elongate my time with her. I'd failed. It was clear Izzy needed to go home. She belonged there. I held onto a bar and shook it. I belonged here. It would hurt like a bitch to say goodbye, but I would take her home. There would be plenty of time later to grieve for myself and all this wasted time and start making decisions for a future that did not include her.

I stopped sleeping. My mind whirled as it spun out thinking about the future. I'd worked what felt like my whole life towards getting to this point right here where I had my sister with me.

I stopped eating. What the hell was the point? Maybe I should sail with Marco. Maybe I should marry Andrews. Maybe I should just stay in this prison and let it rot around me. Lord knows this is where I belonged.

Should

Should

Should. That stupid word again!

I admit that I did all this for me and my life. I wouldn't go so far as to say that all my efforts were in the service of Izzy and her benefit. I wasn't such a liar as that yet. But you work and you dream and you hustle and you beg and you steal towards a goal that will benefit us as a family, and then she fucking makes you pinky-swear to take her home.

It took two days before I could make a coherent thought about proceeding with my life without Izzy in the picture. It was a small choice that became my first step out of depression. I'd go back to school. Maybe get a PhD in something difficult like game theory or string theory. A small decision, yes, but the first decision I'd made in years that didn't revolve around my sister.

I fell dead asleep as soon as I made that decision, as if my brain and soul had just been waiting for common ground.

The high-pitched screams and futile pleas of some wench woke me up. The guards were muscling a local prostitute into the cell the Puritans had just vacated. I didn't know the girl's name, but I'd seen her around enough and dealt with plenty of her clients.

The guards slammed the door and locked it, then walked out mumbling about how minding a prison full of females was beneath them. The prostitute shook the bars and hollered and screamed at the men to come back and let her out. She was giving me a headache. I took off my boot and threw it at the bars dividing our cells. It had worked on the rats.

"Shut up!" I yelled.

The whore finally noticed my presence and made a noise of disgust. "Locked up with the Bitch Captain of the Seven Seas." She slid down

The Bitch Captain (and The Lady)

the wall and sat facing me. "Wonderful." Then she noticed the stockpile of food I had stashed in the cell. "Can I get some of that bread?"

I looked over at the pile of rolls Andrews kept sending to tempt me into marrying him then back at her. "No."

She made a noise of disgust and a rude gesture. I put my hat back over my eyes and leaned against the wall to rest.

It was barely an hour before another damn guard was in with more food. The whore began screaming at him immediately to release her, to call the lieutenant, to give her some food too, to let her go, how this was completely uncalled for. I started threatening that he better stop bringing in all this food, to tell Andrews where he could stick all his generosity, to get me some paper to send a note to Izzy. We were both at the bars shouting our various threats and demands in a tidal wave of high-pitched noise and echoes. He dropped the bowl unceremoniously on the floor and all but sprinted away. The whore and I retreated to our walls.

"Please. I'm starving," she begged.

She was so pitiful I relented. I pushed the bowl through the bars with my feet. The whore gobbled it up then ogled more of my stash.

"Are those wine bottles full?" she asked. If you give a mouse a cookie...

"Yup." I put my hat over my eyes and leaned back against the wall.

"Can I have one?" She draped her arms through the bars and simpered at me.

"Nope." All this crap was getting carted back to Andrews' estate and dumped back on his land. All I needed was a moment's peace from the guards and all these damn visitors and I could get the hell out of here.

The whore wouldn't shut up.

"I service women too." She eyed my trousers. "For some of that wine I could make you feel so good. Make you forget you're here." She made some beckoning motions with her fingers that I ignored. The whore retreated and pouted a little while more. "Even the sea bitch herself must like some kind of company," she tried.

I stayed silent under my hat.

"So, tell me, what tickles the bitch captain's fancy?" She made her beckoning gesture again.

"Information," I answered. "Got any of that up your skirt?"

The whore retreated back to her wall. Most soldiers tend to shut up when they are putting their dicks in paid-for pussy. True enough that men talked more after sex, but this whore didn't look like she was high class enough to sleep with anyone who had any secrets to spill anyway. She pouted and sobbed in her corner until I threw another shoe at her.

"Get your shit together. What the hell is wrong with you?" I took a bite of bread. It was stale now, but I was hungry.

"If you hadn't brought that whore of a lady on your ship, everything would be fine," she sobbed.

"What the hell are you talking about?" I muttered.

"That dark woman got off your ship and started ruining lives," she sneered.

"Speak more." I rolled her a bottle. She cocked her head at me and pulled out the cork.

And then this whore cracked open from the ass up. She spun me a tale of idiocy I never thought my sister capable of. According to the slattern, Izzy had spent exactly twelve seconds in her room before gallivanting around the island, spending my fortunes on hotels, land, more land, street children, stall food, going to exclusive dinner parties, and getting engaged to the very same lieutenant who had thrown me in this delightful prison cell. Roisin (the baggage told me her name between drinks) was good and drunk now.

"You want to know how many married men I see?" she slurred. "They bend me over and damn their vows. So I know he'll be back. He'll be back." She took another pull from the bottle. "He's in love now. Giving her rings. But I know him. I know how he feels." She ran her hands over her body. "And he's solid and strong. And so large—"

I threw another bottle at her (since I was out of shoes) shattering it

The Bitch Captain (and The Lady)

everywhere. The loud clang brought the guards in and they proceeded to yell and go on about behaving and cleaning up. Roisin and I yelled back threats and insults. Roisin also yelled out a few propositions and demands to see the lieutenant commander. No one managed to gain any ground, and we all retreated, the guards to their stations outside the door, me to my wall, and the whore passed out.

My thoughts darkened. Izzy was out of her room. Izzy had spent all of my money. Izzy was sleeping with a ghost...probably many ghosts. Who was I kidding? There was an excellent chance she'd be the next whore thrown in here for public indecency. My blood began to simmer. I'd thought she was safe, sound, and relaxing in her room. If anything, perhaps Gerta might walk her around the town a little to air her out. Izzy's room must resemble Chernobyl by now.

If Roisin were to be believed, though, Izzy was not safe. Izzy was exposed and vulnerable and gallivanting around an island that had proven to be some of the most dangerous territory I'd ever traveled. I couldn't wrap my head around the idea that even after she had witnessed how bad things could turn with one wrong move (see Tavern Rock), she would be so brazen as to try her hand at such risky maneuvers as consorting with nobility at a dinner party. I had to get out of here. Roisin was unconscious.

There was movement at the door. The guard was watching me again. I wasn't going anywhere yet.

Dammit.

Izzy had accepted a proposal. This, I could not understand. Roisin had been very clear on this point, however, as it was the reason she was sharing the fort's hospitality tonight. Roisin had seen the ring and everything. I didn't even know they did engagement rings in this time. Clearly Izzy was up to something. I would believe in Santa before I believed my club-hopping, pot-smoking, pansexual sister actually agreed to marry and commit herself to a man from the 17th century barely a week after making landfall. No, she was up to something.

Her intended was the highest-ranking officer of this fort. Perhaps this was some ill-conceived and misguided attempt to break me out of prison? Could Izzy have warmed to me enough to try and help me escape? Despite myself, I hoped so. If she was trying (however stupidly) to break me out of here, maybe I wasn't so unforgivable. Maybe there was hope for us.

I fell into an uneasy sleep with uneasy dreams.

Gold leaked from my boat, and I couldn't stop it. I'd plug one hole up only to find another. Izzy was there in her bikini, laughing at me as she tossed coins overboard and wrapped jewels in rolling papers and smoked them. I tried to stop her, but she was in her cabin with the young lieutenant, bent over as he drove into her from behind. She panted and moaned as the blue-eyed soldier reached around and toyed with her.

"Oh yeah. That's so good," Izzy said with Roisin's voice. "Keep going." The soldier grunted and moaned.

The noises continued, and I floated up out of my dream to see that Roisin was braced against the bars dividing our cell and had her skirts up. One of our young guards was pumping behind her. Roisin's face was bored, and when she saw me, she waved to get my attention. "Hey, sea bitch. How about some more of that wine?"

"No." I pulled my hat down farther and tried to block out the pitiful sounds of the guard as he came inside the whore. He backed out of her and buttoned up, then handed her a bowl of food.

"What?" she said as she rearranged her skirts and began eating. "You were asleep and I was hungry. Your food is good." She licked her fingers.

Another guard entered and offered Roisin early release if she serviced him. Roisin jumped at the chance. She knelt in front of him and took his dick in her mouth through the bars. The girl was talented, she had him off in no time. The still-quivering guard opened her cell and led her away.

I fell back asleep.

The Bitch Captain (and The Lady)

Izzy was in my dream again. She was an old married woman dressed in all the trappings and finery of nobility with her children and grandchildren surrounding her. She sat on a mountain of my hard work and wealth and glared at me.

"You promised," she accused. "You promised to take me home." Her children glared at me.

I saw myself reflected in the gold and silver she sat on, and I looked exactly the same as I did now.

"I will take you home now." I told her and reached out my hand.

Her son, a blue-eyed soldier with curly dark hair, chopped my hand off. "It's too late now. I'm not leaving." She dismissed me. "I have everything I need here. I don't need you anymore."

There was a wrenching noise behind me, and I watched as Izzy directed that my ship get torn apart board by board and tossed into a bonfire as the Puritans laughed and cheered. The bonfire blurred into a sunset off the coast of a tropical island where Maui sat on one side of me and Andrews on my other. Both offered me their hands and gestured in different directions, a smoking volcano, a foggy shore.

A door slammed. My face was on the dirty brick floor under my filthy coat.

CHAPTER 7

A Sisterly Visit

"Anne? Anne?" Izzy's voice spoke somewhere above me.

My heart sprinted into overdrive as I tried to separate dream from reality. I leapt from the floor and rushed to the bars to get a look at the vision that was my sister in an era where she certainly didn't belong. It was like looking at a collage made from old magazine pages with a photograph thrown in there that didn't belong. That's what I'd done. I'd cut her out of her time and sloppily pasted her into this nightmare.

She was in new clothes. It looked like some recreation of a riding habit. Where had she gotten that? If she didn't belong here, why did she look so comfortable and peaceful? There had always been an energy about my sister, a hustle that I thought we shared. But where I was continually reaching, from my vantage in this prison cell I saw a woman who had a hold on that which was unattainable to me. I reached for her now, wanting to feel if she was actually here or if I was still dreaming.

The guard smashed my forearm with his cudgel, bringing my ire and focus sharply down upon him. After gasping from the pain I let loose on this turd.

"Come closer, you little piece of shit, and I will show you where you can stick that! I will ram it up your ass so hard you'll be shitting out your eyebrows." I was pissed he'd gotten a hit on me. Izzy's presence had eclipsed his, and I'd let my guard down. I shook the bars and dared him to come closer. "Get back here and try that again! You better hope you don't pull the short straw again or I will be on your ass, scalping you! You tiny-brained, buck-toothed, pot-bellied—"

"Anne! Would you stop it and calm down?" Izzy ordered. Her voice was just as I remembered, not old and hate-filled. It was my sister.

I refocused on her and took some calming breaths. I rubbed my arm. That had really hurt, and I was embarrassed to have been caught so unawares. I bit back the tears and just stayed focused on Izzy.

"That was a bit much, Ross." Izzy addressed the asshat pretending to guard her from me.

Ross? She knew the name of this cad?

"You are going to open the door, yes? I can't exactly check on her through the bars, can I?" I looked through the bars at the two of them, trying to discern exactly what this strange relationship dynamic was.

"Lady Isabelle, the lieutenant commander – "

"The lieutenant commander ordered you to keep me safe and do what I asked."

"Yes, my lady." He approached the bars with his cudgel again, banging them and ordering me to step back against the far wall. This time I was ready. My hand flashed out and grabbed his slow, meaty arm and gripped it tight. I yanked him hard against the bars.

"What are you going to do now, chump?" I slammed him against the bars again and got a hold of his cudgel and wrenched it from his grasp. I could smell the fear on him. "I told you not to try this again, and here you are. Now bend over—"

"Anne! Would you please do as he asks?" Izzy asked, annoyed. She had the same tone in her voice as she did when she was cajoling me into minding my behavior for one of our mother's dinner events so that I wouldn't get grounded and we could go out partying over the weekend.

I dropped him, threw the cudgel out my window into the rocks below, and stepped back against the far wall with my hands up.

"Thank you," she said to me, then turned to Ross. "Some privacy, please? We have a number of sensitive female matters to discuss." I

The Bitch Captain (and The Lady)

rolled my eyes as Ross unlocked the door and skittered away.

Izzy entered my cell, leaving the door open, and pulled the guards' stool in to sit on. I mourned the hem of her getup; that was expensive wool, and she was dragging it through the muck.

I hesitated as to what I should do. What I should do was run. I should run hard and fast and now. Izzy was on friendly enough terms with the guards that she might not be punished too severely. Whatever magic she'd used to get in here might just take her out of here as well. The image of her from my dream lingered in front of my eyes, a lurid afterimage superimposed over her body: similar clothing, twisted face.

"Are you alright? I've been sending you food, but I couldn't get in before now. Here." She took some packages from her basket and held them out.

Again, I looked at the door. Run, Anne! I urged myself. But I couldn't leave her.

"Do you need any medical treatment?" she asked.

Run, Anne, run.

"Anne?"

"Food?" Her words slowly penetrated my fevered brain. She'd been sending me food? Not Andrews? "You've been sending me food?" I couldn't help but feel a little betrayed. I thought Andrews…I guess he finally heard my no. His absence sliced like a knife through my gut.

"Who else would feed you in prison?"

"No one." I braced against the emptiness and tried to hold back the devastating loneliness with useless, sophomoric reasoning about how I'd chosen this.

"So, are you okay? I know you were involved with the explosion and everything. Did you get hurt?" she asked.

I was incredulous. What next, asking about the weather? I ran my hands through my disheveled hair and tried to make sense of this visit.

"What are you doing here, Izzy?"

"Obviously, checking on your well-being. I know it's been days, but

I couldn't get in before now. I'm sorry." Izzy glanced about the cell. The place was familiar to me, but I supposed it was an affront to her senses.

"Days." I rubbed at the growing bruise on my arm, courtesy of her new friend. "Days." She shows up here in new clothes, a ring on her finger. It had barely been a week. I had to put a stop to all of her misguided schemes. "Why do I hear that congratulations are in order? That you are taking a husband?"

"Well, yes. I'm getting married." She blushed.

I slid down the wall and rubbed my temples. "Why would you do that?"

"Why do people usually get married? What a question." She must be putting on a show for the guards right outside eavesdropping on us.

"Because they're stupid and naive." I know I certainly was the first time I got married. "Are you stupid and naive, Izzy?"

She didn't answer. I wouldn't press her to reveal her plan when it might land her in here next to me. I'd work on getting it out of her when fewer ears were present.

"I didn't think so. Listen, I didn't leave before now because I figured you'd be in danger. Now you're here and it makes this easier." I got up and moved closer so I could keep my voice low. "Be at the ship tonight. Wait till sunset and make your way over. We can be on the water and far away come sunup. We'll head straight for home – or Portugal if you'd still like to go. I know I would." She started to say something, but this was important. I had to get the instructions across. "We will probably have to resupply in the Azores, but we can definitely—"

"I said no, Anne," she interrupted me.

"No what?" Did she have somewhere else to resupply? Because Arnoldo owed me a favor and I'd love to cash that in this summer.

"No, I'm not leaving," she said.

I glanced out the door towards all the ears just beyond.

"Leaving where?" I whispered. I had no idea what she was talking about.

The Bitch Captain (and The Lady)

"I'm not leaving the Somers Isles," she said.

"The who?" I could not have heard that right. The useless nobility who bought the land only to trade and burn it to the ground called it that. Izzy shouldn't be calling this place Somers Isles. She knew this island as Bermuda. My mind fractured between the 21st and the 17th century vernacular and made my head hurt.

"Here? This island? Later known as Bermuda? I'm staying." She continued sitting like she was indeed staying put here.

"Don't be ridiculous." I brushed her off. "Of course we're leaving." Izzy was not useless or nobility.

"No! I'm building a life here!" She got up and into my face. "I own a hotel, with a kitchen and everything. I sold your guns, Anne. I traded them for a vast quantity of land—"

"You did what?" I erupted. I was counting on those guns. I had a contract to fulfill with Charlie. Not to mention that most of that sale I was planning to gift to Andrews and Helene for the running of the estate. I would not leave those children wanting.

I looked at my sister in fury. She had stolen a sale from me that I desperately needed. I straightened up and looked her squarely in the eyes with a dead calm. "Tell me you are lying, Izzy. I needed that money. I needed that gold."

"What? You wanted to sell the guns, and clearly you weren't in a position to do so. I got 200 acres, Anne! Two hundred! And bonuses—"

Oh dear god, she was serious.

"You sold my cargo for dirt? Why not magic beans!" I hollered.

"Keep your voice down," she said, but I was beyond.

"I killed for that cargo, and you've thrown it away! Do you have any idea what you've done!" My fingers itched. Any other person...any other person and I would have run them through for betraying me like this. I felt spayed, defanged. How was I supposed to address this?

"You are truly unbelievable. Regardless, I am not leaving yet." She sat there letting her skirt grew roots.

"The fuck you aren't." I almost grabbed her bodice to bring her close and under control. "I will be on that boat tonight and I will be leaving and you will be right next to me. That's a promise." I was not spending another night here and neither was she.

"Oh, is it, now? Regardless of what I want, you're just going to drag me away, again? Do I have that right?" She served it right back to me.

"What the fuck do you want, Izzy?" I grabbed her hand and ran my finger down the very thin scar I sliced into her when I'd made my vow to take her home.

"Have you been listening to anything I've said?" She wrenched her hand from my grasp.

"All I hear is that you threw my hard-won cargo to the winds and are planning on marrying a ghost. No, Izzy. I don't understand. All I know is that tonight, within the hour even, you and I will be on our ship safe and free and going home!"

"Ross!" she yelled and backed out of the cell, slamming the door in my face.

This Ross came running in and looked between me and Izzy. He left and returned a moment later with four other guards and manacles.

"Izzy," I said breathlessly as they walked into the cell, "Izzy, call them off." Take care of Ross first, then the one with a slight limp. "Izzy, where are you going?" One was young, probably had little fighting experience. "Izzy, where's Gerta?"

The guards launched on me on cue. I yelled and screamed for her to come back as I managed to throw at least two punches and a few kicks, taking one down. I thought I heard Izzy call something out, but the guards were on top of me and I was screaming my guts out with every insult known to me in every language known to me. I got my hands around Ross's throat before one of them struck me hard and fast on the back of my head. Stars and sparks burst in my vision and I dropped.

The Bitch Captain (and The Lady)

Fish course fork. Meat course fork. Salad course fork. Charger. Dinner plate. Soup bowl. I nudged each piece as I named them, left to right. Salad course knife. Meat course knife. Fish course knife. Soup spoon. Seafood fork. My mother had ignored our algebra, didn't care a lick about languages, but God save my sorry soul if I should get my forks mixed up. I grabbed the butter knife at the top of my setting and dug it into the tablecloth that cost more than my dress, playing with the edge so that an impression was made but no fibers were cut.

"Just sit still and stay quiet," Izzy urged me and took the knife from me. She replaced it in its proper position and smiled at the various guests as they mingled near us.

I plucked at the pale purple satin nonsense our mother had dressed me in and sulked back in my chair.

"Come on, it's not that bad." She gestured to all the grand figures in the ballroom dancing to the strains of a string quartet.

"I hate this stuff."

"I know. But if you can manage it, we can stay out late tomorrow night. So just sit still and don't do anything. Come on, I want to have fun with you this weekend." She reached out and held my hand to stop my fidgeting.

I really tried.

I mostly really tried.

Until this man wandered over to us. He was far too old to be talking to Izzy, and I tensed. Izzy kept her hand on mine, trying to keep me calm. I wanted this man gone. He was drunk and overreaching. Izzy politely refused his advances to "just have a dance," "just have a drink," "just enjoy a little conversation." He called her "beautiful" and had the nerve to try and put a hand on her hair that she'd worked on all afternoon.

I'd had enough. I caught his arm before he could touch her and pinned the sleeve of his cheap blazer to the wall with the seafood course fork. I didn't even draw blood, but everyone was in an uproar and I was grounded.

Chains clinked and clanked as I tried to raise my hand to my aching head. I groaned and sat up as the cell spun around me. Tight manacles chained me to the wall. I had maybe three feet of play at the maximum. When I reached back to the sore spot on my head, I felt dried blood. It was tender. The secondary measures of the Fountain hadn't kicked in, so I couldn't be too bad off, but I would do well to take care of myself until I could drink from my flask.

It was quiet in here. After a couple hours I realized why. I was chained up. There was no longer a need to check on me. I now had all the time in the world to escape. No one was watching, no one cared. I was able to reach some of my food stash and pull it close. Looked like I was in for a long wait. Either I'd be released or I'd be executed.

.
.
.

Had someone cleaned up in here?

Someone had definitely cleaned up. There was a bucket and a fresh shirt. I gingerly mopped at the back of my head with the clean fabric and winced when I hit broken skin. I performed a few concussion tests and decided I was probably okay for the time being. The sun set in my little window, and I watched the stars begin to wink into existence. It was so very quiet.

A song came to my lips, and I crooned the words softly just to hear a little noise. It was an old song, one I hadn't thought about in a very long time. The words came easily, and I sang it softly as I leaned against the wall I was chained to.

I paused when I heard the footsteps. They were heavy and regular, and I had my suspicions who belonged to them. I continued my low crooning as the young lieutenant unlocked the door and stood framed in the archway. He was taller than I remembered, broad, elegant. I could fairly see the blue blood coursing just under his skin, surfacing in full dominance within his irises. He had a certain appeal, I could see that. Izzy always did have good taste in bedmates. The young lieutenant surveyed me as I sang my old song. If he were here to kill me, he'd let me know. Till then, I had no deeds to do and no promises to keep.

"Lady...Anne," he addressed me, the words pained and contorted.

I stopped my song. Well now, this was different.

"Captain," I answered. I did not care for titles or embellishments which carried no honor or meaning.

"No." He refused my rank.

"Something I can help you with, Lieutenant?"

"Lieutenant Commander. And yes."

I clanked as I turned to look at him. The weight of the iron on my arms was beginning to bother my barely-healed shoulder. "Well, spit it out," I encouraged. He blanched.

"I would like to know about California," he asked after composing himself.

"No." He could go to hell. I went back to looking out the window and crooning.

"Lady Anne—" he started again.

"Captain," I corrected.

"If you are of noble rank, the same rank as Lady Isabelle, you will be addressed with your proper title," he insisted.

"Who says I am of the same rank?"

"She does. In fact, she insists on naming you as her family, her sister. Do you name her as such?" He was still and full of tension. This question was the reason he was down here: Were Izzy and I actually family?

"Yes." I turned to look him square in the face. "Lady Isabelle is my sister."

The young lieutenant swallowed in what could be disgust, or possibly terror, and marched out of the prison, slamming and locking the door.

CHAPTER 8

Prison Purgatory

That was it for a few days.

This sucked.

My shoulder hurt.

Sleeping in the chains was uncomfortable. The iron irritated my wrists, and I tried not to scratch at the deepening welts. My stash of food grew increasingly stale and rat-eaten and was not replaced. Izzy had had me chained and bound; it made sense that she'd stop sending me food as well. The guard rotations had all but ceased. The few times guards did come in to toss me a cup of water they were tight-lipped and quick about their duty. Apparently I was to be kept alive...but only just.

I grew concerned that I was being held to make an example to the citizens of St. George's. The whore had been released after only a night and a blow job. The Puritans had been flogged and released after only a day or two. Yet here I remained.

A big, ceremonial public execution would present a problem for me and Izzy. I was inordinately hard to kill. It wasn't impossible to kill me, but it was an involved process beyond the skills of any local hangman.

I sat and sang and badgered the guards with questions they wouldn't answer when they sporadically came to check if I was alive. I received no answers.

Three days later, I toyed with the notion of accepting Andrews' proposal. What was one life sentence in trade for another? Andrews could get me out of here, he'd done it before. I called for the guards, for the lieutenant, for Izzy, for anyone.

It was so quiet here now.

Something was very off about this whole situation. I was unsettled and knew there was some important piece of information missing.

I was hungry.

I was going to die here.

Definitely going to die. Die of boredom if nothing else.

I wonder what Marco was up to.

I smelled really bad.

CHAPTER 9

Prison Company

I heard the commotion begin as soon as their boat docked. Loud, shouting men, cracks of whips, clipped soldier orders. What fresh hell was this?

The commotion moved through the fort until just outside the outer door of my prison cell. It appeared I was to have company. Fuck. Shackled like this, I was sure to be a sitting duck to whomever was placed in here with me. I sat up against the wall and tried to make myself appear bigger – which was a tall order considering how much weight I had clearly lost over the past week – week and a half? Two weeks? How long had I been in here?

The young lieutenant opened the heavy outer door and then the door of my cell. He eyed me appraisingly. There was an electric energy about him. Something was up. I adjusted my hat so I could get a better view of what was happening. The young lieutenant came to a decision and shouted orders to the guards outside. Five bound men were ushered directly into my cell, leaving the other cell completely empty. Something was definitely up.

"Well, well, well," the final man in had the audacity to speak, "if it isn't the Bitch Captain of the Seven Seas." It was Marius. Fucking hell. I could smell his decaying hand.

I was in huge trouble. I placed the rest of their faces as men from the first militia who had come calling for the guns at the Sea Wind. I knew that young lieutenant didn't like me, but this was obscene. These men would kill me, and if I was lucky, they would kill me first. He was kind enough to leave the men bound, at least, although I doubt that would delay them by much.

I looked at the young lieutenant, feeling betrayed despite having no call to expect anything different from the man. Execute me if you want, but be honest about it.

He met my gaze and took a deep breath. "You men are here pending judgement for the assault and attempted rape of the Lady Isabelle," he announced.

I physically jerked and stopped breathing. A haze of fury descended over my vision.

"If by morning you have come to your senses and have found repentance within your wretched hearts, you may beg forgiveness from the Crown. Until then, a pleasant evening." He turned his attention to me. "And, Captain?" My eyes flashed to his face. He stared intently and moved to shield me from their view. "Perhaps you will behave yourself as befits your title. I will return in an hour." The lieutenant deftly and soundlessly popped open my shackles and walked away without a backward glance.

"You attacked Lady Isabelle?" I accused them after the lieutenant was well away. They all laughed and hacked.

"Almost had her too," one of the damned bragged. "On the ground and everything. MacFaddon got her skirt up. Beautiful sight." They laughed some more.

"She'll be wearing Joseph's bruises for a while. Did you see her face when he got her in the belly?" Another of the doomed souls chuckled.

"Her screams were delightful," Marius reminisced, digging his own grave. I would save him for last.

"Beg for mercy," I instructed them all.

They burst out into laughter that quickly died as I stood up and stepped away from my shackles.

The Bitch Captain (and The Lady)

Incapacitate first.

Five of them. Five swift kicks to their barely-protected heads. They all dropped.

Destroy.

I grabbed the heavy chains from the floor and wrapped one around each of their necks in turn, roughly three minutes each did the trick.

Finally, rule number one: dead men tell no tales.

I was panting from the exertion after days and days of confinement, but I wasn't about to ignore rule number one. Not finishing the job good and proper had come to bite me in the ass a few times too many. I ran my fingers along the edge of the wall until I found the thin groove with the thin strap and pulled. Attached to the strap was a good sharp modern blade, not much bigger than a scalpel, an easy-to-hide blade that could reap devastating results.

The men were likely dead, but the deep slices through their arteries assured it. From the looks of things, they hadn't arrived here in the full flush of life. They were thin and mangy, bruised, and one had a portion of an arrow still embedded in his shoulder. I pulled it out and examined the point. Izzy had been involved in some type of archery therapy after her parents died. Mom had signed Izzy up for every type of therapy seven ways from Sunday. Looking back on it, she likely drained my college fund, such as it was, to afford it.

I examined them more closely. There was evidence of an attack. One man's pants were ripped at the crotch with extensive bruising visible beneath. A few had suffered head wounds, and there were burns where musket balls had torn through clothing. My very favorite, though, was the man with severe fingernail scratches across his face. I smiled and fondly touched the marks. "Good girl, Izzy." I felt sure the arrow from his shoulder must be hers too.

The young lieutenant's footsteps sounded outside, and I quickly hid the scalpel back in its place. He opened the door to find me calmly back in my spot, surrounded by the dead men and their blood. He nodded, stepped back outside, and returned with a heavily-laden tray with a delicious hot meal and two tumblers of whiskey.

He handed me a glass (whereas I wanted to dive headfirst into the food), and I accepted. The drink was strong and burned as it went down. He tossed his back then poured us another. We drank. He poured a third but took his to go and left me the bottle and the tray – and for some reason a bucket of warm water and soap. Not that I was complaining, it was just a strange thing for him to do.

I was alone and unshackled. I should leave. I eyed the space in the wall I knew I could remove and be gone, but the smells emanating off the tray and the whiskey on my empty stomach overpowered my senses. I washed my bloody hands thoroughly and dove into the hot meal. Eat first, then escape. I probably had time.

Despite knowing better, I sipped at my third drink between bites. Rule number two was to avoid alcohol and the like. A side effect of the Fountain was my body's intolerance of unhealthy foods and mild poisons such as alcohol. I had a low tolerance and got drunk quickly. It was usually better to avoid the stuff. I broke this rule constantly, but I did try.

"Cheers, lads," I toasted the dead men and drank.

The food was swimming in gravy. There was a pot pie with a rich crust and herbs. Even Izzy would be impressed with this meal. My thoughts began to swim in the gravy, and I leaned against the wall. I wonder if Izzy made this. I don't know who else would have included greens…or a freaking flower on the tray. This alcohol was really strong. I speared some type of meat and chewed it as I imagined Izzy at home in our kitchen beating lard into flour for a short crust. I loved gravy. I sopped up as much as I could into some rosemary bread and chased it with more whiskey.

I needed to go. The food could travel with me, and I had wasted enough time eating. Solitude was a precious commodity which I would be a fool to squander right now.

The Bitch Captain (and The Lady)

As I stood, my cell spun around me. Even for being bad at alcohol, this was a bit much. My first step brought me to my hands and knees, and I crawled over and examined my whiskey tumbler. There was a faint powdery residue at the bottom.

"That fucker," I gasped as unconsciousness stole over me.

When I woke up, I was shackled to the wall again and the dead bodies were cleaned up and gone. I had a splitting headache and clanked as I took stock of my cell. The young lieutenant had left me the food (what was left after the rats got to it), the whiskey, and the soap. I poured a huge amount of the drink into my glass and drank it down to aid me in passing out again. I was a stupid, stupid fool.

The food disappeared. What I could snatch from the rats and bugs and humidity was stale and rotten after a few days. A stray guard appeared every now and then and brought me a drink of water or a small bowl of rice. My wounds from Tavern Rock healed while the welts and sores from the iron shackles grew deep and infected from the constant irritation.

It was quiet.

The guards that did visit were clearly instructed not to talk to me. The guard with the brother on Kent Island usually brought me a bigger portion of food than the others, but even he kept his mouth shut.

The clanking annoyed me every time I moved, so I stopped moving. My scars itched and pained me, so I spent hours trying to disconnect from my muscles and keep my mind on matters outside my body.

I'd been imprisoned multiple times in my life. My longest stint was in the Canary Islands. Officially it was for smuggling jewels, unofficially it was because the local authorities had been tipped off that I'd robbed a big convoy. I was kept in that awful place for several months. Then I was severely flogged, hung, and released. I'd lost a lot that trip.

When I'd finally limped back home to Andrews in my looted and stripped-down ship, he'd been furious. Yvonne was pleased I'd managed to successfully hide the gems, but Angelica and Helene hid my bleeding back from the children and scowled. Yvonne was as equally as delighted with the deep stripes across my back as she was at the chest of jewels I brought the estate.

There was never a question in my mind why I was being held in the Canary Islands. Why was I here now? Sure, I had blown a little hole in a little building, but no civilians had gotten hurt. And who hasn't exploded one wall or another in their life?

I'd been here far too long. It crossed my mind that Andrews could be behind this extended sentence. He wasn't above bribing the officers at the fort to keep me behind bars until I relented and said yes to his proposal. Although, I felt like he would have come to deliver the terms himself if that was the case.

I'm not coming to get you this time. If you get into trouble, you can get yourself right back out again. I mean it, Nan!

He did mean it. He wasn't coming for me, and I couldn't ask him to sacrifice any more of his time for me than he already had.

Today I watched the little square of sun travel across the cell floor and worried the growing welts. The sting brought me focus. I deserved this, I know. I just wish Izzy wasn't in so much danger because of me.

The Bitch Captain (and The Lady)

Today was gray and intermittently rainy. There was no sun to mark the time. The drops splashed through the window onto my floor. I tried to sleep, but the ghosts of the men I'd killed chatted blithely from the straw floor, repeating the story of their attack on my sister. Marius's hand lay stinking and staining the floor with pus. The small droplets of rain weren't going to wash that mess away.

They laughed their sick laughter, and once they were through laughing at Izzy on the ground with her skirt up, they laughed at me. They were plum tickled that they were released from their mortal bonds and there sat The Bitch Captain of the Seven Seas in irons.

"Thought she was so clever, aligning herself with that lieutenant."

"Look where it got her now. Sitting in her own filth. Watching the days pass. Chained to the wall."

"Chained for a sister who abandoned her."

"She killed for her sister, and the prissy little girl hasn't even come to say hello."

"Hope she's worth our stains upon your soul."

"That blade is still within your reach. Why not go ahead and add your blood to the dirt in this cell? Let it mingle with our own."

"Do it to yourself and it just might stick."

"Don't listen to them." The voice spoke clear and strong in my ear. It was Maui's voice. My dear friend. My lost friend. **"They aren't real. They aren't here."**

"Neither are you." Mine was the only voice speaking aloud. My lips were dry and cracked, my throat sore from days of breathing dust and mold and mildew.

"Chin up. She'll come for you. She loves you. Have some faith, Heeny." Heeny. The old nickname made me chuckle. He was the only one that ever called me by that name.

I'd allowed my old friend onto my ship to have one final goodbye with Izzy. His ship was prepped for departure too, and soon we'd both open sails *to speed us in our separate directions. I met him back on deck and looked him over. He looked good, strong, healthy.*

"Have a little faith in me, Heeny." He finally broke the silence. "I really think I can make a difference." He was full of courage and hope.

That was the last time I saw him before he went off to die in his failed war.

"No." The chains clanked as I moved my arms. She'd put these on me. I deserved it, I know I deserved it. "She's done with me. Just like you were done with me too." I closed my mind to all those ghosts and stared out the window.

It was quiet. Quiet was good. I'd choose the quiet over the voices of all the men I'd killed.

I was starving. I was dehydrated. I hadn't peed all day. My wrists were caked in blood. My cell was full of the ghosts of my victims come to laugh at me. Maui didn't return. I had to get out of here. I was going to die.

The guard with the brother on Kent Island came in and shoved a tray through the bars. Water. There was water. I dove on the cup and wet my lips, my tongue, taking small sips, immensely careful not to spill a drop. I looked up at the guard, wanting to thank him, but my throat was closed and his eyes held nothing but pity. He left quickly.

He returned with another cup. I was not going to die this day.

Perhaps tomorrow.

Or the next.

The iron rubbed deeper into my wrists, stinging and rubbing me raw. I wiped the blood on my shirt. I'd lost enough weight that the shackles

The Bitch Captain (and The Lady)

were looser now, not loose enough to slip out of but loose enough to move freely and rub and rub and rub my layers of skin away. I was starving and bloodied and aching.

The scars on my legs screamed at me; the enforced inactivity was torture.

I know I deserved this, but how could Izzy do this to me?

The humidity had increased today, there was a storm brewing. About half an hour ago, the sun disappeared behind the clouds and hadn't come back. The fort sat a little ways back from the shore but not far enough. A major storm surge would flood the prison. The clouds raced in the opposite direction from the winds, and the tides were doing an odd standing march that indicated dangerous undercurrents. All the birds were roosting, not about to risk a flight through what was coming. It was early for a hurricane but not impossible. Izzy and I were supposed to leave Bermuda weeks ago to avoid this entire issue.

A flash of lightning lit up the early evening, and I began a count until the thunder. Nine. When the count shrank to seven, the rain began. Footsteps sounded down the hall, and I hoped that whoever it was was bringing food. I'd licked the last crumbs off Izzy's tray long ago. If only there was any of that whiskey left.

Thunder boomed again.

On second thought, with this storm, better keep my head. I might be swimming before long.

The outer door opened, and the young lieutenant entered the room and looked me over. "Back up to the wall," he instructed. "And stay there."

The hair on my neck stood up. I thought it would be a public execution. I swallowed and shuffled to the wall, my stomach ice. When he shot me, I'd have to play dead and get buried. I closed my eyes and steeled myself for the bang and the pain.

Instead, a different set of footsteps sounded, along with the drag of skirts against the rushes. I opened my eyes and saw my sister. The lieutenant held her close and kept his eyes trained on me as if he suddenly doubted the iron's strength. She looked healthy. I couldn't see any deep bruising, she didn't limp, there was no shine of fever to indicate infected wounds. I let go of tension I hadn't realized I'd been holding. She was okay.

My eyes played tricks on me and overlaid the room with the blood of the militiamen. I felt their souls, swept into the corner, watching and judging me over the shoulders of that rat bastard thief and his cronies.

"Anne." Izzy's voice captured my attention away from their cackling laughs and gurgles through their slit throats. I'd made all my cuts deep.

The moment my name left her lips she began crying and held onto the bars of my cell. The young lieutenant stopped her from leaning too far in, where I had a chance of reaching her. I glared at his lily-white hands holding my sister away from me as she cried.

"I need your help." She at last managed to speak coherently.

"Why? Get attacked by another militia?" If so, at this rate I would leave this journey topping my body count ten-fold. "Glad to see you're alright." My voice was rough from disuse and suppressed anger.

"I am not alright," Izzy cried at me. Oh shit, oh no, no. I had given her a sip of Fountain. Could it have messed with her pills?

"Oh, my god. You're pregnant." I tried to see past the stays on her corset to see if she might be showing. How long had I been in here? It couldn't have been that long. Is this why she wanted to get married? I glared at that young lieutenant. I'd have his balls off the minute I was out of here if he put Izzy through any more trauma.

"What? No. It's literally impossible." For some reason, she added her glare to mine, and the young lieutenant straightened nervously.

The Bitch Captain (and The Lady)

Who was this lady pretending to be my sister? Izzy was in sex ed class right next to me; she knew the consequences of opening her legs.

"Right. Because accidents never happen." I snorted.

"They don't happen if you're being forced to abstain," she muttered.

"Who's being forced to abstain?" My head swam with hunger and confusion. Now who were we talking about?

"The lieutenant commander won't touch me until AFTER the wedding. He's. Very. Disciplined." She glared at him again but this time with an edge of wanting to be disciplined and disciplined hard.

"But you're engaged. And you're...you're you." I moved to the end of my chains to get a better view of these strangers in front of me. The storm had darkened the room considerably. I knew stronger men than this young lieutenant who had happily and gratefully fallen to Izzy's wiles, never to recover.

The young lieutenant wavered under our stares and attempted to back out gracefully. "You were right, Isabelle. I would indeed prefer to stay outside for this." He kissed her cheek and held her face a moment, silently checking in with her before stepping out.

I felt rather the stranger in that tiny intimate moment. This little scene did not coincide with my conjectures as to why Izzy had consented to marry this man.

"He's far too gorgeous to be such a prude." Izzy sighed, watching him leave.

I stayed still. I did not like what was happening. Something was wrong. I was missing information and I knew it would cost me. Izzy met my gaze and I tried to search for my missing pieces in her eyes.

"Anne – I need your help."

Of course. And here are my apples, and branches, and bark. I rattled my chains. "I'm a little tied up right now."

"I didn't want to be kidnapped again," Izzy said and shoved a basket through the bars. I nearly fell over from the smell alone.

I took the basket with shaky hands and pulled out a still-warm pastry.

Izzy kept talking. "You're the only person who can help me, Anne. No one here...."

My stomach growled, and I was completely distracted. I was desperate for calories, and this smelled buttery and full of carbohydrates. I was enraptured by the simple baked good. I took a small bite, savoring the end of my involuntary fast.

I'm afraid I might have missed some of Izzy's words. I must have because when she said, "I discovered slavery today!" I was at a complete loss.

"What?" I said around bites of the pastry.

"Fucking white people!" she screeched. Oh lord, what had I done now? Izzy continued, no longer crying but shouting. "I went to a dinner party last month, and I thought I made a new friend. He was charming, and attractive, and normal, and he was really nice and helpful, and everyone's been talking about how his place is the ONLY possible place for the wedding."

My eyes flashed up. There was only one place on this island that could handle a high nobility wedding. I knew exactly where Izzy had been. Had she really seen him? Had she really met him? Andrews, my Andrews, had met my sister? The image of my two worlds in one room sparked in my imagination.

Izzy continued her rant. "And we went out there today, and you know what I learn? HE HAS SLAVES, ANNE! No one mentioned that wonderful, perfect estate is a FUCKING PLANTATION!"

The word resonated flat and out of tune in my head. She wasn't wrong. Brass tacks, that's what it was. It was a large piece of land worked mostly by people of color, and those people, by all outward accounts, were the property of Graham Andrews. Didn't matter that they were no longer enslaved, no one was held in bondage, or that the terms of their contracts were fuzzy. No one could go anywhere anyway because it was

The Bitch Captain (and The Lady)

a fucking island. If it were known there were free people on our land, we'd face daily attacks as slavers tried to recapture our tenants. Andrews was master in a kingdom full of unwillingly transported subjects. Izzy was right. It was just two centuries early for the image painted by my AP history class. I wondered how I had missed it.

Izzy continued her rant as I attempted to reconcile the images. "You know, he comes across as this remarkably modern, progressive man—"

Nanette, you do not give a man a chance, do you?

"—who has women running his business—"

Shall I propose again now or do we need a drink first?

"—and then you learn that the strong women he supposedly admires so much—"

Be careful, Nanette. One day I just might.

"—are ENSLAVED!" she crescendoed.

I reached up to my wounded shoulder and rubbed; it still ached where it was barely healed.

"And he's definitely fucking all of them. I mean, what the fuck, Anne?" Izzy was pacing a hole in the floor, and thank god she was distracted. I crushed the delicate pastry in my fist.

Those women hated me, and I hated them right back. I loved him. I was there first. Couldn't they all just leave each other alone? I mean, how could he do that to me? My eyes burned and my throat closed and I couldn't swallow. I couldn't release my fist. The pastry squeezed between my fingers.

"—and everyone thinks I'm the one that's weird for not being okay with him owning human beings."

It was a moment before I realized she'd stopped ranting and pacing and was looking to me for a response.

I know he slept with them. I know he had his children with them. I couldn't give him children even if I wanted to. Maybe I could have tried to change, should have tried...

I'll still be a mother. What have you got to love you? A cold ship and a man who jumps into another woman's bed the moment your boat rows away.

Izzy was waiting.

"You went to see Graham Andrews?" I could barely say his name aloud.

"You know Graham fucking Andrews-?" Izzy ripped through a few octaves. "Never mind. I shouldn't be surprised. Apparently you're full of secrets." She turned her attack squarely on me. "Your secrets have secrets. You have secret criminal records in the 17th century, why wouldn't you have all manner of secret friends?"

The lightning flashed and illuminated her face. She was going in for the kill. I'd only seen that look on her face once before, when Mom dared to ask her to stay home for some party instead of going to visit her grandmother. I backed against the wall.

"Mary, Dom, Davies, Graham – "

The names sliced into me.

"Helene and Yvonne—"

The names cut deep. How dare they be so bold as to occupy any space in my sister's head?

"All those pirate buddies of yours! Marco—"

Annie

I stopped breathing.

"—Oh and let's not forget Closer To You My God Cowlishaw, and what you did to his face! You're awful!" Closer's mangled face hung in front of my eyes.

You are unwanted in heaven, hell, and here on earth.

"—This is all your fault! Who just kidnaps someone and takes them to a place like this without any warning? I mean, what the fuck, Anne?" The names were bleeding me. These ghosts were not supposed to haunt her. "And then you're all 'I know what I did, I did what I did, and I'd do it again'?!" Izzy wound up for her final blow. "You're a terrible sister!

The Bitch Captain (and The Lady)

I can't even call you my sister right now. You know who you really are? You are the Bitch Captain of the Seven Seas!"

There it was. The name she should never have known. The name that encompassed all the secrets I'd burn myself at the stake for all over again before letting her know them. I felt the flames stealing the oxygen from my lungs again and attempted to calm myself before spinning off into madness again. The image of Izzy huddled in my tiny ship's kitchen, terrified of the one person who'd devoted her life to protecting her, was burned into me forever.

I tried to stitch myself back together as Izzy fumed. "Feel better now?" I managed to rasp out. "I think you should leave." I couldn't face her any longer. I couldn't leave. I could barely move in this tiny cell with these shackles keeping me close to the wall. The thunder rolled.

"You're just going to have sit there and deal with the horror of my fucking presence. We can both be pissed off together because I'm not going anywhere!" She spoke from outside the bars, giving them a harsh kick.

I had no more words. The ocean roared just beyond the sea wall and began to spray and spit inside the cell. What was a little more salt water to wipe off my face? Get yourself together, I commanded myself. She doesn't know what she's talking about. It doesn't matter how right she is. We'd go home, and she'd forget this ever happened.

Except the looking glass was cracked now. Izzy was across its threshold and was privy to all the ugliness I had worked so long to keep from her. Not the ugliness of the world, the ugliness that had taken root in myself. She'd never be able to unsee it. She was smart not to name me as her sister. This trip was intended to be a farewell tour, and it was living up to its name spectacularly. All I'd done so far was say a crapload of goodbyes.

The rain began to deluge.

"Ian took me out and showed me." Izzy was never good at silence. "Slavery is here, and it's real, and it's awful. And I've been an unwitting participant. You know, I'm building a shipyard. When Michael Davies and Richard Lavigne suggested—"

The absurdity of this statement shocked me into a smile. Izzy blabbered on and on and on about labor practices. The more she talked, the more I felt at home. It was a habit she'd developed at the dinner table. Mom and I could hardly speak to each other for very long before one of us picked a fight. Silence equaled a hot meal and an even-keeled night. Izzy would regularly monologue throughout entire three-course meals. She'd say our lines for us and keep the illusion that we were a happy, functioning family.

The lightning cracked close by, and I saw the sea lit up as if from a camera flash. Izzy was still droning on about sustainable tree farming and not indulging in the slave trade. What did she want from me? According to her, I was nothing but a secretive sea bitch captain. Did she want my secrets? Could she handle my secrets? Could I even speak my secrets out loud? Would she even care to hear them? They were my problems. There was no good reason she would want to take them on. There seemed little point in telling her anything now that she was just going to go home and move on with her life.

"I travel. A lot." I pried this one secret out of myself. I should have said time-travel. I time-travel a lot. This would have to do. My admission stopped the babble, but the wind picked up in the void of Izzy's voice. I wrapped my damp coat tight around myself against the chill.

"Yes. You love to sail."

"I sail." My god, it was like pulling up an enormous anchor. My secrets were never meant to be unearthed once buried. "I meet people. Not all good people. Mostly not good people."

The waves pounded against the sea wall. Izzy was quiet. I'm sure she was confused, but she offered a simple "Alright."

"I keep a lot of secrets for a lot of good reasons." I couldn't do it. I couldn't speak the words. I changed tactics like the coward I was. "It's easier not to get involved in the lives of ghosts. But," I hesitated, "sometimes I can't help it." Like when Graham's hand wandered up my skirts and found exactly what he was looking for. Like when he whirled

The Bitch Captain (and The Lady)

around a dance floor with me, wildcat grin, shocking the guests by passionately kissing me at the conclusion of a waltz. Like when I woke late at night to find him curled around me. Like when he laid his weight on me, kissed me, and sank—

"I wish you wouldn't call them that. Go on..." Izzy's voice doused my fantasy the same as the cold sea water beginning to spray in with each wave. This night was going to suck.

"It's what they are." I shrugged and turned to face her finally. The light was dim, but I could make out where she stood. "It's what you'll be if you choose to stay." I hadn't put that fact together until just now. If she stayed, if she married that man, she'd become a ghost.

Thunder quickly followed lightning. The storm was here.

"What a sad, lonely way to look at things." She stared back at me. "I don't understand you. How can you share a drink or a laugh with someone and think of them as a ghost? You have friends here, Anne!"

I've seen many of my so-called friends' graves; I knew exactly what they were.

"I have moments. I don't have friends, I have moments. And in those moments, I do what I can with what I have before they become gho—memories," I amended for her delicate sensibilities.

"Moments?"

"It means I drink with the ghosts sometimes too." The thunder boomed. "But I don't marry them." No matter how many times he asks.

The wind picked up, and I wondered how long Izzy was planning to stay here. It wasn't safe. Back home, Andrews and the family would be huddled together to wait out the storm. When I was with them during the stormy season, I would tell the children endless hours of stories to keep their minds off the wind and the cracking trees. I wished I was there with them now.

"What do I do about slavery?" she asked.

Jesus. I rubbed my temples. I guess she wasn't ready to leave yet.

"You don't have to do anything," I answered. "It's over. 1833, 1863.

It's done. Over two hundred years ago. It's done." She needed to get out of here. This storm was turning dangerous.

"It is not over. You tell that to Bessie, and the branded men on that boat and the bed slaves I met today. Done my ass." She gripped the bars and looked like she wanted to hit me.

"Get me out of here, and I'll tell them whatever you want!" My hand went absentmindedly to my own brand on the back of my neck, a souvenir of one of my earliest trips down a dark and winding path.

"When I get you out of here, are you going to try to snatch me off again?" The lightning lit up her face, and I saw she was serious. She didn't want me taking her away.

"Oh, Izzy, come on!" I protested. Staying here was insanity.

"I'm building a life here!" she insisted. I wanted to wrap her up and feed her strained peas. She couldn't possibly know what she wanted. She was a baby!

"You just got here!" I exclaimed. This was ridiculous!

"I know! Isn't it amazing!"

"Be real. You are not going to go off and marry Lt. Rando from the 17th century." The infantryman young lieutenant and my infant sister were not in love. They couldn't be. It was absurd.

"Yes, I am, Anne! I love him!" Izzy was pissed all over again now.

"You're going to get married? Without Mom?" It was a low blow, but my arsenal was depleted.

"Well, are you going to go and get her?"

"Hell no!" Pigs would fly and fire rain down from the sky making the most delicious bacon storm ever before I invited Mom on my boat for a journey back in time.

"Well, then, I guess it's happening without her, isn't it?" Wind swept in and blew the rushes on the floor around.

I shielded my face as best I could and tried to find my hat. The lightning cracked close by. Izzy didn't seem to notice or be concerned.

"And without any of the trinkets or heirlooms from my hope chest.

Such is life!" She threw her hands up in the air just in time for a wave to break against the prison wall and a huge spume of water to enter and soak me and half her dress.

Izzy shrieked, startled, as if this was the first time she was noticing the weather and the fact that there was no glass on the window. The young lieutenant burst into the room and swept her into his arms.

"Isabelle." He checked to be sure she wasn't hurt, just wet. "This storm is worsening. You cannot be down here." Thank god he had some common sense to his name.

"Wait, you're leaving her down here in this?!" Izzy gestured to me. The lieutenant and I rolled our eyes in synchronicity. Another spume of sea spray soaked the room and shook the mortar.

"You left me soap. I'll be fine and much cleaner." I grabbed the hunk of soap and pretended to wash my armpits in the spray. If she thought I was in too much danger, she'd never leave. "Get her out of here!" I growled at the lieutenant.

Thunder boomed again, and I was hit in the back with another spray of water. It knocked me as far as my chains allowed me to move. The noise of the storm was fantastic in the cell.

"What?!" She screamed, incredulous.

"Leave now!" I ordered at the same time that the lieutenant pulled Izzy toward the door yelling, "Isabelle, it's not safe for you down here."

"You can't leave her down here like this!" I thought I heard her yell from halfway up the stairs. The storm raged, and I couldn't hear anything other than the pounding rain and the wind and the thunder. I wrapped my coat around me and huddled as far from the window as possible. The sea doused me over and over.

Izzy's little basket of gifts wasn't far. I pulled it towards myself and found a little bowl of pesto and noodles. My favorite.

Three inches of water covered the floor of my cell by the time the young lieutenant returned. I held the basket tightly and tried to stay dry. The winds had died down along with the rain, and a soggy yellow light filled the window. We were in the eye of the storm.

The young lieutenant opened the door and hesitated a moment, looking mournfully at his clean, dry boots before splashing inside. He held a ring of keys.

"The storm is bound to pick up again soon, so do not interrupt me. For your...safety...I will unshackle you until it passes. Your sister will check on you in the morning to witness that you have not drowned, and then you will be chained again. One word, just one, of threat or deceit from you and I will return upstairs and refuse her wishes."

I stayed quiet.

"Good. Back against the wall," he instructed.

I did as I was told, and he unlocked the cell door and waded towards me.

"Whatever you think or believe, Isabelle and I are getting married in ten days. She esteems you highly – though I cannot imagine why – and would like you to attend. I would not." He busied himself finding the key to my irons. "I think you are too great a risk to her happiness. Am I correct? Would you ruin her wedding day and insist on making her fearful and sad on such a momentous occasion?" He held the key teasingly close to my shackles. "You may speak."

"If what she wants, what she really and truly wants is to marry you, then I won't interfere." I watched his face, not his hands, for signs he would follow through with unlocking me.

"You believe her acceptance is a ruse of some sort?"

"I believe that you barely know her. You come from different worlds and are rushing into a commitment neither one of you fully understands." I was risking my freedom with each syllable that left my lips. I needed to just shut up.

"You will earn your release the morning of our wedding. You will behave. And you will be there for your...sister. So help me, you will do this, or I will see you rot in this cell for eternity." He popped the locks of my shackles open and left with my chains over his shoulder. He slammed and locked the outer door, leaving me alone.

I rubbed at the deep sores on my wrists and waffled only a moment. The wind was beginning to pick up, and I was not going to waste this time. I was out of here. I stuffed what I could from the basket into my pockets and yanked the bars I had long ago replaced with vulcanized rubber from the window. I climbed up and out, dropped to the rocks below, replaced the "bars," and began sprinting and planning.

The wind was back and pelted me with the first rain drops from the south side of the storm. The town was boarded up tight and I didn't run into a single soul until close to the docks, where Dom raced up to me, soaked and terrified.

"Captain! Captain! It's gone! All of it!" he shouted while shoving a note in my hand.

Anne,
I've taken the cargo to The Phoenix. I didn't give your guards any choice.
— Lady Isabelle

What the hell was The Phoenix? I crumpled the note into my shirt as I boarded the ship and saw what Dom was talking about.

It was gone. All of it.

Every box, crate, sack, and container of goods I'd carefully cultivated over the past few years was gone.

Fucking Lady Isabelle.

I walked straight to the galley and launched her air fryer into the bay. Then I followed it with a few spatulas and a series of wooden spoons. Fuck! I kicked a hole in a cabinet. All of it was gone. Everything that had decorated my decks and cargo hold was gone. The thunder boomed, and I shook my head to clear it.

"I'm sorry." Mary came up next to me as I surveyed the empty hold. "The lady arrived with her lieutenant commander and many wagons and took everything. I couldn't stop them." Anything that hadn't been nailed down was gone. The boxes of foodstuffs, fabric, various luxury goods like plates and silverware, ivory, china, all gone. Nothing left but the stinking ambergris in the corner. I pulled down the false ceiling in my cabin and breathed a sigh of relief that my strongboxes were still there.

"Dom!" I shouted, and the boy appeared at my elbow. I shoved a bag full of coins at him. "Run to the blacksmith. Buy all the tools and woodworking equipment he has. Get them to deliver it in the next twenty minutes. If he can do it, there's double this amount waiting for him." Dom saluted and Mary watched in terror as I sent her son out into the burgeoning storm. "Twenty minutes. He'll be fine."

There was no sense mourning my lost cargo. I grabbed one of Izzy's precious kitchen knives and stabbed it through the note and into her door. I'd lost cargo before – never to someone I considered a friend, but I could build the stores back up later. It was a pain, it was expensive, but what needed to happen now was getting the hell out of St. George's forever.

While the children sat and shivered in my little kitchen, I did a quick engine check. I fully intended to get us out of this port and far away. In this storm I'd need an engine, not sails. Dom was back in record time with the old, chiseled blacksmith and his enslaved man pulling a heavily loaded wagon. The strong young man immediately began unloading the wagon onto the ship. I watched him with new eyes, thought about his life with new thoughts. Damn Izzy straight to hell.

I called the blacksmith over. "I have a proposition for you." I kicked open one of my strongboxes and watched the strong old man's eyes pop. "I'm building a shipyard far out on the western end of the island. I would like to hire you and I would like to hire that young man."

"My boy? Henry? You want to buy him from me?"

The Bitch Captain (and The Lady)

"Absolutely not. I want to hire him as a free man. You do this and you are both guaranteed good pay and good positions at my shipyard. We'll leave as soon as the wagon is unloaded. You have until that bank of clouds breaks to decide. Then I'm leaving."

The old man went to talk to his apprentice, and before long they both came over to me and shook my hand. The old man needed to make arrangements to move his entire industry to the west before settling out there, so I left Henry in trust of the old man's share of their onboarding pay to be delivered to the blacksmith upon his arrival.

The rain began sheeting down, and I called for Dom and Henry to get everything and everyone below decks. Mary came up to me, her eyes wide and terrified. "What are you doing?"

"We are going west."

"Now? In this? On this boat?" She was ready to bolt.

"Yes. Stay calm. Go down below. We'll be fine." I lied to her a little bit.

"Captain, I can't. I—"

"I killed Marius," I shouted over the wind and rain. Mary sat down hard, and her hand went to her swollen belly. The rain turned her threadbare dress almost transparent, and I saw she was much further along than I'd first suspected. I knelt down to be at her level and grabbed her hands. "I will not leave you in a bad position. I will see that you and your family are taken care of. I promise you that, Mary." I helped her down the stairs to the kitchen and saw a strange sight: a crowd of people in my ship. Their scared faces wet and staring. I had passengers on my ship. It felt wrong. I did not like it. My back crawled and the air felt thin.

"Listen," I started, "I'm going to sail us out in this storm. Stay in this kitchen. Do not mind the noises you hear. Do not come above until I tell you it's safe." I fairly fled back up the stairs and jammed the engine start.

St. George's was a ghost town with its windows boarded and inhabitants huddled inside. No one would be looking out their window at the ship moving against the wind in this screaming storm.

The ship tossed and rolled and bucked against the rudder. I kept us pointing into the waves and upright. I was buying time, if not much distance. Once far from the island, I called Henry and Dom up to begin loosening the sails.

The sea was boiling around my prow. We made slow but steady progress west. I aimed us towards the backside of the storm and attempted to sail us out beyond it. Three hours later, Dom and Henry were waterlogged and grinning and whooping their way up and down my masts, my kitchen smelled strongly of sick, and I was shaking from the effort of steering through a hurricane after weeks of little food and bad sleep. We sailed through the night this way.

When the sun broke through the clouds, Dom, Henry, and I cheered and celebrated. Henry was younger than I even imagined. There were barely five or six years between the two boys. I brought everyone up on deck and ordered the windows opened in the galley. We had an excellent view of the end of the storm crossing over the island. I held on tight to Mary and whispered constant reassurances to her that we were fine. She was still terrified. I encouraged her to go lie down, but the words and concept were foreign to her and she refused to leave my side.

The older boys raised the sails, and we began the true journey to the west of the island. Bettie, Mary's oldest girl, brought me up some food and drink, and I was feeling elated after cheating death over and over again with each wave we crested, so I put the girl's hands on the wheel and gave her an impromptu sailing lesson. The boys looked on with jealousy as I shared my captain-y secrets with her, secrets such as "Sail that way," "Now keep sailing that way." The two little ones ran to and fro on the decks, scaring Mary into paroxysms of panic until I tied long ropes around their middles and the other ends around the railing. They'd be fine.

It was oddly delightful to see so much activity on my lonely little

The Bitch Captain (and The Lady)

ship. Usually she and I crossed these oceans together in silent dedication to each other. In a very esoteric and otherworldly way, I thought my ship felt happier and lighter to have these little voices ringing out in praise and fun about this little jaunt around the island.

Mary held white-knuckled onto the railing next to me. "There!" I pointed out to her the small encampment barely visible on the shore. "That's the location of the shipyard." Mary was unimpressed. "You'll be safe there. It'll be a better life," I encouraged her.

"I've heard those words before." Her voice was thin and shaking.

I tried to rub some warmth into her shoulders but gave up; she was frozen. Instead I went and pulled Izzy's comforter off her bed and wrapped it around my friend. Izzy didn't need it anymore…I added it to the list of things Izzy didn't feel she needed anymore: modern plumbing, denim jeans, suffrage, a hope chest of trinkets, her mother at her wedding, me.

The water was deep off this end of the island. Large ships could pull up close to the shore, which made it ideal for a shipyard. I knew for a fact that Izzy wouldn't own this land for long. Within a century the British Navy would take it over and use it for their own expansion purposes.

I moored the *Try Your Luck* and rowed my passengers the short distance to land. Michael Davies and a motley crew of what looked to be uneducated and malnourished laborers met my rowboat on the shore.

"Captain!" Davies beamed. He was a tall, wiry man with a face that never seemed to grow old. He was a boundless well of optimism despite his repeated failures. "I'm heartened to see you released at last." He shook my hand vigorously.

"They can't keep us down, can they, Davies?" I always responded well to his optimism.

"No, madam, they can't. They try, boy, do they try! But we prevail." He grinned and I was reminded of the energetic teenager tagging after Andrews and me, hoping to pick up the scraps of business we left behind. The two of us had tried to set Davies up time and time again in all kinds of positions, but it never took.

"Let me introduce you to Mary." I brought Mary forward, and Davies kissed her hand. She was still unsteady from the boat. "Mary and her family are relocating here. She's been hired as the grounds manager and will manage the division of labor and distribution of resources." Mary looked at me agape.

"Wonderful!" Davies exclaimed. "I was just ordered to hire women! I'm enjoying the novelty of it all. Thank you for taking this on, Mary!" He kissed her hand again before letting go.

Mary was bewildered. I hadn't told her she'd be employed here as I knew she'd refuse if I gave her time to think about it. Next I introduced Henry, and Dom as Henry's new apprentice. The two boys thought this was a terrific bit of subterfuge and didn't say a word to the contrary. I explained that the older blacksmith was also hired and would arrive in a few days.

Davies invited us all up to the main encampment, and I got a first-hand view of how slipshod this operation was. Mary was immediately in crisis-solving mode and got to work delegating the unskilled labor into minor and major chores to begin setting up a workable camp. She'd managed her huge family and small farm all by herself for years and was a natural. Henry and Dom scouted out a good area for a forge and went out for Dom's first lesson: how to chop a shit ton of wood for forge fires. Dom came back for dinner blistered and happy.

I had planned to drop and run, but the idea of designing and producing my own brand of ship off my own shipyard line was entrancing. I spent three days drawing out designs and construction plans for an ideal merchant ship. Not that I had any plans of giving up the *Try Your Luck*, but these babies would be gorgeous. I grilled Davies on production methods and drafted several letters he was to post to my various contacts throughout the Caribbean and the African coast whom I knew to be expert engineers and skilled shipbuilders.

The Bitch Captain (and The Lady)

Three times I tried to pack up. Three times. I had the anchor up and everything only to remember one last bit of advice and expertise I wanted to impart. Before I knew it, Davies and Mary and I were having dinner together again and discussing the finer points of the assembly line.

Then, of course, the old blacksmith arrived, and I couldn't very well leave without setting him up and introducing him around.

The morning of the eighth day, I had to face facts. I was dragging my feet. The wedding was two days away, and I needed to decide to go home without Izzy or stay and watch her be relegated to the history books. It was shit-or-get-off-the-pot time. Either option meant sailing: Andrews' dock was several hours away, the portal slightly farther. I packed in earnest this time.

"Where to now, Captain?" Davies asked, the same as all the other times he'd walked me to the ship the past few days.

"Home. I think."

"If I don't see you in an hour," he chuckled and patted my shoulder, "I wish you a happy homegoing."

"Thanks, Davies. Don't lose all my money."

"Your money? This is the Lady Isabelle—"

"Until the lady's family money comes in, I am providing the start-up capital. The money you'll be losing is mine," I warned.

His eyes bugged and his mouth gaped open.

"Captain, perhaps I'm not—"

"You are." I held out my hand and shook his firmly. "We all just need the right opportunity, and this is yours. Don't fuck it up." I climbed aboard my rowboat, and Davies pushed me into the water. "Get this dock built!" I shouted back to him as the waves took me out.

Mary had walked down to stand with Davies, and I waved to the two of them, wondering how much of a wager they had on whether I'd really leave this time or not.

I stowed the rowboat upside down on the aft deck and looked back to the island. Somewhere in there was my sister, my 21st-century sister, choosing to stay. I raised my sails, turned toward the wind, and chose to leave.

An hour out, I began the search for my buoy. The last time I was here, a storm was rolling in and Izzy was shut in her cabin, high and furious. I dropped anchor and rowed over to the buoy and hauled up the capsule. I checked to make sure no new notes were added (that happened occasionally) and pulled out a new sheet. I dated it and began.

August 6th, 1649

> *Mary is fine. You killed her husband for her finally.*
> *Blew up the inn.*
> *Burned and cut up the Puritans.*
> *Imprisoned a few weeks*
> *Andrews almost convinced me to marry him*
> *No news of Edmund*
> *Dom is growing up too fast*
> *Izzy married the young lieutenant*
> *You may not return here.*

CHAPTER 10

Home Again Home Again

Quiet. Everything was...quiet.

Mary and her family had filled the ship with noise. Izzy had yammered and sung from sunup to sundown. She had made me laugh, and the leagues had disappeared beneath my hull.

It was quiet now.

Even a month ago, silence had never bothered me on my ship. Why did it bother me now? I found myself humming old tunes and blasting music from my phone once I was free of the portal. The lap of the waves against the fiberglass-and-teak ship wasn't as soothing and melodic as it normally was.

It took about two weeks between leaving Izzy's shipyard and pulling into the bay at home. The house was bright in the morning sunshine, the dock ready and waiting for my ship. There it was, waiting for me as always, another home I thought I'd left behind me only to sail back to, time and time again: Heron's Landing.

Heron's Landing for all your special occasion needs, both great and small! Step back in time and stay at our luxurious historic mansion, where you'll experience delights unavailable anywhere else on the Eastern seaboard. Our boutique resort features unparalleled bay views from every room, culinary farm to table delights prepared by an on-site chef, and a variety of activities on our 15-acre estate.

The old mansion-turned-resort was the same except now Izzy wasn't there waiting for me. She wouldn't come out to greet me at the dock and ask how my trip was or exclaim over how I never seemed to pack enough food. I'd wrecked that for myself. I'd stolen her from her life and turned her into a ghost. Her blood was on my hands now, along with all the others.

I laid out the solar panels to charge on the deck and stowed the sails, all while continuously looking back at the house out of habit. Normally she'd be trotting down the yard toward me. The Bitch Captain of the Seven Seas had finally destroyed the final place she could call home. I patted my ship; it was just the two of us now.

My phone had zero messages. No one here to talk to anymore. It was a Tuesday morning. Mom would be out for some mimosa breakfast with the old biddies. I shoved all my dirty clothes in a sack and hiked up to the house.

Once I got the laundry started, I turned my music up loud enough to drown out the voices in my head and got in the shower. I was a filthy mess. My hair was matted and greasy. Dirt was caked into my soul, I swear. I lathered gently around my wrists and various other wounds and let the hot water run over me until it gave out. I reveled in soft towels and fell asleep in fabric softener-scented sheets.

I woke up when the music was suddenly shut off.

"Anne?" My mother was at the door to my room, her mimosa-drinking dress slightly wrinkled from the drive home in her car. "I thought you were going to be away all summer. It's barely been a week."

I sat up and wiped the grogginess from my eyes. "There was a change in plans." I kept the sheet low around me to hide my legs and grabbed some clothes, an unceremonious jeans and t-shirt combo, and dressed out of her sight in the bathroom.

"Is she alright?" Mom called from outside the door.

"She's fine." I exited the bathroom and tried to ignore how loose the clothes hung on me.

"Well, you are looking nice." She evaluated me. Six weeks of

The Bitch Captain (and The Lady)

near-starvation will help you drop a few dress sizes. It was always irritating to me to come back to this era where life-giving calories were derided and I was hailed as healthy and fit when I'd literally been starving to death.

"I'm hungry. Is there food in the house?"

"No," she answered, pulling out her phone. She was dialing up her hairdresser. "Yes, we'll be right in." Mom tossed me some shoes. "Finished getting dressed. We have to do something about your hair, and then I'll take you to lunch."

"Mom, I don't—"

"Not a request, Anne. I'll meet you in the car." She high-heeled away, and there was no use arguing. God, she was so annoying! I pulled on a pair of tennis shoes and stomped down the stairs to the garage.

We didn't speak the whole drive to the salon. Then I was the only one not speaking as my mom and her stylist, Guillaume, nattered on and on about the state of my hair. Guillaume picked and pulled and brushed and cut and conditioned me into a coma.

I felt unrecognizable by the time he was finished. My hair lay in glossy sheets around my shoulders, and he looked like he needed a smoke and a Medal of Honor. Mom was ecstatic and tipped him generously. I studied myself in the mirror as she paid. I enjoyed the play of light over my hair and swished the locks around to feel how soft it was. I hardly ever looked in mirrors or reflective surfaces anymore. What was there to see? There wasn't even a mirror in my cabin. I'd smashed it a long time ago and never bothered to fix it. I wasn't terrible-looking, and my hair did look really nice. I twirled a lock around my finger. Graham would have thought it looked nice too.

"Ready, Anne?" Mom asked. "I made our lunch reservation just around the corner at Maison de Jouissance." I got up from the chair.

"Great. It's my treat." I was feeling buoyant and pretty. I could pry open my accounts and pay a few bucks for lunch.

Going out to eat was an old trick of ours to reduce the chances of ending a meal in a fight. When Izzy wasn't home, we rarely ate at the table together. We both tried harder not to piss the other one off when we were surrounded by ears. I ordered the heaviest items on the menu and a glass of red. Mom got a light salad with pears and a glass of rosé.

We managed to get through one drink staying on the topic of my hair and Guillaume before Izzy came up again.

"So, where is she?" she asked in a casual-not-casual-at-all tone.

"She's fine. She just – didn't want to come back. She met someone." My eyes began to burn, and I wiped at them.

"And she started spending a lot of time with him or her or them?"

"Him."

"Him?"

"Yeah."

"And that meant she had less time for you?" Mom sipped her wine too casually.

"It's not like that. I'm not jealous. Mom, she wants to marry this guy. She hardly knows him!" My voice cracked, betraying me, just like my eyes. Mom handed me a napkin, and I wiped the stupid tears off my stupid face again.

"Izzy has always wanted a family of her own. It doesn't mean she's leaving you behind." She tried to put her hand on mine, but I pulled away. I couldn't bring my face out of the napkin. My shoulders shook as I inexplicably cried in the middle of this French restaurant.

"Yes, it does." My voice was rough as I sobbed into the napkin. This time Mom patted my shoulder, and I didn't shrug her off.

"No, Anne. Izzy's adding to her life, not subtracting. She'd never leave you." Mom's simple words cut deep. Izzy hadn't left. I'd left. I'd left because I'm a great big coward. I'd left her stranded centuries ago.

"Have they set a date?" she asked.

"Mom!" I cried out. Of all the questions she could ask – should ask! She wanted to know the date?

"It's a logical question." She defended herself like I was the crazy one. Her too-young daughter was getting married to some random guy she had never met, and here Mom was, wondering about dates?

"Yes." It was in two days. Sort of. "She doesn't know what she's doing. She's too young."

"She's older than I was when I married your father."

"And look how well that turned out."

"Tact, Anne," she reprimanded me. "Izzy is different from us. She understands people. I'm not surprised she made a connection so quickly."

"It's only been a week, Mom. This is insanity." It had only been a week for her, at least.

"Feels longer." Our food was delivered, and Mom nibbled at her salad in silence while I went to work on my gravy-laden plate.

"I cannot believe you are okay with this." I stabbed a bite of potato.

"I cannot believe you took her with you." She countered with a pear. "I imagine the wedding is too far for me to attend?" My eyes flashed to her face. She was too cool and collected with that statement. I'd always suspected she knew more about my affairs than she let on.

"Yes." To put it mildly.

"Then I'll have to put together a gift for her. You will take it with you and deliver it."

"Mom, I'm not going." I stabbed another piece of potato but didn't eat it.

"Yes, you are. Isabelle is not getting married without her family," she insisted. "And since I can't go," she paused, weighting the moment with her words, "you will."

We ate in silence until the wine was gone and our plates cleared. My curiosity burned away at me the whole time. "Mom," I ventured, "do you—"

"Whether you want to see it or not, Diane, you are very much like your father." She halted me before I could say anything more damning than I already had. "Now let's go. We have some stops to make." Mom stood up and high-heeled it from the table faster than I'd have thought possible on such thin stilettos.

Over the next few days Mom drove me all over the place. In addition to various wedding gifts and attire, I was able to buy bulk supplies for the ship, which was an unusual relief to my preparation responsibilities. I loaded my ship up with MREs, protein bars, candy, rice, salt, and anything else that wouldn't need refrigeration or that the humidity couldn't attack and spoil. Mom went around the house wrapping items and writing a long card. She had found Izzy's hope chest and pilfered many of her gifts from there.

Then she asked about the dress.

"What's Izzy planning on wearing, do you know?" She was pulling dresses out of her closet.

"I hadn't thought about it." I didn't want to think about it now.

"She'll need something beautiful. Will any of these work?" Mom laid out many of her designer-label gowns, and I looked them over, shaking my head.

"I don't think so. No."

"Surely you can get her something, wherever she is." She continued diving through her closet.

I felt the velvet nap of the closest gown and shrugged.

"What will you wear?" She eyed the gown I was touching. "Would you like that one?"

It was a fancy gown, a rich Merlot color. With a few adjustments I could make it look period-appropriate. Andrews would love the feel of the velvet as we danced. No. Stop. No. I wasn't doing this. I would go to the wedding, give her the gifts, and leave. No dancing. Besides, if I was going to wear a fancy dress, I would wear...

"Wait, I do have something." I left Mom in her closet and went to my ship and pulled out my embroidered gown from under the mattress then returned to the house. I spread the gown out on her bed. Without the petticoats and bustle underneath it didn't look distractingly historical. Mom was entranced. She ran her hands up and down the embroidery and the rich silk underneath.

"Anne, this is beautiful. Did you make it?" She examined the seams and hem. I nodded. "This must have taken you—" She stopped herself and looked steadfastly at the dress, not at me. "It needs dry cleaning. Marchaud's will do a rush order on the dry cleaning for us. Come on." She scooped up the gown carefully, and we were back in the car and driving again.

While we waited for the dry cleaners to work on the dress, Mom took me next door to get our nails done. Hers were pristine, of course, but I couldn't tell you the last time any polish had been on a nail of mine. It was somewhat relaxing, I guess. I only let them put clear polish on. Mom was distracted. She wasn't nitpicking at me or pressuring me for one color or another. She stared into space as the nail tech filed and coated and dried her hands. Overall, we were having the most pleasant day the two of us might have ever shared.

On the drive back home, she continued her out-of-character thoughtful silence until we were in our neighborhood. "You should give her something. It's tradition at a wedding to give the bride a trinket. Why don't you do borrowed?"

"What are you talking about?" I'd been lost in thought too. I hadn't expected to leave again so soon and was checking weather patterns on my phone.

"You know perfectly well what I'm talking about," she snapped.

I put my phone down and raised my eyebrows at her. This was much closer to our usual energy.

"Surely you have some trinket or other that you can let her borrow for the ceremony?" She tried and failed to sound calm.

"I said I'd go to the wedding. None of my stuff needs to be held hostage to make sure I witness the whole thing," I snapped back.

"It's tradition." She stopped the car somewhat short at a stop sign, jerking me forward in my seat. She was angry.

I rolled my eyes and went back to my phone. We were almost home. I had dared to dream I might escape a trip home without fighting with her.

"I'll find something," I mumbled. The concession appeared to mollify her. Once home, I pulled the dress out and wrapped it carefully in cloth and stowed it in its spot under my bunk.

Mom was already up. She was the only one I knew who was awake and moving as consistently early as myself most days. Our similarities started and ended with this morning-person persona. She read the morning news as I studied weather reports and made lists in my notebook. Today was my last day here. The weather was on point for departure, and I'd concluded all my restocking yesterday. I'd be on the water for dinner tonight. A few days to reach the portal, another week once I exited, and then I'd be docking at Andrews'.

Electricity exploded down my stomach: Andrews, Izzy's wedding, Bermuda so close to the stake...I wanted to crawl back under my covers.

"Tell me about him," Mom asked as we sipped our coffee. She wanted more information about the young lieutenant. I hadn't been very forthcoming about the man. One, I didn't know much. And two, I hated him.

"He's fine," I grumbled.

"What's his name? I don't think you've told me yet." Mom had pulled out her wedding card and fancy pen.

The Bitch Captain (and The Lady)

I really wish she'd chosen less flashy paper and colors but, nothing doing, Vivienne St. Germaine was going to write her daughter the card she wanted to write. I refocused on her questions. What was the young lieutenant's name? Huh. That was a head-scratcher.

"Ross? Roger? Something like that." There was a developing storm in the southern hemisphere I was keeping an eye on. It wouldn't hit me here, but would the 17th century be experiencing similar conditions? I made a note in my book.

"Does Ross or Roger have a last name?"

"I don't know. Probably," I mumbled.

"Diane, I am not amused." My mom slammed her hand down and made me jump. "My daughter is getting married. You will remember, and you will tell me about my new son-in-law. Do you really care that little for me and your sister?" Her cheeks were red and her knuckles white around her mug.

I met her stare and felt for the first time how deeply my mother was lying to both herself and to me. She was going to miss her daughter's wedding. The only wedding she'd ever believed she'd get to throw. She was missing her daughter's life – she'd already missed so much of mine. Her manner and words had been light regarding preparations to send me back, but underneath that veneer were depths of sorrow. She was missing everything. I could relate.

I closed my eyes and searched my memory. The young lieutenant had introduced himself to me at the dock. Surely Izzy had mentioned his name when she visited me in prison…

"Ian. His name is Ian. I don't—" What the hell was his surname? "Cov – Cov-something. Covington." It was close enough. When Izzy was done with this fling, she could tell Mom his full name herself. We'd sit around this table together, and she could tell Mom all sorts of stories about her blue-eyed lover, just like she had told Mom about falling in love with my friend Maui when I sailed her to Cabo.

"Ian Covington?" Mom asked.

"Yes." Probably. Mom brought the envelope in front of her and wrote their names in bold silver calligraphy. I did not like seeing those letters intertwined together.

"And he's a soldier?"

"A lieutenant."

"That makes sense. She has a type." Mom made a final silver flourish.

Maui had fought wars too. Telling Izzy that my best friend, her first love, had died in battle was one of my hardest moments. When I thought back on it, that was the start of the two of us drifting apart.

"And he loves her? She loves him?" Mom was thoughtful as she held the silver pen over the cardstock.

The memory of the two of them looking at each other with such trust and tenderness on my last night in prison flashed through my mind. It only served to highlight how lonely I felt. "Yes."

"She loves you too." It was nice of her to try.

I messed around with the toast on my plate and didn't realize she was looking at me until I looked up a minute later. I nodded my head and quickly looked away.

I thought she'd gone back to writing until she asked, "What happened to your wrists?"

I quickly pulled my sleeves lower and my hands away. Mom reached out to lay her fingertips on the back of my hands to stop me. Her small touch was stronger than the iron manacles; I couldn't move. I rarely came to Heron's Landing broken, bleeding, in pain, or wrapped and bandaged. It was a bad idea to expose my mother and sister to the dangerous life I led. Their questions were more vicious than blades.

"Don't hide them—" Mom's voice caught, but I couldn't look past her manicured nails resting on my rough, tanned skin. "Stop hiding, Anne. Talk to me. Tell me—"

"I need to check the cargo hold," I interrupted her. She and Izzy talked. She and Izzy could tell each other things. They always could. I was the third wheel in this family. I needed to go. Nothing was out of order on my ship, but I couldn't be in this kitchen any longer.

The boat was loaded. The tides were right. If I was going to leave before dark, the time was now. I looked up at the lonely house and saw my mother on her way towards me with a bundle in her hands. It was the velvet dress.

"Take it. It'll look beautiful on you." She pressed the dress into my arms.

I nodded my thanks and accepted her gift. While my hands were full of velvet, and before I could protest, she wrapped her arms around me. I stood there in shock.

"Come back to me someday, Anne." She threw caution to the wind and kissed my cheek.

I nodded. "I will."

"Fair winds, following seas," she whispered in my ear.

I hugged her back. When we let go, she wiped her eyes and went back to the house where I'm sure a glass of wine was waiting for her. Once my ship hit the open water, I opened my own bottle and wondered at what I had thought this trip would be and what this journey had actually become.

CHAPTER 11

Home Sweet Bermuda Home

Andrews' dock was on the north shore of his property, and I sailed straight for it. The sun was just graying the horizon, plenty of light for me to sail by. Once my ship was secured, I opened the secret compartment under my bunk that held the beautiful embroidered dress and caressed the threads, admiring my work again. Carefully, I rewrapped the dress and petticoats in the clean fabric.

My hair had lost some of the sheen and lightness Guillaume had beaten into it. I brushed it out and reviewed myself as best I could in my broken cabin mirror. I was sleep-deprived and thin, with bags under my eyes and hollow cheeks, but at least my hair was acceptable. I shook out the velvet dress Mom had given me. As I sailed back here, I'd reworked the design into a simple A-line pattern semi-appropriate for the time. It was not as full or decorated as the other women's were sure to be, but it would do. Time to get dressed. I sighed. Today I was to be a lady.

I layered on a freshly-laundered shift and corset and added petticoats. Together it all shaped and billowed out Mom's rich velvet gown until I was confident and "wedding-ready" for a day in 1649. I put on my soft designer boots and remembered how, just a few weeks ago, they had squeezed against my swollen calf. That wound was mostly healed now. With all the weight I'd lost in prison and on my solo boat rides through the portal, the boots were more than roomy enough. In fact, everything was too roomy. I'd need to see what I could do about getting better nutrition before I lost too much more muscle.

Time to get off the ship, Anne, I pressured myself, but my feet were acting stubborn. It's not like I could hide here. Before long, the household would wake up to the sight of my oh-so-familiar ship docked in its oh-so-familiar place, and I'd be found out. Move, Anne.

How was it that I walked free and easy into taverns loaded with pirates and danger and yet this bright manor in the sunrise caused me distress? I gritted my teeth and lifted the embroidered wedding dress in one arm. In my other arm was the sack that held the many presents from my mother and the one very small one from me – something for her to borrow. Izzy was somewhere up there. Andrews was up there too. I was confident about neither reception. I silently promised my ship that I would be back soon and took a step away from assured safety.

How many times can one person leave a place? How many times can she come back? I knew every inch of this estate, my feet knew each and every footfall. I did not have to think about where I was going. I was going home. The dining room entryway flew open, and Amelia beamed at me from the dimly-lit interior.

"Auntie!" The beautiful girl wrapped me in a hug. "I knew you'd be back."

She might as well have knifed me in the gut. All too soon there'd be a time when I left and would never walk through these doors again. I held her tight.

"I had some trouble in St. George's," I told her.

She helped me put my items on the table and led me into the kitchen. Just as my sister would have done, she brought me a mug of coffee and a little plate of food. She and Angelica were just warming the ovens for breakfast. Soon the whole space would be filled with loaves of bread, pastries, and doughnuts for the whole estate to come and break their fast.

"Auntie Von told us you were in prison there." She lightly ran her

The Bitch Captain (and The Lady)

fingers over the bandages of my still-healing wrists. "I wish you had stayed here. We would have taken care of you."

"I know, Amy." *They need you to say yes just as much as I do.* Amelia was a gentle soul. She was kind to all the spiders in her kitchen and to the butterflies on her flowers yet could butcher a chicken without blinking. "I hope I didn't worry you." I held her hands till she could meet my eyes and put a small smile on her face.

"I know you are strong." Her eyes drifted back to my wraps.

"Almost as strong as you." Now she smiled in earnest. "This," I held up the small pastry, "is delicious. Did you make it?"

"Yes! The lady staying with us – she's getting married today – she taught me about using figs in the pastry. She had so many good things to say about the knives you gifted me." Amelia got up and was dancing about the kitchen much the same as I remembered Izzy doing at about her age. The sudden allusion to my sister knocked the wind out of me. Izzy had been right here. Izzy had been in this kitchen, using those knives, teaching this girl about pastries.

Izzy was upstairs.

Andrews was upstairs.

I owed both of them explanations.

"The gifts on the table, they're for her wedding," I told the young chef.

"Lady Isabelle will love them, I'm sure! Perhaps when she's up, I can introduce you?"

"In truth, I know Isabelle very well. She's my sister."

Crash.

Amelia and I both turned to observe Angelica, just steps inside the kitchen, now surrounded by dropped pots and pans. Amelia sprang to her aunt's side and picked up the iron implements.

"Auntie, you've never mentioned family. I wish we had known, there's so much—"

"Amelia, go find your mother." Angelica interrupted her. Amelia ducked her head and left the kitchen.

"Angelica—" I started.

"She didn't tell us and we didn't know." Angelica slammed a written recipe down on her worktable. The writing on it was Izzy's. She began assembling ingredients. "Yvonne told us she arrived on your ship. Andrews said she spoke with your accent, she knew your words. We are hosting the lady's wedding – "

"Angelica, please—"

"She didn't tell us. She didn't tell us because she didn't know about us. Just like we didn't know about her." The woman aggressively refilled my coffee. "Do we mean so little to you? Does Andrews?"

"Angelica, please. It's not like that. You know you all mean the world to me."

"But just don't tell the world we are here, is that it? Where in heaven's name does she think you've been her whole childhood?"

"I visit her as often as I can." Angelica scoffed at my response and put a plate of sausages and crepes in front of me. Ah, guilt and pastries; it was good to be home.

"And of course Andrews behaved atrociously." Angelica began beating her frustrations into a mass of dough. "If he had known she was your relation – he might have at least saved that plate. I loved that set of dishes." She was upset, and I knew it wasn't entirely about her dishes. Angelica was affected deeply by her family's behavior. She took our behavior as a reflection on herself. When Yvonne, myself, and Andrews were particularly uncouth and wild, Angelica would spend every meal lecturing the three of us and do little things out of spite like refuse to make pasta for a month.

"I'll replace the dishes," I assured her. Clearly the broken dish was my fault – how, I didn't know yet (I was sure Angelica would let me know as she loved blaming me for things). Whatever, I'd replace it anyway.

"The ones with the tiny flowers and birds." Angelica was still pounding away.

"I know."

"Anne." Helene summoned me from the dining room entry. The principal had arrived. I left my plate and coffee and went to take my medicine.

She sat in her chair at the table, and I went to mine.

"You may not ruin this wedding." She leveled a finger at me.

"I don't ruin—"

Helene scoffed and sat back.

"I brought gifts." I gestured to the items in front of me. "I mean to make this affair as pleasant as possible." As stupid as this wedding was, I wasn't going to ruin it for my sister. She would look back on it fondly.

"You will be perfect. You will ensure Andrews comports himself as the consummate host and gentleman. When you sit down for breakfast, you will be the picture of charm and grace." What the hell had Andrews done that I was in so much reflected trouble because of it?

"I will," I assured her.

"The household is waking. Make your way upstairs or make your excuses and leave. If you choose to stay, promise me that you will be a credit to this family." The formidable woman didn't wait for my response. She stood and made her way back to her house in the early morning light.

Izzy would be upstairs in the west wing of bedrooms in the room Andrews reserved for visiting noblewomen. If I turned right at the top of the staircase, I could climb into bed with Andrews and delay being face to face with my sister for an hour...or two...or three. There was still the chance that she would refuse to have me anywhere near her and send me away. If that was the case, there was no need to wake Andrews from a sound sleep.

Left. I turned left.

I steeled myself to accept any verbal abuse Izzy intended to rain down on me and knocked. Fuck. Fuck. Fuck. I should leave.

A small woman answered the door. "May I help you?" The young woman was still in her night clothes and partially hid herself behind the door.

"I'm sorry, I'm looking for Lady Isabelle. Can you direct me to her room?" I knew this house inside and out, and this was supposed to be the room for celebrated guests. Maybe Izzy had opted for one of those ridiculous tents outside. I knew how she felt about this place.

"The lady is not yet awake. I am her maid. I can help with anything you require." The young woman stifled a yawn.

Behind her a small girl – couldn't be older than twelve or thirteen – stirred under a pile of blankets. How many people were in this room? I had planned on seeing Izzy alone, not surrounded by an entourage of strange women. I suppose beggars can't be choosers.

"Lady Isabelle's captain has arrived and would like to speak with her." I put some authority behind my voice to cow the young woman… it worked a little too well. The small maid's face displayed shock…and something else I couldn't put my finger on. At any rate, she opened the door and directed me to the nearest chaise. I was in.

The room was chock-full of expensive wedding gifts, and suddenly my small sack of trinkets felt decidedly inadequate. I held the gown tighter. I knew what the garment meant to me, but in the midst of all this finery, perhaps she'd want something else, something less…less me.

"I have some gifts for the lady as well," I said before the maid could disappear. I indicated my sack and she gestured to the pile. Right. Stupid. Why would my gifts need to stand out at all? I slid the small sack over with my foot.

"Anne?" Izzy's voice, rough and wary, sounded from the dark doorway to the bedroom. She moved into the light slightly. She was scared. She was scared of me. I felt like shit, but I'd committed to being here and so I'd take my medicine.

"The lieutenant invited me. I hope you don't mind." I attempted a calm smile and didn't move. Izzy still looked ready to bolt. "I'm not going to take you away." I put my hands up, open, nonthreatening. She needed more. "I heard you when you said you were building a life here. I'm not going to leave you either. Not unless you tell me to go." Which she might, I cautioned my expectations.

She was choosing her new family now, and despite what Mom said about adding people to her life instead of subtracting them, there was every chance Izzy would take this opportunity to replace me with someone who could actually protect and care for her. Someone who wouldn't kidnap her.

Izzy broke from her trance and embraced me in a hug I didn't realize I needed. I missed her. I wrapped my own arms around her and held on for dear life.

"Thank you, Anne," Izzy cried into my shoulder.

"I love you, Izzy," I whispered quietly so the others in the room couldn't hear. Two more faces had appeared at the bedroom door.

There were few people in this world who openly and willingly touched me. I spent most of my life starved for physical touch; hugs like this quickly overwhelmed me. I'd need to ease back into how effusive my sister was. I backed away for a moment to recover.

"I brought you a dress. I didn't know if you had one." I unwrapped part of the gown and held it out for her.

The four other girls in the room rushed me, and I put my instincts on lockdown so as not to strike them as they swarmed me and took the garment. The maid produced a clothes valet from thin air and displayed the entire thing, petticoats and all, for the women to admire. I recognized one of the women as Lady Catherine, the young wife of the asshole who was so fond of throwing me in prison.

They oohhed and aahhed over the gown, and I felt oddly warm to this funny group of females for their admiration. Years of effort went into this gown. They were enthralled with the intricacy of the embroidery and imaginative depictions of faraway lands. I have to admit I got swept up in their joy and found myself smiling and pointing out different elements of the dress to them. It was an unexpected treat to have my work praised like this. I actually found myself telling a detailed story of how I acquired the thread for certain details in a middle-eastern bazaar.

Izzy stayed back behind the jumping, exclaiming girls. I turned to check on her, wondering if she was disappointed with the gown.

"Wow. You really did go home," she accused.

I backed away from the other girls and wondered how to defend myself. I had needed to escape, and I had seized my opportunity. Was coming back here for her significant enough of a gesture to erase that sin? I loved Izzy but not so much that I would stay chained to the wall in a disgusting prison forever for her. I'll take my punishments, but I'll also take my chance at living when given the opportunity – show me the person who wouldn't.

"Marchaud's, right?" Izzy asked, indicating the newly-cleaned dress. Marchaud's were our dry cleaners back home. "You saw Mom?"

"She sent you something." No sense denying the proof of my homegoing. I opened the small sack of gifts and pulled out the ridiculously extravagant card Mom had written Izzy. I had argued with her over the stationery choice and begged her to choose different paper, different ink, less silver, but she'd have none of it. She was writing her daughter this card, this way, and that was the end of it. I'd relented, banking on the assumption that when I delivered it to Izzy, she'd be alone. This clown car of a bedroom would make it much more difficult to hide and subsequently burn this damning evidence of the future.

Izzy took the card back to her bed in the early morning sunshine and welled up reading each word. I stood in the doorway watching her. She shouldn't be here. This was wrong. She should be with her mother on her wedding day, not four strangers and a murderer, four hundred years before she was even born. The journal didn't lie, though. I had been blown to times and tides I was unprepared for and suffered greatly

The Bitch Captain (and The Lady)

for it. The brand on the back of my neck was only the start of it. It was wrong to take her, it was wrong to leave her; it would have been worse to let her face all of this alone and unprepared.

All that was left to me was to work with what I had. I was here now, and I would stay just as long as I could. Today that meant watching my sister marry a ghost. The young lieutenant had given me my marching orders, and I was going to follow them. I would behave, and I would be there for my sister, to support her through this and catch her when it all fell apart.

I walked into the room with the sack of trinkets and sat next to her on the bed. "Come on. There's more. Let's get all the tears out at once." I pulled out the gifts, one by one, which Mom had labeled "old," "new," and "blue." There was a veil, a pair of shoes, and some earrings. They each dropped like bombs on her. I sat patiently as she absorbed the impacts of these items and squeezed the last gift in my hand. She wouldn't understand it. I knew there was no way she would understand. In order for her to understand, I would have to crack open secret vaults so sunken and protected it might kill us both to dredge them up.

"This one isn't a gift. It's something for you to borrow." I opened my hand and pulled out the small seashell with a tiny hole drilled through it and laced with tough braided grass. It wasn't pretty enough for her, but I tied it to her wrist anyway. I'd only tied it on one other person, and it wasn't pretty enough then either. "I got it a long time ago. I thought maybe you'd think it's nice."

I watched the small shell dangle from her wrist and worked hard to pull my hand away. Regardless of whether I ever saw it again, this tiny thing should not hold such sway over me. Maybe I should have just given her my silver helmet instead. I almost reached for it back but checked myself just in time. Izzy would take good care of it. Still, my stomach flipped as I parted from the small shell. Izzy politely nodded her thanks. It paled in comparison to all her other gifts, I'm sure. I was stupid. I should have given her a jewel or something.

The skinny little girl who I'd mistaken for a pile of blankets earlier interrupted the moment to pull Izzy away from me to admire the gown. The oblivious little urchin, couldn't she see we were having a moment? Izzy was too polite to refuse her, so she let the girl lead her into the sitting room and point out various pieces of embroidery on the gown. I stayed back by the doorway to the bedroom and leaned against the doorframe. This wasn't my crowd. I didn't belong with them.

"Anne," Izzy turned back to me, "this is incredible! Did you do this?"

"Yeah. I had some time on my hands." I grinned and shrugged. I brought that gown out almost every time I sailed and added more details to it. Stitched into it was my life story in pictures and thread. If you looked closely, you could see elements of every place I'd been, everyone I'd met, the important moments, and the small and wonderful ones. I didn't have a journal, I had that dress.

Izzy's maid brought out refreshments. My sister sat me next to her on the chaise and made me participate in the conversation. If it weren't for all the dressing gowns and lack of electricity, we could have been sitting around the pool house after one of her massive sleepovers.

Lady Catherine's handmaid brought in a round of drinks and coffee, and I loosened up a little and offered stories about the dress. They were fascinated when I told them the fabric came from a port in Shanghai and that I'd saved it in my rowboat after a storm capsized my ship off the coast of Jakarta. I'd been so pissed at Zheng that day. It was my ship, I was captain, she sucked at taking orders.

"And you're going to let me wear it for my wedding? That's amazing. Thank you so much," Izzy asked, somewhat breathless.

"I'm going to let you have it. It's yours. You deserve it," I told her. Izzy had accused me that even my secrets had secrets. Well, there they all were, every secret I ever had was sewn into that gown. Even an abstract map of the portal current wound around and through all the pictures. Until I could bear to speak my secrets out loud to her, this was the best I could do. She hugged me again. I guess I could get used to this. I hugged her back.

Loud, pounding footsteps sounded outside in the hallway, and a muffled bass voice demanded, "Where is she?" Then more running. I held my breath. He'd seen my ship. The doors to Izzy's sitting room flung open, and Andrews, disheveled and wild, shouted, "Nanette!" His face broke into a blinding smile.

"Graham," I whispered, physical relief engulfing me just at the sight of him.

He had me in his arms in two steps and swooped me up. We landed on Izzy's recently vacated bed, and he laid me down and covered me with his long, strong body. He kissed me. His arms were tight around me, full of pressure and desire. He nuzzled into my neck, kissing every part of me his lips could reach. His hands ran up and down my arms and chest, hitched my leg up around his hip.

I had spent the better part of two months in lonely torment on a prison cell floor. How many times had I had to let him go? How many times had I tried to say goodbye? Graham held my face for a moment before kissing me again, gently at first and then deeper and with intention. I let the world spin away as we delighted in having each other so close and wanting. I missed this man so much when I wasn't with him, and it was electric to hold on to him now.

Izzy cleared her throat dramatically from somewhere over Graham's back. "Mr. Andrews, if you wouldn't mind? You are interrupting! And we are none of us dressed to receive men at this hour." He paused only a moment and grinned down at me.

"She doesn't like me," he breathed into my ear.

"My sister doesn't know you like I do." I smiled and lightly kissed his lips.

"Sister?" He groaned and dropped his head to my chest and crawled off me. "I'll wait for you outside. Not too long, Nanette, yes?"

I kissed him again and sent him out. "Not long at all."

Izzy stood there incredulous and irritated. "I know," I told her, trying to forestall an argument. "But you aren't the only one I left. I'll be right back." My heart pounded as I quickly walked out of the room, eager to finish what we'd started. Graham caught me round the middle and pushed me up against the wall, kissing me firmly and keeping me in place.

"Dammit," he said, taking a breath. "Sister?"

"Sister," I confirmed. He growled and pulled me towards our bedroom. Graham had me unlaced and in our bed in record time. His clothes had barely made it down the hall and through the door. Only when we were both stripped bare and lying skin to skin on the sheets did he relax and begin to take his time. "May I stay here for a little while?" I asked as I clasped my hands behind his neck.

"Stay here forever." He breathed the words against my lips as he raised himself over me. "Open those legs for me now, Nanette."

And I did.

The sun was high in the sky when we finally finished. I lay satiated next to Graham in bed, letting him trace circles on my areolas with one hand and listening to the wedding preparations in the garden below. I leaned in and kissed him, wanting more of the closeness I had lacked for so long.

"Marry me, Nanette," he hummed in my ear as he softly ran his fingertips over my wrist wraps. I turned my head so that my lips were to his ear but said nothing, just took his ear lobe gently in my mouth, nipping it just a little. He pulled me up and astride him and held onto my hips. "You're not saying no," he said.

"How about, for just this very moment, I keep not saying no?" I leaned in and kissed him lightly, knowing he'd be frustrated with that answer. He brushed his hands over my skin, but we were both sated

The Bitch Captain (and The Lady)

and didn't take it farther. I relaxed next to him, and we listened to the crash of the waves and the birds and the wind and all the preparations below.

"Just for this moment then," he agreed and brought me into his chest. He wrapped his arms around me and held me close. I held him too, feeling as at home and calm as I did on my ship. I loved him as I would a husband. Graham closed his eyes, and soon his breath came steady and deep.

I left him to sleep. Though I was exhausted, there was no time to rest. I had explanations to make to my sister. I washed and dressed and selected an old dress from my armoire to wear for the day in order to protect the velvet gown. It was a sturdy forest green number with a voluminous skirt. The dress wasn't my favorite, which is why it lived here, but I wanted to make sure Mom's gown was in good condition for the wedding. I fixed my hair as best I could and went to find Izzy.

In her room, several people were fussing around the gown, but I didn't see her. Lady Catherine informed me that Izzy had stepped out and wasn't there. From the looks of it, the young woman would never be able to make eye contact with me ever again.

If Izzy wasn't here, there was only one other place she'd be.

Angelica sat out in the dining room, antsy and upset as she heard the chopping and scraping coming from within her domain. Her attitude had not improved since this morning and Izzy messing around in her kitchen was only tallying more deficits into my column.

"The Lady Isabelle is within. She is not to be disturbed," Angelica warned.

"I need to speak with her." I stopped in front of my usual spot at the table and took a calming breath. Angelica crossed her arms and blocked the door.

"Your needs are no concern of mine," she stated while tapping that damn foot of hers.

"Clearly."

"Helene warned you to be a credit to this family and not to ruin this day. Now your *sister* is in there—" we both winced at the sound of a cleaver meeting a cutting board "—cooking." Even Amelia had had to earn her place in Angelica's kitchen. I imagine the idea of a foreign woman, a lady to boot, in there and using her tools, abraded Angelica's very soul.

"Andrews came in – I didn't have time to explain. There's a lot going on and I'm so tired, please—" I don't think I'd slept in over 48 hours. I'd pushed myself hard through the portal and the equatorial Atlantic to get here on time.

"We are all tired!" Angelica exclaimed. "This wedding has to go well. If all you can do is make things worse, then you should just go home. Go home, Hurricane Anne," she stood her ground against me, drawing a line between her territory and mine.

"I am home," I placed my hands deliberately on my chair in front of me.

Her eyes lit with fumes. It was only too clear why they were all stressed about this wedding. It was a dress rehearsal for the real thing. All they needed was me out of the picture. Well, they could all lump it and deal with me for just a short while longer. I'd be gone within the year.

"Do not touch anything in my kitchen," the woman warned and finally stepped aside.

I walked past her and opened the door, stopping only to say, "Hope you had fun at the party last night" before walking into the arena to duel once again with Izzy.

My sister was busy with a thousand different preparations and concoctions. She didn't look at me as I entered. I took a seat and grabbed the nearest bowl and started tasting the cake batter. Gross. Yeast cake. I put it back and looked for something sweeter.

Izzy finally threw a cold "Hello" my way. I sighed. *Your secrets have secrets.* I'd need to tell her something, something big. Not big enough that it would destroy her day but enough to shock her into talking to me again.

"I love him. I've loved him for years. I met him before—" I was about to launch into just how I'd first met him when a parade of servants came into the kitchen to make final preparations for the wedding day breakfast. Angelica muscled her way past me into the kitchen.

"What did you say?" Izzy spoke above the din. "Love? You're in love with Mr. Graham fucking Andrews?"

Angelica shot me a dirty look from across the room before I could hush my sister. Angelica motioned to the door, and I put my hands up and left.

"Auntie!" Magnus wrapped his gangly arms around me as soon as I left the kitchen. "Were you really in a dungeon? Auntie Von said that you were and that there were rats and prison guards and iron bars—"

"Are you having breakfast with everyone this morning?" I cut the boy off before he went into too much loud, pubescent-boy detail about my past few months.

"Yes. As I am heir," his chest puffed with importance, "it is important that I learn how to comport myself at these functions with aplomb and decorum." Helene's voice sounded in a double timbre through his memorized words.

"And what a fine heir you are going to be!" I straightened his collar and he beamed.

"Auntie?"

"Yes?"

"Don't go to prison again, okay?" He wrapped me in another gangly hug.

They need you to say yes just as much as I do. Don't worry, my perfect little one, you'll be right where you need to be soon. I hugged him back.

Please remember this hug, please remember I love you even when I'm not here.

"No more prison," I answered out loud. "I promise." He accepted my words and I'd do my best to honor them.

The dining room was already filling up with guests, many of whom I knew. I lost Magnus to a group of younger attendees. Andrews entered, bathed and dressed in his finery, and I went straight to him. He brought me in for a kiss that Davies promptly interrupted.

"That's what I like to see!" He patted us both on the back hard. "Now, when are we finally going to be here celebrating the two of you?"

"The day, the hour, the minute this woman relents, I will have her in front of a priest, I assure you." Graham pulled me in close, and I put my head back against his chest. If he only knew how much I wanted that too.

The young lieutenant entered the room to a chorus of congratulations and huzzahs.

"Come," Andrews spoke softly to me, "we must introduce you. I fear I've been rather remiss in my hosting duties and must remedy my behavior." I'd rather stab the lieutenant with a fork, but I was attempting to remedy my own behavior as well.

"I know the bum just fine. And he knows me." I didn't dare let slip to Andrews that this soldier used me to kill for him. Andrews would not take that well.

"Lieutenant Commander!" Graham bellowed out, commanding the tall, dark-haired soldier's attention. "I'd like to introduce you to someone." He pulled me forward. "Lieutenant Commander, please meet—"

"Lady Anne." The young lieutenant dared to take my hand and kiss it.

Graham snorted into my hair. He knew I was no "lady". My sleeve fell past a wrist wrap as the young man took my hand; I was still bandaged where his shackles had rubbed me raw.

The Bitch Captain (and The Lady)

"Lieutenant." I lifted my hand out of his and replaced it in Graham's. The young man made his way to his seat.

"Come along, Lady Anne," Graham chuckled into my ear. I swatted him playfully, and he led me to my seat where he pulled out my chair for me and kissed me as I sat down. Graham then went to his seat, opposite me and next to Magnus. The boy waved and I waved right back. He was so cute. The little urchin from Izzy's room was seated across from the handsome boy.

Davies took the seat to my right, and I was thrilled to have my optimistic old friend to speak with during this sure-to-be-awkward meal. The rest of the guests took their seats, and we all waited for Izzy, who was still working in the kitchen. As it was impolite to speak until the guest of honor was at the table, once we were all seated, we were all silent and waiting for her to enter. In the silence, all her sounds of banging and chopping and exclamations from the kitchen were heard clear as day around the table. I couldn't keep the smile from my face imagining Izzy banging away in there. I happened to glance at the young lieutenant, who was also smiling. When our eyes met and we realized we were sharing the same humorous image, our smiles erased simultaneously. The bum.

Finally Izzy emerged from the kitchen, pulling off an apron, and we stood for her. She seemed startled to see me at the table, and I wondered if she didn't want me here. Graham gave me an encouraging smile as Izzy greeted the other guests and took the seat accorded to her. Everyone sat except for the host.

"A toast!" he announced, and everyone raised their glasses. "To the soon-to-be Lady Coventry and the Lieutenant Commander."

"Lady Coventry!" "Lieutenant Commander!" "Hear! Hear!"

Graham continued, "We wish you happy days, happy nights," the men cheered, "fat babies, and full purses."

"Hear hear!" Everyone toasted and drank.

Graham tipped his glass to me before taking a sip. I returned the gesture. As he took his seat, the various servants from all the nobility present in this room began serving food and filling and refilling drinks. I spoke mostly with Davies and Wallington about business matters as Graham handled the opposite end of the table. He even appeared to have a few back-and-forths with my sister without any bloodshed. That was a good sign.

"I say, what a beautiful day for a wedding," Davies bellowed, his voice bounding across the huge table. "Dear Lady Wallington, tell me, did you and the lord truly get married in the midst of a deluge?"

"Dear boy, we rowed to the church itself on Noah's ark!" Lord Wallington chuffed.

"My dress was soaked up to the knees," Lady Wallington exclaimed. "Lady Isabelle, we are all anxious to see what dress you've chosen." She beamed and giggled with excitement as she drank from her wine glass. The stately woman loved a good wedding.

"The lady has informed me that in the land of California, it is bad luck for a groom to see his bride in her wedding dress before the ceremony," the young lieutenant informed the table to various exclamations of surprise and interest.

"It's true. We believe the first time the groom sees the bride should be a wonderful reveal," I volunteered. I was feeling warm and familiar in this place with wine in my belly, Graham across the table, and my sister close by.

Davies piped right up on the heels of this bit of information. "Captain, we'd all love to hear more about your homeland. Tell us more!"

Across the table all the guests seized on this rare opportunity to hear about Izzy's and my homeland. Graham's eyes never left my face, and I found myself talking almost exclusively to him describing the lavish modern ceremonies where there are bridesmaids and groomsmen, where dresses cost more than a year's supply of food, how there is music and dancing well into the night. Graham's expression looked as strained as mine felt. I'd never told him this much about my culture.

"And the dancing," I continued. "In…California we love to dance at weddings." Everyone laughed at that as I knew they would. Graham and I didn't attend many noble functions together, but when we did, we danced. We danced all night, and only with each other.

"We do know that!" Davies said.

"If the Lady Isabelle is anything like yourself, dear Captain, she and the lieutenant commander will need to be dragged off the floor to consummate their vows!" Richard Lavigne shouted out, well into his cups already this morning.

"Consummate?" Magnus asked. Graham leaned over to the boy and whispered. "Oh yeah." The handsome boy flicked his eyes at Izzy's urchin across from him and blushed. Graham sent me one of his wildcat grins. If Magnus learned that grin from his father, the next generation better watch out.

"With your first child expected within a year's time, I assume you'll be handing your financial interests off to the Lieutenant Commander, and Mr. Davies here seems quite well suited to your shipyard. So tell me, are you at all concerned with producing a child at your advanced age, Lady Isabelle?" Lady Wallington asked.

I choked on my wine and snapped my head to Izzy to see how she would react to that breach of cultural protocol and was not disappointed. My sister looked like she might faint dead away. She clapped a hand over her mouth to stifle what surely was about to be a profanity-laden response about minding one's own business.

"Unfortunately," the young lieutenant stood, "this leads me to an unpleasant announcement."

I dared to dream for a moment that he was canceling this wedding.

"The warship *Victory* has been sighted not too far away. She is due into port within a week or two. We will do our best," Ian winked at all the men, the cad, "but our efforts at a family may be postponed until the end of the war."

Did he mean he was planning to leave my sister only a week or two into their marriage to go fight a losing battle? Surely she knew, how could she not know? This information did not endear the young lieutenant to me any further.

Graham stood and shook the bum's hand. "Nothing is harder than saying goodbye to the woman you finally have gotten ahold of." He refilled Ian's drink. "Condolences. God save the King."

We all raised our glass and gave a few good "God save the King's."

Davies quickly turned the conversation towards the new shipyard. I had to remind myself that I'd only left a day or two ago and that Davies likely assumed I did not go home but came straight here. I joined in the conversations up and down the table. I'd done business with many of these people and knew them well, certainly well enough to comment on pieces of their lives and lands and products. Like Graham, I was on my best behavior. Helene would have nothing to complain about. I channeled every piece of instruction my mother had drilled into me about proper table manners and hostess duties. She would likely have been prouder of me in this moment than at any other time in my life.

Eventually the food was eaten, and the time had come to officially begin resting up and dressing for the ordeal later this evening. Graham and I excused the whole table to their rooms and activities, and the servants began the monumental task of cleaning up.

Izzy met me at the door as I stood saying a few words to the Wallingtons while Graham stood behind me, his hand lightly on my lower back. She had a huge fake smile on her face that I read immediately as danger and announced with fake cheer, "We're going to talk." I excused myself and let her lead me away from everyone.

"Izzy, I don't like horses. You know this." I stared down the beast as she set up a stool for me to climb up on this devil monster's back.

The Bitch Captain (and The Lady)

"Too bad. We're going riding because we need to talk. Get up." She hoisted me up.

Horses smell. I really didn't like horses. Even growing up I didn't like them. They are too big and too unpredictable. They kick and they bolt and they throw you off as often as they can manage. Then, after that time I was roped up and dragged behind one, I really stopped liking them.

The fur (or whatever) was prickly and smelled. Izzy put the reins in my hands, and the thing turned its great big head to warn me not to touch it. My palms started sweating. My skin crawled at being up high like this. I smelled dust and dirt, blood and fire. I wiped the sweat out of my eyes and refocused on the land that was in front of my face and not in my memory.

My sister vaulted up onto her own horse like a total badass as flop sweat ran down the back of my bodice. She rolled her eyes at me and moved the animals to action. "Let's go." And we began moving. My horse was tethered to hers and followed Izzy closely.

"Slow down, Izzy!" The wind picked up in my face, and the movement under my thighs felt chaotic. I wanted to get down. I really wanted to get down. "Izzy, this is too fast."

Izzy just shook her head, laughing at my fear.

"Izzy, slow this thing down." She ignored me. "Izzy?" Nothing. "Oh god. Going to die. Fucking horses," I mumbled and cowered on the animal's back.

"We're all walking. She literally cannot go any slower than her current pace," Izzy scoffed at my cowardice.

"Don't you think we should go get you dressed? You are the bride." I knew that dress took no time to put on, but maybe she didn't. "I'm so high up. Isn't there a shorter horse maybe?"

In answer she tossed me a flask. "Drink up and stop being a bitch."

I was really feeling my lack of sleep and early-morning stress now. My skin crawled as the scratchy horse fur touched it. The thing shook its head, and I tensed for it to bolt. A drink might be good. Just a little. My hands shook as I tried to open the little screw top. Maybe it was the horse that was shaking, not me. My heart pounded, and I could feel my pulse through my fingertips. Maybe the horse would keel over and die on top of me.

I couldn't get the flask open. Izzy took it back from me, opened it like it was no problem at all, and passed it back. The whiskey fired down my throat but didn't touch the uneasiness in my stomach. My knuckles were white around the reins. I was so high up. And I really think the horse was shaking. What if she'd put me on an epileptic horse? The horse would fall. I would fall. I would die under this horse.

"You love him?" Izzy asked out of the blue.

"Who?" I'm going to die on this beast. "The horse? Take me home." I fumbled the reins again.

"The horse is a fucking girl. I'm talking about the dude who owns this place." She kept the horses on a steady pace. My heart pounded, and I struggled to stay upright.

"Yes. I love him." She wanted to talk about Graham? Not that I kidnapped her or left her or have been time-traveling for years? She wanted to talk about a boy? "Please, let's go home," I begged. "I'm going to fall off. This thing is seconds from bolting." The horse stared back at me, fire in its eyes and soul as it chewed some grass.

"How can you love someone who dabbles in the slave trade?" she demanded.

I held the reins tighter. Andrews was part of a world where the concept of freedom and agency over your own life was brand new. Slavery was sewn deep into the fabric of society and had been since the dawn of time. A nobleman was created by god, and the rest of us losers were condemned to serve him. The fact that Andrews had been able to buck his lowborn status and achieve wealth was the direct result of this age of exploration and mass trafficking. Societal roles, including slavery, had been fed to him with his daily bread every waking day of his life. His

The Bitch Captain (and The Lady)

kingdom out here was far ahead of its time in many ways except the one that counted most. Andrews didn't know any differently.

But I did, and there was no excuse.

All I can say is that I was a lonely traveler far from my culture and everything familiar. Graham had shown me kindness when I'd been in desperate need. It was all too easy to slip into the conditions of life here. There were no handholds to my upbringing. Nothing even closely resembled the world as I knew it, and no one would have understood me anyway.

"There's no good answer. It started so long ago. I couldn't stop." I'd tried to stop. Lord knows I'd tried.

"That is a dumb answer."

"I know."

"Why didn't you tell me about him when I came to see you?" she yelled back to me.

Thinking of Graham and not the horse calmed me down a little. I still couldn't believe that of all the topics she could rake me over the coals for, she chose Graham Andrews.

"Because I never intended to come back here." Road to hell and all...

"That's not what I asked you. Why didn't you tell me? You had all the opportunities," she accused.

I had to snort at that. When Izzy came into that prison cell, she had barely taken a breath between syllables. When the hell was I supposed to get a word in edgewise to describe a relationship I'd tried to break off over and over and over again over the entire span of our relationship?

"Why tell you about someone I have no future with?" The beast shook its mane. Now, I know I saw in a documentary somewhere that that is a clear sign of agitation and aggression in horses. "Izzy, this horse is really mad. I think we should turn around." She kept leading us steadfastly onward. "Izzy, I mean it. I was never coming back here," I insisted.

"Alright. I hear you," she admitted. Thank god. I relaxed until her next words. "Hold on tight." Izzy sped the horses up.

The wind caught my hair, and I crouched down and held onto the reins for dear life. I hated this so much. I hated this. I hated this. I was going to vomit.

"Are you ready to talk now?" Izzy demanded like a torturer asking where the money was buried or she'd shove the bamboo shoots under my fingernails.

"Yes." What did she want? I thought I was talking. "Just make it stop!" The horse smell was going to choke me. "I'll tell you anything."

"Tell me about Helene, Angelica and Yvonne," she demanded.

I snapped my mouth shut. Not that. I would not talk about that. I could not talk about that.

"For the record, that was barely a jog for the three of us," she reminded me.

"No." I wheezed the word out. I could not talk about them. I could barely think about them.

Izzy sighed, and suddenly we were flying. Tears streamed backwards out of my eyes as horse hooves thundered across the land. Air flew past me, but I couldn't catch any of it.

"Helene. Angelica. Yvonne," she demanded. My thoughts felt trampled.

"Angelica and Yvonne. That's not a thing anymore. Maybe a long time ago, but now they just run his house and business." There was an arrangement there that not even I understood. Yvonne was a one-time deal, but once was enough to bear a child. Angelica...there was nothing real between them, and the affair had not lasted long. Still, they also shared a child.

"Helene?" she asked.

No. I couldn't. Not her.

Izzy raced the horses again before slowing. I was going to puke.

"Helene?" she repeated.

The Bitch Captain (and The Lady)

No. Not Helene. Not her.

Izzy spurred the animals into a sprint again and I held on for dear life.

"Helene!" she demanded as we flew over the terrain.

"I can't!" I shouted. "Don't make me!" I begged. The horses slowed, but the pounding in my head remained. It sounded like waves. I thought we were farther inland. Where had she led us? I tried to look around but couldn't pick out any landmarks.

"Okay." Izzy slowed us a little more. It did nothing to stop the pounding.

My head was killing me. The exhaustion and stress had hit a peak. My head was going to split in two. The sound of surf crashed through my brain, and I put my hands to my head to attempt to hold myself together.

"Two years ago, he asked me to marry him." Demanded, really. He'd gotten me out of prison after Kings Bay and brought me back here. He'd been furious with me. We'd never had such an enormous fight.

Go! Get back on this cursed ship! Leave! But understand this, if you do come back here, you come back as my wife. Do you understand! he had shouted at me.

How long do you wait after I leave to get in bed with her? A week? A day? An hour? I don't have a home. That is not my home! It's hers! Go be with her! I had roared.

"I refused. I told him to choose an heir already and stop waiting for me. I wasn't supposed to come back here. I left." Of course, I did end up coming back because I could never seem to stay away.

"Because you don't marry ghosts?" Izzy repeated back to me the line I'd told her from my prison cell. "I don't understand any of this. Obviously, I'm not a fucking fan, but – if you love him, be with him."

I looked at my sister. How was she so old and so young at the same time? She didn't understand. And how could she possibly understand when she knew so little about what I'd gotten myself into?

"I've seen his grave...and the gravestone next to it. It wasn't my name written there," I told her. My voice sounded thin, or maybe my ears were struggling. The sound of hooves pounded into me with each step. I felt sick. I was going to throw up. I was going to throw up right here on this horse. The horse smelled so bad. My stomach rolled and my chest tightened. I had to get off. I pulled at my feet but couldn't release my boots from the stirrups. I was stuck. It was too hot. My hands shook as I wiped the sweat off my forehead. I didn't feel well. I leaned against the smelly animal.

"When? When did you see his grave?"

"Graduation. Bermuda. You saw it too."

"Oh, god..."

The waves pounded in my head and the sun beat down. "We've been here before. We've been right here. Right here. Their graves – their ghosts– it wasn't my name written there. It wasn't my name."

It was too hot in these pants to be hiking everywhere, but my scars would terrify Izzy, not to mention the fit Mom would throw. My sunglasses did little against the equatorial sun. It smelled really bad here.

"Who was – was it Helene's?" Izzy asked. Her voice was far away and through a tunnel. She was reading a book on a bench just off the path. The waves just kept pounding. Mom complained that this was supposed to be a vacation. In front of me was a stone.

Helene Andrews
1610-1684
Beloved wife
Beloved mother

He wasn't mine and never would be mine. If there were any goodness in the world, it would be my name engraved above "beloved wife" and I'd be dead and buried under it. But it wasn't my name. It was hers.

The Bitch Captain (and The Lady)

I stole my meager minutes with Andrews, holding on for dear life every time I was with him, desperate to let go every time I left.

What was I still doing on this horse? The sky was spinning, my hands shaking. My legs were locked into these stirrups. I clutched at my chest. Was this what a heart attack felt like? I yanked out my knife and started hacking at the reins. I would get off this horse one way or another. I managed to shear off a buckle, and the whole saddle assembly twisted, and I toppled to the ground, tangled in my skirt. I hacked at the green fabric next, gasping and choking as I cut the drawstrings.

Helene Andrews
1610-1684
Beloved wife
Beloved mother

"I loved him first," I wheezed at that damn accusing headstone. Helene stayed resolutely below. She'd won. I was the loser. "Get me out of here." I spun around and snapped off the busk of my corset and tossed it as far away as possible. "How could he do this?" I demanded of the silent headstone. "How could he do this to me?" The wind and sea spray beat against the inside of my head. "She—" My words cut off as my throat closed up.

"Anne, it's time to go. We have reservations at 6:00," Mom whined. The heat was getting to her.

"I can't go. I can't go without him." I threatened my mother with the knife. Then gasped and dropped it as my mother's face swam in and out of focus showing me Izzy, showing me my mother, showing me a noble lady I didn't know. I grabbed my head and stumbled backwards against a tree.

"It's getting late. We have to get back to the house." Mom pulled at me, but I couldn't move. The world was spinning and out of order.

"It was just him and me. Young, stupid, gorgeous him. And me." I slid to the ground.

"Anne, get up."

"I am up."

Mom grumbled and knelt in front of me. She checked my eyes, felt my forehead, then put my head between my knees and rubbed my shoulders.

After that there was nothing but the sound of the waves washing everything away. The ocean is magnificent. It doesn't have a care in the world. That's how I should be, endlessly moving, flowing around any and all attachments, only coming to shore when absolutely necessary. I let the sound of the waves eclipse everything and closed my eyes.

Take me away.

Take me away.

Take me away.

"Just him and me," I mumbled.

"Nanette?" His voice broke through the waves, and I opened my eyes slowly to see his bright blond ghost head haloed against the sun. I closed my eyes again, not ready to say goodbye.

"You don't want me." I exhaled and covered my face with my hands. Graham's ghost sat down next to me.

"Lies, Nan. Lies. I'm here. Come back to me." From far away Graham's ghost stroked my face and held me in that small island graveyard.

I took a long shuddering breath and leaned into him and let him hold me. Ghost or mirage, I was happy to have him near.

"Come on, Nanette, come back to me," he encouraged me.

"I chopped up the dress," I mumbled, stroking the frayed edge of my bodice.

"It was an awful dress." He crooned into my hair.

"Is the horse okay?"

"The horse is fine."

"I want to go home." Wherever the hell that was. Was it that old

The Bitch Captain (and The Lady)

mansion, or my house with Graham by the sea, or my familiar ship?

"I'll take you home. Are you ready to leave now?" Graham's ghost held me safe and secure. I was not ready to leave him.

Something was still wrong. It itched at me. The waves capsized me again and I almost toppled to the ground, I would have if he hadn't kept me upright. What was I missing?

"Where's Izzy?" I was probably supposed to call her. Had I missed an appointment to call? Usually I did all my calls to her at once, dipping in and out of the time stream in one-week intervals. Where was my phone? I patted my pockets, but they were cut off. I'd cut them off with the knife. Izzy was still in bed. It was time for school, but she wouldn't take her head out of that book.

"You need to get dressed," I told her catatonic form.

"I'm not going anywhere until I know you're alright." She zombied at me. She showed me her book; there was a bride on the cover.

Why was she worried? She wasn't supposed to worry about me, not now, not ever. Izzy was the important one. She was so young and hurt, lying there in that hospital bed. I was the lucky one. I was strong and healthy and hadn't lost anyone. *She needs you to protect her, Anne.* They had all told me. *Read to her, talk to her, she can hear you.* Izzy lay in that hospital bed with her grievous wounds from the car crash. She had to be protected. My life was sunshine and butterflies compared to my best friend who had just lost everything. I was the lucky one. *Think of Izzy. She needs you to be strong for her now*, they had instructed me. So I had.

"I'm fine. Don't worry about me. You need to get dressed." I held out her hospital gown for her as she sat in her wheelchair. I heard the waves again. Graham continued to hold me close. Where was I?

The island air chose that time to send a calming breeze my way, and I opened my eyes and saw my hands, wrists wrapped up the same as I remembered, held in Graham's hands. I looked up at him, wondering when he'd gotten here. I squeezed his hands, and he exhaled in relief. I reached to smooth his worried forehead wrinkles. He was getting too old for this kind of worry over me. Lucky for him he wouldn't have to worry about me for too much longer.

"Alright. You sure?" Izzy said. I looked around and spotted her near a horse. What was she doing here?

"Don't worry. I'll be home soon." I said it automatically. The words were out of my mouth without conscious thinking. It's how I ended almost every phone call I had ever made to her. It was complete bullshit. I rarely went home anymore.

Izzy seemed satisfied and took off on her horse with the young lieutenant, who was also here. What had I done? How bad had I lost it that so many reinforcements needed to be called? I groaned and buried my head again.

"I'm okay now," I told Graham, and he appeared to believe me.

"Up you go, Nanette." He pulled me to my feet.

The walk home cleared my head and helped my blood flow again. Graham held me close to his side and I made it back to our house, our room. There he slowly helped me undress out of my torn and dirty gown. It reminded me of when we were first together. To this day he is the only one to have ever seen me and my scarred body in all its glory. He didn't run away from me then, and he wasn't running away from me now.

Graham pulled a clean shift over my body and helped secure the busk on my corset. The velvet dress felt wonderful draped over me, soft and comforting and smelling of a different home and time. Graham ran his hands up and down the luxurious fabric just as I knew he would. If we were back in my times, he and I would spend a few hours on my old corduroy couch watching terrible TV and eating snacks. We'd drive out of town just to see the stars away from the city lights. We'd do anything except put on these layers of clothing to attend a wedding where the wrong actors were cast as the bride and groom.

He sat with me on the small couch next to the window in silence until I was ready to continue the day. I wanted to close my eyes. I was beyond tired, and this day wasn't half over. Usually my days passed so quickly. Suddenly my sister was in my life again, and the hours crawled by, forcing me to experience each and every excruciating minute.

"I have to apologize to her. That was embarrassing," I conceded after enough time listening to the servants setting the tables on the patio.

"That was cruel. What she did to you was cruel. And you are going to apologize to her?" He was incredulous.

"She's young. She doesn't understand." I defended her against him.

"Nanette, she's dangerous. I've seen you take down full-grown men in a fight, and this woman had you on your knees in less than an hour. Be careful. I dislike seeing you hurt." He kissed my still-wrapped wrists.

"I'm always careful." I kissed him.

"Liar." He grinned his wildcat grin, and I left him to get dressed and ready. He would come to escort me to the ceremony later. I passed Angelica in the hallway on her way to make certain Graham was tucked and buttoned appropriately as the host and master of his kingdom. We did not stop to make polite conversation.

For the second time in one day I found myself stalling outside the door to Izzy's room. I was mortified over that embarrassing display with the horses...and after I'd tried so hard to make her wedding breakfast a jovial and elegant affair. Why did I even try? Everything I touched turned to crap. But I was here. I would attempt to apologize as best I could.

I knocked. Once again, the small maid from earlier opened the door.

"Anne!" Izzy quickly replaced the maid at the door and gave me a once-over.

I opened my mouth to apologize, but before I could get any sound out, she hugged me. I was stunned. She was supposed to be mad. She was supposed to greet me with a cold shoulder. I was ruining her wedding day, and I was deeply involved with a man she despised. Yet here she was with her arms around me in an embrace I needed so badly I couldn't find any words. Luckily Izzy was never without words.

"I'm so sorry, Anne. I didn't know – and I would never – I'm sorry. Please, I want us to talk about...all of this, more, later. But only if you're okay with it. Alright?"

"It's not your fault." I hugged her back. She felt like a lifeline. I couldn't let go. "You don't need to worry about me. Just been a long day already. I didn't sleep much the past week while sailing." I don't think I'd slept a full night since I'd left Mary and Davies at the shipyard probably three weeks ago. I disengaged my arms from her, rubbed my eyes, and tried to shrug it off with a laugh. I'm afraid it didn't come out exactly completely sane. "I didn't get you with that knife at all, did I?" I tried the laughter thing again. I think I was more successful this time.

"No, I'm fine. So is the horse." Izzy rubbed my shoulders. "Are you sure you're okay?" she asked. I didn't know how to answer that.

"I'm not the one we need to worry about." I fell back into my old consistent tropes. "You're getting married today. So let's get you dressed, shall we?" I backed away from her and took refuge in the dress. I couldn't look her in the eyes. I was embarrassed and just wanted her to forget the whole thing. Usually after an episode like that I'd be halfway to my boat, making plans to run far and wide. Here I was, already far and wide from home, and I had nowhere to run to. I fussed with the lacing on the sleeves and tried to hide my mortification.

"Anne, stop." Izzy grabbed my hands.

I tried to twist them away. If she held onto me, I was going to cry. I couldn't cry. The Bitch Captain of the Seven Seas couldn't cry. My eyes burned and watered. Izzy wasn't done.

"I'm allowed to care about you too, even if it is my wedding day," she said. Even tepid water on frozen hands burns. "And I really do want us to talk about all of this."

The Bitch Captain (and The Lady)

I sat down hard on one of the chaises and covered my eyes with shaking hands. Shit! What the hell was wrong with me? Why couldn't I get it together?

"When's the last time you slept?" she asked.

"I don't know. I'm fine. Don't worry." I wiped at the stupid, weak tears and forced air into my lungs. When I tried to stand, Izzy pushed me back down.

"Josefa-Maria, can you bring a pillow and blanket?" Izzy called out, her hands on my shoulders keeping me in place.

"I'm fine. Don't worry," I tried to protest, but then the pillow was under my head, and someone was taking my boots off and tucking the blanket around my stocking feet. That was it. I gave up the ghost and passed out.

"Aaaanne. Aaaaanne. Wake up." Izzy's voice sing-songed above me.

I floated back to consciousness and sat up expecting to see our bedroom at home and had a moment of disorientation when I realized I was in Andrews' second-best bedroom in the evening light. Izzy stood by the chaise in a shift and corset, holding a bouquet of fragrant flowers, surrounded by servants.

"How was your nap? Do you feel like you can get up now?" she asked.

I felt much better. I stretched and ran my hands through my now-tangled bed-head hair. Izzy ordered some of the maids around, and before I knew what was going on, Lady Catherine's handmaid was brushing my hair out and re-styling it into something wedding-appropriate. I was still bleary-eyed but felt better than I had in weeks.

Once my hair was done, Izzy confused everyone by sending all the maids and attendants out of her chambers and insisting that it was tradition for the Maid of Honor to dress the bride alone. She told them all that we'd meet them at the chapel. I went along with her charade and bid goodbye to all the girls.

Izzy shut the door, and we were finally alone in a quiet room. Before she could get too involved in dressing, I reached for her hand. How do you thank someone for taking care of you? No one did that for me. All of a sudden, I just needed her. I pulled her in close, unbelievably grateful she was here with me. I kissed her cheek and rested my forehead against hers.

"I'm so glad you're here." And for the first time in our lives, I didn't pull away first.

When Izzy eventually stood up, I followed her to the dress and lifted it off the valet. I gently draped the gown around her and smoothed out the folds, adjusted the laces, and arranged the shift underneath.

"He's going to love you in this." She looked beautiful in my gown.

"He already loves me. At least, he's convinced he does." She admired herself in the mirror. I adjusted all the lacing to better fit her petite frame. I wasn't a giant, but I had more muscle and her waist was smaller.

"Do you know he told me that he would have proposed even earlier, but he didn't want to scare me off? What a world." She grinned as she turned side to side to see more of her reflection.

A laugh escaped me. She really didn't understand this era. "I imagine he wanted to propose as soon as he saw the sun shining through your nightgown in port that first day." It was a miracle he hadn't proposed on the spot.

"What?! What are you talking about?" She pulled me up, her eyes panicked, her grip tight.

"He didn't tell you?" Even I remembered that vision: the sunbeams turning her light cotton dress into vapor and leaving nothing but the silhouette of Aphrodite on a half shell with a joint stuck in her mouth. "Oh yeah, you were displayed in all your glory up there as he came to check on my ship."

"Oh my god. Ian was one of those guys on the dock? And he still liked me after that?"

"Yeah. I'd say so." I'd liked him far less after that, but I suppose during that first day I wasn't as anxious to see him drawn and quartered.

"It's a different time. I'd think he'd be appalled by such a display." Izzy actually seemed embarrassed. Meanwhile, I'd seen her prance down the streets of Miami in a crocheted bra, but here she was concerned about this? Maybe this young lieutenant was something more than I'd thought. There'd be time to mull that over later.

"Men haven't changed so much throughout time," I assured her and resumed retying all the lacing.

"I would like to think there was more to his proposal of marriage than that. Especially since he still won't...you know...yet." She gestured to her body and all the fun her fiancé was missing out on.

I did know. I knew in all too detailed a manner. I frowned and kept lacing.

"One hour left." Then she could go ahead and undo all my hard work here and get down and dirty with that – I sighed. Keep your thoughts to yourself. It's her wedding day. I looked back up at her. "You can do it. Then you can – ugh, really? He's who you want?"

I'm sorry, I just couldn't keep it together. He was a dick.

"I know you two don't like each other very much," she admonished me. "But I do love him. I wish you had gotten to know him the way I have. He really is amazing and – god, Anne, I can't even explain all the things he's done for me. I know this seems crazy, but...I have a really, really good feeling about this. And him. He's so different from anyone I've ever met, for obvious reasons. And it's quite appealing to be with a powerful Roman when in Rome."

I listened to her talk and heard the words of a girl who hadn't let the world drag her down despite its best efforts. Izzy still liked glitter and strawberries and polka dots and kittens, and all these things made her stronger. The fact that she was unapologetic in embracing what she loved, instead of eschewing it to appear more grown and cynical, served to draw people into her life. It even made some people want to keep her with them longer than she was supposed to be in their lives.

While imprisoned I had racked my brain to figure out the piece of the puzzle I was missing in this whole situation. Why was she making these random and unconnected choices? Love. It was fucking love – or, in Izzy's case, non-fucking love. At least she thought it was love and, for now, I'd go along with her. I begged the universe for an ounce of patience.

"I don't see it. But I'll suffer this young lieutenant as an in-law since you love him so much."

"Lieutenant commander, Anne. He's not a lieutenant. And thank you." She went back to admiring herself.

"He's an ass—fine. This...Ian...seems to love you just the same way back." I turned my attention to the veil and where and how to place it on her head. "Your hair looks wonderful. When did it get so long?"

"I know, right? It's hard to tell when it's all curly."

I stuck the pins in place and wondered at her straight hair. "Did you smuggle a hot comb on board my ship?"

"I hardly smuggled it!" Izzy pointed out the metal comb on the vanity next to her. "It fits all of your parameters!"

"Yes, yes. Okay," I grumbled. I did say no electricity. I didn't figure on needing to limit inventions by patent year. Looks like no harm was done. I tugged the veil to get the lace to turn out and frame her face. "Mom wouldn't shut up about this veil as she wrapped it up. Got to hear the whole damn wedding story all over again. I hope you appreciate my sacrifice." The limo mix-up, the sun shower of afternoon rain, how the photographers got the most glorious picture of her at sunset. Blah, blah, blah.

"Right." Izzy twisted around and the veil pulled out of my fingers. I twisted her back and continued my preparation. "Didn't you just leave

The Bitch Captain (and The Lady)

yesterday?" she asked. "That's what Davies told us. But you said you had been sailing for the past week? How did you manage any of this?"

"I've been sailing for three weeks. Time travel. Duh." I smiled to myself. I really hadn't had much time to explain anything after Tavern Rock. It's amazing she hadn't stabbed me.

"Oh. Uh. Okay. Can you give me a little bit more than that?"

"Yeah, what?" I asked around the pins in my mouth. "Like, I sailed home. Mom yelled at me. I sailed back here in time for the wedding? Or do you want, like, science? Because I have theories, dimensions, and branes and—" Izzy blinked at me. "Magic feels appropriate too. Or rather, the old gods still messing about." I rubbed at the wicked brand on the back of my neck out of habit.

The brand was called a Nekydalleon, and my friends and I joked it was called that because it went on your neck, much like Tavern Rock was called Tavern Rock because it was a tavern on a rock. However, the significance went deeper and darker than was appropriate discussion for a wedding day. I dropped my hand quickly from the Nekydalleon to my side and hoped she didn't notice.

"Huh. Well...okay. I guess that makes about as much sense as anything else that's happening. Thank you for giving me a straight answer for once."

"I always give you straight answers. I don't lie to you, Izzy." There, that last pin would keep this damn veil in place.

"You don't volunteer information, either, Anne." Izzy gestured to the room, and I imagined that gesture included Andrews and all he entailed.

I grimaced. True, I had never had any intention of telling Izzy about Andrews ever. Which made me wonder how mad she might get if and when she learned of some of my other stories.

"That's fair." I hid myself behind her veil again, pretending to fix a small bit of stitching.

"How was Mom? And – what did you tell her?" she asked as she ran the delicate veil through her fingers.

"She's fine. Mimosa lunches and all that." I poured a drink for myself and put a piece of cheese on top of bread for a snack. "I told her you were getting married, and she spent the rest of the time in motion getting all this stuff for you." I gestured to all the crap Izzy had on right now.

"That's it? She didn't think it was weird that I was getting married when I wasn't even dating anyone? Or – oh, god, did she think I didn't want to invite her?" Izzy started pacing unconsciously.

"Mom...she...has suspected me for a long time. She never says anything outright, but I'm sure she knows. Apparently 'whether you want to see it or not, Diane, you're very much like your father.'" I imitated Mom's voice as I said that last line while grabbing a few grapes and more cheese. That dig still stung. She could get under my skin unlike anyone else. It was her superpower.

"Wait a minute. Like Da?" she asked.

I nodded and started looking at her jewelry options.

"Anne. When you kept running away – is this what you were doing? Were you coming back here?"

"Yeah. Of course. Here, there, other places. I get around." She already had a lot on. I wondered if she'd be willing to lose that necklace. "When I couldn't navigate the portal right, I would miss days and you all thought that I'd run away. Really I'd just blown my exits." I rambled as I straightened parts of the gown. It was pleasant to talk so freely to her about this. This was closer to what I'd envisioned our trip would include – minus the upcoming husband.

"And you guys think that Da might be here in 1649 too? I mean, that's—"

"What? No." God no. That bastard was long gone to hell and good riddance. I was sure of it. Heaven help him if he wasn't. "I don't know what Mom thinks. What I think is that Dad was a bad sailor and didn't make it through the portal. Not everyone does."

The Bitch Captain (and The Lady)

"But you do think he might have tried?" Izzy kept pushing this line. "Because anything could have happened—"

"Izzy, stop." I cut her off. "It's an impossible question. All that's important to know is that he was a piece of garbage who left in the first place. Nothing matters beyond that." Izzy was destroyed when he'd left. She had been in her bed reading for weeks. She wouldn't even touch a sailboat for ages. She still hadn't left her books behind and escaped into the pages every moment she could.

"Anne, it does matter! Don't you understand? It's crazy here, and anything could happen!" She was pacing again. "Maybe he just got lost or wrecked his boat or something, but – this is amazing news!" She turned back, all smiles, to the mirror. I couldn't argue that the happy expression was the defining accessory for her to wear, but the reason behind it worried me. There was enough going on for her today, I'd hate for thoughts of that man to intrude.

"Maybe. Sure." I straightened the skirt just a little and stood next to her in front of the mirror. My sister looked resplendent in all her finery and now with a smile to boot. I looked old. Ah well, can't be helped. "Are you ready?" I asked.

"We are missing one thing. I really, really wish we could have pictures. Even just a few selfies, you know?"

"I know. This wedding is dangerous enough though. Let's not add a camera into the mix." That devil rectangle was not coming off the ship on my watch. Not after what happened at Tavern Rock. "But maybe we can add a little to your dress here in memory?" There was a small area around her hip near a depiction of a turtle where we could add something. "Maybe a nice ring or," I reached for her hand to see what kind of ring the stupid boy – Hold. The. Fuck. Up. "Hey, is that one of my diamonds?" It was! I had sat in a damn prison in the Canary Islands for three months because of that thing! How had she found it and what was it doing on her finger?

"Yes." She took her hand back and admired the sun sparkling off the rock. "Speaking of you doing nice things for me, your sister, who you love and kidnapped? I need a couple of small favors."

"Uh oh." This wasn't going anywhere good for me. The sound of guests climbing the stairs sped Izzy and her litany of requests up.

"I need you to take Lady Catherine off this island. I need to get some supplies to some impoverished refugees. And I need to get my almost-husband inoculated as best I can before he goes off to war. Will you help me? Please?"

The doors opened, and Izzy was swept away from me before I had a chance to wonder what the hell just happened. Did she say something about Lady Catherine as a passenger? Refugees? However, I did sort of enjoy the idea that I could stick my new brother-in-law with something sharp.

"Wait...what?" I said as the tide of silk flowed back down the stairs. Why not ask for the moon while she's at it? Andrews trotted up the steps and poked his head in the door.

"Nanette? Shall we?" He offered his arm, but I was still reeling from Izzy's departure. "Nanette?" The concern in his voice caught my attention, and I turned to him. He looked stunning. He was washed and dressed in a beautiful brocade ensemble. He'd even shaved some of the scruffiness off his beard.

"You were right," I told him. "She is dangerous." He grinned that wildcat grin and took me in his arms and kissed me.

"I'm glad you slept." He held me close, and I put my head to his chest. "I came to check that your sister was being kind and saw you dead on the chaise. You snore really loudly, did you realize?"

"Liar." I reached up and kissed him.

"Takes one to know one." He grinned. "Let's get this charade over with, shall we?"

"Let's," I agreed and let him lead me out of the house.

I did make one stop before heading to the chapel. It looked like Izzy had tasked me with enough errands to ferry me to hell and back. And

I'd do them because I'd do anything for her. So if I was going to hell, I might as well do it thoroughly. I retrieved my phone from my cabin. This devil rectangle might get me killed, but only if Izzy didn't manage the deed first. I pocketed the thing and met Andrews back out on the dock. Time to go watch Izzy take a short walk in a pretty dress.

Andrews and I were almost to the chapel when that street kid Izzy had taken in came running out to meet me.

"Maid of Honor! Captain Maid of Honor!" the breathless child called to me. "The lady bride needs you." She almost tumbled into me, and I wondered if she'd ever walked, let alone run, in a dress before.

"Go on. I'm almost there." I tried to send the urchin back. Andrews was smirking next to me as I tried to deal with the child.

"No, I am to bring you to her." The skinny thing was adamant.

I kissed Andrews and told him to save me a seat and let the urchin lead me to my sister. Izzy was in the front annex of the chapel pacing and drinking. For the love of god, hadn't she had enough this morning?

"Anne! Oh my god, Anne, what am I doing?" she exclaimed between sips. I'd had enough. I grabbed the flask and tossed it out the door. She had dragged me to this event, she was going to freaking see it through.

"Getting married." I held her hands tight in mine. "If you spill anything on this dress, I'll kill you." So far, the dress still looked fine, but I wasn't going to abide any rum on it after I'd kept it in pristine shape longer than she'd been alive.

"Why did you do that? It was calming me!" she hissed. All the nobility was already assembled just beyond, and we were attracting attention. She continued her hysterics. "No, you're right, I am obviously a crazy person! Being in love with someone doesn't mean that you just marry them! This time is bonkers! And now I can't stop thinking 'What if he only wants to marry me because he saw me naked that first day?'"

"I gotta say, I'd respect him a lot more if that's the reason. It's a good, honest reason." I laughed.

"What?!" she shrieked. I hushed her and pulled her out of view.

"Izzy, I can offer you the chance to walk out of here right now. I can take you so far that you'd never ever need to see or think of this moment again. But you can't say yes to that, can you?" I played chicken with her anxiety. Say yes, I silently begged her.

"No. No, I'm not leaving." Resolve returned to her complexion.

"Then this is your very own moment. Just live it and enjoy it. It's a good one." I patted her on the back and moved to take my seat next to Andrews.

"What did Mom say? When you told her?" Izzy stopped me.

"'Stop being a jealous bitch and go to your sister's wedding.' More or less." I laughed, but Izzy was not impressed. Fine. I could be serious. "Also. That you're different. You have always wanted a family of your own. And that you aren't leaving anyone behind. You're adding to your life. Because that's what you do." Not subtracting, I reminded myself. She was not doing this to subtract me from her life.

"I – I wonder if I'm being unfair to him. I brought up the concept of family planning, and it was such a foreign concept I never even got close to talking about the Pill. He thinks it'll just happen when it's supposed to."

I looked out into the little chapel and saw Andrews sitting with Magnus. If I had met that man when I could still have children, I would have done it. The son next to him would be our son. The name next to his in that graveyard would have been mine. I sighed and rubbed my neck. Fate was a cruel mistress to serve.

"Men are funny about their children," I said, watching Andrews talk with Magnus. "But in order to have any with him, you are going to have to have sex. And to have sex with that—" douche canoe "—Ian, you need to get married first." I spun her towards the opening of the chapel and attempted to take my seat for the third time.

The Bitch Captain (and The Lady)

"Yes. You're right," she conceded.

I smiled. She was looking better. I tried to take my seat again.

"Do you think he's actually going to go through with it?" Izzy ratcheted up her panic once again.

"Yes," I reassured her again. Enough of this. "Wait right here." I left her with her maid and the skinny kid and marched to my soon-to-be brother-in-law.

"Up. Get up now," I demanded. He looked about to talk back, but he was not talking to some lady, oh no. Lieutenant Commander, meet the Bitch Captain of the Seven Seas, your new sister-in-law. "We are getting this show on the road." I yanked him to his feet and stood him at the end of the aisle. "Do not move a muscle. Wait right here and I will bring her to you. You really want to marry her?"

"Yes," he replied, looking deeply offended at the question. There was no softness in his voice for me.

"You owe me one large favor to be named at a later date," I told him and marched my ass back down the aisle to Izzy. I put her arm in mine and began to hum "Here Comes the Bride." "Let's go, Lady Covington."

"Coventry," she corrected me.

"For fuck's sake. Let's do this already. I'm starving." I walked my sister down the aisle. It was a short walk, and at the end I gave her to him. Then it was me who couldn't move. The two lovers gazed at each other, and I didn't matter anymore.

Graham's hand appeared in mine, and he guided me back to the bench next to him, where he kept his arms around me while the priest spoke. Weddings are funny things. You go to watch your loved one make this huge commitment yet spend the majority of time thinking of your own wedding, be it future or past. I picked at the wrist wraps and thought about the man at my side and the children we would never have.

"This should be our wedding," Graham whispered to me. I turned to see his eyes, intense and pained, studying my face for any break in my resolve.

"I know." I smoothed his frown away and kissed him lightly. Graham found the tiny bag in my hand holding the rings. Apparently, as maid of honor I was charged with holding these tokens. Probably a better idea than giving it to that urchin girl. Graham examined them closely before slipping the larger on his own finger, and the smaller one onto me. Neither ring fit our hands, and he quickly returned them to the tiny bag with a laugh then wrapped his arms around me. For that brief moment my insides had rejoiced at the sight of a physical representation of connection between us. I was absolutely sick with the wanting of it.

Helene Andrews
1610-1684
Beloved Wife
Beloved Mother

The minute Izzy said, "I do," I felt lonelier than I had ever felt in my life. She was his family now. I had only just gotten her back and now she was his. Intellectually, I knew she was still my sister, but my heart watched the two of them so besotted and happy and committed, and all I felt was loss. The bride and groom exited the chapel to cheers and congratulations.

"Addition, not subtraction," I murmured to myself as I followed them out of the little chapel, where Izzy tackled and hugged me in front of god and everyone. Her new husband quickly took her away once the receiving line was finished, and I wished her a happy humping in my mind. Hope he was worth the wait, Izzy.

Andrews hadn't come out of the chapel, and I went back in to find him. He was leaning against the altar looking out the back windows displaying the sea beyond. He turned at the sound of my footsteps on the stone and straightened as I walked toward him. He welcomed me with open arms, and we kissed. It was quiet here in the chapel. Most of the guests had begun the walk back to the main house where the reception was just starting up. He leaned back against the altar and held me to him.

"Say yes, Nan." His lips found mine and he almost had me. I kept myself locked against him. "Darling, say yes," he crooned.

Helene Andrews
1610-1684
Beloved Wife
Beloved Mother

"The guests are waiting," I told him and the grave next to his. He kissed me once more but didn't argue. This was as close to a marriage ceremony as he and I would ever get.

Outside the chapel we heard the noises coming from the guest house and grinned at each other. "Ah, young love." I chuckled.

"Lucky bastards." He pulled me in for another kiss while one hand traveled over my chest.

"Come on, Andrews. You owe me a drink."

"I paid you back for that a long time ago."

"Then buy me another." I let my own hands travel, and he shivered and grinned.

"Right this way, *Lady Anne*." The joke killed us both, and we dissolved into laughter.

We were already a round or two behind when we approached the guests. Like a middle school dance, the men were on one side and the women another. All of us waiting for Izzy and her new husband to emerge. The younger, unmarried crowd mingled along the edges of the patio. I joined the men's party where the drinks were strong and the language stronger. I knew these men and had made them plenty of money.

"Captain, shouldn't you be with the women ready to console young Lady Coventry? They should be back soon!" Lavigne guffawed and welcomed us into the group.

"Coventry was in a desperate hurry. If it were me, she'd be bedded and back here already!" Lord Wallington cackled around a cigar and a tumbler of brandy.

"No wonder Lady Wallington always looks so windblown with you speeding in and out of her," I retorted, and all the men exploded with laughter. I took the opportunity to steal the lit cigar right from Wallington's open mouth.

He cackled again and poured me a drink. I drank it down, and Graham was right behind me with a refill. The distillery was right here on his property, and he never bothered to water down the drinks. This would be a raucous crowd by the end of the night. I waggled the cigar in my mouth and took a seat. Andrews sat behind me and lit a cigar for himself.

"At Wallington's age I'm surprised he can get up at all!" Lavigne joined in the fun.

"Trick is to remember them as they were." Wallington leered at me.

"And we'll remember you as you are now." I let the cigar droop sadly downward. Wallington cackled again at the blue-collar humor as did the rest of them.

"Well, Coventry has got himself a live one, heard those screams of hers from here!" Sherman jeered. "Haven't heard noises like that since—"

"You've never heard noises like that, Sherman. Sit down!" I cheered the other men and threw back my drink. "I've seen you try to button your coat." I walked my fingers along his big belly. "I'm guessing your finger work doesn't improve when between a woman's legs."

"Control your woman, Andrews."

"Learn to pleasure one, John," Andrews retorted to the fat man.

"Andrews, this captain of yours, does she talk like this to you?" Talbot ventured.

"Oh no," he spun me towards him and hugged me close, "we do very little talking. Look away, gentlemen, lest you learn something that actually pleases your wives." He kissed me long and deep to the cheers and whistles of the gathered men. Andrews grinned that wildcat grin of his, and I brought him in for another kiss.

I was feeling the effects of the alcohol already. I was a lightweight and these drinks were strong, and I wanted nothing more than to lose myself tonight. The good-natured, if raunchy, banter continued as the drinks were poured and consumed. Andrews kept me close to him, and his face soon grew rosy and warm from the alcohol. Where the hell was the food? I was starving and half-pickled already. If Izzy didn't return soon, I was planning a kitchen raid...or just taking Andrews to bed and never returning.

What felt like an hour later, the huzzahs and whistles announced the return of the newly-married and consummated couple. Izzy must have had a good time. She was doing an excellent Bambi impression walking into her wedding reception. Her new husband was flushed and satisfied and almost as baby-deer-like.

"She can still walk, Coventry. Go back in there!" Lavigne shouted to them and was joined by the hoots and cheers of the other men.

Izzy looked like she wanted to crawl in a hole and die, which was hilarious. She'd obviously had a good time, and if we were home, she'd have texted me a picture of herself smoking in bed to brag about her latest conquest. These buffoons and their blue humor weren't anything she couldn't handle.

"There he is. You look much relaxed, sir!" Davies greeted the new groom with a tumbler and a cigar.

"Couldn't have done a good job. Those silks aren't even wrinkled!" Maynwaring jeered.

He would notice the silks. I rolled my eyes and almost fell over from the effort. His two young sons were either miracles or not related to this man at all.

"I heard the lady myself. The lieutenant commander certainly fulfilled his duties!"

"Sit down and get some new material!" I yanked Sherman back toward his chair, but he fell to the ground, merely guffawed, and continued to smoke his cigar from the supine position.

I expected Izzy to stay with her husband, but the women claimed her and took her into their dour circle. That damn young lieutenant brought his drink over to us. A man with echoes of the lieutenant's genes hovered over him.

"He's still stiff! The lady best prepare for a long night!" Wallington crowed over the noise to loud catcalls and whoops.

"Gentlemen, please. My lady wife is delicate and sensitive to your jests." The young lieutenant was far behind us in cups.

"Right. And I'm Doris Day," I snorted.

"Pardon me?" He looked at me oddly as if he hadn't realized I was here.

"No." I despised him. He stole my sister from me.

Reprieve in the form of Lady Catherine arrived, requesting my presence with the ladies. I looked around to be sure she meant me. "Really?"

"Yes, Lady – Captain. We heard the – well, the sounds she made – it's not polite for mixed company, but I feel sure the Lady Coventry will have need of you." Her voice was hardly more than a whisper.

The men and I exploded in lewd laughter until I saw Catherine's terrified expression. The young wife appeared to be only just holding up to the men, the booze, and the smoke. She'd bolt at any moment.

"Enough, gentlemen!" I shouted them down. "I can imagine your own pathetic mewling the first time you paid to get between a woman's legs." A few of the men shared poor Catherine's shocked and embarrassed expression with that one; many more less-ashamed spirits laughed along with me.

"So that's what I hear from Robert's bed every evening. Too bad there isn't a girl in there with him. Just his own hands and a dream." Young Henry Maynwaring dug into his brother to the cheers of this crass crowd.

"I bet dear Robert will dream of this beauty tonight, and the noises we could get out of her!" Sherman roared as he smacked Catherine on her rear. The poor girl turned to flee, but I shielded her in my arms, feeling oddly protective of this future passenger of mine. I was about to kick the balls off Sherman when Andrews placed a hand on my shoulder.

"Darling, allow me." Andrews decked Sherman so hard the fat man stumbled ass over shoulders into the bushes beyond. The whole crowd cheered and laughed and patted Andrews on the back and refilled drinks, leaving Sherman in the dirt.

"Pay these miscreants no mind, Lady Catherine." I spoke to everyone but her. "They do not have a very discerning scream palate. They wouldn't know the cry of a woman's pleasure from the gas exploding out their backsides!" The men sent up hoots of laughter as I led Catherine out of the cloud of cigar smoke. Ah yes, everyone loves a good fart joke.

I leaned on the young wife to help me cross the great divide to the women – the much quieter, much less boisterous women. I cursed my lily liver as I took my first steps. The alcohol was running thick through me already, and my head was spinning and giddy.

"So, Catie, where are we going?" I drunkenly whispered to her once we were away from the men.

"Just going over here." She pointed the way to the women, struggling a little under my weight.

"No, I hear we're going sailing." I tried to look at her pointedly. She just looked wide-eyed back at me. I tried again. "You and me are getting on my boat. Right? So where are we going?"

The girl was petrified.

"Don't worry. I don't do the alcohol on the boat. That's rule number two. There are five rules. I'm a good captain. Only capsized a few times. So," I leaned on her more as my left leg forgot where it was going, "where are we going?"

She was so cute with her eyes all wide and scared. I could have picked her up and put her in my pocket.

"Anywhere but England. Maybe France or Portugal?" The little girl spoke in no more than a whisper.

"No! Not Portugal!" I whispered back. "I owe Charlie a lot of money." And that guy was not going to let me out of my debt. "Ugh. Fine. You can have Isabelle's bed."

"Is the cabin big enough for three?" she asked as she straightened me up.

"Three what?"

"People."

"I…" I locked my eyes on my darling sister, "have someone to kill. Be right back." Although the killing might have to wait. Now it was my right foot who'd forgotten where it was going.

I didn't know these women as well as their husbands. Lavigne's wife was fine. But the rest merely tolerated my presence and the wealth my ship brought their homes. I'm sure they were perfectly content to have me across the way with the men. Catherine helped me to a seat. The women were consoling Izzy after the supposed death of her virginity.

The killing could definitely wait. I wished I had popcorn. This was the most amazing moment of my life. The women were attempting a 17th-century sex ed class for my sister who had voluntarily sat on faces up and down the west coast of the Americas.

"You don't have to be brave for us, Lady Coventry," Lady Wallington consoled Izzy, who seemed mildly confused.

"Lady Isabelle, the first time a husband has his wife is often difficult," I elaborated, having a hunch it was Ian who probably needed the

The Bitch Captain (and The Lady)

consoling, not Izzy – that young bastard likely never experienced anything like he found between my sister's legs. "He must have been gentle with you. You are lucky." Gentle like a battering ram.

Izzy sat down like she needed a piles cushion, and I was ready to keel over with laughter. I looked over at the young lieutenant with new respect. My brother-in-law caught me looking, and I saluted him. He frowned and went back to smoking. Ass.

The women continued educating Izzy on the mysteries of what husbands want and how they get it, and I was giddy watching her reactions of horror. It wasn't only my lack of nobility that kept these women separated from me. Andrews and I had always enjoyed a more-physical-than-socially-appropriate relationship in public, and my responses to him were beyond foreign to their experiences. The fact that I touched him and welcomed his touches made them uncomfortable for reasons they couldn't explain to themselves.

"Lady Isabelle," I couldn't help chiming in, "the male body is nothing to fear. If you have any questions, I'm happy to answer them. I know you have never been bedded before." Izzy was going to kill me, but at least I'd die happy. I took the drink from Catherine's hand and drained it. Go big or go home.

"I do appreciate all of your kindness. My lady mother prepared me for this eventuality and…I believe I am quite fortunate with my husband," she said.

I hoped to god that young lieutenant felt the same way. I looked over at the young lieutenant again. He had one of Izzy's joints in his mouth. At least they had one common interest. The assface.

"You were quite fortunate with your lady mother as well," one of the other women added.

"California is a rather foreign place," Lady Catherine said to me as she refilled the glass I'd stolen from her. "Captain? Have you seen many male bodies?" The young wife looked at me with such innocence and sincerity – and if she had asked me this question three drinks and a male boasting session earlier, I probably would have not been as crude.

"A lot happens on the sea, Lady Catherine." I couldn't help it. She was too innocent. I lifted my skirt with a finger to look like a huge erection. "There be monsters."

Lavigne's wife shrieked and laughed and fell into me. I always liked her. I laughed into her shoulder, and we found our way back to sitting straight up together.

"Oh no, really?" Lady Catherine gasped.

"I'll tell you a secret." Oh, I could tell her stories of monsters. But I'd prefer kinder memories right now. I looked over at Graham, who was watching me from across the dance floor. "I like their bodies. If the bed is right, there's no reason for fear at all."

"Like Mr. Andrews? You don't fear him?" The young wife looked over at him too.

"On the contrary, he terrifies me." I kept up his gaze, and he stood up and came over.

"Nanette? May I have this dance?" He held out his hand, and I let him lead me away.

And then we danced.

Did I mention how much I loved dancing with this man? Before everything, when it was just him and me, my ship and his small crappy farm, we'd have parties out here. There was music and bonfires and food and dancing. I taught him my dances and he taught me his, and we'd somehow put the steps together. Later, at the many Wallington dinners, we'd spend the whole evening dancing away among the tapers and silks and floral arrangements. Then, as his estate grew and the parties became larger, we still danced. We moved in sync, and I let him lead and twirl me around the dance floor and ignored the wider world.

In my long and wandering life, I had become a connoisseur of last moments. There was a distinctive fear and flavor to last moments, and I was tasting that now. I wouldn't have a whole year with Andrews. This was my last dance with him. I'd be sailing away soon, and this time I really wouldn't be coming back.

So we danced.

The party blurred and circled around us. Beri got out her new violin and played a lively reel that Magnus and I danced to (he was getting as good as his father) while Graham swept Sofia around the dance floor. The girl's feet barely touched the ground as they whirled about. We almost crashed twice, but I ducked low and Graham lifted his daughter high. Then Amelia and I took a spin around the floor while Graham led Josephine. Their mothers all sat to the side and enjoyed their drinks and meals as they watched us cavort. Even Yvonne's face took a break from its usual scowl as she watched her daughter dance. Magnus and Sofia partnered up and attempted some steps together while his older sisters badgered him and noted each mistake.

Lady Wallington snagged Andrews during a brief lull between dances, and he merrily swung the older lady around the dance floor. I looked for Izzy and saw her young lieutenant pawing her over at their table. Right, it was time to get her to explain this Catherine-plus-two-mystery-passengers conundrum.

"Lady Covington," I interrupted the young lieutenant sucking at her neck like a limpet, "I'd like to have a word with you."

They had cake in front of them. My stomach growled. I hadn't eaten yet as Andrews and I had started dancing before the food was served. I had only managed to grab a few bites between the music changes. I was hungry but desired time with him more than food tonight.

"I will kill you, Anne." She moved her neck away from the suckerfish. "Cov.en.try," she corrected me.

"Cov-en-try," I imitated her and grabbed a fork and wondered where to start. I always did enjoy cake, and Izzy's new husband was probably full since he'd been eating her out all night. Just a guess.

"Darling," Izzy turned to her human-sized barnacle, "would you be so kind as to give me a few minutes with my very, very inebriated sister?"

Was I drunk? I held the fork up and tried to sight on the tines. Yes. I was drunk. I giggled and stabbed the cake. I loved wine. Shame I couldn't drink it all the time.

"Jesus, Anne." Izzy put another slice in front of me. She really was a generous soul. She was kind enough to mercy-fuck that lieutenant, which seemed the epitome of generosity to me at the moment. "So what's up?"

"Three," I answered, pointing the fork at her. "Three, Izzy." I couldn't focus on her too long when the calories were beckoning. I never seemed to get enough to eat on my journeys back here. "Good cake. Needs a little more sugar, though."

"It does not!" She glared at me. It definitely did, but I wasn't about to stop eating it. "Three what now?"

"People, Izzy. Lady Catherine plus two. Makes three. I don't take passengers." I counted them on my fingers for emphasis. I missed a few of my fingers on the first try and waved off the effort.

"What? Well, don't think of them as passengers. Think of them as… survivors of the system that you are going to spirit away to safety!" It's a good thing she made good (if unsweetened) cake because she made lousy arguments.

Spit and polish it however you want, passengers were a messy business. Cargo stayed nice and tidy in its crate and didn't ask "Are we there yet?" and "Do you think those clouds look dangerous?"

I shook my head and found more cake. "I'll take care of the sails, but you – you will have to take care of the spirit. Think she'll sleep in the kitchen bunk? Who are the other two? Better not be a man. That rule isn't changing." Every time I relaxed that damn rule it ended badly.

The Bitch Captain (and The Lady)

I'd have to tell Dom soon that he would need to stay away. His older brother was stolen, press-ganged, right off my deck. I wasn't going to risk him too.

"The baby – male, but only a year, so I think you'll allow it – and Bessie."

"BABY!" I almost choked. "Oh no, no, no, no. No babies." She must be out of her damn mind. Babies were worse than men, if slightly less needy. No. No babies.

Izzy actually shushed me and looked around like I was blabbing out national secrets. "Anne. Listen." She grabbed my arm to keep my focus, and I stared at her hand on the velvet gown.

I was really glad she was here. Even if this was her wedding, I was happy to have her with me. Like, I was really happy. She knew me better now and wasn't running or scared. She liked me still. I was happy for that. Izzy had been talking and talking, and I'd missed some of it. I attempted to refocus.

"And they have a baby together," she was explaining. I nodded seriously like I'd heard and committed every detail to heart. "Her husband is the commander, and there's no way she's going to be able to keep passing John Henry off as Bessie's once he's back. And he's coming back on the same ship that's taking Ian. So this is very, very urgent."

"Ugh. I do hate that commander." I'd love to stick it to that son of a bitch. He'd orchestrated the attack at Kings Bay, and I owed him some hurt. One baby on a boat was a small price to pay. "Pompous ass. Fine. I'll do it. How quick can you pack up?"

"Pack up? What do you mean?"

"You're going with me. Duh." Of course she was coming. Why wouldn't she come? She'd have to cull that wardrobe of hers, though.

She smacked my hand away from more of the cake. I sat back and waited. I could be patient. She couldn't guard that plate forever. I kept my fork at the ready.

"I can't go with you!" she protested. "I have business interests here!

I'm running an inn – that we're expanding – building a shipyard, not to mention a house with my new husband—"

"Not leaving this island without you." I interrupted. I was still hungry. "You stay, I stay, Catherine stays. Baby stays. We all—" I loved playing chicken with Izzy. It was too easy.

"We all stay, I get it." She thought for a moment while vigilantly keeping guard on the unsweetened cake.

"Are there any reputable female captains here in the Somers Isles?"

I broke into an enormous smile. "Just the one." I waggled my eyebrows. I was the best captain, hands down, regardless of what lay between my legs. Blink, Izzy. Just give up and blink.

"She's very concerned about sailing with men. Doesn't trust them at all," Izzy mused.

I watched her calculate and kept a steady line on her. She'd blink first. It wasn't even a fair fight. Izzy felt deeply for people, and poor Catherine's plight had clearly sung its siren song deep into my kind sister's soul.

"How long do you think I could successfully hide them? I do have 200 acres," she asked.

"Up to you. It's a small island." Blink, Izzy. I grinned.

"She wants to go to Europe. You mentioned needing to be in Europe by fall…" she continued, thinking aloud.

"I'm not going without you."

"Yeah, you said that. Can we do it?"

"Yes. *We* can do it," I affirmed. Come on, blink, sister.

"How long will it take to sail there?"

"I have a few stops to make." Greenland, France, and possibly Spain if I could squeeze it in. "Probably four months."

"And how long would it take to sail back? Are there any seasonal patterns or anything like that that would delay a return trip?"

Sail back? I blinked. I wouldn't be sailing back. I wouldn't even be sailing close by enough to do a drive-by drop-off. If my sister left

The Bitch Captain (and The Lady)

this island, she wouldn't be returning with me. If Izzy didn't leave this island, I would have to leave her despite the promise I'd made her earlier today. *Your secrets have secrets.* My scars tightened and twitched, and I rubbed my hands over them. Yes, Izzy, I keep things from you, dark and desperate and evil stories that I won't dare allow creep into your dreams.

"Do you have a time you need to be back?" If her husband wasn't here, did she need to be here?

"Maybe next summer at the latest?" She twisted her napkin and looked at her shiny new husband.

"Next summer's not great for me. Can I interest you in a nice 1670 or 1680? I hear their Bordeaux are drinking nicely." I swirled my wine and took a sip in imitation of a sommelier. I was not going to be anywhere near here in 1650. Well, *I* would be here in 1650, but I was definitely not going to be back here in 1650. My current plans included skipping that whole year altogether and hanging out in Aruba 1996.

"You do realize I got married today, right? I'm not interested in a ten-to-twenty-year separation." She had the nerve to look at me like I was the idiot.

"That's not–sure. Yup." She didn't have the concept quite right. I'd explain it to her later.

Izzy continued her mental math, and I sat back and waited. Her answer would determine how long I had left with her.

"You love sailing. Why do you need me, again?" She was an idiot sometimes. My wine glass and I agreed on that.

"Don't be an idiot. I love you, you loser." I laughed and forked some cake from the plate she'd left open again.

"Oh!" Izzy suddenly hugged me.

I was embarrassed to have a female in this era be openly demonstrative towards me. My needs for physical contact were typically fulfilled by Andrews and Andrews alone. Izzy's hugs were of a different ilk, and I wasn't prepared.

"You should have led with that." She squeezed me tighter. "Alright.

I don't think I can tell him any of this. He wouldn't understand."

I looked at the young lieutenant and shrugged. What he did or didn't understand made me no nevermind.

"Tell him whatever you want." I absently picked up my fork and looked for more to eat. The alcohol was pounding around my head. I needed to soak some of it up before it turned on me worse than it already had.

"You're obviously starving. What do you want?" Izzy conjured a servant from the ether, and soon the table was laid with every dish she'd spent the past few days concocting. It was all delicious.

She derided my food preferences and rolled her eyes as I attempted to recall for her every bite of every morsel I'd eaten since the ceremony ended. Most of it was alcohol. The sugar and fat revived me a little, and I found myself spouting all kinds of details I'd never otherwise reveal to her. It was a rarity that I had both slept and eaten decent amounts in the same day.

My spirit was riding high. As I talked, I watched Andrews dancing with Lady Wallington. He spared me a glance that was half incredulous and half "help me" as the older woman grazed his rear. This was a great party. I was having a blast.

"Hey, how would you like to travel east? I have a friend there. Oh! But you know. Yeah, you know."

Izzy had met Zheng some years ago on spring break. That was a crazy trip. I shot Marco for the second time on that trip. I chuckled at the memory. If she did want to go east, I know my sister would love the bustling ports and insane goods sold there. Bet she could make a better cake than this with some of those ingredients.

"I have a boat in port in Madagascar I sometimes switch to in the Pacific. It's a catamaran style, less in-your-face European. I can get into better ports that way." I left that boat on loan to a contact there. He worked independently, sourcing riches off the East African coast, and provided me with a share of his haul in return for use of the ship.

"This amount of traveling would take some time," Izzy mused some more.

"Lucky for you, I specialize in just that very commodity." I smiled as I ate my way through the table.

"So we might even be able to send messages and plan out some kind of itinerary?"

"Well, if you want to portal, just pick a date. Boom. So long as you don't die, you'll be back whenever." There was really no need for messages when you'd be back before they'd know you left.

"Well....I just want to be able to find Ian. Would we be able to go to England?!"

"I try my best to avoid that place. Too busy. Not much sun." I shivered just thinking about the rocky shores and cliffs of that place. The people reflected the poor weather and conditions. There was no mystery in my mind as to why the inhabitants of that island set out to live anywhere and everywhere else in the world.

"Let me try this again. I want to be able to go see my husband. Can we fucking do that?" she snapped at me.

"I mean...sure. But isn't he going to be at war awhile? We could travel the world three times over, arrive back tomorrow. He'd never know you were gone. Why sit and pine for him here, doing needlework or whatever for two years, when we could just skip to the end of the war? He probably wouldn't be gray by then or anything. Just older." Or dead. I stopped my alcohol-soaked brain just in time from including that tidbit. "Besides, London is way expensive." Andrews was now deep into a branle dance with Lady Wallington, and I couldn't keep the smile off my face.

"We'll talk about those details later," Izzy mused. "So you mean to say we could leave, do our errands or whatever, and then come right back? Like almost no time had passed at all? Like you did!" She gasped.

"Well, no time will pass for him. But yeah." Andrews narrowly avoided another bum grope. This was better than any TV show.

"Right. Like you did. Hey! Did you refill the ollas, or are all of my plants wilting?"

"What are ollas?"

"My plants in the kitchen, Anne! The ollas are a watering system, remember? You set them up for me." I tried to focus on her. Plants in the kitchen?

I had a vague memory of her asking for some plant system when I first approached her about taking a "sisterly summer cruise." I'd gotten it but had been in and out of the time stream for at least five years between when she'd made the request and had finally gotten on board.

"I don't remember. But yeah, they're probably dead." Lady Wallington was fairly chasing Graham around the dance floor. I was dying.

Izzy patted my arm returning my attention to her. "Have you had any of the brownies?"

I loved brownies! Where had she been hiding them? "No, but they look good."

"No. Remember, you're not allowed to have any. Not even in 1649.... probably even more not in 1649."

"Why not? I love brownies. Got to be better than that cake." I reached for one, and Izzy got in my way.

"No. Anne? Anne? No!" Izzy hauled me back from the plate.

She started wrestling me but I was a good brawler and I was craving chocolate. She gave me all this food and was going to refuse me a brownie? I was going to get that brownie.

"Mr. Andrews!" Izzy called out, practically sitting on my lap to keep me from her precious desserts.

Andrews gratefully detached himself from Lady Wallington and walked over to us, a bemused and curious smile on his handsome features.

"She can't have any of those chocolatey squares," Izzy informed him. "If you can't control her, she'll be your problem once the stuff kicks in."

"Up you go, Nanette." Andrews lifted me to my feet and held me to him tightly. "Lady Wallington is going to get the wrong idea if I keep dancing with her."

"Good. She needs a good long, hard—" Graham's lips found mine, and I didn't care about brownies or babies or anything else. I returned his kiss and forgot the rest.

"Come along, Nanette." He spoke softly in my ear and whirled me out onto the dance floor, where we began one of our favorite dances, the tango. The food and dancing finally brought a semblance of sobriety to my mind, and I focused on just taking the moment in and committing it to memory.

Andrews and I spun through a reel, dancing circles around the other guests. I toasted Izzy, I toasted Andrews, I toasted the guests. Izzy was having a grand time too in the moments between the young lieutenant dragging her off to screw and coming back to enjoy her party. I remember there was a lot of laughter. I remember there was a lot of dancing.

I managed to snap a few pictures, one of Izzy and Ian dancing, a close-up of Ian holding Izzy glowing in her dress at sunset, Izzy surrounded by the other noble ladies, and a selfish one I took of Andrews, grinning that wildcat grin, just so I'd be able to remember him just like this.

But mostly we danced.

Many of the guests had retired to their beds before Graham and I were close to finishing the evening. When the music hit a lull, Izzy and that new husband of hers came over before the next song began.

"Finally!" she exclaimed, and I turned to see her actually standing and not straddling the young lieutenant. "I've been waiting to say good night to you for what felt like ages." Izzy caught me up in a huge hug that knocked the wind out of me.

Graham laughed at the sight of someone else willingly hugging me.

"You didn't have to wait for me." I pushed her back. "Haven't you 'gone to bed' like eight times already?" The dress was now wrinkled in a distinctive "oh, mighty Ian, have your way with me" pattern. Good thing I gave it to her, or I'd have to burn it.

Izzy elbowed me, and I was thankful for the whalebone corseting protecting my spleen. "We did have to wait for you, because we're well-mannered, and you two are our hosts."

"I suppose we are, aren't we?" The moniker sounded funny to my ear, but there was a certain truth to it. I had seen this house built, grown this estate beyond the bounds of any other on this island, and was intimately involved with its proprietor. I smiled at Andrews, who beamed back at me and placed his hand on my lower back.

"No need for fisticuffs tonight, Coventry?" Andrews asked the lieutenant. I'd have to find out that story later. Sounded fun.

"I should say not, Andrews." The two men clasped hands.

"Don't wear him out," I told Izzy, giving her new husband a depreciating evaluation. "He looks fragile." Izzy flicked me. "Ouch." That kind of hurt.

"So, good night then?" she asked with her eyes on that husband of hers.

I decided to shock the crap out of her and grabbed her and kissed her on the cheek right in front of that lieutenant who thought he might have eclipsed my claim on her.

"Congratulations on your wedding," I whispered into her ear. "I wish—" that I could have had a wedding just like this "—you all the best. Good night." I relinquished my sister over to her new husband and retreated back to Graham.

"I imagine that you will have a pleasant night as well. Good night, Anne. I love you," she said.

Mom should have been here. In my ledger of misdeeds, not bringing her back here for this now officially numbered in the top five.

"Love you too. Go get 'em, tiger." I punched her on the shoulder and watched them walk up to the house.

"Nanette?" Andrews asked as he led me back to the dancing. "What's a tiger?"

"You. You are a tiger. Just with fewer stripes," I told my wildcat man and kissed him fiercely while I still could.

After the newlyweds went off to their bed, I helped Andrews settle the guests into the various rooms and pallets throughout the house. Soon the two of us were the only souls still moving around the place. He led me to our room and held me around the waist as he shut the door. I surveyed our bedroom, feeling for all the world that he and I were the newlyweds, not Izzy and her lieutenant. Andrews moved his hands up to cradle my face and pulled me in close for a kiss. He pressed me up against the door, slowly lifting my skirts and laying claim to my curves underneath, pulling me against him.

"Nanette," he brushed the words against my lips, "say yes to me."

"Give me something I can say yes to," I pleaded.

He retreated back just far enough to look at me, his eyes burning and dilated, as mine surely were as well. A bit of the wildcat crept into his gaze, and he leaned in, overwhelming me with his presence, and whispered in my ear, "Let your hair down. Say yes."

I smiled, only too willing to play the game. "Yes." I pulled my fingers through my hair, undoing the braids and letting it fall free and loose. He stroked the smooth, loose waves, wrapping a lock around his finger.

"Unlace your dress. Say yes." He stepped back to watch.

"Yes." I pulled the laces out and let the outer garment drop and revealed myself in my stays and shift. I undid the busk without him asking and dropped it to the floor.

"Now your shift. Say yes."

"Yes." I pulled the drawstring at the neck and let my shift fall to the floor. Andrews walked around behind me and brushed his lips against my neck. I shivered in the chill.

"Tell me to touch you," he breathed, his lips and tongue at the nape of my neck.

"Touch me."

He clasped my hands around the back of his neck so that my chest was fully exposed and he had uninterrupted access to my body. "Keep your hands here. Say yes."

"Yes."

He began at my hips. One hand came up and massaged a breast while the other traveled between my legs, teasing me, until I was thrusting against him. My head leaned back on his shoulder and my breath came fast as he slipped his fingers deep into me. I cried out a wordless plea.

"Come to bed now."

"Yes."

I whimpered a little as he removed his fingers against my body's desire. Graham lifted me in his arms and laid me in our bed. He stood over me, just looking.

"Close your eyes."

"Yes." I did as he asked and felt a shock of delight as his lips closed over first one breast then the other. I gripped the headboard and moaned.

Find a way to stay, I begged myself, *stay*. I heard his clothes fall to the floor and felt the heat of him over me as he climbed into bed. He opened my legs and knelt between them. I could live here, I could be his wife, *find a way to stay*!

His fingers sank into me again. He stifled my cry with his lips as he kissed me long and desperately while his fingers played within me. I had never lost control of myself so thoroughly. I shook and thrashed and held onto that headboard for dear life.

"Please, Graham. Graham, please," I begged.

"Yes, Nan," he said, removing his fingers and thrusting deep into me with a groan of satisfaction.

We moved in sync, thrusting, pulling away, meeting each other again. You've been alone long enough, find a way to stay. It felt so good not to be alone. It felt so good to be wanted and desired.

Graham held me tight against his body, not wanting any space between us where I might slip away from him. I held him just as tightly back, angling him deeper and deeper into me, knowing how much space I was about to put between us in a few short days. *Find a way to stay*, I begged. *Stay! Stay! Stay!* At last we brought each other to a final climax and collapsed.

The next morning I woke up hungover and naked in bed, with Andrews' bare ass snoring next to me. "Where are my clothes?" I asked him. He kept snoring. I tried to shake him awake, but he flung his arm over me and shoved me back into the pillows. "Shush, Nanette. Go back to sleep." Yeah, that was a much better choice than getting up.

Andrews had all our food delivered to the room, and we lay curled into each other, still naked, for the rest of the day, the night, and into the next morning. We talked about old times and new ventures. When we got tired of talking, we had sex. When we were too tired for either, we slept.

CHAPTER 12

Not my Honeymoon

Neither of us was well practiced in the art of sitting around and relaxing, and the day Izzy was set to leave for her honeymoon, Andrews and I were already up and moving. We smiled over the obvious sex noises originating from her room, and I told him I'd meet him downstairs at breakfast. I threw my dress sloppily over my shift for the short walk down to my boat. The wind off the sea smelled fresh and tempting. Soon, I promised the waves, soon.

I didn't need my full fighting regalia, but I wasn't interested in wearing any more dresses. I opted for a pair of soft linen pants, one of Graham's shirts I'd stolen from him long ago, and a tailed waistcoat with full, slightly more feminine pleating in the waist. I kept my soft boots on, wrapped a well-washed scarf around my loose hair, and grabbed a hat for the walk back to the house.

Before I left the ship, I stopped in the small galley to examine the terra cotta pots Izzy had made me get for her plants. Ollas. I suppose I understood the purpose. The little plants looked wilted and sad. I took a moment to refill the water and shrugged. Either they'd make it or I'd get some space back in the galley.

I brought out my tools and sail-repair kit and scaled the mast. It was a beautiful morning. I sat a moment looking out at the sea then back towards Andrews' kingdom. His land rolled out from the coast in cleared green swathes lined with trees in the distance. Smoke trailed up into the sky from the various tanneries and processing houses on the outskirts of his property, and workers moved to and fro changing the land and creating goods. The sea was glorious this morning. The sun gleamed off the never-ending waves and the clouds piled up high, a sign that the trade winds were active and ready to make my ship fly. I patted the solid mast I was perched on and sighed. That land was beautiful, its king was beautiful too, but it wasn't my land. Somehow I had to start the process of letting go.

A figure exited the house and walked towards the docks. It looked like Bessie, Lady Catherine's attendant. She walked with determined strides all the way to the dock then hesitated at the gangplank of my boat. She looked all around, saw no one, and took a tentative step on board.

"Hello!" I called out to her.

She started and shielded her eyes to look up at me.

"Are you looking for me?" If she wasn't she could go right back up to the house.

"I was – I wanted – Lady Catherine – yes. I was hoping to speak with you," she called up to me. Clearly she was hoping just the opposite. I shook my head and climbed down.

"I suppose we ought to talk." I jumped the last several feet and landed in front of her. To her credit she didn't back away. "Lady Isabelle intimated to me that you and your mistress might require transportation."

"Yes. She – we do." Bessie gave a furtive look back towards the manor and I imagined that behind a glinting windowpane Lady Catherine was watching us, heart in her throat. I decided to take it easy on this Bessie kid.

"Relax. Isabelle wants you on this ship, so that's what'll happen. You have your ship. Listen carefully to these instructions." I spoke quickly so as not to be seen spending too much time with her. "When the *Victory*

The Bitch Captain (and The Lady)

arrives, you and Catherine must be ready. Pack lightly. Take only what you need to survive. No sentiment. Understand?"

Bessie nodded, wide-eyed but full of grit.

"Good. At some point I'll knock on your door and invite you to do something, it doesn't matter, just refuse me loudly so lots of people hear. That will be your signal that it's time to leave. Grab Catherine and the baby and meet me in the alley behind Gafford's square exactly three hours later." I waited for this to sink in before continuing. "Say nothing to anyone. If you get caught, I will deny you. Take only what you need to survive," I repeated.

Bessie was hardly breathing at this point but kept a hard and determined face. She nodded once and took off for the house. I sent up a silent prayer that Bessie could pull this off. This was all on her small shoulders. I had no confidence in Lady Catherine whatsoever. If they got caught, I would see what I could do for that brave girl.

I walked in through the dining room to the unlikely sight of the young lieutenant and Andrews sitting together at the table. Familiar bangs and scrapes from the kitchen indicated that Izzy had finally finished schtupping her new husband (at least for the time being). I kissed Graham lightly on his lips, whispered, "Have fun," and entered the kitchen area.

Izzy had an apron over a dress I didn't recognize and was whirling around the place in a familiar pattern. She blew me a cheerful "Good morning!" as she curtseyed to the oven.

If you looked closely, you could see cartoon woodland animals singing about her latest love session as she cooked a fairytale feast. Guess the young lieutenant was a good lay.

I spied some cooling rolls and butter and sat on the counter to help myself. Andrews' laughter boomed out from the dining room next door, and I looked, bemused, at the door, wondering what he could have found so humorous.

Izzy brushed me away from my spot on the counter to get access to some pans. She moved me again when she pulled some kind of hot pastry from the kiln-like oven and sat me in a proper chair by the fire. There was a simmering pot of some kind of sauce over the flames. I dipped a chunk of roll in it and tried a bite. It was hot and I inhaled and tried to chew and cool my mouth down.

"Yeowch, that's hot." I dipped the roll again and blew on it this time. Still hot.

"At least wait for the compote to cool, Anne! Geez," Izzy rebuked me. All the cartoon animals following her around shook their heads and tsked at my impatience before going back to singing.

"It's cooler now." I went in for a third taste and waited as long as my patience allowed to eat it. "Ouch. Nope. Ouch. Not yet. Damn, that smarts. Ouch."

Izzy smacked my hand away from the sauce and removed the pot from temptation. I went back to the butter like a chump. The men's voices murmured through the wall, and I again wondered what the two of them could be talking about.

"We should probably discuss those favors I need from you." Izzy pounded green stuff into dough.

"Probably." I tried to sneak a piece of the dough, but she smacked my hand.

"I have some crates of supplies. There are these refugees who barely escaped being enslaved, and now they're working at the shipyard – anyway, I just want to help them with a few basics. I've already talked to Davies, and he mentioned that Mary would be in charge of those things. The same Mary from your boat?"

"The same." I stood up and found the pot of sauce. It must be cool by now. I stuck my finger in it to test. "Ouch. Fine, I'll bring the stuff over. Where is it? Ouch." I stuck my delicious finger in my mouth. Worth it.

"I brought the crates and things here. Angelica let me store them."

The Bitch Captain (and The Lady)

"I'll get it over. What next?" The idea that I'd get to see Mary and Dom and the other kids again before leaving this place warmed me.

"Medications. I need to try to give Ian as much protection as I can before he leaves. I figure TDAP, MMR, maybe a few others? Smallpox?" She looked towards the walls and kept her voice low, knowing this was illicit future talk.

"I've got it. But clearly you know that already. I've been vaccinating this place for years. I loved stabbing Yvonne more than I've ever loved anything I've ever done." There was another memory that warmed me. Oh, how she'd screamed like a little bitch. I smirked and replayed the memory in my head a few more times. So good.

"Stabbing Yvonne? What are you talking about?"

"With a needle. Not a knife...not yet."

"You vaccinated your boyfriend's other girlfriends? Concubines? I don't know what the proper terms are. Okay, whatever, I'm not judging the details of your sex life," Izzy said, voice dripping with judgement despite her words. Concubines? As if Helene would ever be at the beck and call of anyone's carnal desires.

"Concubines? God, no. If anything, he was their whore." I pushed the unwelcome but fitting image out of my head. It was isolated out here, and there was a distillery and lots of parties and few options. "And I was vaccinating the kids. I made her sit there and take it to show the kids they'd be fine." God, how I'd relished sinking that needle in her stupid arm. I'd take that memory to my nonexistent grave.

"I see. Regarding our...secret mission. Since we're going to be at sea for so long, I want you to tell me things. Like, all of the big things you've been hiding. Deal?" She was serious. Izzy pinned me to the wall with her eyes.

"Izzy..." How could I begin to explain? "That is a complicated request." I was at a loss. There was no way I could fulfill that request. I could try to tell her some stories, but there were so many others her life would be happier not knowing.

"I'm sure it is. Will you do it?" She didn't drop her gaze. I winced. It was a terrible idea.

"I can promise you that I'll try. It's just complicated." I mumbled, not wanting to outright lie but not wanting to make her angrier with me than she already was.

"Then try now. Tell me something real and don't bullshit around about it," she demanded.

"Like what?" I bargained for more time to think.

"Dealer's choice. Just tell me something you've never told me before." She and her woodland animals crossed their arms and nodded their heads in agreement.

"Okay." Crap. Crap. Crap. I needed something that wouldn't invite a ton of follow-up questions. Something relatively harmless. Something that would distract her. Izzy stood patiently expecting. Then I had it.

"This isn't the first time you've time-traveled." I confessed. Her woodland chorus puffed out of existence in shock.

"What?!" she exclaimed then looked quickly at the door and back and hushed herself. "Really?" she hissed.

"I had to make sure you'd survive the portal. So we did some test runs," I started to explain.

"Do I dare to ask any more details about those test runs?" Her eyes were wary but intrigued.

"Oh, I'm sure you remember it very vividly." I grinned. This was absolutely the right story to tell.

"Anne! Tell me! I'm going crazy over here."

"I took you to a commune in the 1960s. You met my best friend and proceeded to hump his brains out. Is that enough of a hint?" I smiled and laughed out loud as the revelation crashed over her head.

"Shhh!" she hushed me. "Are you seriously talking about Fetu? Cabo was in the 1960s!?" Maui had told her his real name on that trip, Fetu.

"Sure was." I cackled. This telling her stories was more fun than I realized.

The Bitch Captain (and The Lady)

"Well, shit." Izzy sat back and absently kneaded more dough. "I guess...that actually does explain a lot."

"See, I can say things." The sauce in the pot was finally cool, and I spread it over what was left of my roll.

"Yes. Yes, you can." Izzy absently loaded a few plates with steaming food. "Does this have anything to do with that brand?"

I almost choked at the unexpected reference to one of my earliest and most distinctive scars. Along with his real name, Maui had told her far too much on those spring break trips, in my opinion. Maui bore the Nekydalleon on his neck too.

"Was Fetu a part of this too? How did you learn about this? Does it have anything to do with that liquid you poured on my wrist? How does it all work? Anne?"

Well, fuck me. I had banked on Maui/Fetu log-jamming her thoughts with erotic memories. I guess her new husband had done too good a job. Her cup runneth over and her brain was working again. I forced the memories down and grinned at my sister and did not reveal a thing. She got a taste, and if she wanted the meal, she would get herself on my ship when I departed.

"Sounds like it's going to be a fun cruise. See you on the ship." I grabbed two of the plates she'd filled with breakfast concoctions and exited the kitchen. That was actually a lot of fun. What other stories could I tell her...I certainly had enough of them.

Andrews and that new husband of Izzy's stopped talking and leaned back in their chairs as I entered. I placed one of the plates in front of Graham and kissed him. "I've got work to do on the ship. I'll be up later."

"Nanette," Andrews held my hand, "solve a riddle for us. How old would you say you are?"

I laughed. What a question. "How old would I say I am? Or how old am I?" I did my own Cheshire cat impression and chuckled. "Do you know, I've lost count." And that was the god's honest truth, by the way.

"My lady wife asserted to me that she was your elder." Her husband had the nerve to pipe up.

"Did she now? Well, what a mystery." I kept my voice light, kissed Graham again, and left the room. Dammit, Izzy, and after all I did to not maim and dismember your husband every time I looked upon his stupid face. Less than a year and Andrews would have all the answers he wanted. A witch can be anyone and anything. He'd be free to revile my name and ride off into the sunset with whomever he chose.

I left Andrews to his riddle and took my breakfast out to my ship. I sat at the stationary helm and put my feet up, watching the waves sparkle in the morning sun. Against my will, my thoughts drifted out along the rippling tide to the ocean beyond. As I ate, I breathed in the sun and the temperature and the smells coming off the wind. Conditions were excellent to set sail. I turned to look back at the house and frowned. Not yet. I couldn't leave yet. I finished off the last of the crumbs on the plate and set it aside and sighed. Now was the time for work.

I walked the length of the ship checking the conditions of the boards. Inside, I ran all the systems and checked the solar batteries and reconnected my phone after looking at the pictures from the wedding night. I carefully hid it away behind a slot in the windowsill of my cabin. No one who wasn't looking for it would find it there. My ship echoed strangely, empty as the day I bought her, minus the stinking ambergris in the hold. There was little to take inventory of in either the hold or the kitchen or any of my hidey-holes where I smuggled goods and riches. Izzy had cleaned me out.

Back up top I began my sail check. One at a time I raised the sails and examined the attachment points and damage on the sturdy canvas. I was about to climb the mast to inspect the rigging when Magnus ran down the dock and jumped aboard.

"Auntie!" he called out. "Auntie! You ready to play that game?" He had a chess piece in his hand that he waved at me.

"Have some checks to do first. Want to help?" I asked, knowing he'd jump at the chance.

The boy beamed and put the chess piece in his pocket. He loved working on the ship with me. I sent him up the masts to check on the rigging and listened to him whoop with glee watching the world from so high up.

"Focus!" I called out to the young boy. "Don't lose your footing!" He was giving me a heart attack. I was getting too old for this.

I raised the mainsail and had him check from the top down for any tears. We repeated that process on the other mast. Only one tear up top on the mainsail.

"Head on back to the house. We'll have our game after I'm done. I have a lot of cargo to load, and I have to figure out where your mother stored it."

"I'll ask her," he offered.

"Don't bother her. I'll get it."

"It's probably in the barn. I'll go look." And he took off running.

After repairing the sail, I brought out cleaning supplies and began working over the outside and inside. As I'd just been on a journey a few days ago, there wasn't much to do, but better to catch problems early, while in port and in reach of supplies.

I pulled out my notebook, loose sheafs of paper, and old hand-drawn maps I'd made from memory and began making lists. Magnus returned then with a horse-drawn wagon loaded to the breaking point with crates and sacks and bundles I recognized immediately.

"This is my missing cargo!" I glared up at the house. Izzy was just going to gift my cargo? My cargo! To some threadbare ghosts? Did she have any idea what this was worth? These items could fund my trips for years. These items were procured from all over the world and were of the best quality. I groaned. In modern terms, Izzy was looking at gifting hundreds of thousands of dollars of my hard-earned money and effort away as if this was just stuff left over in a storage unit that she needed to clean out. I rubbed my temples and took calming breaths. She was young. She couldn't know.

"What's wrong, Auntie? Did I do something wrong?" Magnus hopped out of the wagon, concerned that I might be upset with him.

"Nothing's wrong. A person just can't know what they've never learned. Let's have that game." I shoved my annoyance with my sister away and refocused on Magnus.

He scrambled back up into his wagon and jumped back down with the chessboard and box of pieces. We played at a small table I set up on my deck, and he beat me soundly several times. I sucked at games.

"You are letting me win, Auntie. Really try this time," he chided me.

"I am trying," I growled in frustration. "Just set the board back up." He laughed and reset the pieces and trounced me yet again.

"So where are you going today?" He indicated the ship and the cargo.

"I'm taking all this over to the new shipyard. Likely stay the night and sail back tomorrow."

"You'll need help with all of that. I could go with you." He was as eager as Dom was to run away with Peter Pan on this pirate ship of fun and mystery.

"I do not think your parents would approve of that." He was cute to want to help but Helene would kill me if I took him with me.

"Your ship is part of our family and our business. I need to learn the business." He puffed his thin chest up with importance.

I ruffled his hair. "Well then, you can learn how to properly stow all this cargo. Come on. Except these crates." I singled out the straw-packed crates of Han dynasty porcelain dishes. Those I set aside for Angelica.

We spent the next hour loading and tying down all my old cargo in all its old spots. As I patted the last of it in a welcome back/farewell manner, Magnus called me back up. There was a ship coming towards the dock.

The ship was a small thirty-foot rig with triangle sails and a shallow hull. The crew sailing her brought her in a little fast and annoyed me by bumping her harshly into the other side of the dock and almost knocking me backwards. I held onto Magnus to steady him, and we both glared at the sailors now tying her off.

"This is a private dock. State your business." I stood in the way of the upstart attempting to leave the dock and head toward the house. He looked somewhat familiar, but it wasn't till he leveled a haughty glare at me that I placed him as a relation of the young lieutenant.

"I owe the bitch captain no answers. Step aside or I will be forced to remove you. You have no claim here," he sneered.

If Magnus weren't right behind me, I would have handed this jackass his own colon on a platter. Instead I attempted to demonstrate that words and tact could be powerful too.

"Let me try this again." I took a deep calming breath. "You will need to explain—"

The young man viciously slapped me and manhandled me back to the other sailors who got hold of my arms before I could recover from the shock. The slap was hard, unexpected, and sharp. Again, these men needed to thank their lucky stars that that precious child I loved was here and I didn't want to encourage the notion that violence was the way to solve problems.

"Auntie!" Magnus tried to get to me, but I put out a hand to keep him back.

"No, girl, I need give you nothing," the man sneered.

"I am heir to this estate!" Magnus blocked their way this time. "You will answer why you are here."

"God save me from the perversion of these holdings." The young lieutenant's relation laughed along with the other sailors.

Magnus crossed his arms and stood his ground. The asshole of a man sighed with annoyance before relenting. "This is the Lieutenant Commander's personal boat. He restored it himself and he intends to sail that – his bride on it for his honeymoon. Now step aside so I can complete the delivery."

"Take your hands off my aunt and you may proceed," Magnus ordered in a fine impression of his father mixed with the eyebrow raise of his mother.

"She is not your relation, boy. She is a whore pretending to an empty throne," he sneered.

"You are wrong. We are family and this is her home. Tell him, Auntie," Magnus pleaded.

They need you to say yes as much as I do. Graham's words rang in my head.

"She knows what she is. No need to hear more from the shrew." The relation spat at my feet.

The sailors all laughed but let go of me and followed the dumbass up to the house. Magnus rushed to me full of concern.

"Are you okay?" he asked. I smiled at my 21st-century vernacular coming out of his 17th-century voice.

"I'm fine. Never worry about me." I ruffled his hair and kissed his cheek. "You were marvelous."

He grinned and stood up straighter.

I collected myself and looked over the smaller ship. Izzy was going to ride around the island in this?

"Go play now. I'm going to have a discussion with the other adults up there." He ran off, flushed with his victory over the small crew, and I trudged up the hill, more and more upset with every step. I was upset because that asshole was correct. I had no claim here. I was an intruder haunting Andrews' life, and I should have been exorcized from this house long ago. My hurt and anger channeled into an explosive direction, and by the time I reached the dining room, my emotions had funneled squarely against the young lieutenant.

The Bitch Captain (and The Lady)

"Your plan is to take my sister on some craft-project boat of yours around the island? With no crew? How exactly do you plan to navigate safely when you can't keep your dick out of her for even an hour?" My cheek still stung. I resisted touching it and focused on the young lieutenant, who pursed his lips and narrowed his eyes.

Instead of answering me, he turned to Izzy and spoke gently to her. "Surprise, darling. I am sailing you around the island, to all my favorite places, just the two of us. As I've mentioned, I've spent several years preparing a personal ship for my own usage, and I believe you'll find it full of the comforts of home."

"She is not stepping foot on that so-called 'boat' until I inspect it," I threatened.

"Nanette," Andrews spoke sternly and drew my attention, "a word, please?" He stood and offered me his hand.

"Just a moment—"

"Nanette. Now." He put a hand on my arm, and I let him pull me away into the kitchen. Andrews waved Izzy's maid out so we could have a private moment. He held me tight until I stopped fuming and resumed a normal breathing pattern.

He put a hand up to my cheek and caressed the stinging skin. "What happened?"

"Nothing."

"Nanette, talk to me," he demanded.

"It doesn't matter. That ship—"

"He's a naval officer!" Andrews hollered. "I'm sure that ship will float around the island just fine. What happened?" He held his hand to my cheek and refused to move it.

"What happened is I came back. I came back and I am not your wife. I have no claim here. I don't belong," I fired back at him and tried to pry his hand from my cheek.

"One more time and maybe you'll hear me. What happened to your face?" His voice was not quiet.

"That son of a bitch out there struck me because I have no business being here. And he's right!" I thundered back, my voice catching on the words barbed with truth, and I turned to leave.

Andrews held onto me. "So make him wrong! Say yes, goddammit! Be my wife. I won't have you hurt on our own land when it was entirely avoidable!"

Izzy came through the door and laid into me, a second barrel in this assault. "I'm very sorry to interrupt what was clearly going to be a successful marriage proposal, but you mentioned that someone struck you? Who?" she demanded.

"Not now, Izzy," I growled at her. My two interrogators side by side.

"Answer her, Nan." Andrews took her side. My sister crossed her arms, and Andrews didn't give me an inch.

"No," I told them both.

"I told you I won't take another no from you!" he yelled.

"Then stop asking!" I yelled right back.

"Why won't you just tell me? You know I'm perfectly capable of getting the information." Lady Isabelle, in all her glory, joined the fight against me.

"Why does it matter? It doesn't matter!" I backed away from the assault. I didn't know why it mattered, but it did. I had nothing. Nothing. No land, no house, no husband, no future. Just this one piece of something that they wanted that was mine. I couldn't give them anything else. I needed this. I kept the answer trapped in my chest, desperate to have something of my own.

"Lieutenant Commander, would you join us please?" Lady Tattletale called out.

"No! Izzy, what the hell? I'm going back to my ship." I tried to struggle past them, but Andrews got his arms around me and held me fast. I hadn't realized I was shaking until I felt the vibrations in his arms. I simultaneously needed him to release me and hold me tighter.

When Izzy's new husband entered, I stopped fighting Andrews and sank back against his chest. It was now three on one.

"Dear husband," Izzy started, "would you be so good as to find out which of your men was so bold as to strike my sister in the face? I would be most grateful." Andrews shifted me closer.

"Was it my valet? Tall, blue eyes, and a blue jacket?" the young lieutenant asked. I kept my mouth shut.

"Anne?" Izzy asked, expectant.

I didn't answer.

"Nanette?" Andrews prompted.

"I can deal with him on my own. Everyone, just leave me be." I tried once more to get away, but Andrews wasn't having it.

"It was him," Izzy asserted to Ian. She whispered something to her new husband then said aloud, "Yes, I am serious. Now, please?"

The young lieutenant left, and I relaxed a little. Two on one.

"Well, that will be handled." Izzy approached me cautiously and kissed me on the cheek.

"Izzy, this isn't your fight," I said to her. She ignored me. I turned my face into Andrews' chest. "You cannot protect me from every danger."

"I could if you'd let me," he responded.

"No."

"Okay! Well, I'm going to let you two get back to whatever the hell you're doing in here." Izzy flounced out of the room clearly as in need of escape as I was.

One on one.

Once more I tried to escape the claustrophobic kitchen, but Graham lifted me up and sat me on the counter and held me close. I struggled, but the rage within me had cooled and the embrace felt nice.

"Dammit, Nan. Just let me hold onto you for a fucking moment," he growled in my ear. I crumbled and held him back.

"It's not fair," I said, even as my throat closed around the words to keep me from saying them. I buried my head in his chest.

"I know." He cradled my face and kissed me.

"I want to marry you." I looked straight into his eyes and spoke the truth. "I want you as my husband. I want to wear your ring. Sit in that chair. Wake up with you every morning."

His eyes burned with desire and his arms tightened around me as he heard all the words he'd ever wanted to hear me say tumble out of me in this charged moment.

"It's not fair," I repeated.

"It can be. Say yes. Please, Nan. Just say yes." He tilted my head up and kissed me again, lightly at first and then deepening with intensity as he stood on the precipice of all his most desperate desires coming true.

Helene Andrews
1610-1684
Beloved Wife
Beloved Mother

"You're not mine. And I'm not yours. No, Graham." I pushed him away. My beloved's eyes turned to stone. I could feel the heat from his heart cool and retreat. For a moment it felt like he might strike me himself.

Instead he turned and walked away from me. He slammed the dining room door on his way out. I sat there, shivering from the reflected chill of the heart I'd just killed.

Through the kitchen window I could see my ship. At least I didn't have to stay here. I had cargo to deliver. I got down from the counter and left through the kitchen exit. Magnus caught up with me as I went down to my ship.

"Auntie, I heard yelling. Father is upset."

"I gave him some bad news."

The Bitch Captain (and The Lady)

"Are you leaving?" He eyed my braids.

"Just to deliver that cargo you helped me with."

"But then you are coming back?"

"I don't know."

"You'll come back." He rushed off to do whatever thirteen-year-olds do in this time, and I kept going to the ship.

The young lieutenant's ship was an affront to my eyes. It hardly looked seaworthy. The ass-faced valet was back on the dinghy working, probably using toothpaste to patch some holes.

I went aboard my own ship and down to my cabin. I needed a minute. I poured myself a drink and put my old helmet from the temple on and let it shut out the sounds around me. Unfortunately, it didn't occlude the vibrations of several people walking down the dock together.

I dumped the old silver helmet on the floor and drank as I heard Izzy's shrill voice demanding answers from someone on the other ship. What the hell was she doing? I knocked back the rest of the tumbler, poured another, then walked up top, already feeling the effects of the whiskey.

I arrived in time to witness Izzy slap the asshole clear across the face. He'd wear that handprint a few days. I took another sip and watched the wanker fail to stifle his tears before storming off.

"That wasn't necessary," I told her. Izzy spun around. I don't think she knew I was here. "But thank you."

"It most certainly was necessary. I don't know where these cowards get off striking women all the time!" Izzy screamed off after him. "A time of chivalry my round ass," she grumbled.

I took the few steps over to her and the young lieutenant. It definitely wasn't necessary, but I did feel slightly warmer to the pair.

"I'd like to inspect your boat. Permission to come aboard, Coving-try?" I stumbled over his name – their name.

"Permission granted," he acceded and stepped aside for me to pass.

I stepped aboard the smaller ship and made note of the condition of the wood, the sails, and the lines. I scowled at the bed tucked in below the deck. There was an itty-bitty galley, just a wood-burning stove top and a small dry sink.

"She cooks. A lot. What's your fire-suppression system?" I grilled him.

"If a fire breaks out, what precautions are in place?" Izzy translated.

"There are buckets of sand there and there." He pointed to a few buckets out of the way. Fine. He passed that one.

I continued on. "Where's the lifeboat? Do you have an accessory boat when this one goes down on the reefs?"

Izzy mumbled under her breath what sounded like petty sarcastic remarks, but when this ship went down, she'd be happy to know if there was a second thing that might float.

"There's a small detachable raft tied off the port side." He pointed out a flimsy concoction of roped-together twigs. "We shan't ever be far from land. The reefs are quite a ways out to sea from my projected course."

"Which is what, pray tell?"

The young lieutenant detailed for me his route around the island and through the small upshoots of land that dot the inner bays of Bermuda.

"How far has she sailed before?" I continued the inspection.

"She's made it out to the western end and back to St. George's."

"Any issues?"

"All fixed." He outlined that the winds had stressed a few of the riggings and the mast, problems that he'd since reinforced.

He then took me on a tour of the ship after that and detailed the ship's condition when he first acquired it and all the work he'd put into the little ship. He'd bought the piece of junk just after arriving on the island and used most of his free time between then and when I'd arrived with Izzy working on the little ship. Since Izzy had come along, he'd been paying a crew to formally finish her off and add amenities that might suit his new wife and her quirky landlubbing ways.

I tried out the halyard, the down haul, the responsiveness of the rudder. He told me there was a keel but a small one. This ship wasn't intended for open ocean; it was strictly for circumnavigation of the island.

He eyed my ship and I bristled, ready for his criticism, but instead he asked a question about the rigging and the pattern I'd wound into the ropes. And just like when the women admired the embroidery on my dress, I opened up a vault of stories about my precious ship.

I ended up pouring a glass of rum for Ian and telling him about the time I'd capsized off the coast of Jakarta. He whistled, impressed with the tale. He asked how the masts held up in storms, and I told him that I'd only suffered one really terrible breakage, which kept my ship out of commission for a whole season while it was repaired. We started sharing stories of crossing the Atlantic, and I impressed him again when I said I'd made the run from Newfoundland to Paris in eight weeks. He told me that he'd scaled the mainmast of the galleon that ferried him here in a sudden squall to repair a line that had snapped. I toasted him. I was impressed and told him so.

It turned out he knew an acquaintance of mine in London, a pub owner, Mr. Colin O'Rourke. He'd seen him just before departing a few years ago. "Did he ever repair the fire damage?" I asked.

"Never. He continues to blame the damage on every party that comes through. I believe it's rather kept the pub afloat financially." He drank and smiled.

"I do believe I've paid for that corner at least twice."

"Three times." He pointed to himself and laughed. He was about to launch into another story when Izzy interrupted. I blinked at her. I could have sworn she'd left.

"Hello! Are you two quite finished?" She was annoyed.

I looked at the shadows on the dock. I supposed we had been going on awhile.

"Of course, darling." Coventry handed me back his empty glass. "Provided your sister is satisfied as to your safety upon my vessel?"

"Fair winds and following seas, Lieutenant – Lieutenant Commander." I amended the rank so as not to annoy her further and toasted them both. "I'm about to head out myself. I imagine the next time I'll see you is in St. George's. Enjoy your time together. It's a gift you got any at all." I wished I had any more time at all with Andrews. I'm afraid I rather punctured Izzy's spirit with that comment.

She hugged me anyway and said, "I love you. Be careful, and I'll see you soon?"

"Right. One moment. A last parting gift." I had forgotten the damn vaccines.

I quickly went down to the cargo area and reached to unlock a complicated mechanism that dropped my medical bag into my hands. I unrolled the leather pack that contained the precious syringe and vials of various medications, antibacterials, and added the vaccinations from my fridge. There were cotton balls and antiseptic in the bag along with a few oral medications. I'd put this kit together when Magnus was a baby. I'd sailed in not long after he was born to find the estate sick with scarlet fever or rheumatic fever, either way something penicillin could easily cure. Andrews and the adults were down and out, and the children were worse. I'd made a decision then that they all needed a little magic. I'd made one of my tightest exits and entrances I've ever managed to date, even spotting my own sails on the current. I brought them medicine. I stayed with them in their cabins. I sat up several nights with Magnus, hot with fever, to let Helene sleep and heal.

They'd all been too weak to protest at first and too astonished with their recovery afterwards to question it. When I began regular vaccinations, they were all skeptical, but the power of my medicine was too strong to argue against. When surrounding farms were wiped out by

The Bitch Captain (and The Lady)

one plague or another while ours was left untouched, even the questions stopped. Every trip back to the future I picked up more and more medical supplies and vaccinated every new baby and person who took up residence.

Magnus had been so sick. I still remembered his hot, heavy baby breath and the raised rashes on his skin and his mother and sisters sleeping soundly on the beds beyond. Even once he got better I held onto him. Helene recovered after a few days and took her child back. The little boy had captured my heart from that moment on.

I repacked the bag exquisitely carefully and headed back. Izzy was actually in the galley grabbing a few odds and ends before I took her 21st-century stores away.

"Here. Everything you need. Do not lose it. Do not sell it. Do not trade it. No one sees this," I instructed.

"Of course. I understand." She nodded absently as she packed small tins into her bag.

"No, Izzy. Hear me. No street children, no refugees, no enslaved people. Ian. That's who gets it. The wrong word in the wrong ear and you will be put to death." Maybe this was a mistake. I put it in her hands, wondering if I'd be able to save her from the stake if it came to it. My scars tightened, and a dull roar sounded in my ears. I shook my head and tried to remain calm despite the smell of smoke. I pulled at my collar and took steadying breaths.

"Yes. I understand. Ian has said as much about some similar topics. I don't know if it will matter, but I have to try to do something to help him." She put the medical kit in her bag.

"It'll matter. You are doing what you can with what you have." It's all anyone could ever do, really.

"Exactly! Like the refugees. Thank you for handling that. They've been through so much, Anne—"

"Literally never mention it again." I was still sour about losing all my hard work even if it was going to a good cause.

"Look what I'm going to surprise Ian with." She held up a canister of tea she'd bought before we'd left. "He's never had tea before. Do you think he'll like it?"

"An Englishman liking tea? You never know." She chuckled at the terrible joke and grabbed a sack of pot to dull the pain of my humor. "Go on that honeymoon already and don't get pregnant."

"I am mildly concerned as to whether or not my pills are up to the phenomenal challenge they've been put to." She was smitten and I was nauseous.

"Get out before I vomit." I pointed the way. She straight up giggled and kissed me on the cheek before skipping out.

I raised the sails soon after booting her horny ass out and told her I'd pick her up in St. George's when I got word the *Victory* was in port. My plan, as it stood now, was to sail to Mary and Davies, unload the cargo, and spend a last night or two with my friends. Then I'd sail to St. George's, pick up Izzy and Catherine-party-of-three and launch us across the Atlantic.

And Andrews?

He had retreated to somewhere on the estate and was better off for not seeing my departure. Maybe he'd continue to watch the horizon for my sails, or maybe he'd feel blessed to finally have me out of his life.

I navigated swiftly away and out into deeper waters, feeling better with each passing wave. I toyed with the idea of setting up my speaker and playing music to drown the voices in my head.

Andrews' kingdom was completely out of sight, and there was a ways to go before I reached the new shipyard. I settled in and tried to breathe and relax and just feel the waves carrying me on and not the afterimage of Graham turning to stone in front of me. I almost man-

The Bitch Captain (and The Lady)

aged it until a lanky teenage boy with my beloved's exact smile dropped from the mast in front of me.

"Hello, Auntie!" He beamed.

"Magnus!" I gasped. I looked up at the mast where he'd stowed away. People never look up. It's why I hide all my good stuff in the ceilings. I groaned. This was trouble. I was going to have to turn around. "What do you think you're doing?" I started lowering the sails to drop speed.

"I'm here to help you! I'm also making sure you come back." He rushed to the edge of the ship and looked over the rail at the hull cutting through the waves. He turned back and grinned in success. "Since I'm here, you'll have to bring me back."

"Exactly. I'm turning around now, and you can swim once we get close enough." I would make him walk the plank, I swear to god.

"Auntie, come on," he whined. "We're almost there. You'd end up sailing through the night. I left a note on Father's desk. And Auntie Von said she'd tell Mother."

I blanched. "What did you tell her?"

"That you needed help and I was going with you." He sat next to me and grinned. "So they know and it's all okay."

"Oh, Magnus, no. This is a terrible idea." I sighted the waves and began the turn back towards the estate.

"You were going to leave. I hate when you leave. I mean, the parties are really fun and Mother stops yelling so much, but I like it when you're here." He scowled and sat with his arms crossed.

"They must be out of their minds with worry." I tacked into the wind and did my own scowling at the waves about the delay this would cause.

"So am I every time you leave." He rubbed his eyes and looked down at the boards. "So is Father," he grumbled. "Even when he yells. He doesn't mean it. We like when you are home with us."

"I know. I like it when I'm home with you too." I sat next to him and put my arm around his broadening shoulders. "But, Magnus, they need to know you are safe."

"I left a note," he grumbled.

My stamina eroded away beneath this guilt trip. That strange, complicated kingdom had entangled me more than I ever realized. Here was this child I had helped raise and feed and teach, and now I was supposed to leave him? It echoed my own past with frightening familiarity.

My father had left me when I was not much younger than Magnus. He and I sailed together. That was our thing. That bastard and I would be out on his boat every spare hour we got. He never left shore without me. Until one day he took that ship out to sea without me, never returned, and I was left waiting on an empty dock looking for sails that never reappeared. If I had known, I would have stowed away exactly as Magnus had done. I would have cheated a few more minutes out of that man as well.

We were over three-quarters of the way there. It would delay me an astounding amount to turn back now. Regretting every twitch of my muscles, I raised the sail back up, tacked around again, and sped us on our way to the shipyard.

He cheered and went to the bow and stood looking like a curly-haired king of the world. I had to admire the gumption of this kid. This little stunt of his did more in two hours than his father had ever accomplished: joined me on an adventure, coerced me into a decision I wouldn't otherwise have made, made me commit to returning home. This kid was going places – wish I'd be around to see it.

I spent the rest of the trip giving Magnus a crash course in sailing. He gave me a crash course in generally having a good time and laughing at myself. We were both sure to be in a magnificent amount of trouble when we returned, but at this point it was in for a penny, in for a pound. We were both reckless enough to decide just to have a good time and enjoy the moment.

The Bitch Captain (and The Lady)

Davies had managed a semblance of a dock at the shipyard, and Magnus raced down it toward the unfamiliar beach as soon as the ship was secured. He whooped and cheered at his recent escape and successful stowaway plan. His joy brought Dom and Henry out, and the three boys were soon fast friends, running in and out among the waves.

The shipyard was taking shape. Temporary structures lined the compound, some for processing and some housing and some for business. The smithy's forge belched smoke and heat I could feel from here. An enormous pile of felled trees lay stacked and awaiting shaping by the tree line. Laborers could be heard felling more of the cedars out in the forest. A warning shout preceded the crash and tumble of another tree down.

Mary came out of one of the temporary structures to greet me. She looked healthy despite the advancing pregnancy. Davies was at her side and offered her his arm to climb over the driftwood and brambles strewn on the beach. After some hearty greetings from Davies, I handed Mary the letter of instructions from Izzy about how to distribute the cargo. She looked it over and said she thought she understood.

"This woman, she is very kind, isn't she?" Mary looked up from the rough paper. Technically she and Izzy had never had much of an introduction.

"She is. To those she deems worthy." I often wondered where I stood on her scale of worth. Since this journey began, I felt part of the small group of people Izzy might cast off into the abyss at any moment.

"Difficult to tell sometimes who is worthy and who ought to be left to the lions," Mary said as she reread the letter.

"I've never been much of a judge of it myself."

"Me either. Probably why I've taken up with you, Captain." My old friend smiled at me. Scarecrow, I was going to miss you most of all.

Mary went to work directing the unloading of my ship and was astounded at the quantity and variety of items my sister was donating for distribution. Let it go, I counseled myself with every crate, box, sack, and stack of goods ferried over the gangplank. Just let it go. It was all going to a better place. Still, each item was linked to a memory linked to a thousand different memories and plans. Let it go, Anne. Just let it go. What's done is done and cannot be undone. And what was done once can also be done again. I'd just have to tighten my belt, lift up my bootstraps, and continue onward.

"Captain," Mary called over to me after opening several crates of fine and exquisitely decorated glassware, "this is unusable here. Might I make a suggestion?"

"It's yours to do whatever you think best." Let it go. It was time to let it all go. The beautiful glass had come from Egypt. It had sailed with me on my ship for four years. I missed it already. I picked up a demitasse cup and caressed it lovingly before placing it back down.

"I'll sell it then. Use the money, reinvest it in the tools we need and housing supplies." She boxed the crates back up and went to speak to Davies about coordinating a sale. I patted the crates one more time before following her out of the temporary structures.

At dinner that evening, Magnus and Henry joined all of Mary's children and Davies around the table. It was a raucous time, and I saw Davies absolutely bubbling over with glee at the antics of all the children and the boastful stories of the young men. Apparently Henry and Dom had taught Magnus some basic blacksmithing today, and the three of them had almost burnt down the place but might also have also stumbled upon the recipe for tin. Magnus's irrepressible good nature matched Dom's enthusiasm and Henry's understated energy perfectly. The three of them made it simply impossible to depart the next day.

Also, I really didn't want to leave.

So we stayed just one more night.

The Bitch Captain (and The Lady)

Mary and Davies and I continued to talk shop long into the night about production and children and wine. I watched the two of them talk in an easy back and forth. Davies was careful with her pregnant body and poured her drinks and saw that her plate was full. Mary laughed at his boisterous jokes and provided him insight where he'd overlooked details. Davies would be good for her, and Mary would be a miracle for him. This was good. I'd managed something good at last.

Perhaps I wasn't supposed to see, but as the evening concluded, Davies reached for her hand and she gave it to him. I left them to each other. My bed felt unusually cold that night. It was time to leave. Tomorrow morning we would go.

I was on my ship (with Magnus all but trussed to the mast) on the morning tide, ready to meet my doom.

"I'll watch the tides for you, Captain." Mary hugged me and stepped aside for Davies.

"Don't be a stranger," he boomed and squeezed me in a huge embrace.

Rule number four: No goodbyes.

"Don't lose my money," I warned them both and raised the sails and waved for all I was worth as they disappeared from view.

One slight detour before we sailed back to reality. I went out into the open ocean and raised my spyglass. There. There was a telltale smudge on the horizon that was the *Victory* finally on approach. I hope Izzy had gotten her fill because, this time tomorrow, her husband would be remanded back to the King.

The Hundred Acre Wood was atypically still and quiet when we docked. The smokestacks and usual sounds and goings-on were noticeably absent. The place was on lockdown. I looked at Magnus and he looked back at me. We both knew we were in deep shit. I tied the ship off and lowered the gangplank. Magnus didn't want to leave.

"We did the crime. Now we'll do the time." I held my hand out to him.

"Auntie, I think this was a mistake," he confessed.

"No question about that. Listen to me. I ordered you to come. I refused to bring you back. This was all my idea. Do you understand?"

"Auntie—"

"No, Magnus. I did not give you a choice. You had to come."

"They'll kill you," he whispered.

"Let them try. I'm hard to kill. It's you I'm worried about." I brought him close and kissed the top of his curly head like I did when he was a little kid. I walked to the gangplank and held out my hand. We'd do this together.

After hesitating and looking out to sea and freedom, wondering if he could make his escape, he finally took my hand. We walked past the main house to Helene's cabin. No one was about anywhere. This was going to be bad. Her cabin sat at the end of the cul de sac, large and foreboding.

I shielded the boy behind me and knocked on the front door. I would deal with his mother. Helene hated me and that would make it only too easy for her to believe the lie I'd tell her about forcing Magnus to come with me.

Only it wasn't Helene who answered the door.

Andrews stood backlit in the doorway, the master of this land, a huge and terrifying presence. His eyes, still stone-like, worse even for the two days of worry and hurt.

"This is not his fault. This is all on me," I told my beloved and his shuttered heart. "I needed help on my ship and he was kind enough to offer and I accepted."

"Lies, Nanette," he growled. "Where did you go!"

"You know damn well I was at the shipyard. Mary and Davies can confirm. I told you myself before I left."

The doors and windows of the nearby cabins opened to hear the show.

"I ordered Magnus to come with me." I stood my ground.

"Auntie—" Magnus hissed in my ear. I shushed him.

"You are not the lady of this house. You have no authority here to order anyone anywhere." Andrews jabbed his finger into my chest.

I had a mind to lay into him with a good right hook.

He read the danger and removed the finger but remained threateningly close. "You took my son from his land and damned the rest of us. You want to sail away on your accursed ship, you go right ahead. But you will not have my child aboard. Magnus!" Andrews turned his attention to the boy. "Is she telling the truth? Did she force you on that ship, or did you leave your mother to join this fool on her damn folly of an errand?"

"Let him be." I continued to shield the child and take Andrews' wrath myself. "I gave you your answer. Did you hear it?"

"Someone will pay for this transgression. Will it be you or Magnus?"

"Me."

"Fine." He grabbed my arm and threw me to the middle of the flagstone clearing between the cabins.

Yvonne and Angelica watched from the door of their own houses. Yvonne must have been tickled pink with the proceedings. Andrews left me there, presumably to go get his weapon of choice.

And indeed he had.

Helene entered the clearing to face me. The woman was a good few inches taller than me, and she matched me or better for musculature. I braced myself. She never broke eye contact with me as she hauled back and struck me clean across the face one way then backhanded me the other. The force of the blows threw me to the ground, and my head slammed hard into the flagstones.

I lay there on my back gasping, sucking in dust and dirt. A grenade exploding inches from me would have been less devastating. I wouldn't be surprised if I was concussed. The woman came and knelt on one knee as I struggled to rise and jabbed me several more times, hard, splitting my lip and sending me back to the stone. I rolled over onto my hands and knees, and blood trickled down from where her knuckles had split my cheek and lip. I swallowed back vomit.

"Leave my family alone," she threatened, low and close to my throbbing face.

"Yes, ma'am," I grunted.

Andrews walked up to determine that blood had been drawn and I was sufficiently punished. "That's enough for now," he ordered Helene to stop.

Andrews left me in the dirt and escorted the mother safely away from me. She grabbed Magnus by the shoulder and dragged him inside their cabin. Josephine and Amelia watched me from the doorjamb, eyes big and bodies frozen to the scene. Andrews followed them up to the door, sharing a final few words of consolation with Helene and remonstration to Magnus. Family, she'd said, leave her family alone.

Bermuda was over for me.

My chest constricted. I couldn't get any air. I didn't wait for permission. I went straight back to my ship and vomited over the side.

My vision blurred in and out with my heartbeat. The floors lurched and swayed under my feet. This wasn't the first blow to my head this journey. I'd been at the point-blank range of the blast in the Sea Wind, and the guards had pummeled me silly when putting me in those shackles. I retched over the side again.

Magnus's mother and her fists of fury had piled on to an already growing list of issues. I gingerly touched my cheek and winced. It was a decent-sized cut. If my hands were steadier, I'd sew it up. I could look forward to a gorgeous black eye on my right over that large laceration on my cheek. My lip was split deeply about half an inch above my canine and was already swelling.

There were clean linen strips, antiseptic, and fresh water in the kitchen that I used to mop myself up. I also found a bottle of wine and my flask of Fountain. I picked both up and brought them up on deck where the three of us had a standoff: I could dive into the oblivion the bottle offered; I could heal myself with the Fountain; or I could live with the pain I so richly deserved. No winners yet.

My thoughts were drawn back to Izzy's wedding, the lovers entwined and absorbed with each other – not just lovers, husband and wife. Family. Magnus and his sisters and parents, framed in a doorway. Family. I dabbed at my cheek again and winced at the sting of the antiseptic. The bottles continued to stare me down. I lost consciousness before I could make a choice.

"Ladies and gentlemen, we are about 100 miles from our destination and beginning the landing process. Please stow your tray tables in their upright and locked position. The flight attendants will be coming through the aisles to collect any trash you might have. Thank you for flying Bermudian Airlines and we hope you enjoy your stay!" The cheery voice was almost enough to make me puke. I sat white-knuckled in my tiny chair while Izzy studied a guidebook and my mother slept. I was drenched with sweat and shaking.

"Calm down, Anne. Flight's almost over." Izzy patted my hand. I hated flying more than just about anything else. I glanced at the map on the tiny screen in front of me then squeezed my eyes shut. I wasn't going to make it. My heart was sprinting in my chest. I hated this so much.

"How's she doing?" the nice flight attendant in Bermuda shorts asked Izzy. The two of them had tried to drug me before takeoff but it didn't take.

"Great! She'll be fine."

"Keep her in her seat, okay?" the flight attendant instructed and continued down the aisle with her tiny bag of tiny trash. I reached for the barf bag and held it like a security blanket even though I had puked everything out in the airplane toilet halfway through the flight and was thoroughly empty.

"I knew I should have made you eat those brownies." Izzy sighed as the plane slowed to descend towards the island.

Oh no, this was it. The engines had died. We were going to crash-land. Statistically speaking, most plane crashes happened just after take-off or on landing. The nose of the plane dipped gently. My seat cushion floats. My seat cushion floats. Why weren't the oxygen masks dropping? Oh god.

"Landing already?" My mother had woken up. "What a lovely flight." She stretched and lifted the window cover. I stopped breathing entirely, and a dull buzzing filled my head. "Girls, just look at that!"

The island was sparkling under our stupid, flimsy plane. Many houses and neighborhoods and even cars were visible as we descended. The airport was right next to St. George's Bay. It looked hot. It looked so hot there. I was going to melt. I couldn't even wear the island's signature shorts. The scars on my legs were too fresh.

The heavy tread of male footsteps down the dock shocked me awake in a panic, sweating. The light was blinding. I grabbed my short sword and had the blade at Andrews' throat before he could take one step aboard my ship. He looked about as rested as I felt. Andrews put his hands up as I walked him backwards down the gangplank, the point of my blade a hair from his artery. His face was unreadable stone.

"Stay off my ship." The words were muddled through my fat lip. I

The Bitch Captain (and The Lady)

didn't care what he had come to say. I wasn't dealing with ghosts any longer.

"I'll go where I please." He spoke to my sword. For a moment he looked wrecked, then hardened his eyes and looked at me. "This is my dock, Anne!" He bit the words out and threw them at me.

I scoffed. It was my dock. I'd fucking paid to build it. But fine, he was so worried about my damn ship using up the stupid fucking dock, he could eat his heart out on the cold coins.

"I need two days. I'll pay." I fished a purse out of my pocket and threw it at him. "That should cover a horse and wagon too." I shuddered at the idea of driving a horse myself but desperate times... "St. George's and back. I'll be gone two days. Then I'll just be gone. For good this time." I kept my voice, eyes, and blade steady.

Rule number four be damned. I wanted to hurt him right now. I wanted him hurt. I wanted to see him in pain and laugh and sneer at him for his weakness. This was just the way to do it.

"Listen close because I'm about to give you what you've always wanted, a goodbye," I sneered and leveled my best one-eyed glare at him, "I'm leaving and this time I'm not coming back. That is a promise. Goodbye, Graham Andrews." My face seized in pain, and I inhaled sharply through it. "Now get the hell off my dock."

Andrews opened the purse and estimated the coins inside. "Fine. I'll have the team and a driver – a proper driver, not you – readied in an hour. Pleasure doing business." He mock-bowed and took my money and left. I did not drop my guard until he was well away.

That was it. A lifetime together and that was our goodbye. My sister got wedding bells and I got...this. I collapsed on the dock.

When I came to, I crawled to the flask of Fountain and took a swig. It might be too little too late, but I had to try. The Fountain's secondary measures were all but imminent. I really wanted to avoid that.

My face hurt so bad. One eye was swollen shut. I touched gingerly at my lip and cheek. The aspirin was tucked behind some of Izzy's spices in the galley, but the Fountain gurgled in my stomach, rejecting the pills. It was high tide and the boat rocked under me, lurching me into the walls.

I'd be gone at least a day and a night. I stuffed some food, a waterskin, more aspirin, and my pistols into a sack then stopped to rest a moment before dressing. The boat was unsteady, and it was making me nauseous. Get it together, Anne. I dressed in my best stomping boots and my Kevlar-lined trench, and belted my weapons around my waist. I wrapped my head with a long scarf in an attempt to distract from my bruised face and stuck my wide-brimmed hat on top of it all. Anyone who cared to look would be hard-pressed to discern any womanly shape or manner about me.

I made sure I had a few ready blades close at hand since my driver was sure to be a prison laborer Andrews hired. Helene would likely not loan any of her people to drive me. While not necessarily more dangerous than anyone else, prison laborers were treated poorly, and from my experience, desperation was the cause of most violence.

When I judged it to be about an hour, I left my ship and headed to the main house. The walk across the lawn felt far today. I was puffing and dizzy when I got to the house and saw the wagon and a team of four horses waiting for me. Four. I swallowed back bile and trudged on.

The driver was in place. He was white (I was right about the prison laborer then) and wearing a slouchy overcoat and brimmed hat. Looks like we'd be a matched pair; my mother would have called us a singing troupe. I chuckled at the image and tossed my bag up.

"St. George's. We need to make decent time," I told him as I climbed in back and settled in for a long trip behind smelly animals.

God, my face really hurt. The team took off, and I winced as the wagon jolted me around. I wondered, not for the first time, if getting the whip would have been better or worse. I imagined Andrews and his whip standing over me. It was not an image I cared for. I shuddered and prayed I might always get my ass handed to me by such lovely creatures as Helene.

Andrews was pretty brave to come and try to talk with me this morning. There were few souls on this planet who had struck me, lived, and voluntarily stood in front of me again. Andrews was a good man. I'd miss him.

Izzy had cleared the money out of most of my hidey-holes on the ship. If I could make a quick stop in Greenland, I could replenish my stores from my lonely mountain. With the ship so light we'd make good time; it would really only add a few weeks. Pain stabbed through my temples when I tried to do the math and I gave up.

Honestly, it was for the best that Andrews and I were leaving on bad terms. I wasn't coming back this time. I'd made him angry enough that he wouldn't miss me and could put his real wife in my dining room chair.

I wondered if he'd marry her right away or if he'd mess around with a few of the eligible debutantes who'd line up for him. I could just imagine some simpering little wisp, the very picture of a lady, dancing her mincing steps at a Wallington party. I imagined her doting on Andrews and sitting in my chair taking little delicate bites and dabbing at her little delicate chin with ladylike precision. I could imagine Andrews slipping off her clothes and touching her little delicate breast. That little bitch. I'll slice her head to toe!

The Fountain sizzled inside my gut, and I grew hopeful that maybe I'd be spared the secondary measures. Helene hit hard, but it was my head smacking into the ground that was causing all the trouble. The horses continued their never-ending clopping down the road. They smelled awful.

I brought out some bread and cheese for a meal but only ended up holding them in my hands until the cheese got melty. Between the concussion and the rocking of the wagon, every time I tried to bring the bread to my mouth I missed. I pitched them back in my bag.

I could remember Andrews slipping my clothes off, touching my breast. I smiled and put my hand to my chest, feeling when his hands were there. My headache eased slightly with the memory. I felt the breeze from our open window and remembered lying in that big bed, running my fingers up and down his skin. I sighed. He could hate me, should hate me, but I would cherish him. I toyed with the idea of giving him a real goodbye, the kind of goodbye that didn't involve a lot of clothing. I moved my hand from my chest to my bruised face and winced at even that small touch. Even if he did want to see this face again, who would I be saying goodbye for? Me or him? No. I had said my goodbye to him. It was done.

My headache only grew worse as we bumped and swayed down the wagon-track roads of rural Bermuda. Enough of Andrews. I focused on my breath and what was left to accomplish. There was Izzy to track down and support as her lieutenant got shipped away. I needed to get Bessie, Catherine, and some kid out of their manor safely and unseen. Speaking of unseen, I couldn't be seen. Any Puritan within spitting distance would rat me out to Closer To You My God, and I hadn't packed my dynamite. The wagon rocked and rolled, and my head felt ready to split open.

"Can we stop a moment?" I begged the driver and barely waited for him to slow down before I hopped off and tried to catch my breath. I stretched and tried to massage the headache away. "How far do we have left, do you think?" I asked the him.

"We'll be there by sundown, Nanette." I spun around to see my wildcat man smiling at me from his seat.

"Stay away from me." I reached for my pistol, but he jumped down and batted it away with the coiled horse whip. My reflexes were slow today. Any other day I'd have shot that stupid hat off his head. Just ask Marco.

"Enough of that, Nanette. You promised me two days. I'm taking those two days."

The Bitch Captain (and The Lady)

"It wasn't an offer. It was a threat." My vision blurred slightly, showing me two men: Andrews, throwing me to the ground to have me beaten; Graham, between my legs driving me wild. My head hurt so bad. "You are a glutton for punishment, you know that? You are supposed to be home, despising me." I groaned and sat down, rubbing my temples. I gave up on the Fountain. It was going to be a rough night.

He crouched in front of me and took my head in his hands for a better look. "Easy, Nanette, easy," he soothed. "It's just a little bruising. I've seen worse. Hell, I've even seen worse on you."

I didn't have the strength for this. I groaned and twisted into the hedges. Andrews sighed and rubbed my back as I dry-heaved. This was a bad concussion. The ground spun under me, and I couldn't tell what was up or down. Next thing I knew I was staring straight up at the sun. Andrews was over me with one hand under my head and looking at me with grave concern.

"Helene's got one hell of a backhand, doesn't she? I speak from experience. You're burning up." He smoothed my hair away to get a better look at me. His assessment did not improve.

Andrews got me up into the back of the wagon and sat me against him. He rubbed my shoulders and arms, and I relaxed into his touch.

"Magnus told us what happened. Helene gets very protective. She was scared to death when you took off with him. You are careless with people's lives, you can't deny it."

"I'm not." The sun was overbright. I couldn't keep my eyes open.

"Stay with me, Nanette, don't close your eyes." He unwound my head scarf and tried to mop me up a little. "He's in a tough spot, that kid. I want to protect him. Open your eyes, Nanette. Holy mother, you're bleeding." Andrews bunched the scarf and tried to stem the blood coming from my ear. He was talking mostly to himself as I had started drifting away from the pain.

"You told me you want to marry me." His words came out as a whisper, as if he were in church and not the back of a wagon.

"Of course I do. I love you," I mumbled.

"But you can't marry me?"

"There's not enough time," I tried to explain.

"Nan, I'd take any time with you at all." His hand gently brushed my swollen cheek, I inhaled sharply. He hesitated, then kissed my swollen lip with more gentleness than I'd ever have believed possible from him. I prayed for more time as if I were the one in church. My prayers would not be answered whether in church or in this wagon.

"Jesus, Nanette, that's a lot of blood." He dabbed at my ear some more.

"I'm fine. Don't worry about me," I slurred.

"I'm not," he lied. "Stay with me. Stay awake. You'll be just fine. You've had worse. Now stay with me." He shook my shoulders, and my head rang. I cried out, and he pulled me against him, wrapping me close. "Sorry. Oh lord, sorry."

I knew I shouldn't fall asleep with a concussion this bad, but I hadn't slept well on the plane ride to Bermuda. If Izzy and I were going to hit the beaches as soon as we landed, I was going to need some rest. How long did the flight attendant say? We'd be there by sundown? Perhaps a short nap.

"I want you, Nanette. I've been wed to you since the start even if we never said any vows. You know that." He shook with emotion.

"I know that." I really did know that. We'd been committed to each other from our first days together.

"I'm your husband whether you want me or not." He brought his lips to my forehead.

"I want you." I held him as tight as I was able.

"You're my wife." His words were reverent and true.

"Yes, I'm your wife," I agreed. He kissed me softly again. I brushed my fingertips against his lips. The pain suddenly eased. I relaxed. What-

The Bitch Captain (and The Lady)

ever pressure had been building broke, and I sighed. I felt liquid trickle down my ear. I wondered where Izzy was. Andrews bent his forehead to my own and kissed the unbruised skin. He held me until I knew no more.

CHAPTER 13

St. George's

The secondary measures of the Fountain took effect in severe cases of life and death. What it effectively does is kill you, then offer you another chance. A reset button. An extra life. Turn it off and turn it back on again.

Andrews was sound asleep with his arms around me when the secondary measures began. I woke up because my lungs stopped. I gagged and tried to inhale, but my diaphragm was paralyzed. I couldn't talk or scream. The secondary measures induced silence before killing you. My heart was the next to go. I went from thrashing about for air to complete immobility as it felt like an elephant was sitting on my chest. My eyes bugged, and I gaped like a fish out of water. This can last four to six minutes. Next was the worst. From the crown of my head a splitting, slicing headache as if someone were drilling into my skull and then force-filling me with water. Moments later I died, right there in Graham's arms.

Then I was struck by lightning. Invisible lightning…I assume. I don't know. I've never seen it. I gasped and opened my eyes to the bright morning sunshine. Andrews was still fast asleep. I felt my face and knew that at least the swelling had gone down. I could still feel some of the large split on my cheek and lip and tenderness around my eye. I didn't have a mirror, but I was semi-confident I still sported decent bruises. They were wounds I could easily recover from by myself. My head was clear, and the leftover wounds from Tavern Rock felt completely healed. I rotated my shoulder all around, enjoying the pain-free movement. The Fountain kept you from death's doorstep but only just. You had to heal and carry the scars of your mistakes forever.

We were on a road overlooking the shore. I hopped down and stretched. Large sails caught my attention. The *Victory* had arrived.

"Nanette?" Graham called from the wagon, startled I wasn't still there in his arms.

"Here. I'm here," I called.

Graham jumped over the side of the wagon and looked me up and down in shock. He touched my ear and my face, felt my forehead. Then pulled me to him in a bone-crunching hug. He shuddered against me.

"I'm fine. I didn't mean to scare you." I kept my arms around him.

He took my head in his hands and carefully observed the bruises and cuts. He was intense in his examination, his lips pressed hard together. Then he relaxed and brushed his lips gently against mine.

"Don't make me let go of you again," he begged.

In answer I reached out and took his hand, intertwining our fingers. He gave me another of those gentle kisses.

"You look...better," he admitted.

"Helene's not as good as she thinks." I attempted a smile, but my lip cracked open again and started bleeding.

Andrews handed me a handkerchief. He was mystified. I'd have to watch him for signs that he was ready to turn me over to the witch-burners. I was safe for now.

He did whatever you do to get horses to pull a wagon, and this time I sat up on the driver's bench with him. He set the horses to a good clip. We rode a while in silence, each of us needing a little time to reacquaint ourselves with how to be together now that the animosity had siphoned off.

"Why did you do this? Why did you come?" I asked as the rooftops of St. George's came into view.

"You've never said goodbye before… and I wanted a better one than that nonsense yesterday. I wasn't going to wake up to an empty bed and an empty dock this time when I could help it." He looked over at my broken face and sighed. "I won't ask you to stay with me anymore. Magnus had the right idea. I'm going with you this time. Staying by your side until you give me a proper goodbye. Will you have me?" I reached for his hand and held it.

"Yes."

We rode through the center of town, and I had him stop just around the corner from Lady Catherine's. I had intended to go to her door myself, but my face was truly atrocious. The poor girl was already upset and terrified, and I doubted my visage would provide much comfort. Andrews might be the answer. He was in town often enough that it wasn't strange to see him out and about, and he was high class enough to speak with a lady and no one would raise their eyebrows. I directed Andrews to steer the wagon into an alley around the corner from Catherine's.

"Since you're part of my crew, I have to let you know we have a few delicate pieces of business to conduct," I said, wondering for just an instant if this was wise. Andrews knew not all of my business was legitimate, but this was the first time he'd see me brazenly defy the law. "We are here to bring a few passengers back. Not just Isabelle."

"How many?" He eyed the wagon, perhaps wondering if it was big enough.

"Two and a half. One's a baby or something. I don't know how old. And Isabelle, of course."

"They'll be sailing away with you?"

"If all goes to plan, yes." It would be a miracle if a plan of mine actually went off without a hitch.

"I never thought I'd see the day you took on passengers." He grinned. "Either business is bad or maybe you're growing up."

"Neither. This is a one-time deal. I promise you it'll never happen again." I turned to him on the bench. Here was the real test. "So now for your part."

"I get a part?"

"I'm not paying you to sit around collecting dust."

"I'm getting paid? Maybe I'll take it out of you in trade." He spoke in a low voice, and a smile played across his lips.

"We'll discuss terms later." I tried to keep my mind focused, but warmth spread between my legs just hearing him mention this. A proper goodbye, he'd said. Focus, Anne. I forged ahead with his instructions. "So if you could go to Lady Catherine's door and tell her you'd love to escort her to the docks to meet her husband this afternoon, that would be great. Tell her you understand if she's busy or feels it's improper, or you hear she's already got a carriage waiting, but since you are in town you thought you'd ask."

"Lady Catherine?" He was stunned.

"Make sure she says no to you. Leave with everyone knowing she turned you down. But be sure she understands it's this afternoon." I examined him for signs he understood or was going to back down.

He jumped from the wagon, reached for my hand, kissed it, and said, "Yes, Captain." He walked quickly from the alley and out of sight.

I'd never been more turned on in my life. A proper goodbye, I mused again. It was intriguing. Andrews was back a few minutes later, almost giggling with excitement.

"I thought the lady was going to faint! She has always been a little scared of me, and here I was, offering to take her on a walk together. She could barely get any words out. Her handmaid came to her rescue and turned me down. I'm sure the girl understood. What next?"

"We're going shopping."

Andrews was having a good time going to all the shops with me as I bought a variety of different items, some for the ship, some to build a fort inside the wagon large enough to house a few runaways. Together

The Bitch Captain (and The Lady)

we practically robbed the town. We put on a two-person show, and the shopkeepers and vendors never knew what hit them. Andrews is a shrewd negotiator on his own, and when you added me into the mix, they were practically giving their goods away. Andrews actually whooped as we left our latest victim shaking and confused as to why it was a good idea to sell us those casks of wine for well below market value.

"Tonight, we will toast our victory!" he shouted and scanned the rows of cargo ships at the docks for our next mark. "Next one, we pretend to not know each other, get into a bidding war, then both walk away."

I laughed out loud and sprinted to get to a ship selling bolts of cotton before he could. It was a good thing all those ladies I was picking up later were small because we got almost that whole shipful of fabric for next to nothing.

"We might need another wagon," I observed as we loaded several barrels of fresh water into the back.

"And horses. I have several horses to replace. Damn Talbot straight to hell for betting against me," he added.

We looked at each other and split into identical grins.

"Me!" he shouted and pushed me into a stack of hay to slow me down as he took off to get to the horse traders.

"Cheater!" I hollered after him. I dusted the hay off and ran after him.

We purchased another team of four horses and a wagon. Andrews was crying with laughter watching me try to drive the wagon down the streets. I gave up. Andrews went to stable one set of horses while I waited on the side of the road flipping the reins around and pretending I was in the wild west chasing down a train.

"Are you looking for me? I have an iron horse to catch, and hell's coming with me." I put on my best cowboy accent and imagined the dry plains sweeping out in front of me. A line of carriages and wagons passed me by, and I recognized Izzy's silhouette inside one carriage.

Andrews hoisted himself up into the wagon next to me and took the reins. "Shall I take us down?"

"Well, get on up here and let's get along little dogie." I kept the accent.

"Nanette?" He looked at me quizzically and I grinned.

"I'm your Clementine." I brought him in for a bewildered kiss then let him do the horses. I felt light. I was not being as cautious as I should, but I couldn't help it. It was a happy day.

He worked out that I was in a playful mood despite the foreign words and kissed me and grinned before ye-hawing the horses down the road.

The *Victory* was moored offshore, and smaller boats ferried passengers and cargo out and back. There were a few reunions happening on the shore, but most of the people assembled were there to conduct farewells. Andrews brought our wagon to a halt at the edge of the sand and the road to wait for Izzy.

Rowboats were pulled high on the sand where various soldiers and sailors were loading them with my crates of guns and powder and various other goods. I said a silent goodbye to the arms and wondered idly what excuses I'd have to make to Charlie for losing his fare. That was a problem for another day.

Izzy was wrapped around her lieutenant, tears flowing already. He had his hand under her chin, speaking consoling words to her. Andrews and I sat watching the departure scene in front of us from our seat on the wagon. Neither of us was laughing now.

"I hate goodbyes," I said as I watched Izzy begin to fall to pieces.

"I know." Andrews was rapt, watching the scene. I know he was thinking about us. How he wished a similar scene would happen between the two of us.

"This? You really want this?" The young lieutenant began to step towards a boat, still holding out his hand to my sister.

"Let's not dwell on it yet." His eyes were still glued to the lovers in front of him.

Graham carefully put his arm around my shoulders, the pressure light and questioning, wondering if I'd accept this gesture from him. I leaned in and held my hand up to his, pulling him tight. The young lieutenant was in his boat now, hands holding Izzy's face, kissing her again and again.

When the boats finally launched and Izzy was one among many wives left waving goodbye to their husbands, I picked up a flask of whiskey and jumped down from the wagon. Andrews followed me to the beach but stayed back out of the way. I went right to her side and handed her the flask. She could barely see through her tears but threw back the whiskey nonetheless.

I stood with her awhile, watching her husband get rowed away to war. It hadn't been three months since we'd sailed into these waters ourselves. Tomorrow we'd be out on the same ocean. Izzy would be sailing the same sea as her new husband but leagues and leagues apart. We stood together until the little boat was out of sight. The other wives vanished one by one into their daily lives and responsibilities as we stayed watching that tiny boat get absorbed into the blue.

"It's time, Izzy. It's time to go." I took the flask from her hands and handed it to Andrews, who had come down to assist me with her. Izzy stayed rooted to the spot. "It's okay. I got you." I tried to coax her to take a step away.

"He's gone, Anne. He's gone," she cried.

The scene and the characters were familiar. I'd been with her the last time she'd lost the love of her life. We'd waved farewell to Maui's ship as she cried and wondered aloud if she'd ever see him again. She wouldn't. She'd fallen apart at the news of his death, and I hadn't seen her for almost a year.

"Let's get you home." I put my arm around her and pulled her towards the wagon. If she couldn't move, I'd have Andrews carry her.

She curled into my shoulder, sobbing.

"The day's not over yet, Izzy. The others are waiting," I gently reminded her.

She nodded imperceptibly and attempted to collect herself. Unfortunately, in collecting herself she saw my bruises in the full light of the noonday sun.

"Anne! What happened to your face?!" She gasped. She grabbed my face and turned me side to side.

I winced and made the mistake of flicking my eyes to Andrews.

"Did you do this to her, motherfucker?" She turned and leveled a devastating glare at him.

I had completely forgotten about my face as Andrews and I wheeled and dealed our way across town today. Of course she'd notice. I was a monster.

"I should have known." Izzy advanced on Andrews, who backed away shooting me "help me" looks. I shrugged, enjoying the show.

"Graham Andrews! Did you do this to her?" Izzy stepped towards him again and gave him a hard, one-handed shove. "Answer me!" At least she'd stopped crying.

"Ow. Nanette, care to step in here?" He was taken aback with the abruptness of Izzy's sudden onslaught. God, I loved that girl.

"No, you don't talk to her," Izzy said. She was right in his face, fists balled at her side, all five feet and four inches of her bearing down on him like he wasn't towering over her. "I asked you a question. What happened to my sister's fucking face?" she said, low, slow, the threat evident in her voice and body.

Andrews may act the gentlemen among ladies but was not born nobility and wasn't easily cowed. "Your captain made a choice. And so did I." He was no longer laughing.

"You fucking bastard." She wound up and struck.

Izzy had been a big fan of '90s rom coms. She must have made me watch a thousand of those formulaic stories. In one of my favorites, the spunky lead teaches an audience of beauty contestants how to defend themselves. Izzy had taken that lesson to heart, and in quick succession, before Andrews had a moment to consider changing his tone, Izzy did a quick jab to his solar plexus, followed by his instep, nose, and last of all, groin.

As Andrews doubled over, heaving and gasping, she yanked the flask out of his coat pocket. "You stay the hell away from my fucking sister." She tipped back the flask and turned to me. "Anne? Would you go find the driver, please?"

"He'll be up in a sec." I kissed her on the cheek. It was rare for me to have a champion. I felt warm and loved. "Get up in the back and we'll head out." I helped her and her enormous dress into the back before going to check on Andrews.

"You've got yourself quite the protector," he wheezed.

"She's the best." I patted him on the shoulder. "Giddyup, cowboy."

"What's that now?" He straightened and tried to shake off the aftershocks of Izzy's barrage.

"Go do the horses. We've still got a ways to go." I walked, he limped, back to the wagon.

I climbed up on the bench next to Andrews and looked back at my sister hidden among the various barrels and crates. She took a long pull from the flask while still examining my face. This was going to be trouble. Andrews horsed the horses and we set off.

It didn't take long for Izzy to collect more words, and she set herself up behind Andrews so he was squarely in her crosshairs. Andrews was a sitting duck for her second wave.

"Anne, do you remember that short story I wrote during Domestic Violence Awareness Month? The one where the aunt disappears the womanizing, abusive husband to save her niece and the children?" She took another sip. "My point is – we can take care of him right now, and, bonus – make it look like an accident!" She cheerfully spoke of his murder like one would ask what you want to eat for breakfast. "It's not as if they perform detailed autopsies here."

"If your sister wanted me dead, she wouldn't need your help, Lady Coventry." Andrews grinned aside at me, probably thinking of the first time I'd met him (second time he'd met me but that's a longer story). We put several men in the ground that night.

"Do shut up. No one's talking to you, driver." I fought back a smile. Izzy was every inch Lady Cov – what was the name? Ah well, she was every inch the noble lady with that line. Bermuda must have given her quite the masterclass in becoming nobility.

"Anne? You know I'm never going to let this go."

"Lady Isabelle," I said pointedly, "it will be a great story for when we are sailing."

"So you don't want me to run my stiletto through his ear?" Izzy caressed a long, thin blade just out of Andrews' sight. "I have this shiny new one I haven't tried out yet."

I gave a nice long pause. Long enough to make Andrews somewhat nervous.

"Nanette?" he questioned.

Izzy had startled Andrews with the vehemence of her words and actions. He was waiting to see whether I'd side with her and he should begin fearing for his life in earnest. Too bad I loved him.

"Let's keep that in our back pocket for now," I said. Andrews might not know what a back pocket was but was relieved I wasn't inclined to violence for the moment.

Izzy grumbled but stopped lurking directly behind his seat. She moved over to rest her head on my shoulder. I was surprised and touched by her affection. This was her day to be comforted. Her husband was on his way to war, and she was supposed to be the one accepting help. Since the secondary measures completed and I woke up, I hadn't given a thought to my bruises and the circumstances around how I acquired them. I loved the man in the seat next to me, but our era began to close

The Bitch Captain (and The Lady)

when Helene struck. I sat there tensed, as if ready for another blow.

I needed to shrug these ugly responses off. I didn't want to think about all that now. I didn't want to think about it ever.

"I'm alright, Izzy. Let's just focus on you tonight. Okay?" I murmured to her.

She went back to her perch between the crates and pulled at the flask again, muttering darkly. Andrews stared straight ahead. I had nothing to add to the situation. Andrews and I, we weren't the apologetic type. We made severely deliberate choices and refused to look back in examination of them. There were much nobler ways to live. Look at Izzy, shanghaied to a time of danger and cruelty, fantastical wealth and beauty, and she was taking care of everything and everyone in sight.

The stable hands got our second wagon and horses all dressed and ready to go. Andrews took over the new team, and I was now on deck to drive this wagon.

"Hi yo, Silver," I whispered and flapped the reins.

Andrews brought his wagon up next to me and did some whistle, heyup noise and whapped them a little, and the horses walked. They walked very slowly, but I was moving forward.

"You're shitting me, right?" Izzy clambered over the seat back to sit next to me. "Move," she ordered.

"Thank god." I fairly threw the horse straps into her face. I did not want to be driving. I figured Izzy wouldn't be up for it and was planning to let her relax and drink in the back. She'd only just said goodbye to her husband, she deserved to wallow. Goodbyes were hard. Andrews' wagon disappeared around the corner, and I was suddenly wracked with nerves, wondering what our goodbye was going to look like.

"Where are we going next?" She only slurred a little.

"Catherine's." The horses sped up.

Apparently Izzy knew the way and was now going to get us there as fast as a horse could go. I closed my eyes and took calming breaths perfumed with the horse stink.

"And slow down, it's not a race." Stupid horses. They'd corner too hard and turn over the wagon and we'd all be trapped.

"Jesus wept, Anne. You're not this scaredy in a car, and those are way faster." She rolled her eyes at me. Cars didn't smell as bad as horses.

"Those have brakes. And airbags." One of the horses took a shit.

"Fair enough. For all the good those do for some people. Trust the horses, Anne. They are majestic animals. They want to live."

"If they were majestic, they'd be in the sea. No." I buried my head and closed my eyes. I would have gratefully walked to Catherine's. Izzy was going way too fast.

"Trust me, at least? Or you can move into the back if that's better for you."

"I'm fine. I'm fine here. I'm fine. It's fine." I tried to breathe through my mouth.

"Uh huh. You're about as convincing as that dog in the burning room, Anne."

"I don't know what that is. Do we really have to go this fast? Aren't there speed limits?"

"Horses, Anne. Organic autopilot?" Izzy tipped more of the flask into her mouth, and I gripped the seat harder.

"Just keep your eyes on the road." I groaned in relief as Catherine's house came into view. Izzy kept drinking from her flask.

"What's the plan here? Do I need to do anything? Actually, I should probably not be seen here, right now. I shouldn't be connected with this." She swayed as she stood and looked around.

"It's all arranged," I assured her. "Pull into the neighboring alley. They will be waiting unless they've changed their minds." They were waiting. Bessie and Catherine, a bundle in a basket, and a few trunks were there waiting for us. Izzy clambered back into the wagon bed.

"I said one trunk." I jumped down to argue with the two young women. "That's five trunks. That's not taking only what you need to survive."

The Bitch Captain (and The Lady)

"Lady Catherine couldn't bear to part with some items." Bessie shrugged and began loading them. We needed to get out of here already. We stowed the two women and the baby in one wagon and arranged the barrels and tarps to hide them. Andrews and I stepped back to survey our work. In one, a broken-hearted Lady Isabelle Covington; in the other, two refugees and a baby.

"I'm going to ride with the women and the baby," I told him. "I can't have you caught with them."

"Yes, being caught with the lieutenant commander's drunk bride and her shiny knife surely won't bring me any trouble."

We played rock paper scissors. He lost.

Andrews went to get the flask and refilled it from a cask in the wagon. "Let's just keep her occupied, shall we?" He took the refilled flask and headed over to my sister. "Drink up, my dear lady. We are riding together. Probably better than letting Nanette drive, though." I flipped him off and climbed into the driver's seat of my own wagon.

Mere moments later we were off...mostly. The leather reins slipped in my grasp, and I jumped at each clop and jerk from the animals. Andrews pulled ahead as my team of horses sauntered here and there about the road as we headed out of town.

"What's happening up there?" Bessie called out to me from her hiding spot. "Are we even moving?"

"Yes. Calm down. The horses must be tired or something." I flipped the reins and tried to recreate the karate-chop noise Izzy made earlier. If anything, they moved slower. "Say, Bessie, do you know horses?" We weren't quite out of town yet, but I could put my hat and coat on her.

Bessie peeked out to see what was happening. One horse had stopped to graze.

"I can do better than this." She looked mystified that I was having such trouble.

"My mother never took me for a pony ride. Blame her." I took off my hat and placed it on her head and wrapped my heavy coat around her thin shoulders, flicking up the collar. "Keep your head low," I cautioned her.

Bessie nodded and took up the reins and at last we were off.

Andrews was far ahead by this point, but there was only one way to go. We'd catch up. Lady Catherine was silent as a spiderweb back there, and the baby only gurgled a few times that I could hear. When I asked Bessie about it, she answered that the baby was an angel and she'd given Catherine some rum. Bessie and I were going to get along just fine.

"Do you like the sea?" I asked her. A dark expression crossed her features, and I cursed myself for being an idiot. "Of course not. This trip will not be like that. I promise."

"Lady Isabelle said as much herself."

"Are you afraid?"

"Yes," she whispered.

"I was too my first time out. My father took me out on this tiny ship to teach me to sail. I was just a small child at the time. We capsized."

Bessie clenched the reins harder.

"We were fine, though." I tried to reassure her. "Got the boat back upright. I figured out much later that he was a terrible sailor and a worse teacher." I don't think I'd allayed any of Bessie's fears. Izzy would be so much better at this. The road curved up ahead, and she and Andrews were thoroughly out of view.

"How about you tell me what you're afraid of?" I tried.

"The dark," was all she answered.

"I'll make you a hammock bed right on top of the deck. Sunshine all day." I did have a great hammock attachment I put between the masts. It was a long trip ahead of us, and I'd like her to be comfortable.

Bessie had the good sense not to talk to me the rest of the trip, and we clip-clopped our way at a good pace towards Andrews' house and the sea beyond.

We reached Andrews' stables well past midnight. He had arrived

The Bitch Captain (and The Lady)

before us and already had people unloading his wagon and arranging the various goods to be brought into his stores or down to my dock. Lady Catherine and her child followed Bessie, wordless with fright, onto my ship. It was my plan to have us all packed and sleeping there so we could leave first thing in the morning. Everyone worked around Izzy, who remained dead to the world in the wagon.

I went down to the docks to store the last of my supplies and felt the excitement a new journey always brings me. It was a good thing sunrise wasn't too far off because I was too amped up to sleep. Andrews arrived at the dock carrying the passed-out Lady Isabelle and met me at the bottom of the gangplank.

"Permission to come aboard?" he asked.

I was at a loss. Rule number five: no men on my boat. Either I let him carry Izzy on for me or I tried to carry her or I let her drunk ass sleep on the dock until she could stagger aboard herself. Andrews didn't drop my gaze until I nodded and led him on deck and then below to Izzy's cabin. More gently than she deserved, Andrews placed her in bed and tucked her in.

CHAPTER 14

Goodbyes

Now we were standing unencumbered in a very close and sacred space. He swept his eyes over the surroundings, lingering on the door to my cabin, a yearning in his eyes. He made a move toward the stairs, but I reached out to stop him. I didn't want him to leave. I wanted him to remember me.

"Wait. I want to give you something." My thoughts lingered on our hands during Izzy's wedding, how I'd longed to have a physical representation of our commitment. It wouldn't be the same, but I wanted him to have a token of mine.

I opened the door to my cabin and rummaged in a drawer till I found what I wanted. High school had not been an easy time in my life. I was very lonely and angry for most of it. When I finally graduated, I remembered wishing Andrews was there to celebrate with me. I held the heavy silver ring with the onyx stone and the St. Christopher's Academy shield stamped into it and a date some 400 years in the future staring up at me from the ring. I threaded a length of leather thong through it and turned to find Andrews.

He was in the doorway. His hands braced himself against my small cabin door and his eyes soaked in every detail of my room. How many endless nights had I wished for him to be right here? I approached him slowly and wrapped my arms around his neck, tying the thin leather into a necklace. He wrapped his arms around me and held me close.

"I have nothing for you." He put his forehead to mine.

He was wrong; he'd given me his life. I picked the hat off his head and placed it on my own.

"There." I smiled as the brim dipped over my eyes. He lifted it off my head and tossed it on my dresser.

"First thing tomorrow I'll find you something. I'll have it waiting when you return." His eyes burned, and I kept my hurt trapped in my heart. I was not returning this time. I just nodded.

It was time for him to leave this place. Without words, I led Graham off the ship, down the dock, and to the sloping sandy beach that led up to the house. It was time. It was time for goodbye.

It was a dark night, no moon, cloudy. The mist was already rolling in, obscuring sea and land alike. Andrews took my shoulders and squeezed. I reached up and held onto his hands.

"Not so long this time, Nanette, yes?" His voice was rough and heavy with all the other words he wished he could say.

I couldn't answer. This was really it for us. In less than a year I'd be dead or branded the plaything of the devil in the eyes of every soul on this island.

"Not long at all," I choked out. Less than a year and a younger me would be riding those waves back here.

"Liar." He moved his hands from my shoulder to my face and brushed his thumbs along the base of my bruises. Neither of us could move. We were trapped on this little strip of beach, this piece of shared custody between the land and the sea, the only place we could belong to each other and still be true to who we were.

"Graham?" He needed no more of an invitation and brought his lips to mine. I wrapped my arms around him, kissing him back, stupid tears in my eyes. After a minute we took a breath and held each other forehead to forehead.

"You were right. Goodbyes are terrible." He could barely get the words out. We kissed again, nervous about going much farther.

Graham eventually stepped back, took his coat off and spread it out on the sand and extended his hand in invitation. This was a terrible, terrible idea. I should turn around and get back on that boat. I should get in my own bed, on my own ship, and attempt to get some sleep before the sun rose. I should not allow Andrews to waste any more of his time on me.

I pulled off my shirt.

He took off his.

He took off his boots.

I took off mine.

And so it went until we stood naked before each other in the misty night. Only then did I take his hand and let him guide me onto the makeshift blanket.

Graham lay back and I straddled him. He sat up to massage my breasts, circling them. I ran my hands down his chest, memorizing him with my fingertips. I leaned over to kiss him, and he divided his time between my lips and my nipples, finding welcome and purchase each place he chose. As his lips left mine, I was warm and ready and wanting him.

He was more than ready for me. He lay back again and, using firm hands, guided me, easing me onto him, pushing up and into me in one strong movement. My breath caught at Graham's sudden presence within me. Our eyes didn't leave each other.

"There you are, Nanette," he said and flexed his hips to hear me gasp.

I sat up, forcing him deeper within me, I looked up to the heavens. Graham looked up at me, breathing hard as I rocked over him. He reached one hand up and stroked down my face then brought me to his lips. I cried out, he was so deep in me. Out of instinct I moved up and away from the extremes, but Graham held me fast.

"No, Nanette, come back to me." Graham pulled me over him once more, thrusting into me, manipulating me until I came, crying out wordless emotion into the fog. Graham encircled me carefully and rolled us over so he was above now. He wasn't done with me yet.

"Say it again," he instructed.

"Yes," I said, opening my legs for him.

He entered me again and stayed steadfastly between my open knees, stroking in and out of me. His lips found my breasts again, and he used his tongue until a second wave of warmth flooded between my legs. I wrapped around him, and he eased in again and again, reaching new places within. He moved strong and steady like the tide. I pulled his weight onto me and opened his mouth with my lips. He shuddered and groaned, holding himself back from his peak in order to extend the time between our being locked together here and when he'd have to let me go.

"I'm here, Graham," I crooned. "I'm here with you."

He moaned and couldn't resist any longer. His steady strokes picked up pace, he was a runaway train now, and I was completely out of control. My legs thrashed as he had his way with me. He called my name in desperation over and over, "Anne. Mine Anne. Nan. Oh, Nanette." Until his body rocked one final time.

We lay there, drenched in sweat, unwilling to move, breathing together, marveling at each other and the torrent of emotion we experienced together.

When finally I could string two thoughts together, I took his hand and led him into the cool Atlantic waters. I let the water wash over me and scrub the sweat off. His hands found me again, fingertips attempting to memorize every curve, pausing between my legs just for the pleasure of being allowed to let his fingers explore freely.

"Say yes again?" he asked.

"Yes," I said and felt his fingers slide into me. I put my head against his shoulder and let him hold me. This was not a gesture of pure sexual desire. He wanted to be close, and I wanted him closer. Graham was gentle inside me. Small movements stroking me, teasing me.

"I don't want to let you go," he said, fingers slowly slipping in and out.

I kissed him. Graham brought his thumb into use and held me tight against him as he brought me to climax a third time. "Don't forget me." He spoke against my lips as I quaked against him.

I looked him square in the eyes. "I wouldn't dare."

Eventually we got back to the beach, dried off and dressed, and held each other close. The sun was starting to rise in the gray sky. We lay against each other and watched the fog begin to burn off. Andrews was quiet for a while, and I turned over to see him breathing peacefully. He looked young to me even though he was every inch the tall, muscular wildcat I'd known for years. Let him rest, I told myself. I allowed myself one more minute to commit his face to memory. I brushed his hair back from his face, wrapped his coat around his shoulders, and lightly kissed him goodbye.

I had one stop to make before boarding my ship and heading away from this island for good. It was early and damp, and my boots were soaked by the time I got to her cabin. What I was about to do was dangerous, but it didn't matter anymore. I was leaving. I knocked softly, knowing the woman would hear it anyway. She opened the door. No greeting. Just an eyebrow raise, waiting for an explanation.

"I'd like a word if you don't mind." I attempted to look as disarmed and nonthreatening as possible. Helene stepped out and closed the door. We walked a little ways to an area overlooking the sea.

"Well?" she finally asked as the sun began to break in the foggy dawn.

"Take care of him for me. Do a better job of it than I have, if you don't mind."

"Do not speak in riddles to me, Anne."

"I'm leaving. I'm trying to say goodbye to you." The woman just watched me warily, waiting for the other shoe to drop. She was a wise lady. "And while I am leaving, and this is goodbye – about a year from now I'll be sailing into St. George's Bay. There, a mob will haul me off my boat, beat me, and burn me at the stake."

She scoffed. "You cannot know the future."

I took off my boot.

"What are you doing?" She moved forward as if to stop me.

"Just look." I took off my sock. The extensive scars covered my toes. I lifted my loose pant leg, raising it over my ankle, my calf, my knee. Up and up I went until the fabric was at the top of my thigh and Helene's eyes were wide and frightened. "This happens next April."

"A witch," she mused. She wasn't scared. Helene wasn't bred on those prejudices of Christianity which eclipsed the possibilities of power in the world. As I understood it, the woman had never considered me wholly human and feminine.

"No, not a witch. But I know my future. And yours." The image of her headstone loomed large behind my eyes. "I tried to let him go. He's hard to let go."

"Yes," she agreed. I'm sure her mind was swirling. Helene tentatively reached out a hand and felt the scars, perhaps to ascertain whether I was a specter or not. "Not a witch. But close."

"Perhaps." I dropped the pant leg and replaced my sock and boot. "I wanted you to know – I need you to know so that when the time comes—" My throat closed.

"He'll be destroyed." She looked at me like I was a monster. Only a cruel, scheming, devious monster could perpetrate such devastation on a person she loved. I swallowed and vowed to myself I would feel it later. I would deal with it later.

"Not if you're there." I shook my head to clear the image of what a grieving Andrews might look like. "Not if you'll help him. Please," I begged.

The Bitch Captain (and The Lady)

"Why did you never say yes to him? All these years...I never understood you." Helene appraised me, and I came up wanting yet again. To her, I had it all...or at least most, and I threw it away time and time and time again.

"Hard to say yes when you know what's written on that gravestone." Helene Andrews. Beloved Wife. Beloved Mother.

"Yours?" She raised her eyebrows, wondering just how strong my magic was.

"Yours." I looked at her and didn't blink. Did she get it? Did she understand now? Did she understand now how I'd stolen their years like a thief in the night?

Helene backed away. She opened her mouth and closed it again, starting and stopping a long list of questions. Finally, she turned to look out at the view of my ship in dock for the final time.

"You will truly die next summer?" she asked as the fog rolled along the small shore.

"No," I answered truthfully. "But everyone must think I'm dead. As you said, I won't visit a hurricane on these lands, this family."

Over our long association Helene had viewed me with suspicion, anger, judgment, fury, and hate. She was a hard person to meet one on one and come away unscathed. I would have chosen any of those aggressive stares over what I saw creeping into her eyes now: pity.

"This is a terrible life you lead." She shook her head and for a moment it looked like she wanted to move closer to me.

"Yes," I agreed and turned to face the horizon with her.

"Why live this way at all?"

"I've lived like this for so long...not sure I know of a different way." My life was a tangled knot that I alone knew how to navigate. As awful as the awful parts were, I loved how I lived. There were wonderful and interesting times to accompany the lows. For instance, here I was, standing on a hilltop with a woman I'd shared the most complicated relationship of my life with, telling her the absolute truth about myself because she deserved the truth. I'd never told anyone this much about myself in such clear language. Fascinating.

We enjoyed the view together here at the end of our relationship. She was relaxed now. She believed me.

"He will not be able to move on from you. He has never managed it before." We were both looking at the sleeping figure on the beach below.

"He will this time. This time he does move on." Helene Andrews. Beloved Wife. Beloved Mother.

"I regret the friendship we lost." She turned to me, no aggression, no pity. It was the face I'd eaten with, drank with, and sang with in our early years together when the complications were few.

"I regret that too. I hope you'll forgive me someday."

"Perhaps. I hope you will forgive me as well." She had never said such a thing to me before.

"I'm glad to have met you." There was nothing to forgive.

The sun finally broke the horizon fully, and I took a deep breath. It was time to go. Time to leave this island and this complicated family and home and life that I loved. I cleared my throat and wiped my face.

"Goodbye, Helene. Throw just... the biggest, best hurricane party ever next year."

"Goodbye, Anne."

I nodded to her and set myself in motion for that ship. No more goodbyes. No more. I put my hat on my head and ignored the tears blurring the periphery of my vision. No more. No more. I strode across the dock and refused any last looks at the land, the house, or the beloved sleeping form of the man I would have cherished as my husband and family. None of this was for me and it was finally time to release my hold.

I wished I could die.

The Bitch Captain (and The Lady)

My ship was quiet, full of scared, mourning women. A small baby's cry from belowdecks was the only evidence there were any living creatures around. I untied the ropes and threw them aboard, following right behind them.

Don't think.

Don't think.

Don't be miles away. Be here.

One foot in front of the other. One task at a time.

Don't think.

Do.

I hoisted the mainsail then poled us away from the dock. The blessed wind filled the canvas right away, and we were off. The sudden motion of the ship brought Bessie out of her hammock to watch the island disappear.

We were well away when I heard yelling from the shore. Andrews, his blond hair flashing through the fog, hollering and waving, was calling for me.

I flashed back to another time on this island long ago when the fog wasn't fog but smoke. Another blond head had run through the crowds and smoke, pushing and shoving the masses aside.

My heart froze. No. No! I hadn't recognized the name that unknown man had yelled so desperately as he attempted to make it through. "Nanette!" that man had called out, over and over...just like this man here at the edge of the dock. I couldn't breathe. The wind carried me farther from him and his cries.

"No," I whispered. "No!" I shouted with all my might. I left the helm and ran aft to yell and wave to him. "Don't go! Don't go to me! Graham, don't go! Graham, no!" But we were too far for him to hear me.

Next year, as I stood tied to a stake and accused of witchcraft and the crowds sang for my death and lit the tinder beneath my feet, there had been one man who tried to break through. But I hadn't met him yet. He called for me. Next year, Graham would be in St. George's, and he'd watch me burn. I couldn't see him anymore. His dwindling form was obscured by the smoke.

I felt like Helene had sucker-punched me in the gut. I gasped and choked and almost jumped into the sea to swim back and warn him.

Bessie came up behind me. "Captain?" I couldn't get enough air. I grabbed Bessie by her shirt, partly to bring her with me to the helm, partly so I didn't fall down. I placed her hands on the wheel and pointed at the embedded compass.

"N. North. Keep it that way." Then went to my cabin and collapsed.

"This is supposed to be a vacation, Anne." My mother yawned as I dragged her and Izzy to yet another historical setting on Bermuda. My mother and sister were bored and annoyed with me. "You've graduated! No more school. Let's go to the beach!" She gave up as I charged through the grounds of the ancient estate. Izzy found a bench and pulled out a book; she'd rather be at a beach too. I found it then. The sea-spray-eroded headstone of the old master of this estate.

Graham Caspar Andrews
1609-1677
Beloved Husband
Beloved Father

I traced his name with my fingers. "Bye, old friend."

"Captain?" There was a tentative knock at my door. It was Bessie. "Captain, we need you." I collected myself and left my cabin. I nodded to

The Bitch Captain (and The Lady)

Bessie and went up to steer. We weren't far out from my buoy, and I was half tempted not to stop but did so anyway. I dropped anchor and rowed out to it. On a fresh sheet of paper I drew a giant black X and cast the rig into the water. Goodbye, Bermuda.

Back on the ship Izzy was waiting for me. "What did you write?"

"A warning." I have no idea what she made of this statement. "Hey," I perked up, "want to see something cool?"

Izzy was fairly listless. She shrugged noncommittally.

"See that land? That stretch from that hill there all around the corner to the tip of the island?"

"Yeah?"

"That's yours," I told her. The sun was showing off now, gilding the place in a mockery of the shit show that it was. "That's all yours."

Izzy approached the rail and stood agape at the sheer amount of property she owned.

"Someday you'll have to tell me how you did it," I said in admiration.

"Did what?" she asked.

"How you sold the British back their own guns and used the money to buy land they already owned." I shook my head trying to guess how she'd masterminded that one.

Izzy looked aghast.

I looked ahead.

No more looking back.

No more.

Epilogue

My watch buzzed on my wrist, waking me up. My twenty-minute power nap was over. I checked the waves and the position of the boat and the wind. Three hours and I'd sleep another twenty minutes. I stretched. All was calm.

I rubbed my hands over my eyes and through my hair and winced as I felt a number of bruises and cuts on my face. When had that happened? My heading was north. North. I sat back and contemplated. Why was I going north?

I was disoriented despite my routine surroundings. I know I had set the rudder toward north, but I couldn't remember why. I wasn't near the portal. The temperature was warm, so I wasn't terribly far from the equator. I rubbed my eyes again and settled in to wait for my memory to catch up with my senses. If the stars were out, I could at least deduce my location, but the bright morning sunlight obscured that knowledge from me. On a whim I turned on the Sat Nav and watched it spin. I turned it off. Whenever I was, it was before the invention of satellites. I was in the past, then.

I got up and stretched. I smelled like horse. Whatever time it was, it was time for soap. I undid my braids and stripped down and opened the port bench where I stashed my bucket and soap. I lowered and brought up a bucketful of sea water and placed it on the deck. My clothes smelled; it would be worth giving them a wash too. I stripped all the way down and dunked everything in the bucket of soapy water.

I looked again up at the sky, wishing my memory would return to me already. I was exhausted. The sky was clear and the ocean calm. Best drop the sails and stay in a holding pattern until I could remember where I was, when I was, and why the hell I was going north. I dipped the soap in the water and began lathering. Once covered in foam head to toe, I kicked the ladder into the water and dove in. I floated for a while and worked the soap out of my hair and off my skin. The water wasn't too chilly, so I was for sure more south than north. I climbed back onto the ship and spread my towel out to dry off in the sun. It was quiet and warm and beautiful. I could spare a few moments from my memory as the sun baked warmth into me.

"Captain?" A voice spoke from the hammock strung between the masts, shocking the hell out of me.

"Son of a bitch!" I exclaimed. "Who the hell are you! What are you doing on my ship!" I grabbed for the nearest blade, a short sword, and pointed it at the young woman's face peeking above the hammock sides.

"Captain!" she exclaimed, eyes wide and frightened. "It's me! Bessie!" Her voice was pinched in fear.

"Who?" I kept the blade steady on her when I heard more footsteps race up the stairs. The hackles on my neck raised and I was in full fight or flight mode in the space of a heartbeat. Intruders were on my ship! How did they get here?

"Anne!" Izzy's familiar voice called out to me, and I whirled to face her. She was in a cotton nightgown, and my sprinting heart calmed at the sight of her.

I remembered now. I dropped the sword. We had just left Bermuda where Izzy had gotten married. We were heading to Greenland with Catherine, her baby, and her handmaid Bessie. Bessie, who I'd promised would not have to sleep belowdecks, so I'd strung up the hammock for her. I rubbed my eyes as it all returned to me.

"Son of a bitch," I said again, this time whispered to myself, as all the gory memories returned in full color. I touched my cheek again, gingerly now, remembering how Helene had punched the shit out of me.

"Anne?" Izzy called to me again, and I looked up and saw her eyes glued to my body, wide and appalled.

Shit, I was naked, naked and scarred.

Read Izzy's side of the story in:

(The Bitch Captain and) The Lady
Izzy's Story: Bermuda

www.ingramcontent.com/pod-product-compliance
Lightning Source LLC
LaVergne TN
LVHW091701070526
838199LV00050B/2235